Walking on Eggshells

Caroline Langford

Published by Rogue Phoenix Press, LLP
Copyright © 2025

ISBN: 978-1-62420-839-3

Credits

Editor: Amanda Armstrong

Dedication

To my wonderful mother Shirley Hale

'*Live like a king, even if you can't afford it.*'
— Joe Leslie

Prologue

IRENE

1971, Israel

I let out a groan of pain as I touched my chest.

A moment of panic engulfed me. *The kids. Are they okay? I have to find out.* I strained to lift my head but was too weak even to do that. I squinted, trying to get my bearings, my eyes out of focus. To my left lay the bleary form of a woman, tubes and wires trailing from her body, a machine blinking softly beside her bed. To my right, another woman swam into view, sitting up and reading a magazine.

'*Boker tov,*' she said, smiling.

'Sorry. English only.' My voice was hoarse. The words came out as a croak.

'I said good morning. How do you feel?'

'Not too good.'

'It's okay,' she nodded, 'I will get someone for you.'

Lying back in bed, I struggled to recall what had happened.

A pretty, young nurse, her dark ringlets tied back, walked over to me and lifted my arm to take my pulse. 'Shalom Irene. My name is Shula, and I will help you. Do you have pain?' Her voice was soothing.

I struggled to sit up. 'Where are my children?' I could feel my weak and fluttering heart thumping against my ribs.

'You don't worry. All is good. Dr Levy will be here soon to talk to you about your condition, and someone will come and speak to you about your children. Now, you must rest.'

I sat back against the pillows, dozing on and off until I heard footsteps and the rustle of cloth. Next to my bed stood a short, bald man in a white coat, eyeing the readings on the machine attached to me.

'Oh, you are awake. Good. I am Dr Levy. I operated on you when you arrived at the hospital.' He smiled. 'You were very lucky. You were shot in the chest, but the bullet missed your heart by a fraction of a millimetre.' He held his fingers up to demonstrate. 'Any closer, and you would not be with us. That is what we call *mazel*. Luck.' He looked pleased with himself. 'I am confident you will make a complete recovery. Now, do you have any questions?'

'Yes, I need to know about my children,' I said, straining to speak.

'Of course, but they are fine. Do not worry. Also, your husband is here.'

Joe.

'Joe's outside? Can he come in?'

'No, no. You see, unfortunately, he had a major heart attack, but he is recovering in the ICU. He will need to be here for some time. You may visit him when you are able to get out of bed. I will come back later and see how you are. *Shalom.*' He patted my hand and left.

I sank back into the pillows, exhausted, a dull, hot pain throbbing in my chest. *I never learn, do I? It's always trouble with Joe.*

Part One

(Childhood)

Children are to be seen and not heard.

Chapter One

JOE

1932, London

I hated them boys. I hated school. I hated everything. Why did I have to be smaller than everyone else? It wasn't fair. I was six years old but looked about four. From the first day, all the other children pointed and laughed at me, calling me names. 'Sissy boy,' they shouted, 'who's a sissy, eh? Leslie is.' I could feel me eyes burning. I scrunched them up cos I didn't want to cry, but it happened anyway. That made them laugh even more and then they got close up, and I thought they were going to hit me. I was so afraid that I wet meself. Their jeering made me sob with shame and I ran, as hard as I could, out of the school gates and into the fields. I stayed hidden in the damp barley till it was time to go home.

The next day I was called into the headmaster's office.

'Leslie.' Mr Crabtree's gravelly voice was cold, 'You have disobeyed the rules and absconded from school grounds.'

I hung me head. I couldn't speak.

'Have you nothing to say for yourself? Very well then. You will receive your punishment and that will be the end of it.' He opened a tall dark wood cupboard and took out a huge cane.

'No,' I yelped, but it was too late.

The headmaster bent me over a chair and raised his cane up high. Down it came over me arse and legs, two, three, four bloody times. I could hardly sit down after that.

'Go back to your classroom and don't let me see you here again. Understood?'

'Yes sir,' I gasped, me eyes watering.

Every day it was the same thing; the boys laughed and catcalled. I arrived and left feeling stupid and puny.

After weeks of it, I decided to tell me father. Maybe he'd go to school and beat them all up. Yeah. That would be great.

I ran home and found him in the sitting room smoking his pipe, the crumpled newspaper resting on his lap.

'Pa,' I cried, 'All the boys in school are laughing at me. They call me a sissy.' Tears dripped down me face, wetting me shirt.

My father put down his pipe and stood up, towering over me. He rolled up the sleeves covering his massive arms, his face turning the same dark red as the flames burning in the grate behind him.

'Boy, I've about had it with you. Come with me. Right now.' Grabbing me ear, he dragged me into the kitchen. 'I'm going to teach you a lesson you won't forget. It's time you stopped blubbing and start acting like a man.'

I yelled and struggled, but his pinching fingers held tight. Our old bulldog, Bully, with his rolls of fat sagging down and drool all over his brindle-striped fur, was lying on the rug by the warmth of the oven door. Sensing trouble, he waddled quickly out of the room, snorting with the effort.

Pa stood with his arms stretched out. 'Okay, boy, today you will learn how to fight. Punch me. Come on, come on!' He beckoned, his eyes mean and hard. I stood frozen to the spot. Sense told me I had to move, to do as he said, or it would only be worse.

I didn't know what to do. I tried to throw a jab, me arm flailing, but Pa caught me fist in one hand and punched me in the stomach with the other. The air whooshed out of me like a popped balloon as I crumpled on the floor, doubled over in pain. If there had been air in me lungs I would have cried out, but I could only cough.

'Get up, boy, and hit me. Come on.' He stood over me with his beetroot red face, so I dragged meself up and gave it another go. I did me best, but every time he hit me, it left me gasping for air. I lay whimpering on the floor, me nose running, clutching me aching belly.

At last, he was finished.

'That should do it. Now you'll be a man.' Pa looked down at me, curled on the floor. He shook his head, lit a cigarette and left the kitchen. I heard him calling out, 'Bully, come up, come on, it's okay,' in that soft, kind tone he only used on the dog. I loved Bully, I did, but sometimes I wanted him gone, because truth be known, both Ma and Pa preferred him to me. It was because Bully had an enormous pair of balls, and I didn't have any when I was born. Well, I did have them, but they were up in me tummy, and I had to have an operation to make them drop down.

Pa wasn't happy about that. Balls were very important to him. He was often going around saying; 'A man may not have material gifts, but the best present he can possess is a magnificent pair of testicles.'

'After the operation,' Ma told me, 'Your pa came in the room and opened up your nappy to inspect the goods. What he saw didn't impress him one bit, I tell you.' Her mouth went small and wrinkly like she was sucking on a lemon. I'd been upset when she told me that, even though I wasn't really sure what it meant, but she said, 'It's not the end of the world. At least you're good looking.'

But being good looking didn't help me with the school bullies, did it? By the time I was eight, I had barely grown two inches, but the boys lost interest in me. There was a new boy in school. His name was Howard, and he was so overweight, he looked like Humpty Dumpty with glasses. Boy, did he get it every day from the bullies, and even though I was relieved I'd been left alone, I felt sorry for him. Still, he shouldn't've stuffed his mouth with grub all day, like he did, should he?

I didn't have a problem with eating too much. What Ma cooked was bloody horrible. I don't know how she made it taste so bad, but when I went over to me friend Tom's house, his ma was always in the kitchen wearing an apron and cooking up delicious food: sponge cakes, warm treacle puddings, apple pie and custard, all sorts of goodies. When she smiled and offered me a second helping, I wished more than anything that she was me ma. She would stroke Tom's hair and ask him how it was in school and what he learned that day. My ma never asked me anything like that and I don't remember her ever touching me hair or giving me a kiss. She ignored me most of the time, except to complain or criticise me.

One day, when Ma had gone shopping, I was sitting at the table in our old dingy kitchen on one of the old wooden chairs that always left splinters in me bum. I wasn't allowed to get down until I'd finished me dinner. I'd been sitting there for ages, but there was no way I was going to put those brussel sprouts in me mouth. They tasted like a cat's arse.

Pa was doing his one-handed push-ups on the floor, like he did every day. He was so strong; he made Popeye look like a weakling. I was pushing the food around my plate with me fork, when all of a sudden, he jumped up, clapped a hand on the back of my chair and barked in me ear, 'You eat your supper, boy. You want to be like this all your life? Like a sissy?'

Even though I knew he could thump me one, I said, 'No. I won't,' and I crossed my arms over my chest and stuck out my jaw. Pa turned red, but I carried on. Somehow, that day, I wasn't afraid. I wasn't backing down. 'I'm going to run away and join the circus.' I told him. He put his face close to mine. I could feel his hot, sour breath on my eyelashes. When he spoke, it was quiet and dangerous. 'Go to your room, right now, before I belt you so bad, you'll work in the circus as a deformed freak when I'm finished with you.'

Well, I was happy cos I didn't have to eat any more of that shit. As I got down from the table, me elbow accidentally knocked me plate, and all the sprouts tumbled to the floor, rolling everywhere. Pa went bloody bonkers. Before I could make it out of the room, he'd undone his belt, screaming, 'Right boy, this is bloody well it. I'm going to thrash the living daylights out of you.' I scarpered up the stairs as fast as I could. I knew I had to make it to me room before him, but I tripped on the fifth step and fell right in front of him. He grabbed me by the arm.

I was already crying, begging 'Pa, no. I'm sorry, Pa. I'll eat them,' but he wasn't having any of it. He took his thick leather belt, wound it around his hand, raised it above his head and whacked it down on me arse, over and over. My bum had red and purple marks all over it. I hardly slept that night because I couldn't lie still or stop the tears.

The following morning, when I came in the kitchen, he was sitting at the table reading the newspaper. I winced as I lowered myself into a chair and grabbed a piece of toast, cold and burnt to a crisp, from the toast rack.

'Good morning, son,' Pa boomed as usual, like nothing had happened. It was just a regular day for him.

Education wasn't a big deal in our house. Money mattered most— getting it, mainly. Pa owned an antique and silver business and went around London buying and selling. 'Because of my hard work, I put food on our table and clothes on our backs. That is something to be proud of,' he told me. 'I hope one day I can be proud of you, too.'

I would be over the moon if Pa would look at me with respect. Now that would be something.

When I turned fourteen, Pa pulled me out of school. 'Anything you need to know; I can teach you. You will come and work with me. There is no better education than to experience life itself.' That suited me fine. I'd had it up to here with Arithmetic and books, so without hesitation I accompanied him every morning after that. Together we visited the silver and antique shops and, day by day, I got to know the value of each item, and how to spot the manufacturer and production date from the hallmarks. It puffed me up to be introduced to everyone as his son, following in his footsteps and all. Truth was, though, all of it bored me to tears. Once I got the hang of things, I started to lose my enthusiasm and concentration. When Pa caught me outside sneaking a fag and reading a comic, he threw a wobbly.

'Can't you do anything right? I hand you a career on a platter and you piss all over it. I tell you, boy, I don't know what's to become of you.'

It wasn't fair. Just because Pa's business was chronically dull, it didn't mean I was a failure. There had to be something I could succeed in.

For as long as I can remember, since I was just a little kid, the one thing that could always grab my interest was the circus. I lit up when it arrived in town. The smells and the sounds of the wild animals and the colours and antics of the clowns, with their enormous noses and shoes, would get the blood pumping through my veins. I used up all my pocket money on tickets to see the show every day. I would sit on the edge of my seat, feeling the sawdust under my feet, inhaling the excitement. Sometimes I sneaked out of school just to walk around the grounds and watch the acrobats rehearsing. When the season was over and I had to go back to my daily routine, grey and endless as the winter skies above me; it left me with a longing I couldn't fill.

I was reading the newspaper one morning when I spotted an advertisement. My heart skipped a beat. The circus was due to open in a week. That meant they must have already arrived. I leapt out of my chair, grabbed my cap and jacket, and raced out the door towards the village green. I was on a mission. I was going to get a job with the circus, and I wouldn't take no for an answer.

There it was— the big top. It was just as I remembered it, its canvas walls striped like a peppermint candy cane, with pennant flags fluttering at the peak. The circus caravans surrounded the green in a comforting circle. I breathed in the familiar smells of candy floss and manure. My pulse quickened with apprehension. It was such a lively scene. There were people coming from all directions. A young fellow led an elephant down a soft sawdust pathway, another led an enormous brown bear, followed by a line of several clowns, two dwarfs, and an obese lady who needed a shave. I took a deep breath, approached, and cleared my throat. 'Excuse me, can you tell me where I can find the manager, please?'

'You mean Benny?' asked a clown with a teardrop painted on his face. He smiled. 'Over there.' He pointed to a white caravan.

I nodded my thanks, went over and knocked on the door.

'Da,' a deep voice answered. I pulled open the door. At the back of the caravan, sitting in a huge, winged armchair was a bald, heavyset man with a massive bushy red moustache. He was sucking on a dead cigar between gigantic rubbery lips.

'Why you come here, boy?' he said in a heavy foreign accent.

'I'm looking for a job, sir,' I said, trying to sound confident.

Benny grunted, picked up a magazine and began leafing through it without looking up. 'No jobs. Go away.'

'Please sir. I'll do anything you like. You don't have to pay me much, but please let me work here. Just give me a chance. Please.'

'How old you are?' Benny plucked the cigar from between his teeth and squinted at me.

'Fourteen, sir.' Sweat trickled down my neck and back. I hoped he couldn't see it.

'You want work in circus so bad?'

'Yes, yes, I do. Honest, and I can be a great help to you all. I'll work hard as anyone.'

Benny studied me as he looked me up and down. Finally, he smiled.

'Okay. I have son your age in Moscow. Alex. A good boy. I know you boys. When you want something, you must have it. So, I give you job. You come tomorrow six in the morning, okay?'

'Yes, sir. Thank you, I won't let you down.' I clasped his hand, shook it, and walked away with a huge smile on my face. *I'm going to work in the circus. It's a dream come true. Pa will be so impressed, so proud I'm making my own way.*

I burst into the house. 'Hey Ma, where's Pa?' I called, almost running into the kitchen. I was having a hard time keeping still.

'He should be home soon,' Ma said, raising her eyebrows. 'What's going on? You look like the cat that got the cream.'

'I'm not saying anything until Pa comes home, cos I need to tell you both at the same time.' I sat down and waited, my foot tapping the ground in a constant rhythm. The moment I heard the key in the lock, I flew out of my chair and raced to the front door. 'Pa,' I shouted, 'Guess what? I got a job. Got it all on my own.'

'Hang on a minute, son,' Pa waved me away. 'Let me take my coat off. You're like a dog waiting for his master.' As if on cue, Bully came waddling out.

'But Pa, I want to tell you what happened today.' I was buzzing with anticipation.

'Just a minute. Let me spend a moment with my lovely Bully.'

I fiddled with my sleeve as Pa crouched down and rubbed Bully. 'Who's a beautiful doggie, eh? You are, my love.' Bully squirmed with delight.

'Okay, son. So, what's this job then?' he said, getting up and hanging his coat on the hook by the door.

'It's in the circus, Pa.'

'What?' he scowled. 'What are you on about?'

'You know, the circus in town? On the green. It's back. We've seen it tons of times. Anyway, I went down there and spoke to the manager, and he gave me a job and I start tomorrow.' I beamed.

'Doing what?' Pa frowned. 'And how much are they going to pay you?'

'I don't know. I'll find out. But I know you're going to be ever so impressed.'

He scoffed. 'I'll be impressed the day you bring in lots of money and can fight like a man.' He turned to Ma who was coming out of the kitchen, the conversation over with, 'Now Liz, what's for dinner? I'm starving.' He walked away.

I stood, looking after him. *I may not earn big money for starters, I* thought, *but when he sees me swinging by my teeth on a high rope trapeze, his mouth will hang open, and he'll eat his words.*

The next morning it was hard to get out of bed at such an ungodly hour, but I grabbed my clothes, got dressed in the dark, and let myself out, racing the two miles to the village green. I arrived, huffing and puffing, at ten minutes to six. The sun was just rising, and I spotted Benny sitting on the steps of his caravan drinking a coffee in the dim light.

He lifted his chin. 'Good morning, boy. What is your name? I forget yesterday to ask you.'

'Joe Leslie, sir.'

'Well, Joe Leslie. You ready to start new job in the circus? You ready to learn? Yes?'

'Yes sir, boss.'

'See that man over there?' He pointed to a fellow across the green wearing an undershirt, standing over a bucket, shaving himself with a razor. 'That is Vladimir. You go to him and tell him Benny said for you to start work, ok?'

I walked over. 'Good morning,' I said to Vladimir, and removed my cap out of respect. 'I'm Joe, and Benny said to tell you I'm ready to start work.'

Vladimir glanced at me and kept on shaving. 'You wait one minute, then we start. You no afraid of animals, right?'

I laughed, 'Me? Afraid? I'm not afraid of anything.'

'Good, soon we start.'

Animals, eh? Maybe I'll be a lion tamer. "Joe Leslie and his fierce cats". Yes, then Pa will notice. Or maybe, "Joe Leslie and his dancing bear."

Vladimir wiped his face on a towel. 'Come with me.'

Already I could smell the manure. *Benny must've seen in me a natural talent. A leader. One who can control wild beasts.* We entered a large tent. I stopped in my tracks, amazed. Inside, like a great grey house, stood a gigantic elephant. She swung her massive head towards me and blinked her gentle brown eyes.

'This is Elana,' said Vladimir. 'She my girlfriend, so you be good to her. You see shovel over there? Go take it.'

I rushed to get it.

'You see that kaka?' He pointed to a steaming pile of dung. 'You clean it up. That is your job.'

'Elephant poo? For how long?' I asked. *It was probably a test, for my first day.*

Vladimir flashed a grin that was missing several teeth. 'Every day, all day. Every time Elana does kaka, you clean it up.'

I didn't dare say a word. I nodded and lifted the shovel.

At night when I came home, Ma wouldn't let me in the house until I had hosed myself off. She covered her nose. 'You're not coming in here like that.' Pa just laughed and laughed.

Every morning it got harder and harder to drag myself out of bed. There wasn't a part of my body that didn't throb or ache. I would collapse into a deep sleep as soon as my head hit the pillow.

On the day Elana had the runs, I just couldn't cope. It was coming out of her arse quicker than I could scoop it up. I went home covered in poo from top to bottom, stinking to high heaven, exhausted and thoroughly demoralised.

The next morning was the official opening. There were crowds of people waiting in line, and I could hear them buzzing with excitement from behind the animal tent, where I was hosing myself off with freezing cold water. As I sat on a wooden crate, shaking the water out of my ears, Benny dropped by.

'Joe Leslie. Today, after Vladmir and Elana finish their act, you must go in the big top and clean up the kaka she has done. Okay?'

'Yes sir, boss.'

Vladmir came in dressed in a red and gold costume and draped a matching cape and headdress over Elana. She looked very smart. They both did.

'Good luck,' I told them, as Vladmir clambered up on Elana and steered, lumbering her over to the big top. I followed behind and stood in the shadows. I prayed that Elana might have constipation after yesterday's attacks, so I wouldn't need to go in and clean, but luck was not on my side. I watched as piles of poo poured out of her as Vladmir rode on her back. I clutched the shovel in one hand and the bucket in the other as they did their final dance to the music under the swirling lights.

Once they had left, I raced over to the steaming heaps at the same time the clowns appeared. The crowd clapped and cheered watching them bouncing around with their floppy, over-sized shoes and honking noses. As I was bending over, trying my best to fit all the muck into the container, I heard shouts from the audience.

'Hey Leslie, sissy boy. That's right. Shovel it all up.'

I looked up, cringing at the sight of the class bullies, the whole lot of them, sitting in the front row, pointing at me, laughing their heads off. I clenched my jaw shut and carried on with my work. When I was finished, I headed to the exit, staggering as I carried the overflowing bucket, and lurched to avoid the clowns that were in my way.

'Sissy boy can't even carry a bucket of shit,' one of the pock-faced bastards shouted at me.

I stopped. Turning around, I stood there for a moment, staring at him, my eyes like slits.

'Sissy boy. Too weak to carry a bucket of shit.' He hooted again.

I didn't know what came over me. All I knew was I'd had enough. I marched straight over to him and, in a flash, dumped the whole bucket on his head, grinning like crazy. He spluttered and gagged as masses of elephant dung splattered over him, covering him from head to foot. I roared with laughter, turned and left; my head held high. With poo all over me, I headed over to the manager's caravan.

'Benny, I'm sorry, but I just can't anymore. I quit.'

To my surprise, he smiled and laughed. 'It's ok, Joe, my Alex does not like shit either. Good luck with whatever you do.' He said and handed me my wages.

I walked home, hosed myself off outside and went in search of Pa. He was with Ma in the kitchen.

'Pa, I just want you to know that I've quit my job.'

He snorted over his newspaper. 'Just as I expected. You couldn't hold down a job.'

'I could Pa. I tried, really, I did, but the boys from school turned up and laughed at me.'

'And I suppose, as usual, you cried like a baby,' he sneered.

'No. I emptied a bucket of elephant shit all over one of them.'

'Did you indeed?' Pa put down his newspaper. His face broke into a grin. 'Well, that's something else. Pull up a chair, and Ma, put the kettle on. Let's have a cuppa together and you can tell me all the details.' He took a cigarette packet out of his shirt pocket. 'Here lad, take one. I gotta say, for the first time, you've made me proud.'

I had never felt so happy as I did at that moment. I was beaming. It was the best day of my life.

Chapter Two

IRENE

1942, London

I clung tight to Mummy under the umbrella, trying to stay dry. At least now that I was five, I was allowed to wear my best coat when we went out. It was red and a bit itchy, but it had big shiny red buttons and was much warmer than my boring old brown one with the frayed sleeves.

'Come on Irene,' Mummy said as she prodded me in the back. 'Can't you walk faster? We don't want to miss the train.'

Well, maybe she didn't, but I did. I wanted to turn right around and go home and keep everything the same. I knew it was dangerous to be in London, what with the bombs and everything, but my daddy kept us safe. That was his job. He was in the Home Guard. Every time we went down to the cold, smelly underground shelter, my daddy was always waiting for us, looking so handsome in his uniform.

We were all still here, weren't we? So why did I have to go away to the countryside?

'Mummy,' I begged as we scurried towards Hackney station, 'please let me stay home. I promise to be a good girl.'

'*Mamaleh*. I've already told you,' Mummy crouched beside me and lifted my chin, 'It's too dangerous. I need to know that you are safe. It breaks my heart, but when the war is over, which Daddy says will be very, very soon, we can all be together again.' She brushed my cheek, stood up and hurried on.

I stumbled behind her, trying to keep up, with my Mickey Mouse gas mask bouncing over my shoulder. Under my arm was my lovely doll, Missy, dressed as a beautiful ballerina with a pink tutu and shoes to match. I couldn't leave her behind, not ever.

15

We passed rows of grey houses that looked just like ours. They even had chalk on the pavement. I loved playing hopscotch on the street with my friends. We were outside all year round, every afternoon, even if we got wet in the grizzly old London rain. And on Friday nights, the whole street was filled with the wonderful smell of chicken soup and schmaltz herring. That's when we knew Shabbas would soon begin.

As we entered the bustling station, a man in a bowler hat, a newspaper tucked under his arm, pushed past us and two old ladies shuffled by. I saw a lot of other children too, holding tight to their parents' hands like I was. Except they were crying; they weren't brave like me. Legs and coats clattered and swirled past me on all sides as people carrying fat, shiny suitcases rushed to the same platform as we were.

A whistle started to blow and Mummy ran even faster, pulling me along, her shoes clip-clopping. A smart-looking signalman was waving his arm on the platform. The train was ready to leave, so Mummy pulled open the heavy door of the carriage, puffing away, and pushed me in. She ushered me into a seat and we sat down to the sounds of doors slamming, and voices shouting, 'Cheerio!'

With a jerk, the train pulled out of station and chugged along, getting faster and faster until it was racing down the tracks. I pressed my face close to the window to watch the houses flying past as rain pelted hard against the glass. Before long, the grey gave way to a sea of green, speckled with brown smudges. Seeing so many fields and trees and animals was strange. I'd never been out of the city before. I watched the sheep standing in the rain together, and horses too. One cow stood all alone in the middle of a pasture. I felt sorry for her.

'I think they should make umbrellas for cows,' I said to Mummy. 'They could tie them on their backs, so they wouldn't get the milk wet.'

Mummy laughed. 'What a good idea. Aren't you clever, eh?' She opened a basket, handing me a cheese sandwich. 'Now, your aunt Sarah is clever too. She's a teacher. I haven't seen her for years, but when we were little, she always had her nose in a book. And she's got a nose on her, believe you me.' She winked.

When we were finished eating, we sat back, and Mummy stroked my hair. I loved when she did that. It made me feel like all the bombs and bad things had gone away and I was safer than safe. "Safe as houses",

Daddy said, but I'd seen the houses all in bits with windows and walls all gone. They weren't safe at all.

'In the country, there will be lots to eat and no air raid sirens,' Mummy said. 'You're going to have a lovely time. Trust me. I know what's best for my little girl.'

Maybe it wouldn't be so bad after all.

After a while, I'd had enough of looking out of the window. I wanted to get up and walk around the carriage, but instead I was stuck in the prickly chair with nothing to do. I stuck out my legs and looked at my new, glossy black shoes with a silver buckle. *Look everyone*, I said in my head, *look at my new shoes. Aren't they pretty?*

Mummy elbowed me in the ribs. 'Irene, stop swinging your feet. You're bothering the gentleman.' I looked across at the man with his glasses at the end of his nose, who gave me a frown, and then went back to his newspaper.

'Sorry,' I whispered, rubbing my side, trying not to cry. I sat in silence for the rest of the journey.

When we arrived at Rye station, I was happy to get off the train. It was even colder and wetter than London, so out came the umbrella again as we hurried along the lane to Aunt Sarah's home. Even though it was early afternoon, the sky was dark like it was evening. The trees looked like black figures and their branches twisted and waved. The only sounds came from the pitter-patter of the rain, the howling wind, and our shoes tap-tapping on the cobbled path as we dashed along. I shivered as I hung onto Mummy's arm. Rye looked very different from Hackney. *Where are all the buildings and shops?*

It wasn't too far before we reached a small, red-bricked cottage with a thatched roof and little walled front garden. There were no plants in it. I waited as Mummy tapped on the front door and watched her breath come out like cigarette smoke.

The heavy wooden door creaked open. Out stepped a tall, bony lady with a large, hooked nose. My eyes grew wide. *She looks like the witch from Hansel and Gretel.* I tugged on my mummy's skirt. 'I don't want to stay here,' I whispered, but she shushed me and hugged her sister.

'Sarah. Oh, it's so good to see you after all this time.'

'Yes, it's been too long,' Aunt Sarah said, and moved back. Her voice was nothing like Mummy's; it was high and loud and her mouth was a thin line.

'Come on in, but please wipe your feet,' she said, wrinkling her nose at me as she led us in.

It was even colder inside the cottage. I gripped Mummy's hand as we went into the parlour and sat on the small, hard sofa. Horsehair poked out of the rough fabric and prickled my legs. I wriggled and mummy stilled me with a firm hand on my arm.

'I'll just get us some tea. I won't be a moment,' Aunt Sarah said, then left the room.

I glanced around. There wasn't anything in the room except two wooden chairs and a small table. The walls had no paintings, decorations, or even a mirror. *Witches can't look in mirrors because they will see how ugly they are, and that will make it break into a million pieces.* It was nothing like our living room, with its big comfy sofa and fluffy pillows. I blinked back tears. My chest felt heavy.

'Mummy, please, can we go home now, please?'

'Darling, you know that's not possible.'

'Then stay with me here. Don't leave me with her—'

'Mamaleh, you know I can't. We've talked about it. I need to know that you are safe, and here you will be.'

'I know, but I don't care about horrible Hitler and the bombs. Please take me home.' Tears splashed against my mother's neck as I gripped her as strong as I could.

'Darling,' she pulled my arms down, 'please don't make it harder than it already is. I'm asking you to do what you're told. Now, sit quietly and behave.'

I bit my lip, trying to stop crying, but it wasn't easy.

Aunt Sarah returned with tea and two dry biscuits on a tray. She picked up the teapot and began filling a cup. 'Milk and sugar?'

'Yes, please. Thank you so much for taking in our Irene. It's a weight off my mind, knowing she'll be far away from danger.'

'Of course, we are family. It's what one does. Don't worry, she will be fine, and I shall make sure she keeps up with her studies.'

'Yes, I told Irene how clever you are.' Mummy laughed as she stirred her teacup. 'Not like the rest of us, eh?'

'Nonsense,' said Aunt Sarah, shaking her head, but her thin mouth twitched into a faint smile.

'So, you like it out here? Better than London?' Mummy asked.

'What's not to like? Just look around. Moving away from the filth of the city was the best decision I ever made. Here there's clean air and healthy living.'

'What about work? How do you manage with the war on?'

'Children still need tutoring. I tell you, when I arrived, the village was so pleased to have a teacher with my credentials. I have a great many students wanting private lessons and fortunately, they pay well.'

My aunt droned on, but I didn't listen. Instead, I imagined screaming, running out of the house all the way back to the station. It made me desperate to bite my nails, but I knew I couldn't.

Mummy stood, pulling me up with her. 'I had better get off if I want to be back in time to make your father's tea.'

'Mummy, please. No—' I wrapped my arms around her waist and squeezed. I couldn't let her go without me.

'Irene. Don't make it difficult for me.'

'Come on, Irene,' said Aunt Sarah, pulling me away.

'No!' I screamed. 'Don't go Mummy.'

'I suggest you leave now Pearl. Don't worry. I'll calm her down.'

I stood sobbing as Mummy walked to the door. She looked back for a moment, and I saw tears rolling down her face. I wiped my nose on my sleeve.

'Irene, let me get you a handkerchief. Come with me.'

I followed Aunt Sarah into the kitchen where a big, black oven stood against the far wall, smoke puffing out of the top. I had never seen anything like it before. A kettle and an empty saucepan lay on the flat surface.

'This is a wood-burning stove. Look *at this*.' Aunt Sarah opened one of the doors. I could feel the heat from the raging fire burning inside. On the opposite side of the room stood a table, two chairs, and some strange-looking plants hanging on hooks from the low ceiling. I stared at them, wondering what they were.

'These are medicinal herbs and I will teach you how to identify them. We'll pick them from the fields and then dry them to make teas.

Now, let me show you upstairs.'

More witch's spells and potions, I thought and shivered, despite the heat from the stove.

I followed my aunt up the creaking staircase to the dark landing. Aunt Sarah opened a door. 'This is my room.' Except for the bed and the dark brown curtains covering the window, the room was empty. There was nothing happy about it at all. I held my doll close and rocked her back and forth. She closed the door and opened another across the hall. 'And here is your room.'

It was the size of a cupboard. Against the wall was a small bed on a wire frame with an old woollen blanket tucked in. The small window above had the same brown curtains as my aunt's room.

'Come along.' We walked along the corridor, and my aunt opened another door. 'This is the bathroom.'

I almost wet myself at the sight of the toilet; I'd been holding it in for hours, but I was too shy to say anything.

'Why are you jumping up and down?'

'I need … I need to use the toilet, please.'

'Of course, but make sure you flush properly and wash your hands afterwards. I'll meet you downstairs.'

~ * ~

Even though I was horribly sad to be away from my parents, the countryside was a lot of fun. I ran up and down the lanes and there were lots of trees to climb and squirrels to watch as they scurried up the branches and collected acorns. A bushy-tailed fox even appeared in the garden, looking just like a stuffed toy with its little ears and pointy nose— nothing like the bony, ragged sort we got in London. I made daisy chains, wearing them around my neck and wrist till they wilted. The breeze felt wonderful on my face as I ran barefoot through the field, laughing when the grass tickled my legs. I even found a pond where I could watch frogs leaping in and out of the water. It never got boring.

What wasn't fun was Aunt Sarah. She was terribly strict. At the crack of dawn each day, my first job was to go into the chicken coop and collect the eggs. The hens frightened me with their beady eyes and scaly legs. They kept trying to peck me, but my aunt would send me back if I returned with an empty basket.

'I know it's hard,' my aunt said, 'but it's important in life to fulfil your responsibilities. Make sure you come back with a full basket.' Sometimes I stood crying with the chickens all around me. 'Please don't peck me, please,' I would squeak, but they didn't care, they just guarded their eggs.

Afterwards, I had to help Aunt Sarah prepare breakfast by stirring lumpy porridge. I hated eating it because it had no taste. When I asked for sugar, my aunt replied, 'You need to learn to like it as it is.' I never did. There was also one piece of toast, on which I could put a teaspoon of raspberry jam. I was often hungry after finishing breakfast, but when I complained, Aunt Sarah would insist, 'It is far healthier to leave the table wanting more.' When she wasn't looking, I would stick out my tongue at her. So there!

After our meal, we would clean the house from top to bottom. I would pretend I was Cinderella from the fairy tales Mummy had read to me each night. I'd loved hearing her voice. It didn't matter how many times I'd heard them before; it was always a special, quiet time before I fell into a deep sleep. *I miss my mummy.*

From nine until noon, I had to study the three R's, reading, writing, and arithmetic. I was a fast reader, but numbers were a struggle, which made Aunt Sarah's mouth get all wrinkly.

'Concentrate Irene. Add the numbers together, then subtract from the total. It's quite simple.'

It wasn't for me. I tried and tried and I still didn't understand it.

'My patience is wearing thin. Now come on, try again.'

When I finally got the hang of it, she gave me an even harder sum to do.

Lunch was turnip broth, or something else just as nasty, that had been simmering on the stove all night. I'd pull a face at the steam rising from my bowl, because it smelled disgusting, but I had no choice. I needed to eat it if I wanted to get down from the table.

After washing up, Aunt Sarah taught her private students, and I had to be quiet until four. That was my favourite part of the day. I could do whatever I wanted, so I would go outside, exploring every brook and tree

I could find.

Sometimes, I ran down the lane to visit my new friend, Mr Reeves, who I'd met one day when he was working in his garden. He was a writer from London and was very tall and gangly, almost like a tree, and always wore dark clothes. His face would break into a big smile when I came to visit. Sometimes, we would go inside for tea, and we would sit and have wonderful talks all about poetry, art, and dance. I would pretend I understood because I liked the sound of his voice— deep and calm like my daddy's.

'Irene, come and sit on my lap and I'll give you a cuddle.'

I was a bit shy, but I really wanted to, so I climbed up.

'You are so pretty. Such a pretty girl,' he said, stroking my hair.

I smiled. I felt so special. When it was time to leave, he would give me sweeties that I hid away from my aunt. Late at night, when she wasn't around, I would gobble them all down. They were delicious.

Every afternoon, there was a poetry lesson. It was so boring. I had to prop my chin up with my hands to keep from falling asleep.

'Take your elbows off the table,' Aunt Sarah would snap. Then, after three different poems, Aunt Sarah pointed the ruler at me. 'Now, Irene, tell me what you think about these wonderful words.'

'Well,' I said, cocking my head in thought. 'I think they can't be real poems because they don't rhyme.'

My aunt's face went bright red. 'Stupid child,' she said and banged the ruler down on the table. It made me jump. Was she going to hit me? 'Now Irene. Think again. Tell me your opinion.'

I didn't know what to say, but I knew I had to say something to make her happy. 'Um, I think they are very clever and, um, nice.'

She smiled. 'That's right, they are, and tomorrow and all the days after, we will read many more.'

After tea, it was bath time in ankle-deep water that was hardly warm at all, then lights off at seven-thirty.

And so, the days passed.

~ * ~

I kept getting tummy aches and my bottom was itchy all the time.

It wouldn't go away, so I had to tell Aunt Sarah, who sniffed the air like there was a bad smell.

'I'll make an appointment with the doctor.'

The next day, she took my hand, and we walked into town to a crooked old building. Aunt Sarah led me up some narrow stairs and inside. As we walked through the door into the stuffy little room, she marched over to the man in a white coat who sat behind the heavy desk.

'Doctor, I need your help.'

'Of course. Please sit down. What's the problem?'

'This child doesn't stop scratching her behind. It's disgusting. You must do something. I cannot abide it.'

'Not to worry,' the doctor said. 'This is quite common among young children. The girl has worms. She probably picked them up, running barefoot in the fields. What she needs is a good dose of castor oil and then she'll be good as new.' He smiled at me and opened a big jar of lollipops and gave me one. It was worth going to the doctor and getting such a treat. But as soon as we were outside, Aunt Sarah snatched the lollipop out of my hand and dragged me along the cobbled lane and back to the cottage. Her face was bright red and her fingernails dug into my arm. I didn't know what I had done to make her so angry with me.

As soon as the door was shut behind us, she grabbed my wrist. 'You filthy, dirty child. Worms? Parasites? It's beyond repulsive. I've a good mind to send you home, but I won't be that cruel. As of now, I don't want you near me.'

She yanked me by the arm to the small cupboard under the stairs. Prying the door open, she squeezed me inside like a piece of meat being pushed through a sausage machine. The door slammed shut, and the key clicked. Her footsteps faded away.

It was so cramped and dark in there, with musty old woollen coats smothering me and stiff, stinky shoes underneath. I could hardly breathe with the smell of wet rubber and old socks filling my nose. I held onto Missy and rocked her. I had never felt so alone or so sad.

'Mummy, help me, please. Mummy.' I cried and cried until my throat hurt. I kept listening for footsteps on the stairs, hoping my aunt would change her mind and rescue me.

'I'm sorry. Please, let me out.' I sat there with my nose running and my legs all tingly and numb. A long time later, nothing had changed except I badly needed to wee and it was hurting my tummy.

'Please, somebody. I have to go to the toilet.'

Silence.

'Please, I really need to go.'

'Please, please, please.'

After a while I gave up shouting, because the wee came out all on its own, streaming hot down my leg and wetting everywhere I was sitting. My clothes were cold, damp, and smelly. I tried to move away from it, but there was nowhere to go. I was so tired. My eyes drifted closed. I slept and woke up, each time hoping someone would rescue me, but nobody came.

Then, at last, there was a sound of the key scraping, and the door creaked open. I almost went blind from the light as I climbed out with stiff legs and stood on shaky feet.

'Now you will take your medicine and then we can go back to normal. Open your mouth.'

I kept my mouth shut tight, but my aunt was stronger and forced it open. 'Come on Irene. Take this.' She poured a huge spoonful of castor oil into my mouth.

It tasted foul. I gagged and spat it out, shaking my head, trying to get rid of the taste.

'Naughty girl. This time you will swallow. This is good for you.' Her bony fingers pinched my nose closed, so I had no choice but to gulp it down. It was disgusting. The worst taste in the world. I hated Aunt Sarah, hated, hated her. She was mean and nasty and I was so angry with Mummy and Daddy for sending me away, for leaving me alone with her. I stamped my feet on the ground. I wanted to break something.

~ * ~

One day at Mr Reeves', I noticed a photograph of a pretty woman beaming on the mantelpiece. The lady had short hair like a boy and wore dark clothes, the same as Mr Reeves. When I asked who it was, Mr Reeves gave me a sad smile.

'That was my dear wife, Angela. She died in an automobile accident a few years ago. I miss her so much, it hurts.' He put his hand on his heart.

I didn't like him feeling sad, so I climbed onto his lap to make him feel better. 'When I'm all grown up, I'm going to be a famous ballerina.' I told him.

'Yes,' he said, stroking my hair again. 'I think you will be the most beautiful ballerina in the world.' His eyes looked dreamy as he breathed heavily. 'Your curls are so gorgeous, my precious little Irene.'

What he said made me have a giggly feeling inside. *He thinks I'm precious. I think that means I'm special.* When it was time to go home, he kissed my cheek. 'I promise to get tickets for the ballet company when they next come to town.'

I love Mr Reeves.

A few days later, when I arrived at Mr Reeves' cottage, he opened the door with a bigger grin than usual. 'I have some wonderful news. The Sadler's Wells ballet company is coming to town, and I've bought tickets for us to attend.'

I jumped up and down and pirouetted on the spot. 'Oh, thank you. Thank you.' I held my doll up high for him to see. 'We're going to see ballerinas just like Missy.'

A thought crossed my mind. I stopped smiling and looked at the floor.

'Why Irene, whatever is the matter?' Mr Reeves asked.

'Aunt Sarah won't allow it,' I said, 'I know she won't.' I could feel my lip trembling.

Mr Reeves smiled. 'Don't worry your pretty head. Let's go over now, and I'll talk to her.' He took my hand, and we went out of the door. We arrived at the cottage in time for the afternoon poetry reading. Aunt Sarah answered the door with a book in her hand.

'So nice to meet you, Mr Reeves. Thank you so much for bringing the girl home, but there was no need. She knows the way.'

'Miss Golding, I wondered if we could talk a moment. There is something I need to discuss with you,' he said.

'With me?' Aunt Sarah's voice was squeaky as she patted her hair. 'Of course, do come in.' She led him into the parlour. 'Please have a seat.'

He sat down, draping one leg over the other. My aunt sat opposite with her ankles crossed and her back as straight as a ruler. I sat on the floor watching the grown-ups and listening to their every word.

'It's so lovely to have a chat. I've heard so much about you, and I wanted to say how kind it is of you to take in the child.'

Aunt Sarah's cheeks went red. 'Oh, it was nothing. I am just doing my duty for the war, and for my sister, of course. It's the least I could do.'

'Now, don't be modest. Everyone is doing their bit, but unfortunately, I can't serve my country in the way that I should. An old injury.' He rubbed his thigh like he was in pain.

'No, don't be silly. You contribute by writing your books. Allowing people to escape into stories and forget their trouble for a while. I think that's a great service.'

'Thank you. Though, lately, I'm having some problems with my writing.' He leant forward and lowered his voice. 'Can I confide in you?'

'Me? But of course, please feel free,' she said with an almost girlish giggle.

'Writer's block, I'm afraid. Haven't been able to write a bloody word. Sorry,' he said and glanced at me. 'I sit in front of the typewriter for hours on end until I get into such a rage that I want to break something.' He clasped his hand into a fist.

'Oh my. That's not good.'

'It's happened to me before. I almost became a drunk, but this time I am trying hard to resist the bottle of whiskey calling my name.'

'That is dreadful. We must find a solution, and fast.'

'Well, once, when I was at my lowest, a good friend suggested a change. I took his advice and went to France for the weekend, and do you know what? It revived me. A complete cure in such a simple way.'

'Well then. What do you think might help, Mr Reeves?'

'Please call me Arnold, I insist.' He smiled at her. 'I noticed the ballet is performing in town. I thought if I could spend an evening with you and your charming niece, it might just get the creative juices flowing once again.'

'Then we shall attend the ballet, Arnold. I refuse to take no for an answer.' Aunt Sarah stood, chest out, face flushed.

Inside, I felt a burst of excitement and silently cheered. Mr Reeves caught my eye and winked.

The big day arrived, and I skipped to the theatre, clutching Missy to my chest.

While we were standing in line, Aunt Sarah turned to me. 'Give me your doll. They don't allow toys in there.'

'But I need her. I want to show her the ballet.' I held on to Missy as tight as I could.

'Irene, don't make a scene. I'll put it behind that bush. No one is going to touch it.' Aunt Sarah grabbed Missy out of my hand and tossed her into the bushes. I thought I might cry, but I knew I mustn't. I wanted to see the ballet so badly. Aunt Sarah took my hand and led me inside.

When we walked into the grand hall, my eyes widened. I gazed upwards. Birds and butterflies were painted on the high ceiling, as though they were floating in the air. I thought it was the most beautiful picture I had ever seen.

We sat not too far from the orchestra, who were tuning up. There were so many sounds of violins and other instruments and of course all the people chatting with their friends. I could feel the excitement bubbling up inside me. I sat between my aunt and Mr Reeves. They were talking together, but I didn't listen. There were too many interesting things to see, like red velvet walls with giant matching curtains hanging down the stage. Grown-ups in fine clothes, and painted faces on the ladies.

A hush fell over the room as the orchestra began to play the opening notes. The lights went down, and the curtains slowly opened as twelve ballerinas danced onto the stage. I sat on the edge of my seat to study their beautiful costumes. They were dressed just like Missy, with white tutus, matching headdresses, and pink ballet shoes.

Music filled the room, and it was so lovely, it almost made it hard to breathe. I watched, taking in every detail, wanting to fly around and float like a fairy. *If only I could dance like that. Maybe I will when I'm all grown up.* Mr Reeves handed me a toffee, which got stuck in my tooth, but I left it alone because the story was so sad it made me cry. Aunt Sarah nudged me in the ribs, shushing me, but I didn't care. The finale was so wonderful. I didn't want it to end, but the audience clapped, the dancers left the stage, and the lights came back on.

'This is the best day of my life,' I said to Mr Reeves, who squeezed my hand and smiled as we made our way out of the building.

Outside, I hurried to the bush, bursting to tell Missy all about the magic of the ballet. Bending down on my hands and knees, I pushed aside every leaf and twig, digging deeper until dirt covered my hands. I couldn't believe it. She wasn't there. 'Aunt Sarah,' I shouted, 'come quick. I can't find Missy.' My heart was pounding in my chest.

My aunt took a quick peek into the bush before yanking me off the ground, leaving a red mark on my arm.

'Ouch,' I yelped.

'Stop making a scene,' Aunt Sarah hissed, 'You are embarrassing me. It's just a doll. It's not the end of the world.'

'It is, it is.' I said, and I sobbed out loud.

Aunt Sarah took my arm and we headed home, my feet dragging as I wept for Missy. Mr Reeves walked with us. 'Poor little poppet.' He whispered to me.

Arriving at the cottage, Aunt Sarah put out her hand. 'Thank you, Arnold, for a lovely evening. Irene, what do you say?'

'Thank you so much, Mr Reeves,' I said between hiccups.

'It was my pleasure. I'll see you soon. Good night.'

The door closed and Aunt Sarah grabbed me once more. 'You ungrateful little brat. I try to give you a nice time, and you end up humiliating me with your dramatics. I have no choice but to punish you again. Tonight, you will sleep in the cupboard.'

'No, Auntie. Please, no,' I screamed, my whole body shaking.

She didn't care and shoved me right back into that dark, smelly place. 'Good night.' She said and locked the door.

~ * ~

Weeks became months, the seasons changed, and Aunt Sarah's daily routine dragged on. I'd given up waiting for my parents to come and save me. Their letters were full of love, but it was just words. *They don't love me. If they did, they wouldn't have left me with her. It's cruel and selfish and I hate them.*

After lessons one day, Aunt Sarah made a clicking sound with her tongue. 'Tomorrow you are going home.'

I couldn't believe my ears. Home?

'You should know I don't approve. The war isn't over, but your mother says she can't go on without you.'

I didn't know what I was feeling. I was happy and angry at the same time. *No more Aunt Sarah and her horrible cupboard.* That felt wonderful, but I was so furious with Mummy and Daddy. I wanted them to be punished for sending me away, I wanted them to feel sad and angry like I did. I decided I would tell them I wouldn't be going with them. That would shock them. Maybe it would make them cry.

The next day, after very little sleep, I sat on my suitcase in my bedroom, tapping my feet on the floor and biting my nails. I heard the doorbell, but I stayed put. *I'm not going downstairs.*

Aunt Sarah called up in her sharp voice, 'Irene, come down at once!' I didn't have a choice.

I crept down the stairs as my aunt opened the front door, and there they stood— my parents. My Mummy, with her same lovely smile, and my Daddy, with his twinkling eyes. It made me want to rush into their arms, but I didn't. I bit my lip and stared at them.

'Pearl, Manny. How nice to see you. Please come inside.'

Mummy bent down. 'Mamaleh. Come and give me a cuddle.'

'No,' I said, and I turned on my heel and followed Aunt Sarah into the parlour.

As my parents and aunt sat down, I stood, back against the wall, looking at them. Daddy looked troubled, his eyebrows knitted together and Mummy's eyes were wet. It was too hard to see. I felt a lump bob in my throat like an apple. I couldn't hold back anymore. I ran over to Mummy and jumped on her lap, throwing my arms around her. I wanted to stay right there forever.

'Mummy,' I sobbed.

After a tight hug, she placed me on the ground. 'My princess, let me look at you. Oh, you've grown. What a sight for sore eyes.'

Daddy offered me his hand, which I held. 'Have you been a good girl and behaved yourself?'

'Yes, Daddy, I have, but it's not nice when Aunt Sarah puts me in the—'

'Irene. Let your parents relax for a moment.' Aunt Sarah glared at me. I wanted to stick out my tongue, but I didn't dare.

'Where's Missy? You're not too old for your doll, are you?'

Mummy's voice was barely a whisper.

My eyes filled with tears again. 'I lost Missy. I'm so sorry. Please don't be angry.'

Her brow wrinkled. 'My darling, of course I'm not angry.'

'Aunt Sarah put Missy behind a bush, and then when we came out, she was gone.'

Aunt Sarah cleared her throat. 'Yes, well, you know children and their vivid imaginations. She insisted on taking the thing everywhere. I knew she would lose it, but she wouldn't listen. Stubborn is what she is.'

Mummy stood up, her face bright red. 'Our Irene is not stubborn. She's just a little girl. My little girl. Don't you ever talk about her like that again.'

Aunt Sarah slammed her teacup on the table and stood up. 'This is the thanks I get for all I've done for you and your husband?' Her voice echoed throughout the room. 'I take in your child. Give her an education, despite the challenges of teaching a poverty-stricken, illiterate, disease-ridden child. I've turned my home upside down, but I did it with gladness as we are blood. That is what one does in such a situation.'

I was holding onto my daddy's leg when he jumped up and took my hand. 'Irene,' he said, in a cold voice, 'collect your things. We are leaving.'

'But, Daddy, I want to say goodbye to Mr Reeves.'

'Who is Mr Reeves?'

'We have a literary genius living next door,' said Aunt Sarah. 'He's published many books. A wonderful man.'

'Yes,' I said, 'Mr Reeves is ever so nice. He gives me sweeties and strokes my hair when I sit on his lap, even though sometimes it's a bit lumpy.'

'What!' Daddy roared. 'What sort of place have I left my poor daughter in? I will never forgive myself. You should be ashamed of exposing a young child to such perversion. Where is this man?'

Mummy held him back by his arm as he steered us towards the front door.

'Manny, you mustn't!'

Daddy took a deep breath and turned to stare at Aunt Sarah. I had never seen him look so huge and frightening before, or seen his eyes grow so dark.

'Now, you can have the peace and quiet of the lonely existence that you seem to prefer. May it do you all the good you deserve. Goodbye.' He slammed the door in Aunt Sarah's shocked face.

~ * ~

Back home, my parents and friends smothered me with kisses and cuddles, which helped me forget about the horrible year with the wicked witch. I felt safe in the daytime, but alone in the dark at night, I found it hard to breathe and I would cry out. Mummy would rush in and gather me in her arms. I would beg her to stay, so she would stroke my hair until I drifted back to sleep.

One night, after a few days back at home, I woke to shouts coming from downstairs. Daddy was yelling at the top of his voice. I'd never heard him so angry before.

'That woman is never to darken our door again. She is dead to us, you understand. Tear your shirt and sit shiva for her.'

Mummy was crying, which cut through my heart. 'But Manny, she's my sister,' she sobbed.

'Then it's lucky you have others. What that sadist has done to our little girl is unforgivable.'

I sat on the bed, biting my nails. *Is it my fault they are fighting? Maybe I shouldn't have told Daddy about what Aunt Sarah had done?* My breath came out in quick bursts as I held on to my new doll, Missy Two. She was also a ballerina with a tutu and pink shoes, but you could braid her hair, and she had eyes that blinked. She was even better than the Missy I had before.

Daddy shouted, 'I'll be back later,' and the front door slammed with a thud. Not long after, Mummy peeked into my room.

'Mummy,' I sobbed and held out my arms to her.

'It's alright, *Mamaleh*,' she said as she cuddled me. 'Daddy's just a little angry because he loves you so much and doesn't like anyone making you unhappy. Everything's going to be fine, I promise.'

~ * ~

School was so much better than being taught by my aunt. I went to classes with my friends, and we giggled and chatted in the playground during breaks. My best friend, Dora, always sat with me for lunch, and I told her all about my new doll and Mr Reeves, and how he always made me feel happy whenever I was with him. I didn't tell anyone about the cupboard. It gave me bad dreams to think about it.

My seventh birthday passed, and I entered Year Three at primary school. With a new year came new subjects and I found a new favourite: needlecraft. We were learning how to design and sew a skirt. I picked a light blue material with petals scattered all over it. It was pretty and the cloth felt lovely in my fingers. I cut out the shape from the pattern, but I kept pricking my finger on the needle when I was sewing up the seams. I had to be ever so careful not to get blood on it. The day I finished; I added a blue lace trim for the hem. It was so exciting. I couldn't wait for Mummy to see what I'd done all by myself.

I dashed into the house. 'Mummy, Mummy, look what I made.' I couldn't stand still as I showed her the floral skirt.

She gasped and tore it from my hands, ripping it into shreds. 'Don't you ever dare do that again,' she shouted. 'You stupid, stupid child. Is this what your God-given looks are for, to be a dressmaker?'

I didn't understand. 'I'm sorry,' I said in a small voice, the tears gathering in my eyes, 'I thought you'd like it.' I looked at the pieces of material scattered on the floor in front of me. All my hard work gone in a flash.

'Well, you thought wrong, didn't you?' Mummy snapped. She glared down at my wide, tearful eyes and let out a sigh. She put her arm around me and led me to the kitchen table. Her voice softened. 'I'm sorry, darling. I shouldn't have lost my temper, but you need to understand some facts about life.' She held my face in her hands. 'Look at you, such a beauty, destined for greatness. Your gorgeous hair, with its thick, shiny curls that any woman would kill for. Your eyes, any man could get lost in.'

I wrinkled my brow.

She smiled. 'Someday, you'll meet a prince, and he's going to be crazy about you. What man wouldn't? Beauties like you don't grow on trees.' Lowering her hands, she looked out of the kitchen window. 'I was never like that. We were so poor that I hid my face in embarrassment. Wearing clothes passed down from neighbours, with moth holes and God knows what. All eight of us shared a meal best suited for three people. Going to bed on an empty stomach hurt, but the shame was worse. I wanted to dance, to forget my troubles, but my mother couldn't afford to send me to classes.' Her face grew wistful. 'I was talented, and jaws dropped when people saw me dancing. What a waste.' Her eyes clouded with anger. 'Instead, I had to earn a living by taking in dresses for repair, just so our family could eat.' Her fists banged on the table. 'That's humiliation.' She let out a sob. 'It just wasn't fair.' As tears streamed from her eyes, I shifted uncomfortably in my seat. It was hard to see.

'But you don't have to do that anymore?' I said and put my arms around her.

She wiped her eyes with her apron and looked at me. 'Of course not, thank goodness. And as for you, my darling, it's a different story. You will never have the shame of being nothing but a seamstress.' Her thumb stroked my cheek. 'Despite the fact that your father is such a miser. God forbid, he should have to pay out a bit of money for his only daughter,' she spat. 'Well, he can kiss my big round *tuchas* because I have scrimped and saved money for you to attend Miss Fisher's Theatrical Academy when you turn ten. Only the finest go there. Nothing is too good for my special princess.'

I listened, though it was hard to understand. I knew we weren't rich, but there was always plenty to eat. Though sometimes, whenever my friends wore a new dress, and I asked if I could have one as well, Mummy would hold me and say, 'Don't blame it on me. If it were possible, I would give you the world. Never forget, I am your very best friend'. Then she would pull away, narrowing her eyes. 'Your father, now that's another matter. He's a stingy, hard-bitten man who has trouble putting his hand in his pocket, even for his own flesh and blood'.

I disagreed. My daddy worked so hard each day in his shop, *Bloom Antiques*, where he bought and sold silver and jewellery. Once, he had managed to get hold of a chocolate bar and, taking a knife, he cut it into three parts and gave me two. When he smiled at me, it was even sweeter than chocolate, but when he took out the strap, I wished I could undo whatever I'd done to make him so angry. The beatings hurt, but the disappointment in his eyes was worse.

I looked at my mother's kind face. I wasn't sure I understood, but I wanted to please her so badly. Picking up the pieces of material, I placed what remained of my skirt into the rubbish bin under the sink.

'Good girl,' Mummy said, 'you're so special. You'll make me proud.' She kissed me on the cheek. 'What a beauty. Now, Daddy will be home soon, so go on upstairs, wash your face and comb your hair. You know what he'll do if he sees you've been crying, don't you?'

I shuddered. *Please, not the strap again.*

~ * ~

Three years passed, and I had to agree with Mummy; the new school was so much better than the last one. The school uniform was stylish and well-fitted, and there were no more boring classes like science and geography. Instead, I studied elocution, French, and deportment lessons—learning to be a proper lady.

I would bounce out of bed each morning, eager to get to my daily studies of dance, mime, drama, and singing. We did a public performance at the end of each term, and of course, Mummy insisted on sitting at the front, pointing up at me. 'That's my beautiful daughter. Such *naches* I have. Please, God, you will have such pride from your children,' she would announce in a shrill voice to anyone nearby.

There was something magical about dancing on stage. When the music played, I would lose myself in the experience, and all my shyness would disappear. It was a shame I couldn't sing a note. I would've loved to join the musicals, but there was ballet, tap, and modern, all of which I loved.

Miss Fisher, wearing her blue leotard, her sleek silver hair tied up in a hairnet, taught her dance classes with an iron fist. She insisted on complete silence and commitment to the craft. If anyone so much as sneezed, she would raise her cane and strike their ankles, making lots of girls cry. Compliments were rare, and if someone received one, she strutted around the dance floor like a proud peacock. I longed for such a reward, but it hadn't happened yet. It didn't stop me trying.

All the girls were grateful to be studying at Miss Fisher's Academy.

Joan, Jill, Leoni, and Mary had been there since the year before, but they started chatting with me on my first day. They told me they wished they had curly hair as theirs was straight as a ruler. It made me feel special. They all spoke like the queen and were up to date with the latest fashions. During break, we would leaf through women's magazines together.

'Isn't this gorgeous?' said Leoni. 'I would die to have a dress like this.'

'That model is so thin. I want to look like that. No cakes or sweets for a month,' Jill said as she put her hand on her stomach.

It was wonderful to have such friends to talk with, friends who loved to dance and wore fine clothes. I longed to have such stylish clothes but knew that would be impossible. I felt a flicker of understanding for Mummy as I looked down at my dreary skirt and top in shame.

Chapter Three

JOE

London, 1944

The war was in full swing by the time I was eighteen. Sure enough, the envelope dropped onto the doormat. I'd received orders to report to the Armed Forces for my medical examination that summer.

Arriving in central London, I stood outside behind a long line of men waiting to go into the dull, grey brick building of the army recruiting offices. I was feeling hopeful. Maybe I could finally prove to Pa that I was a fighting man. Lighting a cigarette, I listened to the lads chatting in front of me.

'My fiancé won't stop crying night and day, telling me she loves me. I tell her I'll be back, but she just won't stop.'

'I know, I've got the same with my girl,' said another lad.

Bloody hell. I didn't have anyone who cared that much if I went away, or even if I died. Maybe Ma, but I doubted it. She was a cold fish who never showed me any warmth. *And Pa might even be relieved if I snuffed it, no longer having a useless, loser sissy of a son.*

After about an hour of queueing, I went inside to find everyone milling about in a crowd.

'Excuse me, mate. Do you know where I need to bleedin' go?' I asked a passing lad, who pointed to a piece of paper pinned to the wall.

'Find your surname on that list over there. It'll tell you the assigned room.'

Pushing my way over, I perused the list until I found my name under the L's. I was to go to room seven.

I sat, waiting outside the door, my legs twitching until it was time to go in. I always hated when there was nothing to do except stare at the walls. It gave Pa's voice a chance to echo in my head, criticising me. It was something I constantly tried to block out by joking or telling a story.

I bit my lip. I was so desperate for Pa's approval, and I knew the only way to gain it, was to go and fight in the war. *Who are you kidding? They won't want a puny, sissy boy like you.*

The door opened, and a lad walked out.

'Joe Leslie?' A nurse stood in the doorway in stiff, starched ironed whites.

I jumped up. 'Yes ma'am, that's me. I'm here.'

'Follow me.'

I followed her into the cold and bare exam room.

'Take off all your clothes except your underwear and wait for the doctor.' She gestured with a clipboard.

I did what I was told, feeling like a prize idiot in nothing but my underpants, but I straightened up when the military doctor came into the room.

'Good morning, I'm Dr Crowe. This won't take long. Just have to check you out, see if you are fit.'

'I'm as fit as an ox, Doc.'

'Good. Let's begin then, shall we?' The doctor prodded, tapped, and listened to every part of my shivering body as I stood there with my knees knocking together.

'Please wait for the nurse to return,' the doctor said, then left the room.

'Well, do I get dressed or what?' I asked the silent room. Scratching my head, I figured I should wait. I didn't want to do anything that could be a strike against me.

The door opened, and the same stout, scowling nurse walked in again. In her hand she held a syringe the size of her arm. One look at that and the ceiling whirled above my head. I clamped my hands onto the table to steady myself.

The nurse shook her head and tutted. 'Now, don't be such a child. I'm just going to take a little blood. You'll have to face much more than this in the trenches.'

I held my breath, trying not to pass out and make a complete fool of myself. With my eyes scrunched up, I could feel my heart pounding in my chest as I waited for her to finish. I felt a rising wave of nausea as the needle slid under the skin in the crook of my arm. At long last, she pulled it out and put a small bandage in its place. When she left the room, I breathed a sigh of relief, then got dressed as quick as I could before walking out on shaky legs.

The following morning, I sat in the doctor's office on the edge of my seat, jiggling my foot as I waited for my results. The doctor eyed my chart. 'I have gone over your tests and found that a clerical position would be the most suitable. Although the army needs every able-bodied man, there is no reason to send everyone to the front lines.'

I hung my head in shame. *What am I going to tell Pa?*

One of two things would happen to me when I felt small or defeated. One was to react with violence, and the other was to tell a joke. Considering that hitting the army medic might not go in my favour, I opted for the latter.

'Not to worry, Doc, I'm an expert typist. I'm sure there's a great demand for two words a minute.' I pulled a stupid face. 'Hey, have you heard about the guy who goes to the doctor and says, "I have this terrible problem. Every morning at nine, I have to move my bowels." And the doctor replies, "That is perfectly normal. Most people would be more than happy to have your problem." The man says, "You don't understand, Doctor. I only get up at ten."'

The doctor roared with laughter. Oh, I liked that, so I went on. 'Listen to this one. A woman walks down the street with a duck. A drunk goes by and says, "That's the ugliest pig I ever saw." The woman says, "I beg your pardon. This is a duck, not a pig." And the drunk says, "I know, I was talking to him."'

The doctor was in fits. 'You're funny son, you really are. I have the perfect position for you.'

I left the doctor's office with an order to report to ENSA – The Entertainment National Service Association – on Monday morning at eight. Pa might not be too happy, but as far as I was concerned, it was my lucky day.

I'd been assigned to Major Dresden, who seemed intimidating with his big, bushy moustache, but he had a friendly voice and a contagious laugh.

'So, I'm told you're funny,' he boomed, fixing me with his piercing blue eyes. 'That's good. You'll be part of a group of men. Some sing, some dance, and others, like you, will make the lads laugh, keeping them entertained and boosting morale. You will meet with the others on your team tomorrow morning and rehearse throughout the day. Then there will be a show in the evening.'

I was filled with enthusiasm, so I rose early and headed over to the rehearsal area. I introduced myself to the other men. There were ten in all. Most were budding Frank Sinatra's or Bing Crosbys; at least, they fancied themselves as such. They weren't bad, just needed a bit of practice. The other comedian, Percy Sykes, looked friendly enough. He did impersonations. They were good, especially the one of the King, but I wasn't worried, as my act— the one I'd conjured up the hour before— wasn't anything like Percy's. We wouldn't be treading on each other's toes.

I planned to tell a few jokes, then a couple of funny stories about the war (made up, of course) and then finish with some more jokes. All of that had to be no longer than fifteen minutes.

Not only did we all have to perform, but we also had to set up the stage and take it down after every show. While helping to set up for that evening, Percy and I got talking. He'd been performing for over a year and had a lot to tell me.

'Oh, for sure it's fun, but it can be right hard too. Sometimes we travel to other army bases, and often we have to crack out two shows back-to-back, then onto the jeep for another show somewhere buggering else. You'll miss a fair few dinners, but it's worth it to see the smiles on the lads' faces. Rumour has it we may go abroad soon. That could be dangerous, performing under enemy fire.'

A jolt of excitement shot through me. Standing on a stage with bombs flying overhead? Now that had to impress Pa.

~ * ~

As the months flew by, I stood on the makeshift stage day after day, and had everyone rolling on the floor, splitting their sides, whenever I opened my mouth. I couldn't get enough of the applause. I finally had proof I was worth something. It made me feel like a king. No one dared to call me puny anymore. After years of walking with my head down, I could now hold it up with pride.

The soldiers would clamour around me as I sat in the mess hall and talked till the cows came home. They hung on to my every word. Of course, there were a few who resented the attention I was getting and threw in a snide comment here and there. I was more than familiar with bullies, and I ignored them. Having a few wankers green with envy was flattering. No one had ever been envious of me before.

I was sleeping in my bunk one morning when someone grabbed my shoulder. 'Hey, Jew boy, wake up!'

I slowly roused myself from sleep and rubbed my eyes. *What? How does he know I'm Jewish?* It's not like I kept it a secret, but because of the war and all, I didn't exactly go around announcing it, and with my fair skin, I thought I blended in well with the other guys.

It had happened before. My Pa and Grandpa were also blonde-haired and blue-eyed. When Ma had brought Pa home to meet her parents and announce their engagement, they hit the roof. One glance at Pa was enough for them to erupt into a rage. Of course, it was all cleared up, and they had a good laugh about it over the years. Looking like your regular Aryan had come in handy at times. True, we lived in a mostly Jewish neighbourhood in Stoke Newington, but when Pa went out to trade, it helped to look like a gentile. Otherwise, as a Jew, people would suspect him of trying to swindle them out of money.

I sprung out of bed. 'What did you call me?'

'I called you a Jew boy. You gonna make something out of it?' The soldier gripped my shirt.

'You know what? I think I will,' I said and punched the fucker straight in the nose. I'd had enough of being beaten and intimidated, of feeling small and weak. Blood trickled down the man's face.

'You fucking Yid. Look what you've done. I'm going to fucking kill you.'

I saw red.

I jumped on the other man, punching, slapping, and kicking him. I didn't care what was dirty fighting and what wasn't. Hell, I even used my teeth, sinking them into his ear. He screamed blue murder, but I kept going.

The struggle attracted quite a crowd as my fans rushed into the barracks and stood around, egging me on. 'Joe! Joe! Joe!' It filled me with an incredible burst of strength, like I could conquer anything. With every pound of my fists, I could sense the soldier weakening underneath me, growing limper, until he lay crushed and bleeding on the ground. Eventually, my fists pounded on by themselves, as the darkness closed in around me and I collapsed into unconsciousness.

~ * ~

I opened my eyes and jerked upwards as a sharp pain cut into my wrists. *What the hell?* My gaze shifted downward, landing on the handcuffs securely fastened to the edges of the cot. A soldier in uniform was sitting by my bed.

'What's going on?' I demanded, my voice hoarse.

'You're in the sickbay, but the doctors say you're well enough to stand trial tomorrow morning.'

A trial? Oh fuck. Bloody hell, that's all I need.

They held the court hearing in the officer's headquarters. I entered with Major Dresden, my defence, who directed me to a table on the left side of the room.

Looking around at the paint flaking off the white walls, the smell of defeat filling the air, I wanted to run as far away as possible. *Why did that fucking turd of a soldier have to ruin the only good thing that has ever happened to me? Am I not allowed to be happy? At least the scum got what he deserved.* I felt lucky that all I'd suffered was a black eye and a broken hand.

My mouth was dry, like sandpaper. Licking my cracked lips, I reached for the jug of water in front of me. The wonky table rocked, and, as if in slow motion, the jug and two glasses went sliding to the floor, shattering into pieces as water splattered everywhere. *Fuck!* I bent down to pick up the broken glass, but the major hissed at me. 'For God's sake, boy. Leave that alone and sit up straight.'

Straightening up, I glanced at the prosecutor on the other side of the room. The serious expression on the man's thin, pock-marked face made me want to slap him silly. He was one of those pompous types that I despised, the sort which made me feel small and meaningless. Facing us at another table was Colonel Smythe, the judge for the hearing. I'd seen the colonel a few times but never interacted with him. I didn't know much about the man; except he was high in the ranks and had a lot of clout. He was pudgy and his uniform looked like the buttons might fly off at any minute. I couldn't picture him running exercises at the Front. *Fat people are jolly*, popped into my head and I became hopeful he might be sympathetic. I soon changed my mind.

Colonel Smythe glared at me with beady eyes and his voice echoed throughout the room. 'You have inflicted terrible injuries to another soldier, given him three broken ribs, a fractured nose, and a concussion. Soldiers should be fighting the enemy, not each other. There is a war on, and such behaviour is unacceptable. Do you have anything to say for yourself, young man?'

'He called me a Jew boy, Your Honour,' I shouted, running my finger around my sweaty collar.

'Silence! Do not raise your voice in court. Clearly, *you people* have a problem controlling your tempers.' The colonel's lip curled. 'I sentence you to two years in a military prison on the charge of assault in the first degree. I hope you use this time to learn how to act like a proper Englishman. Case adjourned.'

The bang of the gavel filled the room as I heard Pa's voice in my head.

Once a failure, always a failure.

~ * ~

'In you go,' said the guard.

I stepped into cell number forty-three, flinching when the heavy gate clanged shut behind me. Unmoving, I held my rolled-up, filthy mattress under one arm as I eyed the cramped surroundings. It was the size of a bathroom. There was a bunk bed along the left wall, and on the right was a metal washbasin and a toilet bowl. That was it.

'What're you in for, mate?' A gravelly voice drawled.

I glanced at the muscular guy lying on the top bunk. 'Fighting.' With a thud, I tossed my mattress on the lower bed frame and then stretched out on top. I couldn't bring myself to talk to anyone. It took all of my energy just to keep from crying like a baby.

A blonde head peered down. 'Fighting, eh? How long they give you?'

I peeked at the upside-down face. 'Two years. Two whole fucking years just for breaking a bastard's nose.'

'Christ! They've got it in for you, don't they?'

The man jumped down and offered his hand. 'The name's Johnny, Johnny Reed. What they call you?'

'Joe Leslie,' I said, deciding I felt a bit better talking to someone after all. 'What are you in for?'

'Me? Shit, I just missed my wife and kids. I've got two boys, four and six, and the missus is expecting another any day now. I just wanted to see 'em. It'd been over three months since I'd seen 'em last. I kept asking for leave, and they kept refusing, so I just left.' Johnny shrugged. 'They gave me six fucking months. I've done two already, but it goes so slow. I'm about to go crazy. Fucking Army.'

My prison sentence dragged on and on. I spent most of my days lying on my bunk, dreaming of the moment the iron gates would open and I could walk out a free man. Until then, I crossed off each day on a scrap of paper.

Four months in, they released Johnny Reed. I fell into a lasting gloom. Even though Johnny was not exactly a genius, I'd enjoyed our talks about women, boxing, and football. It didn't matter what the subject was, as long as I had someone to chat with to pass the slow-moving hours and minutes of my sentence.

Charlie Johnson was the new replacement for the top bunk. He wasn't the most talkative of fellows. A typical conversation usually involved him grunting yes or snorting no, which suited me just fine. So long as the communication stayed civil, and I didn't need to worry about my backside. I'd heard rumours about what happens behind bars.

Sundays were visiting days. My parents had turned up twice the first month, but it had been seven months now since anyone had come. One Sunday morning, while I was poking at my cold porridge, a guard shouted, 'Joe Leslie! You have a visitor.'

I made my way along the dimly lit corridor, passing cell after cell, each identical to my own with the rusty iron grids. A few prisoners pressed their faces against the bars, heckling me as I trudged past. Keeping my head down, I ignored them while the guard banged his baton on the cell doors.

There was novelty in the departure from the daily drudgery, and I was curious to see who had arrived. I supposed it was my parents. As much as I was eager to see them, the shame I felt when I saw the disappointment in their eyes was worse than my prison sentence.

The guard led me into the visiting area and I plonked myself down at a table, lighting a cigarette. My heart was thumping in my chest.

A familiar figure marched in and slapped me on the back, then sat down.

I cringed. 'Hi, Pa. You're looking well. How's Ma?'

'Son,' said Pa. His grin was so wide that I could see his large white teeth. 'Today I come bearing good news. You remember the Cohen boy from across the road?'

'The one that always had his nose in a book?' I remembered how boring the boy was. We'd always been encouraged to play together, but I would almost fall asleep listening to him droning on about science and archaeology.

'That's the one. Isaac's his name. Well, he's all grown up now and a solicitor at some fancy law firm in the West End. Anyway, your mother bumped into his mother the other day and told her what had happened to you. So, Isaac filed an appeal, and guess what? He says because of good behaviour, he's confident he can get you out of here by next week.'

I didn't know whether to laugh or cry. After chatting a bit more with Pa, I went back to my cell, grinning so much it hurt.

Isaac Cohen was as good as his word. The following Wednesday, I thought my heart would burst with happiness as the iron gates slammed shut behind me. I was free.

~ * ~

It was back to the army and entertaining for me. It was like coming home. Except, on my return to the base, everything looked different. The barracks were almost deserted.

'What's happening, Corporal?' I asked a soldier walking by.

'Where the hell have you been? The war's over. It's over! Churchill just announced it on the radio. We're free, mate, no more uniforms, no more orders. Take your stuff and get out of here.' He chuckled and clapped me on the shoulder.

I stood rooted to the spot, rubbing my forehead. *Over? That's not good. What the fuck do I do now?*

The soldier looked at me, puzzled. 'What are you, dense or something? Get the fuck out already.'

With a sigh, I walked over to Major Dresden's office to say goodbye. I found him sitting at his desk, smoking a pipe. 'Ahh, Private Leslie, you've returned just in time to leave,' he said with a wink. 'So, what are your plans now, boy? You must continue performing. You always had us all in stitches, especially Private Green, who had eleven of them.'

I didn't think it was funny, but I kept my cool. I was in no mood for a fight. Besides, I liked the major. He was a decent bloke with a good sense of humour, most of the time.

'I'm not sure. I'll have to look for a job. Maybe in the theatre.'

The major gave me a warm smile. 'I have a good friend, Ed Sotherby, that I've known since I was a lad. He's a director in the West End. Go and meet him. Tell him I sent you.' He jotted an address down, handing it to me. 'You never know. Perhaps I will see your name in lights one day.'

I wasted no time. That afternoon I took a train straight to London's West End.

~ * ~

The Glotsby Theatre was an imposing building. Built in the 1800s, it held a mysterious atmosphere of importance. Inside, I took in the magnificence. Red carpets and plush seats surrounded the huge circular stage. Large oil paintings representing various plays and theatrical productions of the past hung on the velvet wallpaper. I stood, mesmerized by the velvety quiet that, every night, would come alive with lights and laughter.

'Hello?' came a soft voice from the back.

I jumped. 'Oh, sorry, I didn't see anyone there. I'm looking for a Mr Sotherby.'

'You've found him. How can I help?' he asked, walking from the back of the stage to the edge. Ed Sotherby was a handsome man in his early forties with sandy hair and green eyes. He wore a cravat around his neck, which I found a bit odd, but theatre people were known to be eccentric, I supposed.

'Major—Mr Dresden said I should come and see you. I need a job.' I scuffed my shoes against the ground. 'I've been performing with the army troop. Now, you ask anyone, and they'll tell you how funny I am. I can show you,' With more confidence than I felt, I stared Mr Sotherby in the eye.

'Well, you don't waste any time, do you?' Sotherby laughed. 'You may be in luck. I'm holding auditions for a new musical and am looking for a young lad like you.' He gave me a once over. 'If Dresden likes you, then I'm willing to try you out. Be back here at three.'

'Thanks so much, Mr Sotherby. I mean it, thank you, thank you!' I skipped out of the theatre, whistling a merry tune.

~ * ~

'Okay, girls, pay attention. Let's rehearse the song again,' Ed shouted.

Surrounding me were fifteen long-legged beauties dressed in army uniforms and wearing helmets. I stood with my back straight, saluting the flag, a big grin on my face. I couldn't believe my luck. Just me and all these girls, and all I had to do was stand and salute, then join in as we sang 'God save the King' at the end of the show. We did eight shows a week, making enough money to pay my rent and have some left in my pocket.

'All right, that's it for today. I'll see you all tomorrow, nine a.m. sharp, for the dress rehearsal,' Ed hollered as the song ended.

I followed the girls as they made their way down to the dressing room. It was my favourite time of day, with half-naked women, who never seemed to care if I was there. In fact, they seemed quite fond of me, hugging me close and giving me pecks on the cheek. I had a huge crush on Jane, a tall, ravishing blonde with enormous knockers— a real stunner. She hung onto every word I said as though I was the King himself. I tried my hardest to entertain her because her laugh was the most beautiful sound I'd ever heard.

Jane was sitting at her dressing table, wearing nothing but her underwear and stockings. She reached for a cigarette when I approached. As quickly as I could, with shaking hands, I whipped out my box of matches and lit one, holding the flame up for her.

'Thanks, darling.' Jane puffed on her cigarette.

'Hey,' I mumbled, 'I wondered if maybe you would like to come out for a drink with me tonight? That's if you're not busy or something.'

Jane laughed. 'You sure you're old enough to drink, luvvy? I wouldn't want to corrupt you.'

I could feel the heat rising in my cheeks. 'I'm older than I look and more experienced than the lot of you.' That was an outright lie. I'd never even kissed a girl, and at nineteen years of age, I cringed at the thought. I was desperate to lose my virginity once and for all, and tonight was as good a night as any.

'Well, let me see.' Jane peered at me. 'You're in luck. I happen to be free and would love to go for a drink with someone so experienced.'

I swallowed hard. *Bloody hell. What have I gotten into?* 'Righty-o. I'll meet you at the Bull and Fox whenever you're ready.' I grabbed my coat and rushed out the door before she could change her mind.

When Jane entered the pub, all the men's heads turned, their eyes following her as she walked over to me. I ran my fingers through my hair and gave her my best smile. I was trying to figure out how one began sex. *Could you say, 'here's a beer, now take off your clothes'? I don't think so.* Sweat trickled down my back as I stood. 'I've got a pint for you, luv. Here, take a seat.' Trying to keep my hands steady, I pulled out the chair across from me.

'Perfect. I've wanted this all day. You must've read my mind. Do you read minds, Joe? Can you tell me what's on mine?' She grinned at me.

I was sitting in what I imagined was a sophisticated, manly pose, with my legs apart as I dragged hard on my cigarette. 'Why don't you give me a hint, and I'll see if I'm right.'

'That's cheating, naughty boy. I'll have to punish you if you keep this up.' She leaned over the table, giving me a glimpse of her ample cleavage. I licked my lips and took it as an opportunity to make a move.

'You see, I can read your mind. You were thinking that you needed to come back to me flat and give me the punishment I deserve. Right?' I flashed a cheeky smile. *Bloody hell, I'm good.*

She sniggered. 'Oh, you are naughty, aren't you? I'll just finish my drink. Then we better get to your place. I'll give you something you won't forget in a hurry.'

Chapter Four

IRENE

London, 1949

I sat in front of the mirror as Mum adjusted my hair ribbon. 'Hold still and stop fidgeting. One has to suffer for beauty.'

I loved my parents' tiny bedroom, with its lacy curtains surrounding the window and the white puffy eiderdown covering the bed. It was so cosy. I would've loved to jump up and down or roll around on it, but it would never be allowed.

Mum stepped back. 'Ah, what a picture you are. A princess. A queen!' Her face became serious. 'Listen, my sweet. Daddy has some very important clients coming over today. They own a big antique business in the West End. I want you to look pretty, and to speak clearly, remember your elocution lessons. They might buy some of Daddy's silver, so we must make a good impression.'

I nodded. 'Yes Mama.'

Later, while we were busy in the kitchen getting everything ready, the kettle's whistle almost drowned out the doorbell.

'Hurry up. Put out the best plates and don't forget a doily under the cake.' Mum fumbled to untie her apron before rushing to the front door. I listened to her high-pitched voice echo throughout the house as she attempted to speak the King's English.

'Hello, so nice to meet you all. My dear husband has told me so much about you.'

There were other voices, but I couldn't make out what they were saying.

Mum dashed back through the swinging doors. 'Quick, help me bring out the tea.' She picked up the polished silver tray laden with a teapot and several cups and saucers. 'Come along, stop dawdling, and stand up straight. You want people to think you have a hunchback?'

I smoothed down my dress and followed her into the living room with the fruitcake, setting it down neatly on the coffee table next to Dad, who was sitting in his favourite armchair.

'This is my daughter, Irene. Irene, say hello to Mr and Mrs Leslie and their son, Joseph. I am told he is quite famous.' Mum pushed me towards them.

'How do you do, Mr Leslie?'

Stanley Leslie was such a big man that my hand was almost crushed as he shook it.

'Just fine, my dear, thank you.'

I warmed to him at once, but his wife was another matter. I winced as Aunt Sarah's haunting image appeared in my head. This woman had the same hawk-like nose and thin lips. When she spoke, I was taken aback. Her tone was soft and sweet, so very different from the witch.

'Nice to meet you. My name is Elizabeth.' She put out her hand.

'Nice to meet you too,' I replied, shaking hands.

I turned to introduce myself to the son.

He winked at me and said, 'You, doll, can call me Joe.'

I felt my ears burning and a blush creeping into my cheeks. He was as handsome as a film star, with his blond hair and glittering sky-blue eyes. I couldn't remember ever seeing anyone so gorgeous.

'Irene is at theatrical school. She's such a talent!' Mum's accent dropped in excitement, but she was quick to correct it. 'She *is* a true star.'

I tried not to wince at her fake-posh delivery.

'Her teachers tell me she is gifted, like me. I gave up my career to look after Mr Bloom, but one could say that the apple does not fall far from the tree.' Mum laughed, her bitterness almost coming through. 'Irene, put on your ballet shoes and show our friends how well you dance.'

No. Please no. My body went stiff, my eyes wide, as I crossed my arms.

'Now, don't be shy. You've performed on stage on so many occasions. Another few people should not bother you.'

I glared at her, my jaw tense.

Joe covered his mouth, looking like he was about to burst into laughter. I prayed he wouldn't; it would be devastating.

'There's no need to trouble the girl,' Elizabeth interrupted. I felt a wave of gratitude towards her.

'Nonsense. Irene loves to perform. Don't you, dear?' Behind Mum's fixed smile gleamed daggers, daring me to refuse.

'Of course, I would love to,' I said through gritted teeth before hurrying out of the room and upstairs. *Why does she always do this to me? It's so embarrassing. And in front of Joe. He's so grown up and good-looking. He'll think I'm a little child.*

With ballet shoes laced and tied, I stood by the door with my shoulders slumped. 'Ready,' I mumbled, hoping no one would hear.

'Ah, there you are, precious.' Mum walked behind me, pulling my shoulders back as she nudged me further into the room. She strode over to Dad to give him a sharp prod with her elbow. 'Manny, would you be so kind as to play some music on the gramophone?'

Dad sat up with a jolt, his pipe about to fall out of his mouth. 'Oh … yes, dear, whatever you say.' He crossed to the record player sitting on the sideboard. Opening up the dark oak cabinet, he eyed the collection of records stacked neatly inside.

'How about Swan Lake?' Mum suggested, holding her hands together. 'She always dances it so much better than the other girls in her class, doesn't she, Manny?'

'Yes, dear,' Dad said under his breath.

Since I had no choice, I straightened up and plastered a smile on my face as the music began. I felt everyone's eyes on me as I leapt into the air, landing gracefully on my toes. Joe smiled as he puffed on his cigarette.

I burned with embarrassment. I desperately wished Mum would stop insisting that I perform for her guests. After the last time, I'd begged her, never again, but here I was.

Finishing with a curtsy, I stood to one side. There was a lot of applause.

Joe whistled. 'Bloody good there, girl. You've got the moves.'

Stanley scowled at him. 'Calm down, boy. There'll be none of that, thank you very much. We don't want our friends here thinking we are commoners, do we?'

'Of course not, Pa.'

I went upstairs to change my shoes and look in the mirror, hoping my face wasn't too red. By the time I came back down, satisfied my colour had returned to normal, the men were discussing silver, which didn't interest me. I joined Mum and Elizabeth on the sofa.

'Darling,' Mum said, her face glowing with excitement, 'I just learned that Mr and Mrs Leslie's hobby is ballroom dancing.'

'Oh, yes,' Elizabeth said. 'We go weekly to the dance halls. Perhaps you and Manny would like to join us sometime?'

'We would simply adore to,' Mum squealed.

'How about next Saturday night?'

'That would be lovely. Oh, wait a minute. What about Irene? I can't leave her home alone. It's not proper for a girl of her age.'

'Not to worry,' Elizabeth patted Mum's arm and gestured to the men. 'We can get young Joe to sit with her.'

I thought I might pass out.

After the guests had left, I helped Mum clear the plates, all the while trying not to scream. Eventually I said, 'You can't leave me alone with Joe. I wouldn't know what to say to him.'

'Don't be silly. You don't have to talk to him. He can listen to the wireless or something while you read a book.'

'But Mum—'

'Enough Irene. It's all arranged. This is important for Daddy's work. I will not have you ruining it with your petty complaints.'

Alone in my room that night, I sat on my bed, biting my nails, as my thoughts charged through my mind like a racehorse. Being alone with someone was hard enough, let alone making conversation. Not knowing what to say to a hopelessly handsome adult man who made my legs weak and my heart pound in my chest was something else altogether. I felt half terribly afraid, certain I would make a fool of myself, yet somehow, I felt a fizzing sort of thrill, too. It set my head spinning and an odd warmth blooming in my stomach. I'd never experienced a feeling like it before and I didn't know what to make of it.

I tried to concentrate on my studies all week, but the upcoming meeting was always in the back of my mind. The teacher had scolded me twice for not paying attention. I wanted to confide in my friends, but I couldn't quite describe what I was feeling. I was sure they would only laugh.

Before I knew it, Saturday night had arrived, and the doorbell's chime sent shivers down my spine. I stood at the bottom of the stairs while Mum bustled to the door to let the Leslies in.

'Good evening,' Stanley bellowed, his large frame filling the doorway. 'All ready to go?'

Dad called me over as he popped his hat onto his bald head. 'Irene, show young Joe to the sitting room and make him a cup of tea.'

'Of course. Please, follow me.'

'Bye, darling. We won't be too late,' Mum shouted as the door banged shut.

I led Joe into the living room. *He looks even better than last time, and his blue shirt and slacks match his eyes perfectly.*

He settled himself on the sofa and looked around. 'Where's the television set, luv?'

'Oh, I'm sorry.' I laughed, embarrassed. 'We don't have one. Well, not yet.'

'Then we shall have to make do with a bit of light entertainment. Don't worry. I can provide that. Ever heard the joke about the drunk who goes into a hotel and asks for the keys to room four-three-four?' He paused to light a cigarette, inhaling deeply.

I opened the cabinet to take out an ashtray, placing it in front of him on the table before sitting across from him, the cup of tea forgotten.

'Anyway,' Joe continued, 'Ten minutes later, a man goes to the desk, smothered in blood, and says, "Can I have the keys to room four-three-four?" The desk clerk says, "I am sorry sir, but we gave those keys to someone else." And the drunk says, "Yeah, that was me. I fell out of the window."'

I tried to keep my composure, like a lady ought to, but I couldn't stop myself. My smile escaped and I doubled over, laughing so hard that I found it hard to breathe.

'You liked that, did you?' Joe grinned, 'Well, I'll tell you another after you go and make me that cup of tea.'

I darted into the kitchen and put the kettle on, hoping it wouldn't take long to boil so I could listen to more of his wonderful voice. When I returned, Joe was leafing through the newspaper Dad had left.

53

'Now, that's a spread,' he said, pointing to the tray in my hand. 'Fruitcake, my favourite. Everyone tells me I'm a bit of one.'

I almost dropped the tray because I couldn't stop laughing. Joe told one joke after another all evening. Some were so naughty that I blushed. Dad wouldn't have approved, but I didn't care. I was having a fantastic time and didn't want it to end, but time flew by, and before long, my parents returned.

Stanley and Elizabeth waited by the front door for Joe. I followed him out. His eyes sparkled as he squeezed my hand. 'I had a smashing time, kid. I'll be waiting for you to grow up, so do it quick.'

I thought I might faint.

I dashed to my room the minute they left. I sat at my dressing table and looked at my flushed face in the mirror. 'He'll be waiting,' I whispered to my reflection. 'He said he'll be waiting!' My stomach exploded into cascading butterflies. Sleep took a long time coming that night.

At breakfast the next morning, Mum placed a steaming bowl of porridge in front of me, but I couldn't even swallow a mouthful. 'Did everything go well with the Leslie's?' I asked.

'Oh, yes,' she said, pouring hot water into the teapot, 'Daddy is selling them quite a lot of silver. He's very pleased.'

'And did you like them?'

'What's not to like? They're wallowing in money. Please, God, one day, you should have as much as them. You should have seen them last night, spending it like water.' Mum shook her head in amazement.

'What did you think of their son?' I asked, pushing my food around the bowl, hardly daring to look up and gauge her reaction.

'A looker, no doubt about that, but no class. They've been lucky, though. Grew up like us in the East End, but now they live in Kensington with all the wealthy folk.' She frowned. 'No. They might be loaded, but no breeding. Their table manners, ugh. Elbows everywhere, talking with their mouths full. I was so embarrassed. Thank goodness I've brought you up better.' Mum sat down next to me and poured herself a cup of tea.

'He is funny. Their son, I mean?'

'Yes, quite a lark, and he couldn't keep his eyes off you.' Mum cupped my face. 'My beauty. A few more years and the boys will be lining up.'

'Don't be silly.' I giggled, taking the dishes to the sink to hide my burning face.

I never forgot about Joe. He often appeared in my mind whenever I passed a blonde man in the street, but slowly, over time, he faded to nothing but a pleasant memory.

~ * ~

At fifteen, my mother's words proved to be well-founded. Boys were chasing after me after me in droves, but I didn't know if I liked it much. It always ended with me pushing them away, brushing their seeking hands from my waist or ducking a kiss. It was like wrestling with an octopus— once one grasping hand had been removed, another appeared to tighten its grip. Couldn't they just sit and talk without all the fuss?

I mentioned my little problem to Mum one evening and immediately regretted it. Taking me by the shoulders, she sat me down for a heart to heart.

'Darling,' she began, looking straight into my eyes, 'men only want one thing. They'll try to jump into bed with you, then once they get it, off they run. Your virginity is a priceless jewel.'

'What's a virginity?' I asked. I thought I might've heard the word before, but I wasn't sure what it meant.

Mum looked uncomfortable. 'There's plenty of time for all the details later. Let's just say it's a special place in your …' She pointed in the direction of my private parts.

I couldn't look at her in the eyes, instead I made a point of studying the floor.

'Now, listen.'

I forced myself to pay attention, though I would've preferred listening to a lecture on the life stages of ants rather than being exposed to Mum's rantings.

'Guard it like the crown jewels. The man that gets it should be able to afford it. Let him court you, take you to dinner and buy you expensive presents. Even after all that, you still mustn't give it to him until he's put a diamond on your finger and you have taken your marriage vows.' She nodded her head. 'Trust me, darling, you'll thank me for it.'

My head was spinning. I had so many questions, but none I could put into words.

Mum cleared her throat. 'All you have to know my dear, is to keep your legs crossed. Don't let any boy go near there.'

'Mum! I wouldn't. I couldn't.' Crossing my legs, I placed my hands in my lap for extra protection. I was horrified at the idea.

'Good. Now, let's go and get dinner ready.'

Following her into the kitchen, I wondered about the special place between my legs called a virginity.

~ * ~

On the morning of my sixteenth birthday, I sprang from my bed and raced to the mirror to see if I looked any different.

Sixteen. A grown-up.

I shivered. *Something wonderful is going to happen today. I just know it.*

I joined my parents in the kitchen.

'Happy birthday, princess. Come and eat your breakfast before it gets cold.' Mum led me to the kitchen table, where a hot bowl of porridge was waiting, a giant blob of sweet raspberry jam spreading on top. Mum only got the jam out on special occasions. I tried to swallow a few spoonfuls, but I had too much energy to sit still.

'Here, darling, this is from both of us,' Dad said with a twinkle in his eye. He handed me a small package wrapped in shiny brown paper, tied with a red silk ribbon.

'Thank you.' I gave them each a long hug before carefully unwrapping the paper. I knew they couldn't afford extravagances, so it was a rare gift. I opened the thin blue box inside.

'Oh!' I gasped, 'It's beautiful.' Inside was a heart-shaped silver locket, two tiny panes of glass inside that could hold a miniature photograph. I lifted the delicate chain and fastened the pendant around my neck at once. 'Thank you so much. I love it.'

'Something to match your beauty, my darling.' Mum smiled. Then she clicked her fingers. 'Oh, I almost forgot. A parcel arrived for you.' She set down a professionally wrapped rectangular box in place of my porridge.

'For me? But who sent it?' There was no return label.

I didn't waste any time. I ripped off the wrapping paper and found an expensive-looking box of chocolates in a creamy box with gold edging. After the sparse years of rationing, they were a rich treat. I picked up the card that was enclosed. On the front was a picture of a bulldog with a cigar in its mouth. Inside, looping handwriting read: *Happy birthday, sweet sixteen. I'm still waiting, Joe Leslie.*

I couldn't believe it. I broke into a huge smile. 'It's from Mr Leslie's son. How on earth did he know it was my birthday?'

'Dad and I ran into Stanley and Joe on Tuesday as we were leaving the silver vaults. Joe asked how you were, and I mentioned you were to turn sixteen today. I must say, he took quite an interest,' Mum said with a smug smile. 'Oh, and by the way, he said he might be in the neighbourhood today, so I suggested he should pop in to say hello.'

I felt jittery. 'I … um … should have a bath, I think.'

'That's a good idea. Remember what I said, Irene. Guard the crown jewels. You know what I mean,' Mum added with a wink.

'What's that all about?' Dad asked.

'Never you mind. It's between us women.' Mum smiled at me before I ran upstairs to the bathroom.

I stood in front of the bedroom mirror, eyeing my yellow top and red flared skirt with its patterned waistband that Mum had sewn for me. *Why can't we afford something else? It's so embarrassing having to wear the same clothes every day.*

The doorbell rang. I gave my cheeks a quick pinch for some colour and tried to steady my breathing.

'Irene,' Mum shouted, 'your friend is here.'

I tiptoed downstairs clenching my sweaty hands behind my back. Peering around the living room door, I spotted Joe sitting on the sofa, one knee over the other, puffing on a cigarette. He looked devastatingly handsome, more so than I remembered.

'Hello, luv. Don't you look pretty? All grown up now.' Joe smirked, catching me staring. My face flamed with heat.

'I was just telling your parents that as it's such a nice day out, I thought we could take a drive and grab a bite to eat somewhere.'

I was at a loss for words. My mouth was dry. 'Would that … er …

be all right?' I managed at last, glancing at my mother, my fingers crossed behind my back.

'Of course, darling, but make sure you return at a decent hour,' Mum playfully scolded Joe, wagging her finger.

'I understand, Mrs Bloom. Irene's a growing girl. She needs her sleep. No need to worry.'

My face hurt from smiling as we climbed into his dark green Jaguar. It was so luxurious. The seats were deep and plush, the soft cushions covered in rich brown leather. Joe drove with one hand on the steering wheel and the other out of the window. He talked and smoked most of the journey while I listened, carried away on his dreamy voice.

An hour later, we arrived at The Wesley Country Inn, about twenty miles outside London. We ate a traditional English lunch of roast beef, Yorkshire pudding, peas, and potatoes. I couldn't believe that I was actually eating meat. It had been years. Rationing was still in practice, so meat was a delicacy. I almost felt guilty that my parents couldn't enjoy it as well, but what could I do? Take it home? Of course not.

I loved how Joe took charge of everything. He ordered the meal, told me stories, and insisted that I eat all the food on my plate. It all tasted delicious. I had forgotten how satisfying it was to tuck into a roast.

I noticed many diners staring at Joe, murmuring amongst themselves and felt silly not knowing quite what he did, and why they might be so interested. I was too shy to ask. I knew he worked in entertainment and television— he had said so several times on the ride over— but since we didn't have a television set, I knew little else.

After eating, we strolled through the village, browsing in the quaint shops on either side of the cobbled street. One particular shop caught my eye. The latest fashions were draped over mannequins in the window; the designs and colours were captivating. I was about to ask Joe about the red dress when I realised he had vanished. He was no longer beside me. I looked around and found him peering into the antique shop across the way. I hurried to join him, and as he took my hand, I felt a bolt of electricity fizz through me. It was like being struck by lightning.

Joe smiled. 'Let's go in here and check it out.'

The bell rang as we entered the cramped shop, brimming over with bric-à-brac. A balding man wearing a three-piece suit and a yellow cravat emerged to greet us. 'May I help you?'

'We're just looking around, sir. Seeing what you got.'

'Of course. Please, go ahead. I am here if you need me.' The salesman returned to the counter.

We wandered through the shop. Since we both grew up in families that dealt with silver and antiques, it was second nature for us to spot quality pieces. I picked up an old atlas and began leafing through it, as Joe went to the counter to inspect the jewellery displayed under the glass.

'Irene, come over here and look at this,' Joe called. 'What do you think?'

He pointed out a cameo brooch with diamonds around the edges.

'Oh, that's lovely.' It was. It had lost none of its lustre and each diamond was precisely cut, identical to the others.

Joe smiled. 'Then it's yours.'

'Oh no, no, I didn't mean …' I stammered.

'Hey, mate,' he said to the salesman, 'wrap this up for me future wife.' He turned to me and bent close, his blue eyes looking straight into mine. 'Happy birthday, kid,' he said, planting a kiss on my cheek.

A tingling crept up the back of my neck, spread across my chest and into my cheeks. It was the most delightful sensation I'd ever experienced.

After the drive home, we walked to the front door. Joe took my hand and kissed it.

'What a *boat* you have, and what *mince pies*.' He grinned.

I frowned, taken aback. 'Sorry, I don't understand.'

'Boat race rhymes with face. Mince pies rhymes with eyes. You gotta learn the lingo if you wanna keep up with me.'

'Cockney?' I asked. I'd heard Dad mention the men joking in the warehouses.

'Of course, my *china*. China plate rhymes with mate.'

'Oh, I see.' I laughed.

'One last thing before I leave, do you *Adam and Eve* in *turtle dove*?'

I cocked my head to one side, trying to work that one out.

Joe kissed me on the cheek one more time, then turned and walked away.

'Adam and Eve – believe. Turtle dove – love. Night, Irene.' He shouted.

I stood there, a smile glowing on my face, in no hurry to go in the house.

Over the coming weeks, every day, a bouquet of blooming, fragrant flowers would arrive for me. I was thrilled. It was terribly romantic and Mum agreed, but Dad often sighed, his brow wrinkled.

One evening at dinner, after Mum had placed a dozen red roses in the centre of the table, Dad exhaled loudly. 'Enough already. Are you sure this is a good idea? Of course, it's flattering, but Joe is twelve years older than our Irene, and I don't like his line of work.'

'But, Dad,' I moaned.

'Don't be silly,' Mum said. 'He is perfect for her.'

'Perfect?' Dad threw up his hands. 'How can you say that? You're the one that went on about their low class and bad manners.'

'Maybe I did, but manners are the least important when you've got the money they have. Besides, our Irene can teach him once they are married.'

'I give up.' Dad huffed, returning to his soup.

I sat back with a smile of satisfaction and gazed at the roses.

~ * ~

One afternoon, some months later, I went out with Joe.

'Where are we going?' I asked.

'We are going on a little drive, kid. That's all I'm gonna say for now.'

I didn't know what to think but felt excitement bubbling up.

'This is mysterious. Where are you taking me?'

'We're just going to go down this road here.'

Joe pulled onto a tree-lined street and parked in front of a grey, two-storey house with bay windows.

'See that house over there with the for-sale sign?'

'Yes.'

Joe looked pleased with himself. 'I'm going to buy that house for us for when we get married.'

My mouth fell open. I felt my stomach leap. 'What do you mean?

What are you saying?'

'I'm saying, you daft cow, that we're going to get married. You and me.'

'Married?' I was confused. *Is he proposing?* I was fairly certain that, in these situations, the man usually got down on one knee and offered a ring. That's how it went in books.

'Yes, of course, married. You passed the test, luv. I'm going to marry you. I've been around the block a few times, and the fact that no man has ever touched you suits me just fine. You're easy on the eye and Jewish, too; that's important to me. You have all the qualifications to make me a perfect wife. So, whatcha say, eh?'

'Does this mean you love me?' I asked with hesitation.

'Of course, I bloody loves you. I'm proposing to you, aren't I? Come on, give us a kiss and let's go and tell your parents.'

This was the big kiss I had been waiting for. My very first one. I puckered my lips and moved to his, but he turned his face and kissed me on the cheek. I felt a flicker of disappointment. Oh well. Perhaps next time?

Mum squealed when we told her the news, but Dad just stood. 'The weather forecast is for rain tomorrow,' he said.

'Dad,' I frowned, 'that's all you have to say?'

He looked at me and I saw concern in his eyes. 'What do you want me to say, Irene? You are much too young. Besides, I can't afford a wedding. I expected you to get married in your twenties, not at sixteen. I have a little fund that will come to fruition on your twenty-first birthday, so it's out of the question until then.'

I felt like my shining bubble had burst.

Joe stepped forward, 'Don't you worry, Manny. I'll pay for it. It'll be my pleasure. It's the least I can do now you're giving me your beautiful daughter.'

I held my breath, waiting for Dad's reaction.

'Well,' Dad exhaled, 'I suppose I can't object. *Mazal tov.*' He gave a small smile and shrugged.

The excitement of planning the wedding filled the house and, before long, even Dad was caught up in arranging the band, the food, and, most importantly, choosing the Rabbi.

My heart sang. I couldn't have been happier

Chapter Five

JOE

1954

I sat in my dressing room, smoking a cigarette, waiting to be called to my adoring public. I looked at my face in the mirror, flashed my famous smile and chuckled. *Who'd ever thought, eh?*

The early days in the theatre seemed so long ago. If it hadn't been for Ed Sotherby giving me the lead in the play, *Heartache*, I wouldn't have been discovered by the top agent who got me an audition to host a game show on TV. Lady Luck was in; they loved me, and it turned out to be the number one hit. *Give Me A Break* ran for three years until I starred in another winner, *Lump It Or Leave It*. The pay was great, and I was able to rent a huge modern flat and even get my suits tailor-made. Life was grand.

After taping the show, I liked to go outside and watch the girls fighting over me. Some of them practically tore off their clothes. 'Joe, I love you,' they would scream. I remembered Jane with the big tits and how I was desperate to have a girl like her, until I discovered that apart from her spectacular body, there was nothing else. Besides, I had my pick of all the best girls clamouring around me every night. For a while, I loved seeing other blokes looking at me with envy, but in time, the novelty wore off, leaving me feeling empty. Still, being a star did have its perks. It certainly made me feel better about myself.

After the show one day, I popped into one of the other studios to see what they were filming. It was a daily drama with a busty blonde that everyone was drooling over. The show wasn't bad, but not my cup of tea — too much of a soppy tearjerker. When they'd finished shooting, I walked over to the actress, bold as brass.

'Allow me to introduce meself. I'm your competition,' I said with a smirk.

She burst out laughing. 'Of course. I'm quivering in my boots.' She put out her hand. 'The famous Joe Leslie. So nice to meet you. I'm Sheila. Sheila Rand.'

'Should we add a 'y' to the end of your name, eh?' I said with a wink.

From that day on, we were inseparable. We'd have coffee together after we finished filming each day and got on like a house on fire. We loved to joke about the idiot fans who were prepared to do just about anything to have a night with one of us. The best part was that I didn't fancy Sheila at all. She was too tall and loud for my liking, but I loved her humour. I found it was great to spend time with a woman with none of the mucky bits getting in the way.

'So where do you live then?' I asked.

'I have two homes,' Sheila said, patting her shiny blonde hair which, cemented by hairspray, barely wobbled. 'One in London, Mayfair, and the other in Royal Crescent Mews in Brighton, next door to Sir Larry.'

'Ooh, fancy. Rubbing noses with the toffs, eh?'

'Yes.' Sheila laughed. 'I'm in Brighton during the summer and on the occasional weekend but spend the rest of my time in London.'

Sheila introduced me to her other friends, and before long, I was spending every night playing poker with the gang.

One late afternoon at the studios, we sat having our usual coffee. Shelia opened her compact mirror and applied an extra layer of dark red lipstick. She snapped it shut and smacked her lips together. 'So, Joe, am I hearing right? You're getting married? Is this one of your jokes?'

'I have never been more serious in all me life,' I said, reaching in my shirt pocket for my cigarettes.

'I don't believe it.' She studied my face. 'You are serious, aren't you? Well, to who, for god's sake?'

I lit up, exhaled, then sat back with a big grin on my face. 'She's perfect for me in every way.'

'What the hell do you mean by perfect? Good in bed, I suppose.'

'Hey, watch it.' I wagged a finger at her. 'Don't you talk about my intended like that. Irene's her name, and she's perfect. She's sweet and gorgeous with dark brown curls and innocent eyes that look at me like I'm the best thing since sliced bread. Best of all, no one's ever touched her before. Clean as the driven snow.' I took a long drag on my cigarette and exhaled smugly.

'Bloody hell,' said Sheila, 'you really are smitten.'

'She's wonderful, and to top it off, she's Jewish.'

Sheila cracked up. 'Since when did that matter to you? My bacon-eating Jewish friend.'

'I know. I know,' I waved her away. 'I don't expect you to understand. It's just me old man always harped on about marrying in the faith, even though we never followed any of the other rules.'

'Well,' said Sheila, planting a lipstick laden kiss on my cheek, 'if you're happy, then I'm happy. I can't wait to meet her. You'll have to bring her to one of my *do's*.'

'For sure. Now let's go back to your place and get the boys in for a few hands.'

Part Two

(Marriage)

The most important rule a wife must follow:
Never, ever contradict your husband.

Chapter Six

IRENE

1958, London

The brand-new West End club was the place to be seen. It was crawling with the most fashionable, glamorous people that London had to offer and was the perfect opportunity to wear the expensive, sparkly black dress that Joe had bought for me. My confidence was high and I felt good. Joe had told me I looked gorgeous in it.

We were out with friends and Joe was in a good mood, telling his jokes and making everyone laugh. I didn't mind sitting on the side, studying the beautiful models at the bar who were all draped in the latest fashions.

At first, I had been sick to my stomach with nerves, horrified by the thought of meeting Joe's friends— what if they hated me? I needn't have worried. They were warm, welcoming people and before long I had relaxed in their good company. Spotting another friend, Joe introduced us and we were soon chatting happily. Suddenly, she pointed at Joe's orange juice. 'Now I think of it, I can't remember you ever drinking anything stronger than that.'

Joe's eyes widened. 'Oh yeah, that's because I once got a fishbone stuck in me throat. Since then, any booze burns something horrid.'

That didn't make sense to me. 'But you always told me you don't drink because you're allergic,' I said.

He laughed, one of his fake high-pitched ones. 'My wife, such a lovely girl, but stone deaf.'

Looking straight at me, he emphasised each word. 'What I said, *darling*,' — beads of sweat were shining on his forehead— 'is that I became allergic *after* the fishbone got stuck. Understand now, luv?'

I dropped my eyes to the floor, staring holes into my shoes. 'Of course, Joe, I must have misheard, silly me,' I said, my voice low.

I looked up as he laughed and pointed at me, rolling his eyes and mouthing 'idiot'. I felt my cheeks burn. *No, that's not true. How am I meant to keep up when he changes his stories on a whim?*

As soon as we left the club, he grabbed my arm and dragged me to the car. Opening the passenger door, he tossed me inside, then slammed it shut. Throwing himself into the driver's seat, he pressed his nose against mine and screamed so loud the windows rattled, 'Just wait till we get home!'

As soon as we walked through the front door of our home, he gripped me by the throat and slammed me against the living room wall.

'How many times do I have to tell you, eh?'

He glared at me, his eyes slits, as his fingers dug deeper into my throat.

I blinked rapidly, trying to clear the haze from my eyes. *Is this it? Is this what dying feels like?*

'Can't breathe,' I wheezed, scrabbling at his hands, desperately trying to pull his fingers off.

'Never, ever, contradict me in public. Do you understand?' he said through gritted teeth, a bright red vein throbbing on his forehead.

'Yes.' My voice was barely a gasp as tears splashed onto my cheeks.

He dropped his hands, only to hurl me to the floor.

Massaging my stinging neck, I coughed and spluttered, trying to gulp in mouthfuls of air.

He sunk onto the settee and looked down at me, cowering near his feet. 'I'm sorry, but you have to learn to shut up. Now, go and make us some tea. I'm parched.'

Why, oh why, do I never keep my big mouth shut? If I had just kept quiet, none of this would've happened.

~ * ~

As time passed, I learned to be grateful for what I had. In fact, I felt fortunate to be married and living in modern times, unlike my parents, stuck in the suffocating traditions of the past. We had a television set with two channels, a luxurious Jaguar, and, best of all, indoor plumbing; no more freezing to death in the middle of the night when you wanted to spend a penny.

Our home was stunning, situated in the best part of London, with four bedrooms, a huge living room, and a kitchen with all the latest gadgets, like an electric kettle and a refrigerator that made ice cubes. I even had a new twin-tub washing machine, something none of my friends owned. When my son, Boris, was born two years earlier, all I had to do was put his dirty nappies in the machine, then lift them out with wooden tongs and place them in the second one. They came out sparkling clean a few hours later. It was like magic.

Life was now a far cry from how I grew up in the East End, with only one set of presentable clothes and my parents scrimping and saving to send me to a decent school. I used to cringe at my scruffy shoes and hand-me-down dresses when other children wore brand-new clothing. At night, I would lie in bed, dreaming of beautiful houses, exquisite clothes, and delicious chocolates. Since being married to Joe, I had all that and more, so I needed to cherish it and be thankful.

I waddled into the bedroom, holding my huge pregnant belly, and peered down at Joe sprawled in our double bed. He'd insisted on having an afternoon nap over four hours ago and as always, he was dead to the world. As I watched him, his face so peaceful, I had a sudden urge to crawl in beside him. I'd do anything for a cuddle, some warmth and affection, but there wasn't enough time. We needed to get going to Sheila's party.

Why does he need to sleep so much? It couldn't be normal. If he wasn't in a half-daze, he was full of energy and raring to go. It was exhausting trying to keep up. He could be like an exploding volcano when irritated, so I was hesitant to rouse him.

I gently patted my stomach as my baby gave me a quick kick. In all honesty, both times I'd fallen pregnant, I'd wondered how Joe would react, given his condition. It wasn't a subject I enjoyed, but he often talked about the operation he'd had for undescended testicles. The doctors had told him they had fixed the problem, but there could be a chance he might be sterile. The first time I found myself pregnant, he'd sat me down and demanded I tell him who I had slept with. It took weeks to convince him I had only ever been with him, no one else. Then came a complete change of mood, and he walked about like a rooster, chest puffed out, telling everyone that he'd got his wife pregnant.

I knew I would have to take a chance and wake him up, whatever the outcome. Biting the nails of my right hand, I gently shook Joe with my left.

'Joe, you need to wake up.'

He grunted, pulling the covers over his head.

'Joe, the party is starting soon. We have to leave.'

No response.

I let out an enormous sigh. 'Please, Joe.'

'All right, woman,' he mumbled, 'Bring me my pills and a ciggie. I'll be up in a mo.'

I always did what he requested. He made the rules, and I needed to comply. My duty as a good wife was to love, honour, and obey, just as my mum did and her mum before her. Joe insisted I fulfil my womanly role by looking after the home and our two-year-old son, Boris. Our nanny fed and bathed him, but he kept me busy the rest of the time with his energy and curiosity. Boris could spend hours in the garden, digging in the dirt, showing me worms he found. When I'd shriek in horror at the revolting, wriggling thing in his hand, he'd roar with laughter. He was such a delightful boy and so handsome. He had my curly dark hair and his father's blue eyes. I loved cuddling him, kissing his chubby cheeks; his giggles were music to my ears.

Joe's job was to take care of his dogs, Belvedere and Guinevere, two fat slobbering bulldogs who spent most of their time stretched out in our bed. Their disgusting, short, stubby hairs clung to everything like magnets. I had to shake out the sheets and hoover the carpet every morning. *I do like them, really, even though they smell, but why can't they be like normal dogs and sleep on the floor?* Joe refused to discuss it, no matter how I felt.

If we had to have dogs, I would've preferred a sweet little fluffy one I could put ribbons on, but he insisted on bulldogs only; it was the breed he'd grown up with. I'd lost count of the nights I lay awake listening to them snoring and passing wind, wondering who he loved more. Maybe it was better not to know the answer.

I was painfully aware that everything I did sprang from my desperate need for approval. An ache deep inside me craved validation, a pat on the head, a smile that told me I was valuable and wanted. Without it, it was as though I didn't exist. It all started with my father. He only had to glance at me in disapproval, and my cheeks would get hot as I huddled in the corner with my stomach in knots and my shoulders hunched. I tried so hard to make him proud, but I often did the complete opposite. Out would come his belt, and he would give me a good hiding, although it was never good— believe you me. I never knew what I had done wrong, but if I cried, he would tell me he would give me something to cry about. It would anger him if I made too much noise, so I tried to be as quiet as a mouse, but sometimes I couldn't help myself.

Things weren't much different being a wife. I was still careful not to do anything wrong, making sure Boris kept his voice low whenever his father was around, and I had every meal ready on time. It was all worth it when Joe was happy. He became charming, funny, and affectionate. He liked to pinch my bottom, tickle me, and have conversations with my breasts, which he named Tom for the left and Jerry for the right. He could make me laugh for hours. But when the black clouds appeared... I didn't even like to think about it.

If you are married, there are rules a wife must follow, duties they must tend to, like housework and childcare, but for Joe, there was one rule that was sacrosanct. Never, ever contradict him— especially in public. Unfortunately, it would slip my mind sometimes, like a fool, and then I would have to endure my punishment. I never forgot each episode of violence, nor did I become immune to them, but my memory was selective sometimes, which made me careless.

I first experienced Joe's rage when I accidentally tripped over one of the dogs, and she yelped. Joe was in the middle of talking to someone on the phone, which he slammed down to race over to Guinevere. I told him she was fine, but Joe viciously kicked my leg and yelled, 'Now you know how she feels.' I had an enormous bruise for over a week. After that, I was careful to step around the dogs, but they were everywhere, hanging at my heels.

Now, as I stood listening to Joe's breathing, I knew it was imperative I had the correct pills, a glass of water, cigarettes, and a lighter when he woke up. *Wait a minute, is it the blue or the purple pills in the evening? I'm almost sure the blue ones, no, maybe the purple? Oh, gosh. Fine, I'll bring him both, then he can choose.*

Joe sat up, picked out two purple tablets, and swallowed. Lighting a cigarette, he leaned back on the pillows. 'What's the time, me darling?' He smiled at me, and, as always, butterflies danced in my stomach.

'Quarter to seven.'

'What?' he screamed; the smile erased from his face. 'Why the fuck didn't you wake me earlier? We're going to be late, and as usual, it's your bloody fault.'

He jumped out of bed and left the room, leaving his cigarette smouldering in the ashtray.

'Sorry, but I tried to wake you,' I said timidly.

'You're always sorry, aren't you?' he shouted as the bathroom door slammed shut.

Stubbing out his cigarette, I sat at my dressing table with my makeup, hairbrush, and face creams, all the things that usually comforted me. I loved painting my face and fixing my hair. *What's the matter with me? Why do I do the wrong thing time and time again?* I wasn't only angry with myself but livid with my mum and her stupid beliefs. She brought me up to believe I was beautiful and perfect and that any man would worship me. Well, she was wrong.

I looked out the window at the dull and dreary sky and felt the same greyness settle in my heart. I knew Joe would calm down eventually, but each time, it took its toll, like a wound that kept scabbing over, sore and inflamed, becoming a scar that was hard to ignore.

Joe started singing in the shower. Good. *Happy Joe* had returned. I listened to his song while applying my bright red lipstick. Tonight's version sounded like another variation of his usual.

'It might be a big one,
But it's got to have a kiss.'

I shook my head. *Why does he feel so compelled to sing about sex when he prefers sleeping instead of making love?* It was clear we'd done it. My enormous stomach was proof, but I could count the number of times it had happened on one hand. He once told me that even if you had the best box of chocolates money could buy, you didn't want to eat them every day, or you'd feel sick. I didn't understand. *Can you get a stomach-ache if you do it too much?*

I was a virgin when I married Joe, so I didn't know what to expect, and Mum wasn't much help. She just said, 'Lie back and put up with it. As long as he gives you diamonds, you'll be all right.' She was wrong again. I didn't need to just put up with it. I rather enjoyed it, but Joe never seemed interested.

One of Joe's friends gave me a nudge once. 'You don't want your hubby taking too many of those pills. They can affect the libido.' I didn't know what that meant. It sounded like an exotic fruit. Confused, I just nodded. I found out the real meaning a few years later, then shuddered with embarrassment every time I thought about it.

Joe whistled as he approached the bedside table to light another cigarette. He stood there, dripping wet, wearing nothing but a towel. I could spend all day staring at him. His piercing blue eyes and sandy blond hair made me weak with desire. All my friends swore he looked just like the film star Paul Newman. I disagreed. He looked ten times better.

With a laugh, I pointed to the pieces of tissue paper stuck to his chin. 'You've cut yourself shaving again.'

'I know. It always happens to me. I don't think I'll ever get the hang of it. Perhaps I should've become a butcher.' He walked towards the closet to find something to wear, turning back for a moment to give me a cheeky wink. 'Blimey, you look smashing. Good enough to eat.'

I melted. That was all it took. One look, and I forgot about all his shortcomings.

Truthfully, I was proud to be married to Joe Leslie: game show host, actor, and entertainer. If you switched your TV on at dinnertime, you would see my husband filling the screen. Wherever we went, women would giggle and pat their hair, but it was me he would come home to. Well, that's what he told me.

Once we were dressed and ready, we went downstairs.

At the front door, Joe played with the dogs as they growled, snorted, and drooled all over his blue three-piece suit. Nanny Green stared in silence; her lips pursed. She had started working for us the day Boris was born. The plan was for her to stay and help with the new baby. I was always very careful not to do the wrong thing in case she left. I didn't have the confidence to raise children alone. Having someone else take responsibility gave me a sense of security and I depended on her guidance and wisdom.

Nanny liked everything spotless. Her silver hair was always combed into a neat bun at the back of her head, and her uniform perfectly starched and laundered. She often remarked, 'A clean body makes a clean mind.' I wasn't sure my husband lived up to her expectations.

Nanny turned to me, ignoring Joe, as usual. 'Do not worry about Boris, Mrs L. He has had his evening bottle and should sleep through the night.' Nanny always emphasised each word precisely, as though it was of utmost importance. She wrinkled her nose. 'It seems the dogs are shedding again. I will lock them in the kitchen.'

Joe winked, popping a Polo mint in his mouth. 'No worries, Nanny. Mrs L has always dreamed of having a fur rug. Let the dogs shed all they want, and soon we should have enough for one.'

Once outside, Joe muttered, 'That bloody woman is an anti-Semite.'

'How can you say that? She's always pleasant to me.'

'Yeah, right. A saint until another Hitler comes along, and then I guarantee she'd turn us in as quick as a wink. Fucking Nazi,' he spat. Grabbing the car door handle, he yanked it open.

I wished he wouldn't go on about that sort of thing. The war was long over, and from my experience, no one was expecting us to hide in attics anymore, but he insisted every one of them was our enemy, as though Nazis were waiting around every corner. His father was the same. He always told us to behave better than the gentiles, so they wouldn't have a reason to blame us for every little thing. I disagreed. *Aren't we all alike?* It didn't matter what religion a person followed. We all felt pain and sadness. We were humans. If only he would see it like that.

As we approached Sheila's place, we wove along the meandering driveway, already packed with many expensive cars, all overshadowed by an impressive mansion. The first time I visited, my jaw nearly dropped. It was the biggest place I'd ever seen. Huge, glittering chandeliers hung from the high ceilings, casting a golden glow over the rooms. I still wasn't sure how many rooms she had. I'm not certain Sheila knew either. Every bedroom had a fur rug; even the bathrooms had one. I believed it was the ultimate luxury to sit on the loo with your feet buried in a fur rug. I once took off my shoes and stockings to feel the softness. It was divine.

The party was in full swing when we arrived, crammed with people standing around, chatting. In one corner, the record player belted out music as several couples danced in a frenzy, knocking over anyone or anything that stood in their way. The air reeked of smoke and liquor, making my stomach churn. Those things didn't bother me most days, but when I was pregnant, that was another matter.

As we entered, Joe announced to the crowd in a loud, dramatic voice, 'I'm here. Your troubles are over.'

Everyone looked up and within moments Joe had an audience. He was well known for his silly antics and wild tales and always wound up the centre of the party. Never needing much encouragement, he embarked on his latest story. 'You won't believe it but ask Irene. She'll tell you it's true.' He lit a cigarette, inhaling deeply. 'Last night, I was walking along the street when…'

I tuned out. I'd already heard it more than once. Besides, looking at all the beautiful faces was far more interesting.

Removing myself from Joe's side, I started to mingle, regretting it moments later. Despite being obviously pregnant with my massive belly, men were making passes at me left and right. I had to wrestle wandering hands off my body at least three times, and the smell of alcohol on their breath was enough to make me want to join a nunnery. I was ready to return to my husband, elbowing sweaty bodies out of my way en route to Joe. The surrounding crowd had big smiles on their faces, listening to his every word.

'So, I had her there in front of me, and I says, "You can look at me all you want darling, I've been blind for the last ten years",' said Joe, amongst roars of laughter. He noticed me standing nearby. 'Anyway, I've got me a real stunner now, haven't I? Hey, woman, come here and give your old man a kiss.'

With my face and ears burning hot, I kissed my husband, trying to find something witty to say back, but I couldn't think of anything. He had such an effortless way with words that I couldn't help but admire. I often studied him, desperate to learn how to be funny and entertaining, rather than a shy little mouse.

'You can see I've done me duty for queen and country.' Joe

chortled, pointing to my pregnant stomach.

'Joe, stop,' screamed one girl, doubled over. 'You'll make me wet my knickers.'

'Well then. I'd better continue with the story— hang on, here's Sheila.'

Sheila was Joe's best friend. At forty-three, she was tall, blonde, and had an incredible figure. The look on men's faces when she descended the staircase proved that age was not a problem for them.

Joe assured me he'd never touched her, nor did he want to. 'I don't fancy women with big tits. It's like a bloody cow. Nah, whatever fits in the hand is enough for me.'

Yet everyone, including Joe, fawned over her because she was an actress on that program, *Promises*. I watched it a few times, but to be honest, I thought it was shallow, overacted rubbish. Of course, I would never tell Joe that.

Sheila clapped her hands and announced in her most theatrical voice, 'Ladies and Gentlemen, you will be happy to know that the games are about to begin. Follow me. Everything is all set up and ready.'

I winced. *Oh, no. Not again.* I'd just about recovered from the last one.

I nudged Joe. 'Shouldn't we be going home?'

He frowned. 'Don't get your knickers in a twist, darling. We'll stay a bit, and then we'll be off.'

He grabbed my arm, pulling me upstairs with him. At the top, in front of a large, dark brown wooden door, rows of chairs were arranged like a mini cinema.

Sheila shushed from her seat in the front row. 'I'm sure you are all wondering what Auntie Sheila's up to this time. Well, Naughty Sheila has put a two-way mirror on dear Thomas and June's door.' People snickered and giggled. 'Now, perhaps we'll find out why my overnight guests wanted an early night. Is everyone ready?'

Her butler stood up and removed the wood panel from the door.

I gasped. I couldn't believe my eyes. We were looking straight into a bedroom with a couple writhing naked on a four-poster bed. The young woman mounted her lover as though she was taking part in a rodeo.

Although muffled, I could hear their groaning and shrieks. I had never witnessed people in the throes of passion before. I was appalled and disgusted, but at the same time, curiosity got the better of me. Those poor people were being watched, examined. This was worse than her last party when they played pass the parcel. The prize was a sex toy. I'd had no idea what it was, nor did I want to know.

Not knowing where to look, I covered my eyes with my hands. *What's the matter with me? I'm a grown-up, married woman who needs to behave the same as all the other adults.* I placed my hands back on my lap.

Grabbing my arm in excitement, Joe whispered in my ear, 'That randy old sod is starting round two. Good for him.'

Squirming in my seat, my face burning and my eyes on the ground, I prayed the performance would be over soon. *They can't go a third round. Surely not.* Luckily, it ended when the couple turned out the lights.

Unclenching my hands, I rubbed my knuckles as everyone rose and dispersed into various rooms. The atmosphere was hot and humid, but Joe was oblivious. 'Come on, woman, it's time to leave.' He took my hand, and we went downstairs.

'Shouldn't we say goodbye to Sheila?' I asked.

'Nah. She's got other things on her mind if I know her.'

The butler opened the front door, bowing us out, and we went out to the car.

As we sped along in the Jaguar, I asked, 'Where are we going? This isn't the way home.'

'Got to see a man about a dog, me darling. You try to get some rest; you're sleeping for two now.' He chuckled, patting my swollen belly. I didn't find it funny at all.

Joe parked outside The Blue Casino a few minutes later. The shabby white building was used for illegal underground gambling. Joe didn't care if it was legal or not. He just wanted to play.

It wasn't fair. Last time, Joe had made me sit in the car for almost five hours.

'I won't be long, so don't sulk. I've told you plenty of times that you're too young for this, so just count some sheep or something.'

He gave me a quick kiss before racing off to the craps and roulette tables.

Listening to the sound of the rain as it drizzled and spattered on the roof, I felt a kick. 'The rain never stops, does it?' I said to my baby as the condensation dripped slowly down the windowpane.

Chapter Seven

JOE

The Blue Casino was home away from home, with lush maroon carpet your feet sunk into as you walked between the polished tables. The walls were a beautiful shade of blue that matched my eyes, and chandeliers hung everywhere. *What am I saying? It's better than home.* Women dressed in furs and men in tuxedos crowded the tables, which filled up the cavernous room with its selection of games; poker, roulette, craps; you name it, they had it. It was a gambler's paradise. I didn't drink, but if I wanted to, they had the best selection of whiskies in England, single malt, scotch, and bourbon. All you had to do was click your fingers, and some sexy wench would bring you what you wanted. The fact was, they wanted you drunk, so you would spend all your money without realising it. Lucky for me, I always gambled stone-cold sober, having my wits about me at all times.

The best thing about The Blue Casino was that there was no one here to nag me. I was free to do whatever the fuck I wanted.

Stepping through the thick oak doors, I relaxed instantly. It was just how I liked it, full of cigar smoke and ladies' perfume, the sound of dice hitting the table, and people cheering. All the regulars were in. Deborah, the seductive cigarette girl, walked over with her selection. I gave her a peck on the cheek. 'Hi, luv. You're looking as lovely as ever.' She giggled. 'I'll take a pack of B and H, okay, darling?'

I waved to a few mates as she handed me a packet.

'Hey, Joe, wanna join the game?' a lad shouted.

I shook my head, going straight to the roulette table. I had a gut feeling that twenty-two was going to be a winner.

The thing I loved most in life was gambling. I didn't care if it was cards, roulette, or whatever, as long as I was king when my numbers came in. There was no feeling like it. Everything else faded away when I was on a winning streak; it was abso-blooming-lutely marvellous.

For me, gambling was medicinal. I spent most of my days and some of my nights so wound up nothing could make me relax, but when I was sitting with a deck of cards in my hands, all the stress melted away.

It wasn't easy being me. Most people I knew went through their lives with the same boring daily routine, all safe and secure. Not me. I had demons living in my head. My fucking father, for one, criticising, judging. Try as I might, I couldn't get rid of him. The only way I could blot him out was to escape into a game of cards. When I won, it was like I was sticking my finger up to him.

Reaching the roulette table, I settled in beside my mate, Steve. I met him when I first came here almost five years ago. He'd always be here, no matter what. He didn't seem to have a life outside these walls. Unlike other blokes, I found it easy to talk to him, and he always took an interest in what I had to say. He won a lot, too, so there was a chance it would rub off on me if I hung around him.

'How you doing, man?' Steve slapped me on the back as I sat down.

'Just fantastic. I can feel it in me bones. Tonight's the night.' I grabbed my chips, kissed them on both sides for luck—it was my ritual—then placed them all on number twenty-two.

The croupier called out, 'No more bets, please,' and the ball started to spin.

I sat back and watched, my leg twitching under the table, then leaned forward to grip the table's edge. *Come on, twenty-two, you can do it. Come on, come on, darling.*

The ball started to slow.

Here it comes. Yes! Yes! Almost… Fuck! Twenty-bloody-one.

'Christ, that's unbelievable.' Outraged, I banged my fist on the table. The ice in Steve's drink clinked against the glass.

'Bad luck, mate.' He patted me on the shoulder.

'I'm going again.'

I bought more chips from the croupier, ignoring the vision of Irene's disapproving face that swam in my head, and placed the lot back on twenty-two. *This time it's going to work. I'm certain of it. It has to.*

The ball started to spin again. Round it went, slowing down. *Here it comes. Yes! Yes! No!* I couldn't bloody believe it, not even close. I put my hands on my head, trying to squeeze away my father's voice. *You're worthless. That's what you are.*

I clenched my jaw so hard my teeth hurt.

'Come on, mate, let's go get a drink,' Steve said, leading me to the bar.

I ordered an orange juice as we sat down.

'I think you'll need something stronger than that.' Steve chuckled.

'Fuck that. You wanna hear something ridiculous? Every time I lose, I have my old man's voice in my head telling me I'm worthless. I know it's stupid. I'm a grown man, famous, on TV, married to a smashing wife, got me a son, and another kid on the way. Still, the bastard doesn't approve.'

I grimaced. *What's the matter with me? Telling mushy things to my mate, he'll think I'm soft.* I needed to talk to someone to sort out the mess in my head that was making me crazy. If it wasn't the old man in there judging me, it was Irene and her parents. I wanted to explode. *Can't they see that I'm a good bloke? That I'm a talented genius, and they need to make special allowances for people like me?*

Steve was the only person I felt might not judge me. I could've been wrong, of course, but for some reason, I didn't care.

'That's tough.' Steve nodded. 'Didn't you ever want to hit him back or criticise him too? Give him a taste of his own medicine?'

'Sure I did, but I don't hit old men, and that's what he is now.'

'Well, screw him. Let's go back to the table. You can try for number twenty-two again.'

Yeah, why the hell not? Third time lucky, right?

Chapter Eight

IRENE

I sat up with a jolt as a searing pain shot through my stomach, taking my breath away. I groaned, clamping my eyes shut until the cramps subsided. *Where am I?* I couldn't get my bearings for a moment. Then I remembered. I was in the casino's car park, waiting for Joe to return. I must've dozed off. I sat in the cold, dark car, my body trembling. As the coat I was wearing did little to warm me up, I wrapped my arms around myself and squirmed uncomfortably. The chair beneath me was soaking wet. *Wait…Oh, no.* I gasped. *I think my waters have broken and labour has started. It can't be. I have at least three more weeks.*

Another contraction began, and I clutched the door handle, almost cutting into my palm with my fingernails as the pain intensified. After it had passed, I sat back, taking deep breaths, my head in my hands, massaging my forehead. I whimpered. *Think, think, what to do?*

I needed to find Joe, but he never allowed me into the casino. He always said I was too young. Twenty-one was the minimum age, and I still had three months to go until my birthday. *Surely there are exceptions? Emergencies, for example?*

The rain saturated me as I stepped out of the car and hurried across the parking lot, clutching my enormous belly. A dull-lit lamp shone above the building as I pried open the massive oak door with all the force I could muster. Squeezing through, I entered as a gust of heat blew across my frigid body.

An overweight man in a tuxedo sat behind a table in the foyer. 'Are you a member, Madam?' he asked, peering at me over a pair of ludicrously small horn-rimmed spectacles, perched on the end of his nose.

I waddled over to the desk, my teeth chattering and hair dripping water onto his table. *What must he think of me?*

'I'm not a member, but my husband is. His name's Joe Leslie.'

'Yes, I know him, but how old are you? We don't let in anyone under twenty-one.'

What is wrong with him? Is he blind?

'I'm twenty, but please,' my breath was coming out in short bursts, 'I need Joe. The baby's on its way.'

His eyes widened as he shot up, knocking over his chair. 'Oh, right, I understand. Well, that's a different matter. Stay here. I will run and get him.'

As he opened a door behind him and hurried out, I heard the sounds of people cheering and laughing. At any other time, I would have loved to go in and see what gave Joe such a thrill and made him run off at all hours.

The door opened again, and Joe rushed through with the doorman.

'Irene? Are you nuts? What're you doing here?'

'We need to go to the hospital. I'm sorry, but it's time,' I said, my eyes cast down.

Joe exhaled forcefully. 'Bloody hell. What, now? You gotta be kidding. I'm on a winning streak.'

'Sorry, Joe, but—'

Another agonising pain ripped through me, and I hunched over to grab hold of the table with both hands.

Joe paled. 'Well, don't have the bugger here. Come on, woman, let's go.' He took my arm.

The man behind the desk whispered, 'I think you may need to wait until the contraction is over.'

Joe glared at him. 'What makes you the expert? What are you, a doc or something?' he snapped.

'Three children, I suppose it does make me somewhat of an authority.'

The pain subsided, and I straightened up.

'Come on then.' Joe took my hand, pulling me outside and into the car. He drove to the hospital like a maniac while I held onto the door for dear life. It was so uncharacteristic of him to be rough on the Jag, his pride and joy, but I couldn't help but feel a flicker of warmth. He'd chosen me over her this time.

Even though I could see he was panicking, he told joke after joke along the way to keep my mind off the pain. A few of them weren't exactly appropriate for the situation— like the one about a woman who gave birth to a baby with only one leg and no arms, and the father said he could turn the baby upside down and use it as a can opener. Still, he was trying to make me feel better, and I couldn't have loved him more than I did at that moment.

Swerving into the nearest parking spot at the hospital, he forced the hand brake up, ran around to my side, and helped me out as if I were a delicate flower. I felt so special. It wasn't often he treated me with such care, and I loved it.

We'd been at home when I went into labour with Boris. After my water gushed all over the floor, Joe had to sit down with his head between his knees. He thought he was going to pass out. Instead of worrying about myself, I rushed about, bringing him water and a cold towel for his head. We had to call my parents in the end, who drove me to the hospital. Mum stayed with me, holding my hand, which was a comfort. Joe turned up after Boris was finally born twelve hours later. Once he learned he had a son, he strutted around like a prize-winning boxer and dashed off to tell his mates. I hoped that this being the second time, he had become more resilient. After all, he had managed to get us to the hospital without fainting.

We hobbled into the wide, white foyer of the massive building and searched for signs to the maternity ward. It was on the third floor. Joe wrapped his arm around my waist as he guided me into the lift.

'Sorry, me darling, I can't come up with you. These female things make me feel a bit *Uncle Dick*.'

Joe tried teaching me cockney rhyming slang when we were first married. It was like learning a new language. I never quite got the hang of it, but I knew uncle dick rhymed with sick because he said it a lot.

Men weren't allowed in the delivery room, but to have someone waiting with me until then would be comforting. 'Of course, but couldn't you stay until they take me in?' My lip quivered. I didn't want to be alone.

He let out a deep sigh. 'Oh, alright, me darling, let's get this bun out of the oven already. But don't shout at me if I faint. You know I can't stand the sight of blood.'

The lift doors opened, and we stepped out onto the delivery ward. There were lots of photographs on the walls of mothers with new babies, rattles, and balloons. It would've been a jolly place if not for the screams coming from several rooms we passed on the way to admissions. A plump attendant with greying hair was at the desk, talking on the phone. She held a finger up to us.

In pain, I leaned heavily against Joe. He glanced at me with wide eyes, then banged his fist on the desk.

'Hey, the missus is about to drop a load any second. We need help.'

The woman hung up, unperturbed.

'Name, please.'

'Mrs Irene Leslie.'

'How often are the pains?'

'Um, I'm not sure. I think every few minutes, maybe two?'

'Oh.' Her face became serious as she put down her pen and rose from her chair. 'Come along, dear. Follow me as quick as you can.'

I gripped my husband's clammy hand in mine.

'No husbands,' the nurse told Joe. 'This is no place for men.'

She pointed to the waiting room designated for expectant fathers. 'Wait over there with the others.'

He rolled his eyes. 'Fine, but how long you reckon it will be?'

The nurse pursed her lips. 'It will take as long as it takes.'

She took my arm and led me away. 'Now, off we go, Mrs Leslie.'

I looked back at Joe, silently begging him to join me, even though I knew it was impossible.

He blew me a kiss. 'Hurry up, luv. You know patience isn't me strong suit.'

Chapter Nine

JOE

Damn. The nurse could've told me how long it'd take. Maybe I could've raced back to the casino and got in a quick game or two. Just sitting around was fucking torture.

Tapping my foot on the ground, I scanned the room. It was the same old, white-washed walls they have in every doctor's waiting room. Yeah, there were photos of babies on the wall, but I preferred to look at pictures of bulldogs. Far prettier. On the chairs against the far wall sat a group of men with faces as miserable as mine. I had to laugh inside my head at the fella opposite. He looked like a right clown. *Doesn't he know that stripes with polka-dots are a bad idea?* I owed my fashion sense to my lovely Irene. She always made sure I was dressed to the nines.

Polka-Dot Tie, with his striped shirt, kept glancing at me. The moment I walked into the hospital, from the girl at the desk to passersby, people couldn't help but blush and stare at me. I was privileged to be able to give them a spark of interest in their otherwise dull, boring lives. I bet they went home and couldn't stop going on about me.

Polka-Dot Tie was clearly trying to find the courage to talk to me. 'Excuse me, but you look so familiar. Do I know you?'

I chuckled. 'You know me, but I don't know you. Try to work it out.' I posed with my head up and plastered on my famous smile. I could see his brain working in slow motion as he turned bright red.

'You're not … um … Joe … something. Hang on, are you Joe Leslie?'

'That's me.'

His face lit up.

Soon all the other lads dragged their chairs closer. A few shook my hand and introduced themselves. I couldn't remember their names, except for Jenkins, who had the worst case of spots I'd ever seen. He looked like a photo I'd once seen of the craters on the moon.

With all the attention I was getting, it wasn't so boring after all. I couldn't wait to tell Irene how made up the lads were to meet me.

A guy with ginger hair beamed. 'I need to pinch myself. It's really you from the telly. When the missus hears who sat next to me, she'll pass out cold.'

The others mumbled in agreement.

We all looked up in anticipation as a nurse entered the room.

'Mr Rogers?'

One lad jumped out of his chair. 'Yeah, that's me.'

'Congratulations, you have a son. If you'd like to follow me.'

Everyone cheered as he rushed out, leaving us to the waiting game. All eyes were back on me.

'So, how did you start in the business? I've always wondered how you lot become famous,' one bloke asked.

'Yeah, tell us,' the others chimed in.

Smiling, I lit another fag. *What a great way to pass the time, an audience with my fans.* 'Well, I started in the army, the entertainment corp. I put on a comedy show for our boys every day. It was fantastic. Everyone was rolling about laughing, and they all loved me. Except for one fella. Who the hell knows what he had against me.' I shrugged. 'Anyway, this bastard came over and smashed me in the face for no reason whatsoever, so I did what any decent person would do and beat him silly.' I smirked as the men nodded in agreement. 'Then I had to appear in military court, and the judge, this ponce, sent me, listen to this,' I paused for dramatic effect, 'two fucking years in jail. Crazy, eh?'

Shock etched the men's faces.

'You were in prison, Joe?'

'Yeah, I did porridge.'

'Did anyone try, you know, on you?' one guy asked, making a wanking motion with his hand.

'Nah, I just made certain never to pick the soap up from the ground.' I scoffed. 'Any roads, I performed in the theatre after that. I did a show called *Heartache*. It was a smash hit, so me manager, who handles only the best top stars—'

The same nurse came back into the room. *Who is it for this time? Is it me?*

No, it was Jenkins, but he sat glued to his chair. 'I gotta hear the end, Joe.'

'What are you, bonkers? You have a new daughter. Get off with you.'

'Can I at least have an autograph for my wife? She won't believe who I was talking to.' He handed me a pencil and a scrap of paper. 'Could you make it out to Nancy?'

I scribbled a few lines.

'Good luck to you, mate.'

He trudged behind the nurse, who'd been waiting impatiently.

I sniggered as soon as he left. 'I wonder if his kid was born with spots all over her face as well.'

They all cracked up.

'Go on, what happened next?'

I was enjoying myself so much that I could've sat there all night. It wasn't good to keep my adoring public waiting, so I continued. 'So, me manager arranged for me to work in television, and I turned into a star overnight. You remember the program, right?'

'*Give Me A Break*, yeah, I loved that, never missed an episode.'

Everyone agreed it was their favourite show.

'I did that for three years. Can't believe it now. After that came *Lump It or Leave It*, and the rest is history.'

Polka-Dot Tie was embarrassed to admit he hadn't seen it.

'Oh, it's great. The best,' said Ginger Guy. 'They have someone on, and she or he has to decide who is behind the curtain, and it's always one of their friends. If they guess correctly, they win all these fantastic prizes, but if they are wrong, they have to pick a card with a number on it. Then Joe hits them on the head with this huge hammer, as many times as it's written on the card. That's when the audience shouts out …' Ginger Guy turned to me.

'One lump or three,' I announced in my best TV voice.

'What, Joe hits them with a hammer? Don't they end up in the hospital?'

Everyone laughed.

'Jeez, you're stupid. It's a blow-up one,' said Ginger Guy, rolling his eyes towards me.

In came the nurse again. 'Mr Leslie?' she asked.

'That's me.' I yelled and jumped up from my seat.

'You have a daughter. Please follow me.'

I marched down the corridor until I found Irene's room. She was sitting up in bed with a big smile on her face, holding the baby like it was a prize or something.

I bent down and gave her a kiss on her cheek.

'Hello, me darling, aren't you pretty? Let me look at her. Gotta check it's mine, right?' I said with a wink. I was kind of pleased I had me a daughter. It fitted in with the perfect image of a family. I glanced at the bundle in her arms. 'Bloody hell, bald and no teeth, a copy of me old grandfather. This one can't have come from me, not good-looking enough.'

Irene looked hurt. 'Joe, that's cruel. I don't care what you say. She's lovely. You agreed I could name her, so I want her to be called Lorraine.' She held the baby to her chest, stroking her round head.

'What? Like the quiche? Bit posh, ain't it? Beans on toast sounds better,' I said with a cheeky grin.

She held up a finger, shaking it at me, before bursting into laughter. 'Beans On Toast Leslie,' she giggled.

I changed the subject to more important issues.

'Hey, darling, guess what? The boys in the waiting room were shocked when I walked in. Their mouths dropped open. I made their day, that's for sure.' I chuckled. 'They weren't even interested in seeing their kids. They only wanted to talk to me. You should have seen what they looked like; Polka-Dots, ginger hair, and spots. One of them had a schnoz on him like a fucking rhinoceros.' I clamped my fist over my nose and held it up high.

We were laughing so hard we didn't notice Irene's parents arriving. Irene must have had the matron make a phone call.

Pearl raced over to the bed and let out an excited squeal. Manny stood nearby, gazing down at Lorraine with a look of pride on his face.

'My darling girl, well done. The baby is as exquisite as her mother,' he said, kissing Irene on the head.

I almost split my sides. 'You gotta be kidding, right? The only person she looks like is Henry VIII.'

Pearl picked up Lorraine, sat down in the chair, and rocked her gently. 'Don't listen to your father. He doesn't know what he's talking about. You are magnificent, that's what you are, and I intend to spoil you to bits.'

There was a knock on the door, and the doctor walked in. 'Mrs Leslie, how are you feeling?'

'Fine, thank you, doctor.'

Nodding, he picked up the chart at the end of her bed. 'Good. All being well, you can go home in a few days.'

'Hey, Doc,' I said. 'Heard the joke about the woman who goes to the dentist?' I didn't need a reply. 'She sits on the chair and says, "Is it going to hurt? Otherwise, I think I'd rather have a baby." The dentist says, "You better decide, as I will have to adjust the seat."' I grinned broadly and waited for the laugh, but it didn't come.

The doctor coughed, his mouth a thin line. 'Yes, well, hilarious. I will be back in the morning, Mrs Leslie.' He left the room, white coat billowing behind him.

I muttered, 'Bloody doctors. They've got no sense of humour.'

Pearl returned Lorraine to Irene. 'We also need to be leaving. We'll come by again tomorrow. Bye, *Mamaleh*.' She gave Irene another quick kiss, nodded in my direction, then took her husband's arm before leaving us alone.

I pulled up a chair and took out a cigarette.

Irene waved the air as though I'd already lit up.

'Darling, I'm not sure that's a good idea around the baby when she's so small.'

'Oh, alright then. Anything to please me woman.' I put the cigarette behind my ear and blew her a kiss.

She took a deep breath. 'Joe, I've been thinking.'

'You have? Let me call the newspapers.'

'I'm serious. Now that we're a proper family, the only thing we're lacking is religion. It's important. I think we should start having Friday night dinners with the candles, bread, and wine like I did growing up. I know I never talk about it much, but they are fond memories that I want the children to have as well.'

'You can't be serious.' I groaned. 'Told you before, luv, I'm a Jew, and that's who I am, but I like me bacon. There's no need for all that.'

'It's for the kids. I want them to have a sense of belonging.'

'They belong with us. That should be enough for anyone.' I was done with the serious stuff and was itching to get back to the casino.

'Please, darling, say you'll consider it, not only for the children but for me. To make me happy,' she said, batting her eyelashes and smiling at me coyly.

I was powerless when she did that. She looked so damn beautiful.

'I'll think about it. Now, you get some sleep. I'm gonna pop over to Sheila's, tell her the good news.' I got up, gave her a quick peck on the cheek, and was out of there before she could say anything more.

I didn't fancy the Friday night business, but if it put her in a good mood, and made her grateful to have me, then why not? Besides, who was I to turn up my nose at bloody good food?

Chapter Ten

IRENE

1959, London

Mum and I lit the candles, covered our faces with our hands, then recited the sabbath prayer together, '*Baruch atah Adonai, Eloheinu...*'

Mum hugged me afterwards. 'Good Shabbos.'

We headed into the kitchen to check on the cooking. The aroma was heavenly. I loved my mum's cooking. Even during the war, she would conjure up delectable dishes with the bare minimum of ingredients. I don't know how she did it, but she had a special touch.

We brought the dishes out into the dining room. The candles flickered, and with the lights dimmed, the room was filled with a comforting, warm light. The familiar furnishings, like the old table we'd sat around for so many meals, and the antique candlesticks, surrounded me. I breathed in the safe, soothing smell of home: beeswax, linen, and bread.

My family stood around the dinner table while my dad said *Kiddush*, the blessing of the wine. He finished, took a sip from the cup, then passed it around. Once we were all seated, he placed his hand on the challah and recited another prayer before pulling off a piece of the bread, dipping it in salt and eating it. He tore off several more pieces for us.

'Good Shabbos,' he said to us with a smile. We returned the greeting, then Mum and I served the chicken soup with matzah balls.

'You've got magnificent balls, Pearl.' Joe snickered.

'Joe!' I hissed.

'It's true. No one's balls are as good as your mum's, I always say,' Joe said as he stuffed one into his mouth.

Mum shook her head and raised her eyes, but I noticed a small smile on her lips. It was clear from Dad's face that he didn't find it funny.

I looked around with pride. My husband, wearing a kippa on his head, was sitting beside little Boris, who was trying hard to eat his soup without spilling, while Lorraine sat in her highchair, nibbling on a piece of bread. She looked like an angel with her golden curls and bright blue eyes. This was my lovely family, and I couldn't be more content.

'Mummy, I ate all my soup.' Boris smiled at me, proudly holding his bowl up.

'Well done, darling. Now, let's give you some chicken and potatoes.'

Mum served the next course, and we all tucked in.

Joe gobbled down his food in minutes. 'That was delicious, but I gotta run.' He stood up.

'Where are you going? It's Friday night,' my mother said with a stern look.

Joe popped a Polo mint in his mouth. 'I promised Sheila and the lads a quick game or two. Won't be home too late.' He came over and kissed my forehead. 'Smashing grub, darling. I'm so full I can barely move.' He whistled as he crossed the room. 'Well, I'm off. Make sure you don't stay too late; the dogs need their dinner. See you.' With a wave, he left.

'Where's Daddy going?' Boris pouted.

'He has things to do. You'll see him in the morning,' I said, stroking his hair.

Mum sighed. 'I don't understand why your husband can't stay home for one night, especially on Shabbos.'

'Joe needs to relieve stress. He works very hard and deserves a little entertainment.' I needed my parents to understand how necessary it was for Joe to relax.

'In my day, a husband stayed at home with his family at all times,' Dad muttered.

Not wanting to spend the night defending or excusing my husband's actions, I turned back to my meal.

In the last year, my life had improved in leaps and bounds, and I was back in love with my husband. I didn't want my parents meddling.

Joe was full of affection, complimenting me on my face and figure almost daily. I would wait with bated breath for him to come home each night in anticipation of his amazing stories, like how he rode on an elephant down Oxford Street with a chamber pot on his head. He explained he did it for publicity for the family business. It worked. Several newspapers covered the story.

Joe's show was still getting terrific ratings, which put him in a jolly mood most of the time. He would even spend some evenings with the kids, rolling about laughing. Being a bit of a kid himself, he liked to crawl on the floor with the dogs and children climbing on top of him. Joe was even there for Lorraine's first steps, something he missed with Boris. This version of my husband was delightful, and the way I looked at it, going to Sheila's was preventative medicine. I didn't want to do anything that might bring back the old Joe. I'd had enough of that for a lifetime.

Lorraine started to fuss, so I went over and took her out of her highchair and sat down with her on my knee.

'You obviously need Nanny on Fridays as well, it seems,' Mum said in her critical tone of voice, which always grated on my nerves.

'I can manage.' I huffed, bouncing the baby.

'You're lucky to have her. I don't know what you'd do without her.'

On that, I agreed. Nanny had told me that when Boris turned four, she was leaving. She never stayed after a child reached that age.

'What about Lorraine? She's only just turned one,' I'd asked her.

'Sorry, Mrs L, but my rules are my rules. It makes no difference to me. Once a child is four, I'm out of the door.'

Suddenly, she was a poet.

Boris's fourth birthday was in three months, and I shuddered at the thought of having to cope alone. It's not that I was lazy. It's just that I relied on Nanny for everything. Boris was due to start pre-school in a few months, but Lorraine would be with me full-time. To be honest, I did like my leisure time, to put my feet up and read a book or go shopping in town without distractions. It wouldn't be the same with the kids around.

'The truth is, Mum, Nanny plans to leave after Boris's birthday.'

'That's not good. Well, you better make sure not to have any more children.'

'No,' I muttered, thinking how careful I would need to be. It's not that we did it often, but Joe was unpredictable and could suddenly get frisky. Usually, it was to get something from me, like trying to end a bad mood I might be having. I had grown wise to his little manipulations, but I didn't mind as I was happy to have a bit of physical contact. One thing I was certain of was that I had to be very cautious. I was finished with having children.

Three weeks later, I woke up feeling sick but dismissed it, thinking I'd eaten too much rich food the night before, and it had passed by the time I'd brushed my teeth. The next morning, the nausea came again. A terrible thought dawned on me as I sat at my dressing table: I had missed my monthly. *Oh no, it can't be.* I thought back to when we'd last made love about two months before. The entire act had been over in a few minutes. *How can you get pregnant from that?*

I cherished my children, but two were more than enough. My figure had just returned, and I was enjoying being myself again. *What am I going to do?* I needed to confide in someone.

There was no point telling Joe. He wouldn't have any solutions. He would just claim that women's issues were my problem. I knew he didn't want any more children, either. He had a son and a daughter, which he said was picture perfect and just fine. My mum would just say she told me so, and I never discussed such personal matters with my friends. Quite apart from anything else, they knew Joe as well. Instead, I kept to safe subjects like fashion and the latest films. Maybe I should talk to Nanny? After all, she'd been around women and children for years. She might know what to do. *Yes, that's a good idea.*

Joe was at work that afternoon while I was in the nursery with the baby. When Nanny came in with the clean laundry, she turned to me.

'Mrs L, I am afraid I might be coming down with the flu, so after I feed Lorraine, if it is all right with you, I will go and rest.'

'Of course, Nanny, you do what you need to do. I hope you'll feel better soon. Though I wish I knew what to do for my problem.' I sighed heavily.

'What is wrong, Mrs L?'

'I think I'm pregnant again,' I said, fighting the urge to bite my nails.

'Well, that is wonderful. Congratulations.'

'Thank you, but oh God, I have to admit, I'm not happy.'

'Not happy? Every child is a blessing. Do not worry. You will come around to the idea, and once it is here, you will be thrilled.'

'Yes. Maybe you're right,' I said, resigned to my hopeless situation. I started to walk out with my head down. *What can I do? I need help. I'm desperate. She has to understand how I'm feeling.* I turned and walked back to her. 'Nanny?'

'Yes, Mrs L,' she said, taking the safety pin out of her mouth to fasten Lorraine's nappy.

'I just can't go through with it,' I whispered, bursting into tears. 'We have two perfect children. I don't want to spoil it. I have no room in my heart for a third. There is no way I can have another baby. I will go insane if I do.'

Nanny looked surprised, but she put her arm around me and asked softly, 'Are you sure? Sometimes it can be a mistake.'

I shook my head. 'No, I'm certain. I am sick and tired in the mornings, exactly how I was with the last two.'

'I don't want you to worry yourself, Mrs L. It is not good for you.' She picked up Lorraine, put a bottle in her mouth, and rocked her slowly.

The room was silent.

Nanny is such a kind woman. A flash came into my head of Aunt Sarah. How different they were from one another. I wonder what Nanny would have thought of Aunt Sarah, what she would've said to her if she knew what she'd done? I had told no one about my past. It was too horrible to even think about. I preferred to keep it all contained in a neat box in my head. It was safe in there.

'Maybe I can help,' Nanny said. 'My younger sister got in trouble a few times, and she swears by this method. It is not something I approve of, but it does work.'

I was all ears. 'What is it?'

She took the bottle out of Lorraine's mouth and held her to her chest, patting her back with her gentle touch. 'You must only do it if you are one hundred per cent sure you do not want to keep it. There is no going back once you start.'

'I am certain.' At least, I thought I was. 'Please tell me.'

My mouth dried and my stomach clenched as I listened to her instructions. Her solution, though simple enough, sounded harsh. But what choice did I have? I had to do something. If I didn't, there would be another baby in seven months. *What if Joe finds out? You know what, it's none of his business. He's not the one burdened with the kids all day.*

'So, you might have a little bleeding, but by morning you should be right as rain, and no one's any the wiser.' Nanny tapped a finger on her nose.

'That's it? That's all I need to do?'

'Yes, dear. Now, if you don't mind, I'll be off to bed.'

'Of course, you go on up. Don't worry about me and thank you so much.'

By the evening, I had concocted a plan. I just needed to get Joe out of the house. The children were fast asleep, and Nanny had taken a hot brandy and some aspirin and was dead to the world, the house vibrating with her snores.

'Bloody hell, she's louder than the dogs. No wonder the old hag never manages to get any,' Joe said over the dinner table.

'Don't be unkind. Nanny's a lovely lady. She's just not well.' A lightbulb flashed in my head. 'You know, I'm not feeling too good myself. I think I'll have an early night after supper.' I touched the back of my hand to my head as though I had a temperature.

Joe stood up and moved away from me, not wanting to catch whatever I had. 'Well, if that's the case, I might pop over to Sheila's. You don't mind, do you, luv?'

Perfect. 'No, of course not. You enjoy yourself, and I'll see you in the morning.'

I let out a small sigh of relief. It was all working out as planned.

As soon as Joe departed, I grabbed the bottle of brandy and a glass from the drinks cabinet and went upstairs. I started the bath, turning the tap all the way for the hottest water. While it was filling up, I crept into the nursery and retrieved Nanny's knitting needle from the basket she kept in the cupboard. Racing back to the bathroom, I poured myself some brandy. Although I hated the taste, I swallowed a few large gulps, repugnance tightening my face.

Removing my clothes, I lowered myself into the tub, inch by inch, and watched my skin bloom bright red in an instant. I held my breath and sunk deeper into the scalding water. The needle sat on the side, reminding me of what I needed to do next. Studying its pointed tip, I shuddered.

Sweat poured into my eyes and mouth, leaving a salty taste and continued down my face, neck, and chest before disappearing into the water. The walls swayed as weakness overwhelmed me. I couldn't take any more. As I stood up, the world spun and I clutched onto the sides of the bath until it evened out, the needle in my jittery hand. *Can I really do this? Do I have the courage? I could stop now, and no one will know.* But I couldn't. Another baby was out of the question.

I sat down on the edge of the bath, my teeth chattering. *Go on. You can do it. You have no choice.* Taking a deep breath, I opened my legs and, with one swift movement, plunged the needle inside as far as I could. I gasped as tears streamed down my face. With my free hand, I covered my mouth to muffle my screams. The stabbing, stinging, burning pain was sheer agony. *Enough.* I pulled out the needle, and with it came a huge gush of blood, pouring down my legs and into the bath, turning it a dark red. Nanny had said there might be some bleeding, but this was a waterfall, and it wasn't stopping. I took a towel and placed it between my legs, but blood saturated it within moments. *Oh my God, what have I done?*

Despite the room's warmth, my body was freezing. I shouted out, but my voice was no louder than a whisper, and even Nanny couldn't hear me. *I need help. I need Joe.*

Slipping down, I lowered my hands to the floor and crawled into the bedroom, the blood following me on my journey to the telephone. My weakening fingers grabbed the receiver, and with whatever strength I still possessed, I dialled Sheila.

She answered with a laugh. 'Hello.'

'It's Irene.'

'Hello, Irene. Want to talk with Joe? Though he might not want to talk to you. He's been losing every game. Watch out, he's in a stinking mood. I'll just go and get him.'

I could hear Joe swearing in the distance on his way to the phone.

As Joe spoke, as if from inside a tunnel, I fought against the darkness.

'Irene, what's up? Thought you were sleeping already.'

'Joe, come quick… Ambulance…'

Chapter Eleven

JOE

My darling Irene called right in the nick of time. I had a great excuse for leaving. It had been a horrible night. Sheila was on a winning streak, the bloody cow, and I had almost emptied my pockets.

I wasn't that worried about the wife. It was a known fact that women were prone to hysteria, crying over every little thing. I was sure there was nothing wrong with her that a few pills couldn't cure, but I dialled the ambulance, just in case.

The house was quiet when I arrived, except for Nanny's snoring. I walked upstairs and opened the bedroom door, but the room was empty. *Where the fuck is she?* I was about to search elsewhere when I saw a shape in the gloom. I switched on the light and screamed. There, lying on the floor, was Irene, covered in blood.

'Irene?' She didn't stir.

Jesus Christ. I thought I was going to pass out right on top of her. Picking up her arm and trying hard not to throw up, I checked her pulse. Maybe I felt it, or maybe it was mine. I couldn't be certain. *Where's the fucking ambulance?*

There had to be something I could do. I raced out to the corridor, yelling at the top of my voice, 'Nanny!'

No one answered.

Back in the room, I stood there like a right idiot before figuring out I'd better try to stop the bleeding. I grabbed a towel and soaked it with water from the bathroom sink, almost tossing my dinner when I saw the bath filled with red water, blood running in rivulets down the sides. I raced back to Irene and pressed the towel down on her privates. It was drenched in her blood in seconds.

The doorbell rang. *Please, let it be the ambulance men.*

98

I dashed downstairs and was relieved to see them standing in the doorway.

'She's upstairs. Come on, hurry,' I shouted in a panic.

They followed behind me. Once in the bedroom, they got to work, checking her pulse and listening to her heart. They stuck a needle in the back of her hand and attached a tube and bottle to it, which one guy then held up in the air.

I had to turn away as they put her on the stretcher. It was a right mess. Everything was dripping all over the place. It was carnage. I dropped into the armchair and hunched over my knees to keep from feeling *uncle dick*.

'You're not coming with?' asked one of the lads, his eyebrows raised.

'No thanks, boys. I'll leave it to the experts. I would just get in the way. Me wife's going to be alright, isn't she?'

'The doctor will check her over, but we must go. She's lost a lot of blood.' They carried her down the stairs and into the ambulance. I followed, standing by the front door as they drove off, sirens blaring.

As the sound echoed into the night, I sunk to the ground. There was too much blood everywhere, making my head hurt. The dogs ran over to me, snorting with concern. They could tell something was wrong as they both struggled and wriggled, trying to climb onto my lap and lick my face. I held them a moment before we all went upstairs.

They dashed into the bedroom.

'No! Stop!' There was blood all over the carpet.

'Up, now.' I clicked my fingers.

They heaved their large, chubby bodies onto the bed, grunting with effort, and sat there staring at me.

What the fuck am I supposed to do now? I had no sodding idea how to clean it up, and there was no way I could sleep near that horrible mess. I'd have nightmares. I took a stack of towels from the airing cupboard and plonked them down on top of it. 'No one can ever say I don't help with the housework,' I told the dogs. 'Okay, that's good enough. Your Ma can deal with it when she returns.'

As I lay in bed next to them, I tried to concentrate on the newspaper, but I just kept reading the same line. I hated the guilt churning inside me, but I couldn't go to the hospital. I was never any use in medical situations. Besides, Irene was unconscious, so she wouldn't even know if I was there, would she? No point in both of us suffering.

I wanted to go; really, I did. I knew a husband should be with his wife in difficult times, but when it came to bodily fluids like blood and guts, I was a coward. I hated admitting that to myself. Irene looked after me so well. The least I could do was support her when she was poorly, but it wasn't my fault. I was born that way, I suppose. Every time someone cut themselves, I almost fainted. It was a phobia, a handicap, and I didn't know how to overcome it. It was a good job I never saw any action in the Army.

What if it's serious? What if she never comes home? No, no, that won't happen. I swallowed a couple of Valiums and switched off the light. *She'll be back, right as rain. She has to be. I need her even more than the dogs, and that's saying something.* I groaned. *This is stupid. Of course everything will be fine.* After tossing and turning for a few more minutes, I turned on the lamp. *Fuck, I can't sleep.* I opened the bedside table drawer and pulled out the phone book.

'Hello, I am enquiring about my wife, Mrs Irene Leslie. She arrived a short while ago.'

I waited on hold for several minutes until a nurse answered, 'She's had extensive internal bleeding, but her condition is stable. We're keeping her here for a few days for observation. Visiting hours are from ten a.m. to twelve noon tomorrow and from four p.m. to six,' the lady said and hung up.

What a relief. Cuddling up to Guinevere, I felt my pulse slowing as the pills kicked in. *Now I can sleep.*

I was deep in a dream when something heavy thumped onto my waist. I shot up like a rocket.

'Guinevere, stop that.'

A little voice giggled in the darkness. 'I'm not Guinevere. I'm Boris. You're silly, Daddy.'

I turned on the light and tried to focus. His rosy face was leaning over me.

'Where's your ma? Go call her,' I mumbled.

'I don't know where she is.' He stared at me as he sucked on his thumb.

Oh, shit. Right. She's in the fucking hospital. 'Well, run off and get Nanny then.' I shoved him off the bed, but he climbed back on.

'She won't come out of her room, and I'm hungry, and Lorraine is crying.' His little lip quivered.

'Fuck. Nanny's got the flu or something. Shit, hold on a mo. Don't start crying.'

I picked up the receiver and dialled my in-laws.

'Hi, Pearl. Listen, I need a favour. You've got to come over here and look after the kids. Irene's in the hospital.'

Pearl's scream almost burst my eardrums. It was so loud I had to pull the phone away. 'No, calm down, all's fine. She's just got some female thing. She's going to be okay, but I need help. I can't be looking after these kids, and the nanny is ill.'

She droned on and on, so it was a while before I got another word in. I watched Boris climb on Belvedere, trying to ride him like a cowboy. The dog never stirred, just slept right through it. 'Well, if you insist on visiting Irene, can Manny come over? There are things I have to do today, like work.' I was getting impatient. *Can't she see my problem is urgent?* 'Please, Pearl, tell Manny to get over here now.'

She eventually agreed, but not before telling me I needed to take more responsibility. *Who the fuck does she think she is? I'm the most responsible person I know, working hard and bringing home the bacon.* With that problem solved, I moved on to the next one. 'Hey, Boris, do you know how to fry eggs?'

After I'd had a hot bubble bath for at least an hour and a half and read the papers back to front, I arrived at the hospital. I held my breath because of the sickening, sour smell of disinfectant that filled the air and clung to my clothes and went into the shop and bought the biggest bunch of roses they had. Armed and ready, I headed over to reception.

'Hi, luv. The name's Leslie.' I smiled at the nurse behind the desk. 'Me old lady's here. Her name's Irene. Well, that's what she tells me.' I chuckled. 'So, where do I find her?'

The nurse blushed a deep pink. 'R—Room three-oh-four. It's just down the corridor.'

Smirking, I headed to Irene's room. I rather liked that effect I had on people.

I stood at the door, watching my wife as she lay in the hospital bed. I couldn't tell if she was asleep or in a coma. A big glass bottle full of blood hung above her, attached to her arm by a long tube.

My legs shook as I walked over to Pearl, who was sitting in a nearby chair reading a magazine. She looked up to give me one of her disapproving faces, her eyes all narrowed. *Screw her.*

'How's she doing?' I called out.

Pearl whispered, 'Shush, keep your voice down. They gave her something for the pain. She finally fell asleep a little while ago.'

I ignored the old bat.

'Hello, me luv.' I nudged Irene's shoulders. 'Wakey, wakey.'

Irene opened her eyes, squinted, then looked straight at me. Realisation dawned on her face, and she burst into tears. *Silly bugger.*

'Oh, Joe,' she sobbed.

'Now, darling, no need for all that mushy stuff. Here, look what I brought you.' I showed her the roses. 'These flowers, they inform me, are the best they got in the shop. Cost a pretty penny, but nothing's too good for me wife.' Placing them on her lap, I passed her my handkerchief. I noticed Pearl was frowning at me, but I didn't pay her any attention as I held my wife's hand.

'What's wrong with you, anyway?' I asked. She was about to speak, but I cut her off. 'You know what? Don't tell me. You know all this stuff makes me feel a bit *uncle dick.*' I shivered.

I preferred to be in the dark about what happens to women's bodies. How they put up with bleeding all over the place every month mystified me. If I was a woman, I'm certain I would've passed out twelve times a year if I had to deal with that.

'You coming home soon? You need to be there.' I didn't want to beg, but I was bordering on it.

Pearl gave a bad-tempered, disapproving 'Harumph.'

'I think maybe in the next day or two,' Irene said, her voice weak and wobbly.

'Well, hurry up and get better.' I picked the roses back up. 'In the meantime, you can think of me as you admire these beautiful flowers I bought you.' I bent down and carefully kissed her forehead. 'I gotta go, luv, but your mum's here.'

I handed the flowers over to Pearl. 'Here you are. I'm sure you'll find a vase or something for them. Bye.' I headed out the door. *Better head over to Sheila's and see if I can win my money back.*

A doctor approached as I was coming out of the room.

'Mr Leslie, may I have a word?' he said in a hushed tone.

'Sure.'

We moved to one side.

'I wanted to say that I'm sorry for your loss.'

'What do you mean? What loss?'

'The baby, of course. It was very naughty of Mrs Leslie to do what she did, but I've spoken to her, and she promises never to do such a thing again. However, I am required by law to report it. It is a criminal offence.'

My head was spinning. *What baby? Is he saying Irene was pregnant and got rid of it? A criminal offence? Shit! Did that mean porridge? How will I be able to carry on without her?*

I painted on my famous smile. 'Look, Doc, me wife is a lovely woman but a bit of a daft cow. She probably didn't even know what she was doing. I'll give her a good talking to.' I stared him straight in the eye. 'And if there's *anything* I can do for you, just say the word. I'm sure we understand each other, right?'

'Yes, of course. As I said, I am required to report any criminal incidents, but I am not required to report the tragic *miscarriage* that your poor dear wife suffered.' The doctor gave a small smile and inclined his head.

'Right. Thanks, Doc.' I nodded slowly so he could see I understood what he was saying.

He cleared his throat. 'My wife is a big fan, and I wondered if you might write a special, personal autograph for her. She will be thrilled.' The doctor beamed.

'It would be an honour. What's the charming lady's name?'

He handed me his notepad, and I made a point of writing more than my usual scribble of *yours truly, Joe Leslie*, by adding how I was a massive fan of her husband and all that crap.

He thanked me and firmly shook my hand. *Phew, at least I've nipped that in the bud.*

I headed out, swallowing two Valium on the way. *Bloody hell,*

Irene, what have you done?

Irene came home a few days later— not a day too soon. I'd been fuming and had trouble sleeping, which put me in a foul mood. Stuck with the screaming kids, I was about ready to throttle someone, and that bloody nanny, with her condescending tone and ugly mug, wasn't any help.

The business with Irene was eating me up. It gave me a racing heart in the middle of the night, and I worried I might end up in the hospital as well. *Has she slept with someone else? I'll fucking kill her if she has, but she can't have. Why would she? I should be enough for her, unless she's suddenly become a raving nymphomaniac or something.* The only way Irene could be pregnant would be from someone else, because we hadn't done it in ages, had we? The image of her naked in bed, rolling about with another geezer, made me want to smash something, punch her fucking face in, and kick the other guy in the bollocks. I couldn't relax, and no amount of pills helped.

As Irene entered the bedroom, she looked pale and shaky and sank into the chair at her dressing table. She glanced at the stain on the floor where I'd made Nanny clean up.

'You okay? You want a cup of tea or something?' I asked, using my sweet, gentle voice. 'Maybe a biscuit?' I smiled, pausing a moment before looming over her, putting my face to hers. 'Or a cock? Not mine, of course, someone else's, who knocked you up and got you to stick fucking knitting needles up your fanny!' I roared.

Her face went bright red.

'It's not like that at all Joe,' she said, her voice faint, 'It was your baby. I swear, I didn't do anything with anyone. I just couldn't bear being tied down with another child.' She grabbed my arm, but I pushed her away.

'Oh, yeah? Well, I don't recall us doing any hanky-panky lately.'

'We did, just once, a month or so ago. A quick one, but it was enough to do the trick.' She held her hands together in front of her like she was begging.

'Yeah, a trick, alright. Listen, you telling me the whole truth?' I shook my finger at her.

'I swear, darling, it's the truth. I would never betray you. Never.' Her eyes were wide.

'Because you know what I'd do to you—' I grabbed her throat, 'if

104

I ever found out you were sniffing around elsewhere?' The image of her with someone else appeared in my head again. It made my blood boil. She needed to know I meant business.

'I swear on the dogs' lives that I'm telling the truth.' She gasped as tears fell, wetting my hand. I ignored them. They didn't move me. Well, maybe a bit, but I didn't weaken. She needed to know who the boss was.

I held her there and glared, only letting her go when I saw from her terrified expression that she'd got the message.

'Okay then. Just so long as we're clear, I don't want a repeat of this ever again.'

I calmed down enough to feel shitty that I'd once again turned to violence. I hated the man I turned into when I was pissed off. I reminded myself of my father and the thought made my stomach turn over. But I was powerless to control it. I promised myself, right there and then, that I would never raise a finger to her again, and I meant it. I wanted to be a better man.

Wiping the tears from her face, I kissed her gently on her soft lips.

Truthfully, I believed her. She had no need to shop around when the services at home were of such high standards. Right?

Chapter Twelve

IRENE

Brighton, 1961

Brushing Lorraine's shoulder-length curly hair was a daily challenge. As soon as the brush encountered a knot, her piercing shrieks could be heard throughout the house. It should have been a happy room with its matching curtains and a bedspread of pink bunnies and butterflies, but the noise coming from my daughter made it sound like she was in a slaughterhouse. I was ready to collapse, but I still had to dress the kids for our family outing along the seafront. My husband didn't like to wait, and my struggling daughter didn't help matters. Sometimes I had to resist the temptation to cut all her hair off.

I hated this job, but someone had to do it since Nanny had departed four years ago. I was exhausted. The vacuuming alone took hours, courtesy of the shedding dogs. Even though they had short hair, it still clung to all our furniture and clothes like tiny needles. If that wasn't bad enough, Joe often came home with big, raw, meaty bones, presenting it as though it was a box of chocolates, speaking love words to them he never afforded me. He would stand there, the treats in his hands, while the dogs drooled in anticipation. He would throw the bones onto the carpet, beaming while they scurried for their treasure, which they would bring to the sofa to eat in comfort. I begged Joe to please feed them outside, but he told me I was cruel, saying, 'How would you like to eat out in the freezing cold?'

After the vacuuming, I still had to make the beds, wash the breakfast dishes, make lunch, and then clear that up. When I asked if we could employ a cleaner, Joe said he would think about it. *How long does it take for him to decide?*

'We're almost done. Stay still. It will be over much quicker if you stop squirming,' I told Lorraine, feeling the muscles in my neck tightening.

'Irene,' Joe called up from the living room, 'aren't you ready yet? Christ, how long does it take? I wanted to leave half an hour ago.'

I finished putting a bow in Lorraine's hair.

'Now let me comb yours, and we'll go out,' I said to Boris.

With both children ready, I took their hands and went downstairs.

Joe was pacing, looking tense. 'At long bloody last,' he said, crunching on a Polo mint.

Even with his impatience, I wasn't unhappy. Life had treated us well in the last few years, most of the time. Joe had his moments, but once they passed, I could relax and enjoy our life. I adored Joe when he was jolly. It was his other side that was unbearable. I sometimes wondered if it had anything to do with all the pills he consumed. There was such a variety of colours, and I had no idea what each tablet did. I asked him about it once, but he shrugged it off and told me thousands of people took them, so there wasn't a problem and that I should worry about more important things, like what's for dinner.

Joe had decided we should move to Brighton the year before, saying he preferred to be a big fish in a small pond and that it was only an hour away from London by train. He also liked having his friend Sheila nearby in the summer months. We'd found a lovely four-bedroom house with a large garden, and I had worked hard trying to convince my parents to move down and find a small place nearby. I succeeded and not long after we moved in, Mum and Dad found a cosy little bungalow. Walking there took only a few minutes, and the kids loved it, especially as they'd adopted a ginger cat named Noddy, who would purr and rub against everyone.

I liked Brighton. It was a vibrant town with winding lanes of shops and plenty of upmarket restaurants. Everything you could get in London, you could get here, but in a smaller area. People were friendlier as well. They actually smiled and chatted when I went into the post office or the bank. The kids loved the sweet shops, especially sticks of rock, which they sucked on for hours. While I worried about the state of their teeth, I enjoyed the fragment of peace.

As it was a glorious day, I wore my new blue dress. It was shorter than anything I'd ever worn before, and I felt a little daring and wild. Joe had bought me a new Singer machine for my birthday, and I'd sewn the cutest matching outfit for Lorraine. I was quite proud of my work.

Boris held his father's hand as we walked down to the seafront while Lorraine and I strolled behind them so she could pull the leaves off the bushes we passed. Arriving at the beach, we stopped to marvel at the bright blue sky and how the sea twinkled in the sunshine. When you lived in a place like England with its constant rain and endless grey skies, a sunny day was sheer joy. Seagulls squawked overhead as we leaned against the railing to look out at the pebbled beach. A row of small donkeys with children on their backs passed us by, a weary old man tugging them down the shore. Families with their dogs sauntered along, and couples walked arm-in-arm down the pier.

Continuing our stroll, the smell of fish and chips, candy floss, and hot dogs filled our nostrils as we reached the stalls. We quickly came across a Punch and Judy puppet show.

'Mummy,' Lorraine squealed, 'I want to watch. Please, can I?'

'Of course you can. Go take your brother and sit with the other children on the ground.'

Lorraine ran ahead and took her brother's hand, pulling him towards the small group of children gathered in front of the red and white striped tent.

Joe shrugged and headed over to the nearest bench. I joined him and watched as the children roared with laughter when Mr Punch tried kissing Miss Judy on the cheek, but she turned away and hit him on the head. I loved seeing the children enjoying themselves.

I glanced at Joe, trying to catch his eye, but he was busy looking at the passers-by. People were smiling at him as they recognised their neighbourhood VIP. Turning away, I rolled my eyes. *When will it ever be enough for him?* Weather permitting, the weekly outing along the seafront always gave him a tremendous boost to his insatiable ego. I couldn't understand why the more successful he became, the more his insecurities increased. It was when Joe was at his lowest that he was his most vile.

The show ended, and the children raced over to Joe. 'Daddy, you should have seen funny Mr Punch.'

Boris tugged on Joe's jacket. 'Can we go on a donkey? Please, Daddy, please.'

'How about some ice cream instead? What do you think of that, mate?' Joe smiled.

The children jumped up and down with glee. 'Yes, please, Daddy.'

'Let's go to the Townhouse, okay, luv?' he asked me as we stood up.

'That's a good idea, darling.' I held the children's hands as we walked over to the traffic lights and waited to cross the road.

The Townhouse was a popular café packed with locals, a large percent of which were Jewish. Joe loved that. It gave him a sense of belonging, especially since they always greeted him with big smiles as they shook his hand or waved at him. People always expressed their pride in having such a celebrity living in their midst. He would go home happy and content, and I would be guaranteed a peaceful evening.

Stepping inside, the powerful aroma of coffee infused the air amongst the sounds of conversation filling the small room. Finding a table was challenging, so we squeezed in beside an elderly couple.

'Afternoon,' said Joe, bobbing his head, waiting for the moment of recognition on their faces. The couple gave him a polite nod before returning to their discussion. Joe leaned over to me and whispered, 'These old geezers need new glasses. I'll just do them a favour and give them a jolt.'

Busy trying to stop Boris from emptying the saltshaker onto the table, I looked up as Joe flashed his famous smile and said to the old couple in his best TV voice, 'Excuse me, would you mind passing the sugar?'

The old man reached over and handed it to Joe. 'One lump or three?' Joe winked, delivering his trademark line.

They stared at him for a moment in visible confusion, then returned to their coffees.

Joe scowled before putting a smile back on his face. 'Maybe you didn't hear me.' He chuckled. 'I said, *one lump or three.*'

The man stared at Joe with a puzzled expression. 'Not sure what you are talking about, son. Sorry.' He turned to his partner and raised an eyebrow.

Joe shoved his chair back and stood. 'That's it. We're leaving. Now. I'll wait outside,' he barked.

I cringed, hoping we weren't making a scene. 'We haven't even ordered our coffees yet, and you promised the children an ice cream,' I said quietly, trying to steady him.

'Too fucking bad. Just come out already.'

Damn. Watching Joe storm away, I could see he was on the verge of one of his black moods, so I swallowed my disappointment while trying to keep the little ones quiet. I bought the kids their ice creams as quickly as I could, and we headed back outside.

'Oh fantastic, now they'll be dripping it all over the place,' Joe snapped as he leant against the wall, smoking a cigarette and sulking.

I had so wanted the day to be a nice one, but with his ego wounded, it was clear that a dark cloud was on the horizon. Honestly, I was tired of always having to be the one to make him feel better. I had enough on my plate with the kids, the dogs, and the housework. I needed a little respite, some peace, but I feared it wasn't to be. I was always walking on eggshells, never knowing when the volcano would erupt. Sometimes, I wanted to go back home to my parents, but I had married him, for better or worse, and I had to stick to that, no matter what. That's what my parents had taught me, anyway.

I longed for the old days when Joe was playful and loving. He could make me laugh for hours. Once, he tied L plates to Boris's pram. We would walk along the road with everyone pointing and cracking up as they passed us by. 'Hey,' he would say when anyone stared, 'we're new parents, just learning.' It was such fun. Then, one day, when we were in the middle of town, he decided he had to go off to the casino, which left me walking home red-faced, unable to shout out witty remarks like he did and subjected instead to laughter and strange looks.

I spent the rest of the day trying to keep the kids entertained and out of Joe's way. By nightfall, I was physically and emotionally drained. Sitting at my dressing table, I massaged cream into my arms and elbows while Joe lay in bed, reading the papers and chain-smoking. The storm had been brewing for hours, and I was tired of wearing a fake smile and speaking in a forced, upbeat tone to try and defuse the bomb that was Joe. We could go months with all being well, and then, out of the blue, something would turn him into a sullen, nasty beast. I didn't know how to prevent it.

With a sigh, Joe reached over to his bedside table to sort through his many bottles of medicine. He picked one up, looked at it, put it down, then reached for another.

'Irene, what've you done? Have you rearranged me pills? You know I need them in a certain order.'

'I haven't touched them.' I showed him my empty hands.

'Yes, you have.' He shot me a warning look before studying each bottle's label like a scientist examining a specimen through a microscope. After a moment, he punched his fist down on the table. 'I need the ones that put me to sleep. The blue ones. I can't fucking find them. Where are they?'

'I don't know.' I put the cream back in the drawer and slammed it shut. 'You know what, Joe? To hell with your pills. Why do you have to take them all the time? What's the matter with you? No one else I know needs so much medication.'

'You wanna know why I take 'em?' His eyes narrowed. 'Because I have to put up with you, that's why.'

'Really?' I walked over to him, my hands on my hips, my nostrils flaring.

He glowered at me. 'Any man that would have to live with you would probably need double the amount I take.'

I wanted to slap him or say something so hurtful that he would understand how it felt to be spoken to like that. 'Well, I'm surprised you don't have something in that pharmacy of yours that might help with your problem in the bedroom.' The words were out of my mouth before I realised I had spoken. I shocked myself. *Who am I?* I didn't recognise this fierce, fearless woman.

Joe leapt from the bed and stalked towards me. 'What did you say? What the fuck did you just say? How fucking dare you speak to me like that?' His mouth was half open in shock.

'I've had enough of it always being about you. Mr Joe Leslie. The most important person in the world.' I couldn't stop myself. I was on a roll.

His lip curled. 'Yes, that's right, and you are married to him. Let's call a spade a spade. You're a whore who married me to get all the fame and money and everything else you could.'

I couldn't take it anymore. The anger, the hurt and the years of fear boiled over. 'Don't you talk to me like that. I will not tolerate it. You know what? I'm going home to my mother. She at least knows how to show love, something you are incapable of doing.'

Joe's face turned red, and he grabbed my arm. 'Shut the fuck up! I don't need this right now, you hear?'

'Oh, I hear, alright. A pathetic little man who—'

He slapped his hand over my mouth; I could smell the stench of cigarettes on it. Beads of sweat glistened on his forehead, and his bright blue eyes blazed down at me.

'If you don't shut up, I'll—'

I forcefully peeled his hand off me. It was amazing how much strength I'd suddenly acquired. He looked stunned for a moment.

I snarled, 'You'll what? You don't even have the courage to do anything. You're just a …' then I said the one word I knew would hurt him the most, '*Sissy!*'

'You cunt,' he roared, gripping my arm even tighter.

He took a deep drag of his cigarette, blew the smoke into my eyes, and in a violent, hateful flash, stubbed it out on my arm.

Shrieking, I tried to pull my arm away, but Joe held on with force, burning me again and again before throwing me to the ground. Grabbing his coat, he crashed from the room, the floors vibrating with his every step.

I lay on the carpet, shaking as huge, angry welts bloomed on my arm. At that moment, I hated Joe with every part of my being. He was evil. I was desperate for something awful to happen to him. A malicious smile spread across my face, imagining him in a car accident, lying on the side of the road, bleeding out and in pain.

Struggling to breathe, I curled up in a ball, my heart pounding in my chest as I heard the front door slam shut, then the sound of the car starting. A sense of deep, awful loneliness pierced through my inner core. *I could die right here, and no one would know.* My eyes shifted to the bed where the dogs were snoring away without a care in the world. Nothing had disturbed their precious sleep. *Why would it?* Joe loved those smelly, ugly creatures far more than anyone else. He would never harm them or even raise his voice, but he could do whatever he wanted to me.

I tried blowing on the wounds to cool them down, but the pain intensified. Blisters were rising on my skin. After some time, I pulled myself up and went to the window. There was no sign of Joe. I prayed he was far enough away that he wouldn't be returning home for some time. I sat back down at the dressing table, staring at my blotchy face in the mirror, wincing at the inferno of pain radiating from my arm. It was clear that things needed to change. I couldn't stay with a man who treated me like that. I had made too many excuses for him. It wasn't healthy for the children. *What if Joe strikes them too?* There was no way in hell I would let that happen. I would do everything in my power to protect them.

A sudden longing for my parents swept over me. I pictured them with their arms outstretched, embracing the kids and me, Mum serving her delicious food and pampering us. We could move in with them. I was sure they would be happy to have us. Then maybe I could find a job and earn enough money to get us a small place somewhere. In my mind, I imagined peace and serenity. It made me feel stronger by the minute.

Getting up, I put on my coat, flinching as the material grazed the burns, and rushed towards Lorraine's room. I stood for a moment outside her door to take a deep breath, then entered with a forced smile on my face.

'Wake up, Lorraine. Let's go for a walk,' I said in the merriest voice I could muster, as I turned on her light.

She peered up at me, bleary, confused and rubbing her eyes.

'Come on, let's go for a midnight stroll. What fun.'

I helped her out of bed and sat her down to put on her shoes, not bothering with socks, then we went to wake Boris. He nearly fell back to sleep while I was buckling his boots. I gently tapped him awake. 'I need to do a tinkle,' he said, so we waited till he returned from the bathroom. I was twitchy. We needed to be out of the house in case Joe returned.

I led the sleepy, stumbling children down the stairs and bundled them into their coats before we stepped outside.

'Let's walk fast to keep warm,' I said as we headed down the road, through the dark and the glow from the weak streetlights.

Since my parents' house was only a few minutes away, we made it there in no time. I couldn't wait to go inside. The desire for safety was burning as strongly as my blistered arm. *Mum and Dad will save me.* I banged on the front door with all my force. It opened with a creak, light spilling onto the porch. My dear mother, her hair in rollers, peered out, looking a little shocked.

'Darling, what are you doing here in the middle of the night? And with the children, too?'

'Oh, Mum.' I broke down, holding her as close as I could.

Dad came to the door, tying his dressing gown. 'What's going on here?'

'Joe and I had a terrible fight,' I sobbed.

'Irene, stop this nonsense.' He took me by the shoulders and removed me from my mother. 'All married couples have fights, but that doesn't mean you take your children out this late at night. You need to go home right now. Your place is with your husband.' He shook his head as he looked down at Boris and Lorraine. 'The children will catch their death. What were you thinking?'

The kids held onto my coat. Lorraine gazed up at me, sucking her thumb.

'But, Dad, look.' I pulled up my sleeve and, between sobs, showed him the deep welts. 'He burned me with his cigarette,' I whispered, trying not to let the kids hear what I was saying.

Mum gasped, pulling the children to her, trying to shield them from the view.

Dad's face was blank. 'Irene, I told you to go home. Take the children right now.'

'But, Dad, I'm scared. I don't understand. You're my father. You said you would always look after me.' Wrapping my arms around myself, I sniffled like a child.

His voice softened. 'I'm outraged by your husband, but, my darling, you know how important rules are. A wife's duty is to be with her husband, no matter what. I'm sure Joe is sorry and will never do it again. I will speak to him tomorrow. Now, go home and put these children to bed, then you can put some iodine on those burns.'

He turned to my mum. 'Come along, Pearl. Time for bed.' He said in a stern voice while holding the door open, waiting for her.

Mum looked at me with a pained expression and mouthed the words 'I'm sorry' before she turned and made her way into the house. The door snapped shut behind her. I stood facing it with my mouth open, my body shaking with my tears. This was the second time they had deserted me. *First, they left me with the wicked witch, and now they leave me with a man who burns me. What kind of parents are they?* It took all my strength not to scream as the feeling of abandonment overwhelmed me.

I had no choice but to put my arms around both kids and head home. The moon had risen full and bright, lighting up the pavement as we strolled along. I was in no rush.

'Mummy?' Boris asked into the silent night. 'What did Daddy do to your arm?'

All at once, my self-pity came to a halt. My children were the important ones, not me. Looking down at their little faces, I studied them, hoping I hadn't scared them.

'Oh, that's part of the game we are playing.' I laughed, trying to disguise the tightness in my throat. 'The Midnight Game. We go over to Grandma and Grandpa's house in the middle of the night to wake them up. Fun, isn't it?'

'But you've got bubbles on your arm.'

Boris tried to poke them, but I tugged my sleeve back down, frantically trying to come up with a good excuse.

'That's right. They are magic bubbles. Daddy put them there. They are a gift from the fairies.'

Lorraine piped up, 'I love fairies. I want bubbles on my arm too.'

Oh my god, what have I done? I searched my mind for an appropriate answer. 'Fairies only put bubbles on *mummies'* arms. Here we are, back home. Now, let's get upstairs and go straight back to bed,' I said as I unlocked the front door, thankful to see Joe's car still absent from the driveway.

I prepared a cup of warm milk for the children, praying that they would go back to sleep quickly. I needed time on my own to collect my thoughts. Once they had settled down, I returned to my bedroom, undressed, and got into bed. My mind swirled.

Why is it my duty to be with my husband, no matter what? Who made these senseless rules? Not a woman, that's for sure. How is it allowed that a man can harm his wife, and she has no choice but to accept it? I'd always been an obedient child and respected Dad, trusting he knew what was best for me, but for once, he was wrong. *If anything happens to me, it will be his fault.* If Joe killed me, then how would Dad feel? That would show him.

My arm still throbbed. *No one loves me.*

I clenched my jaw, wanting to break something. I felt trapped, like a caged animal with no way out. But what could I do? Nothing. Absolutely nothing.

It had been stupid of me to say *sissy*. I knew it was a trigger for Joe, for his temper, but how could I have known he would use me as a human ashtray? I needed to restrain myself and keep the peace until I could come up with a solution. *Just pretend. That's something I can do. I have to.* As long as Joe was happy and his ego was satisfied, he wouldn't have his outbursts. If I kept him content, at least there would be calm in the house. I could pretend to be his obedient wife and do my duty, while I tried to find a way out. I promised myself I would figure out how to take my children and go far, far away.

I dozed on and off throughout the night, waking at the sound of the car pulling into the driveway. My heart pounded as I heard Joe's footsteps coming up the stairs. The door opened, and I felt him approach the bed.

'Darling, are you awake?'

I couldn't reply. There was a great big lump in my throat.

'Listen, I'm sorry. I won't do it again, I swear.'

I still didn't answer, keeping my eyes shut.

'Please, darling, talk to me. Say you'll forgive me. I know it was wrong. I shouldn't have done it. I'm sorry, okay? I do love you.' He stroked my hair and kissed my neck.

I opened my eyes and looked directly into his. 'Really, Joe? You're sorry? I'm in so much pain. You burnt me! You say you love me, yet you act like I'm someone you hate. You went too far this time.'

Joe hung his head and mumbled in a small voice, 'I'm a prize shit. I'm ashamed of meself. It won't happen again. I'm so sorry. Please don't leave me. Please.' His voice sounded like he was on the verge of tears, something that I'd never heard before. It should've moved me, but it didn't. A rush of power flooded over me instead. All at once, and for the first time, I felt in control. It was time for my performance.

I sat up and bit my lip. 'I'm sorry too. I shouldn't have said what I did.'

He smiled, then ever so gently, kissed the welts on my arm, one by one. 'There's a good girl, me lovely Irene. Now, get your clothes off, and let's have a cuddle.'

It's working. I'm an actress just like Sheila, or maybe even better.

Chapter Thirteen

JOE

I paced back and forth on the edge of the cliff. *Fuck. Fuck. Fuck.* I couldn't believe what I'd done. *Jesus fucking Christ, I burned her.*

I kept kicking the tree trunk beside me, ignoring the throbbing in my foot, staring wildly into the dark. *What the hell is wrong with me?* I shook my head, trying to get rid of the image of her shrieking and the smell of burning flesh. It was as though a devil had possessed me. I had no control over what I was doing.

I tried lighting a cigarette, but my hands were shaking too much and the sight of the thing made me want to give it up.

I'd felt like shit warmed over after that humiliating experience in the Townhouse. *Why didn't they recognise me? Everybody knows who I am, especially in the Townhouse.* I liked to give my local fans a chance to see me off-screen. They got such a kick out of it. *None of this would have happened if it wasn't for those senile old bats. Fuck 'em.*

I envied people who walked around with hardly a care in the world, but what happened in the Townhouse was like a slap in the face, a castration, a public flogging. I could feel everyone looking at me, laughing, thinking I was a loser. That old man did worse than insult me. He ignored me, turned away. It made me wanna thrash his wrinkled mug. My anger had scared me, so I scarpered and tried to calm down. *What if I'd hit the old geezer and ended up in the nick?*

Back at home, I'd still been holding it in, doing my best not to let the demon out. I was determined to just go to sleep, but for that, I needed the blue pills. They were the ones that calmed me down and put me out, but Irene had moved them. When I asked her about it, she denied doing anything and started nagging me about my habit like I was some junkie. I still kept my cool. My restraint was impressive, but she went on, implying

I couldn't get it up or something. I grabbed her, just wanting her to shut up and leave me in peace, but then she said the *word*. If I hadn't had a cigarette in my hand, I don't know what I would've done, maybe just pushed her to the floor, but at that moment, I wanted to hurt her. Really hurt her, as much as she'd hurt me. The burning gave me a release.

Moving away from the tree, I sat on a rock and listened to the waves. I got up, paced, and sat back down. I couldn't settle. I didn't want to think I was a bastard, but my fucking father's voice popped into my head. *Never, ever, lay a finger on a woman. They are gentle creatures who need our love and support. Only cowards hit women.* Dad had told me that after I pulled a girl's pigtails in primary school. *Is that what I am? A coward?* My heart squeezed painfully at the thought. I swallowed a couple of Valium, but it made no difference. There had to be something stronger.

Standing up, I took a piss, aiming it off the cliff while imagining it spraying on every single person I hated. It was a long list. It was a long piss. Suddenly, the fucking wind changed, blowing towards me. *Great, on top of everything else, I now have piss-damp trousers.* After thinking a moment, I decided to head over to Sheila's, knowing she was in Brighton and sure to be up; the woman never slept. *Maybe I can find some relief while also giving my clothes time to dry.*

Gary, a mate of mine, greeted me at the door. It was good timing as well. I was getting low on pills, and he always had a supply. He was the one who started me on the uppers and downers in the first place. I met Gary at one of Sheila's parties years ago. Before him, I dragged my feet around, not really functioning, then he showed me the magic of the Purple Hearts. Boy, did I move after that. The drugs were amphetamines, uppers, speed, or whatever you like to call them. One or two of them, and you could race faster than a greyhound on the track. Of course, the downside was they made you edgy and gave you insomnia, but that's what they made Valium for, right? Once Gary persuaded me to try just one, life became so much better. I could work non-stop, sprinting around all day long. I was invincible. I could do anything I wanted as long as I kept taking the tablets.

Gary, the walking chemist, smiled at me, wearing his signature small, round glasses and pin-striped suit. I grabbed his arm and pulled him aside.

'Listen,' I hissed while looking around, checking we were alone, 'I need something a little stronger than usual. It's me nerves. I can't settle them. Got anything that might help?'

He perked up. 'You may be in luck, my man. This new little pill does wonders for people like you.'

'What's that supposed to mean? What you getting at?' I asked, giving him a dirty look.

'What I'm saying is that it calms you down, stops the jitters from the purple ones. You following me?' He gave me a smile that showed his crooked teeth.

'Yeah,' I agreed, 'sounds right up me alley. You know what? Give me a few for now and let's see how I do, okay?'

After I paid him, we went to join the others in the games room.

Sheila greeted me with a hug before looking me up and down. 'You alright?'

'Yeah, I'm fine. Just need to unwind a bit. It's been a long day.'

'Right, if you say so.' She sniffed the air, then took my arm. I hoped she wasn't smelling my pissy clothes. 'Come join us for a bit of poker.'

We sat down amongst the guys. 'Hey, boys. What's the stake?' I asked with a grin, swallowing one of the new pills. Before long, my whole body relaxed, and I'd forgotten all about Irene and our fight. Hell, I didn't even care if I won or lost the game. That pill was perfect, just what I needed.

The sun was coming up as I drove home hours later. I was well and truly knackered by then, and the pill had worn off. I started to worry. *What if I've fucked up royally, and Irene wants to leave me? What if she's already left. She said she would. What if she's taken the kids?* The car swerved, almost hitting a tree on the side of the road. I gripped the steering wheel and forced the car back into the proper lane. I couldn't let Irene leave me. She needed to know I was sorry and would never do it again. I'd make it up to her somehow, buy her a new dress or whatever she wanted. *There's no life without her. She's the best woman in the world. My strength, my light, my love.*

Irene was asleep when I entered the bedroom. I dreaded waking her, but I had to fix things fast and make her love me again. I apologised, ate humble pie, and she eventually came around. Then we made glorious love before I drifted off in her loving arms. It was the best night's sleep I'd had in ages.

Chapter Fourteen

IRENE

1965

Was it really four years ago that life had me all frazzled? Tied in knots? With the kids older— Boris nine, and Lorraine almost seven— I had plenty of time for myself. It made all the difference in the world.

I had played my part well. Joe was content, and I almost believed myself after a while. Pretending I was happy while putting up with his foul moods made things so much easier. My life wasn't too bad with Joe. Like the dogs, he was affectionate and cute if you fussed over him. It was quite simple, but it worked. After that night with the cigarette, there hadn't been a repeat, and I planned to keep it that way.

During dinner that evening, Joe ate in silence. Something was wrong. The dogs whined and drooled, begging for morsels, but he ignored them. I almost felt sorry for them. Almost. Once we had finished, I went upstairs and got the kids ready for bed. Back downstairs in the living room, I found him looking over a stack of bills, his face pinched.

'I make good money. Where's it all going? You need to stop spending so much.' He ran his hand through his hair and shook his head.

I felt a stab of worry. For the last few months, debt collectors had been knocking on our door several times a week, and I had run out of excuses. Since I wasn't sure what to say, and lying wasn't something I was good at, I had to smile and flirt, which left me feeling grimy. Once, I heard Joe answer the phone in a high-pitched woman's voice. 'Mr Leslie has gone away. We don't know when he'll be back. Goodbye.' Then he smirked at me. 'That dealt with them alright.'

It shouldn't have been happening. I knew we should've had enough for the end of each month, but despite my frugal budgeting, it always disappeared. It was clear to me that Joe's gambling habit was to blame. When I confronted him about it, he accused me of being a hysterical female on the rag before reciting his motto, *'Live like a king even if you can't afford it.'* That meant we always had top-of-the-range electrical equipment, the biggest house on the street, and the finest clothes money could buy. There was no such thing as scrimping for Joe Leslie. He liked me all dressed up on his arm, making heads turn and the other men green with envy. I loved it, of course. Who wouldn't? But it was an extravagance we couldn't afford. It wasn't as if he didn't earn a good salary. We should've been living well. The worry had me biting my nails, something I hadn't done in a long time.

'Listen,' he said, leaning back in his chair, 'I want to produce my own TV shows. I've had enough of following orders from idiots who have no idea what they're doing. It's time for me to do what I do best: be in charge.' He lit a cigarette and inhaled. 'I have a meeting tomorrow, so keep your fingers crossed.'

'Producing? Don't you need to study for that?'

'Don't worry your pretty head, darling. Yours truly has what's known as natural talent. Most wankers have to learn, but not me. I have a great feeling about this.'

He turned the television on and switched me off.

'I'll just check on the children,' I announced to the room and Joe's deaf ears.

Several evenings later, after the children went to bed, Joe and I sat at the dining table. While I watched him gobble down the chocolate cake I had made that afternoon, I wondered why I bothered trying out new recipes; the way he ate, he couldn't even taste them.

'Guess what?' he announced with a mouth full of food. 'We're moving to Australia.'

'What?' I almost fell off my chair. 'I don't understand.'

'Don't you remember? I told you I had a meeting today. It was with the Australians. Well, they chose me, your magnificent husband, to produce their next TV show in Melbourne.' Joe beamed. 'It's only for eighteen months, but it's a start. Think about it, sunshine, kangaroos, and more sunshine.' He took a sip of his coffee. 'You know the idea I had for a new program? Well, they love it, and not only am I going to produce it, but they want me to host it too. Double the salary, ain't that great?'

He lit a cigarette and sat back, looking satisfied.

'We leave in two weeks. Don't worry about the furniture, they're giving us a house with everything in it. Fan-fucking-tastic.' Rubbing his hands together, he looked at me, waiting for my reaction.

I bit my lip, almost drawing blood. *Australia? I've never even left England before.* I didn't want to go to a faraway country, leave my parents and have to raise the kids without any help.

I chose my words wisely. 'Can't we at least think about it? It's not good to suddenly uproot the children like this.'

Joe glowed with anger. 'Fucking hell, you ungrateful cow. I work my fingers to the bone to provide the best for you, and when I try to better our lives, you go and whine about it. What have you ever done in your life? Nothing. All you do is take, take, take.' Slamming his hands on the table, he rose.

I flinched.

'I'm going out. Don't bother waiting up for me.' He grabbed his cigarettes and lighter and left.

Shaking my head with a loud sigh, I got up and made myself a steaming cup of tea while trying to make sense of it all. *Don't I have any say in the major decisions for our family? Am I never allowed an opinion?* I thought about my parents' marriage. Mum took care of the house while Dad worked and supported the family. Everything was predictable. Friday night was the big dinner. Holidays were with the extended family. No surprises.

Being married to Joe Leslie was like being on a rollercoaster. Once more I turned to thinking about taking the kids and leaving once and for all, no more abuse, mood swings, or unpredictable explosions. But where could we go? I was certain my parents wouldn't take me in. With no money and nowhere to escape to, I'd hit a brick wall once again. Dead end. There was no choice but to follow him. Do as I was told. Do my damn duty.

Chapter Fifteen

JOE

The harsh wind blew right through us as we stood in the queue at Southampton docks, waiting to board The Majestic. As lightning flashed in the distance, the dark grey sky looked like it was going to pour down. The air was filled with excitement as families chattered around us. Shivering, I pulled up my coat collar as thunder rumbled overhead. *This English climate is one thing I won't miss.*

'Hey, kids,' I shouted above the noise, 'Look. Isn't she grand?' I pointed upwards towards the gleaming white liner. Lorraine and Boris craned their necks, their eyes open wide. We looked like tiny ants compared to the size of the gigantic ship.

I showed them the leaflet. 'Listen to this, "*The vessel spans over eight hundred feet, and its capacity holds over two thousand passengers and nine hundred crew members. Lavish feasts and entertainment around the clock make the long journey across the ocean feel like an island of calm. The trip's highlight is The Crossing of the Equator Ceremony, an initiation rite commemorating a person's first crossing of the equator in the court of King Neptune. Forget your everyday woes when you sail with us.*"' That was my intention, and it had come not a moment too soon.

My heart skipped a beat as I thought about the future. I wouldn't have to put on a fake smile or behave for every Tom, Dick, or Harry. Sure, they treated me well at work, but they had to; it was their job. I knew behind their polite, welcoming faces, they looked down on me and thought me a phoney. I never told Irene how I felt, but it was always with me, that feeling of not being good enough. Even when they praised me and told me how talented I was, I never believed them. I knew they were empty words. I knew that the second I turned my back, they were laughing. *Poor sissy Leslie, what a fool.* That would all be behind me soon. I was starting anew.

They could kiss my arse.

And so could my in-laws.

Manny had come over the morning after the burning business for a heart-to-heart. He thought he was giving me a piece of his mind, telling me that if I ever did such a thing again, I would regret the day I was born. It was a fucking joke. He stood there, glaring up at me as I towered over him, and I'm not exactly a giant at five foot nine. What did he think he could do? I'd just nodded, wanting to resolve the whole thing as quickly as possible and be in Irene's good books again.

Now, I glanced at my wife and noticed the poor thing was welling up. She'd never left England before, so she didn't know what to expect. I'd popped over to France a few times after the war to get some decent grub, so I was well travelled in comparison. I took Irene's hand and squeezed it to let her know I understood. She smiled at me as tears rolled down her face, then leaned her head on my shoulder. For those few minutes, there was peace in my heart.

The queue moved forward, and I clapped my hands. 'Come on. It's our turn to board.'

We teetered up the wonky gangway and stepped into our home for the next few weeks. It was a floating wonderland, twenty-four hours a day. *What paradise.* I planned to give my wife a few bob to spend in the shops, and then I'd celebrate by checking out the secret gambling rooms. My mate Jimmy, who'd sailed the previous year on the same ship, told me that there were the regular game rooms where people played Bridge and such, but if I wanted more, I was to speak to the Entertainments Officer, he would guide me in the right direction.

'Lorraine, Boris, stay with me at all times.' Irene wouldn't let the children out of her sight, the silly cow. *Doesn't she realise there aren't any roads or cars? Let them run about all they want.* They were free to explore all the nooks and crannies, and best of all, no school for almost a month. It was heaven for kids. They gazed in wonder at the hustle and bustle of all the other passengers boarding as we made our way to our cabins.

'We're travelling first class— only the finest for the Leslie's. Our stateroom is on A deck. It's the best you know. All the other poor buggers are on the lower levels, under the sea.'

Once we located our room, I unlocked the door and smiled. It was even better than I'd hoped. There were twin beds with crisp white covers and matching curtains that hung above the porthole. On the dressing table was a vase of flowers and a handwritten notecard welcoming us onboard. The other side of the room had a two-seater couch with big cushions and a desk with pens and paper, perfect for taking notes whenever I got inspired. It was clean and fresh and airy. *How's that for luxury?*

'Look at this, darling. Posh, eh?'

Irene seemed pleased, immediately sitting at the desk to reapply her red lipstick.

We checked out the kid's room next door, which was identical to ours ——much too good for them. They raced around, opening cupboards and peering through the porthole.

'Enough, let's go back upstairs and say goodbye to England.'

The observation deck at the top of the ship was partially covered, sheltering us from the increasingly heavy drizzle. Passengers chattered away, waving to their friends, while waiters scurried about serving drinks to the crowd. We hadn't even left the shore, and the party had already begun. People threw streamers and balloons, which the kids tried to catch, jumping and laughing at the colourful paper flapping in the wind. It was a jolly time. Even Irene smiled for a few minutes, which was a bloody relief after having to listen to her nonstop snivelling the past few days. I knew she was upset about leaving her parents, but she needed to cut the apron strings and look to the future. I hadn't had any problem saying 'cheerio' to my folks. I'd popped over a few days before and told them I was off across the sea to better myself. They didn't seem too interested one way or another, just muttered something about me sending them a postcard when I arrived. I would've preferred a bit of fuss, but that was how they were. I was tired of hoping they would be different.

Every few minutes, the loudspeaker boomed, *'All ashore that's going ashore. All visitors ashore.'* The remaining guests stepped off the ship in dribs and drabs before the crew pulled up and secured the gangways. A loud blast announced our departure as the tugboats started to guide our ship out of port. I started jiggling the coins in my pocket as the boat moved. As soon as I could, I planned to send the family exploring before checking out the gambling situation.

I looked over at Irene and the kids with a big grin.

'Off we go, fighting the waves. Watch out, fishes, here we come. Destination: Melbourne.'

The kids giggled as they leaned over the railings and stared at the cold Atlantic Ocean churning beneath us, while Southampton dock became smaller and smaller and England was a grey line on the horizon.

I took a deep breath, tasting the salt on my lips, loving how the sea air rippled through my hair. I thought I was going to burst with excitement. We'd had a busy few days. I'd left Irene to do the packing. She knew what to do; I would've just got in the way. I spent most of the time over at Sheila's. She was upset I was leaving but was a good sport, giving me a nice send-off party with the mates. We played a few hands before a whole lot of people turned up. Sheila put on some music so people could dance, and even a few strippers arrived to liven things up. It was a lot of fun, but I didn't go near the girls. I had more important things to do, like buying supplies from Gary so that I had enough pills for the voyage and a bit more besides. I didn't fancy a long stint stuck on a boat without them.

I felt guilty that I didn't invite Irene to join the fun, but I didn't need her ranting about the naked women, especially as she was in one of her moods. I didn't trust myself not to lose my temper and do something I would regret if she nagged on and on.

Her parents were giving her a hard time about leaving. *Well, fuck them.* It was none of their business. They should've been happy that I was making their daughter's life better by moving to a place where the standards were higher and she could enjoy the fruits of my labour.

All of that was in the past. I had high hopes for our future and could hardly contain myself.

Chapter Sixteen

IRENE

I had never been so ill in my whole life. I spent our first night aboard lying in bed with my head spinning and insides churning, praying someone would kill me.

Joe awoke the following morning, stretched his arms, and declared, 'That was the best sleep I've had in ages. I didn't even need a sleeping pill. I feel fan-bloody-tastic.' He noticed me huddled up on my bed. 'Oh, yuck. You're as green as a frog, luv. Not to worry, it only lasts a few days, or so I'm told. You don't mind if I run and get something to eat, do you? The sea air has given me an appetite for a generous helping of bacon and eggs.'

My stomach turned, and I groaned. 'You go ahead. I'll be fine. Take the children with you.'

There was a knock on the cabin door, which Joe answered. Shutting it, laughing his head off, he handed me a package. 'They're giving out sick bags. I hope I got enough. I asked for twenty.'

I didn't have the strength to respond.

Joe was right. It was hell for a few days, but once the seasickness abated, my appetite and energy returned with a vengeance. Waking up ravenous, I spent the morning popping from restaurant to restaurant, testing out the mouth-watering variety of foods. I had never eaten so much. Forget dieting. You could eat to your heart's content. Afternoon tea was my favourite, with scones, sandwiches, and beautifully petite cakes, each topped with feather-light cream. On my own, I stuffed my face and had a great time people-watching. It was such a relief to be myself again.

After planning out the rest of my day, it dawned on me that I was free to do whatever I liked. For the first time in years, I didn't need to cater to my family's whims— only mine. I spent my time enjoying the blue skies and bright sunshine as the children raced around with their new friends, engrossed in the numerous activities available. They were so busy I hardly saw them. On a rare occasion, one of them would find me to ask a question, but they didn't seem to need me much at all. I revelled in the freedom, though at first it felt strange and precarious, as if it might be snatched away at any moment.

After the kids went to bed, Joe and I visited the nightclub. The atmosphere was electric as couples danced, crowding the floor, while a live band played. We joined in doing the Twist and Jive. All the passengers stopped what they were doing to watch us. I loved the attention and could've twirled around until the sun rose, but Joe didn't have the same enthusiasm, wanting to get back to his games. After he left, I had my share of offers for a dance partner, but I refused. It would have been improper for a married woman to accept. Instead, I returned to the cabin alone.

As I laid down in bed, leafing through a magazine, I wondered what would happen if, for once, I plucked up the courage and asked Joe to forego the gambling. I suspected his temper would erupt. Best not to test it out.

The following days kept us busy as we docked at several ports. It was wonderful to hold my family close as we discovered unknown places.

First on the list was Rotterdam. With only a few hours ashore, we managed a quick tour of the city. It was such a charming place, with its ancient port and narrow, winding streets, but Joe wasn't very interested in seeing much.

'I've had enough of walking around. I want to eat now,' Joe grumbled.

'Alright,' I said, 'but where?'

'Hold on.' He smiled at a couple walking by arm in arm, 'Excuse me. Would you know of a good restaurant nearby?'

The lady pointed to a building across the street with a sign above the door in Dutch. Joe gave her a thumbs up.

The restaurant was small but cosy, and luckily the waitress spoke English, since we couldn't understand a word on the menu. We ordered some soup with peas and lentils that came with enormous pieces of hearty rustic bread and then followed with some rich fruit pastries and meltingly fine chocolate. It was delicious, and when we'd finished it all off, Joe seemed to be back in good spirits again.

'I'm so full.' He laughed. 'Have you noticed, I'm either ravenous or bursting at the seams?'

'Yes, I have. Black or white, never any grey with you.'

'I don't like grey, it's boring. Anyway, we better go for a stroll, or we'll be waddling up the ship's gangway.'

Walking around the corner, we discovered a market at the end of the road. It was choc a bloc, full of everything and anything imaginable, except perhaps the kitchen sink.

'Can we get some?' Boris asked, pointing to a stand full of clogs. 'Please?'

'Okay, mate. What colour do you want?'

'Blue,' said Boris.

'Pink,' said Lorraine, jumping up and down.

We found the right sizes, paid, and made our way back to the ship.

After a few minutes, Joe shouted. ' Take those fucking things off. I'm getting a headache.'

The children pouted, but I whispered to them. 'Do as Daddy says. You can wear them later when he's not around.'

The next stop was Las Palmas in the Canary Islands. I fell in love with it. The weather was perfect— balmy but not sweltering— and the air was so fresh and smelt green and lush. The sun warmed our bodies and put smiles on our faces as the children pointed excitedly at the palm trees. After walking the streets and looking at various shops, none of which held Joe's interest, we sat outside in the sun at a busy restaurant. We wanted to try out the local cuisine, which included octopus.

Lorraine wrinkled her nose. 'Yuck. All those legs. I'm not eating that.'

'Darling, you need to be open to new experiences.'

'I'll try it, Mum,' said Boris, poking his tongue out at his sister. 'I'm not afraid.'

Lorraine frowned. 'Nor am I,' she said, taking a piece. 'I'll try it too.'

We all agreed that it was scrumptious.

'You know that whenever you eat any type of meat, it always tastes like chicken?' Joe said with his mouth full. 'If that's the case, then what does chicken taste like?' Joe lit up as the children giggled. I loved this side of him, rosy-cheeked, mischievous, and making us laugh. I hoped it would continue throughout the voyage.

~ * ~

We had twelve days until the next port of call, and I had finally plucked up the courage to put on my brand-new bikini and check out the pool. It was such a lively atmosphere with all the loud splashing and laughter and the excited whoops as someone jumped off the diving board and pummelled into the water. A whiff of tanning oil and alcohol filled the air as I wound my way through the lines of chairs until I found an empty sun bed. I sat beside a dazzling woman wearing gorgeous diamond earrings, a matching necklace, and enormous rings on both hands. I stole glances at her as she lay in the sun. It was hard to be sure of her age, but she was definitely older than me. Hoping I could match her deep, golden tan, I applied lotion to my arms and legs before lying back. When the waiter appeared, I ordered a martini with a suppressed giggle. In my favourite book, the heroine always cradled one in her hand, her little finger sticking out— so sophisticated. I'd always longed for the opportunity to do the same. Why not now?

A deep Australian accent interrupted my thoughts. 'Who have we here, then?'

Shielding my eyes from the sun, I smiled at the tall, blonde, muscular man standing before me.

'Cat got your tongue? You must be new. Thought I'd met everyone. Have you been holed up in your cabin? Shame such a lovely woman would deprive us of her presence.'

My face felt hot. 'I … eh … Yes. I'm Irene. Actually, it's my first time here. I've been ill.'

'Oh, poor you. The old *mal de mer*.' He moved in closer, sitting on the edge of my lounge chair. 'Well, it's nice to meet you, Irene. My name's John.'

He offered his hand, and I shook it. What a firm grip. What a handsome fellow, and how refreshing to be talking to somebody besides myself for a change.

The waiter arrived with my drink, and John ordered himself a beer.

'So, why are you going to Australia then? Visiting the kangaroos?'

He laughed, displaying his very straight white teeth.

'Maybe I will. I might even slip in its pocket and go for a ride.'
How daring am I?

John grinned. 'Well, Irene, you can ride in my pocket whenever you fancy. Just say the word.'

I burst out laughing. I was used to flirtatious men, but John was bolder than most.

An overweight, hairy man approached, his belly bulging over his tiny bathing suit in a pathetic effort to cover his maleness. I averted my eyes. *Doesn't he realise how awful that looks?*

'Hey, John, what have we here? Did you catch us a mermaid?' There was no doubt that he was intoxicated based on his slurred speech and heavy eyelids.

'Larry, you leave us alone. This is my catch. Go and fish elsewhere.' John shot him a threatening look.

Larry faked a shudder. 'Oh, mercy. Our golden boy is getting angry. I'm going. Don't get your knickers in a twist.' He staggered off, tripping over the older woman in the next chair.

'Do you mind!' she shouted in a very upper-class British accent. Sniffing as if something most distasteful was under her nose, she adjusted her sunglasses before returning to her tanning.

'So, where were we before we were so rudely interrupted?'

Seeing John's smile, I suspected the journey might not be as awful as I'd feared.

Every afternoon, I sipped my martinis as the warm breeze caressed my skin. The pool had become my regular spot, with John and the others, who would compliment and admire me. I was in control for the first time in my life; no husband or parents firing orders at me, no children making demands on my time, and best of all, no housework. I was free to do whatever I fancied, and I did. It was liberating. I was the centre of attention for once, not Joe, and I loved it.

John kept up a constant campaign to lure me back to his cabin, but I refused. It was tempting, though. He was very attractive, very attentive and wanted me, unlike my husband, who preferred gambling. I battled with my morals, but the flattery was becoming addictive, boosting my confidence. No more blushing or stammering.

One night, after the kids were safely tucked in bed and Joe was gambling, I ventured out on deck to see who was around. I'd never been outside at night before. It was exciting. It felt like I was doing something forbidden, though I wasn't sure what and truly, there was no harm in it. With the low lighting and Frank Sinatra's voice crooning 'Luck be a lady' from the speakers, it felt like another world entirely. No children, no teenagers, just adults enjoying themselves.

The gang was at the bar, laughing and joking. I'd been missing out on all the fun.

John's wide smile made it clear that he was happy to see me. He waved me over and ordered my usual. Everyone seemed to have already knocked back more than a few. I finished my drink and downed another to catch up. I was becoming quite fearless. After the third, John placed another martini in front of me. *Why not? You only live once.* Somewhere deep down, a spark of warning flashed in my mind. But before I could blink, the glass was empty again. I giggled as another appeared and vanished as well.

'It's magic. A disappearing act. I must be a magician,' I said, trying not to slur, but my mouth was on strike. John put his massive arm around me and stroked my hair as I leaned against him. It felt so good. I wanted it to last forever, but then he caressed my arm.

'I've been meaning to ask about these marks. Are they scars?'

'What marks?' I covered the burns with my hand.

'These.' He moved my hand away and gently ran his fingers along the bumps.

'I'm an ashtray, didn't you know?' I laughed, swaying. 'You are a saint or maybe a king.' I tried to point my finger at him. 'Where's your crown, King Joh …' My eyes closed, my legs gave way, and I slumped against him.

John held me up with his powerful arms. 'Let me help you downstairs.' I didn't have the strength to resist, nor did I care to.

My feet walked one after another without completely touching the ground as John led me through the corridors. I pointed left towards my room, but he steered me in the opposite direction. *Maybe he knows a shortcut. He's so clever.* I stumbled a moment as we passed an old couple and burst out laughing. They gave me a dirty look, which I ignored as I held onto the Australian's arms of steel.

As we approached a cabin, John took out his keys. I squinted at the door number, trying to focus.

'This isn't mine. Where are we?'

'Don't you worry, pretty lady. You rest. Everything will be alright soon.' Opening the door, he guided me into a tiny room.

'Why is this cabin so small, but you're so big?' I giggled.

John picked me up, placed me on the bed, and removed my shoes. I wiggled my toes, relishing their freedom while he rubbed my feet. It was heaven.

'Oh yes, please. That's so nice.'

Feeling sleepy, I was glad to be lying down. 'I'm just going to close my eyes for a minute,' I said as a deep sleep overcame me.

Somewhere in the distance, I felt hands turn me over and unzip my dress, caressing my body as my clothes melted away. *This isn't right, but it feels...*

Some hours later, I bolted upright, suppressing a howl at the pounding in my head and the pressure burning behind my eyes. *Where am I? What's the time?* In the faint lighting, I noticed a small desk and a chair with a man's jacket hanging on it, and on the floor, a suitcase overflowing with rumpled clothes.

Hearing heavy breathing beside me, I spun around, regretting it instantly as I fought back a wave of nausea. With my hand on my head, I peered at the shape lying on his back beside me. *Oh my God. That's John.*

'No, no, no,' I whispered, pulling the blanket aside. The frigid air froze my nude body. I searched frantically for my clothes.

John stirred while I was rummaging around on the floor.

'Hey, pretty lady, how are you?'

'Fine.' I averted my eyes. I couldn't bear to look at him.

Despite my throbbing head, I dressed as quickly as possible, flung open the door and dashed out of the room without a backward glance. Running along the corridor, I searched desperately for signs to my cabin. After staggering around yet another corner, I noticed a waiter pushing a trolley up ahead.

'What time is it, please?'

'It's two-thirty, Madam.' He smiled politely.

'What? In the middle of the night?' I felt the blood drain from my face.

'Yes. Do you require any help?' He frowned with concern.

'No. Nothing, thanks.' I hurried past him.

What have I done? How do I explain this to Joe? I prayed he was still out playing cards.

Reaching our cabin, I unlocked the door with shaking hands. Entering the room, I flicked on the light and froze. Sitting in the chair was my husband.

'Where the fuck have you been?' he snarled.

I had no idea what to say. The words wouldn't come. 'I … um … felt sick. I think my, my seasickness has come back, so I went out on deck for some fresh air.' My entire body was rigid with fear.

'You felt sick, did you? I'll give you something to feel sick about.'

As Joe flew out of the chair and stormed over to me, each footstep clapping like thunder, an enormous wave of nausea turned my stomach and, without warning, I vomited all over the carpet.

'What the fuck?' Joe jumped back to avoid the splash. 'You disgusting cow. Clean this up.' Edging towards the door, he barked, 'I'm going out.'

I ran into the bathroom and turned on the shower. Standing under the steaming water, I scrubbed between my legs as hard as possible, clawing at myself, desperate to erase John from my body. *Oh my God, I've been such a fool, gallivanting around, acting like a single woman. What was I thinking?* I continued to wash until my skin was red raw, but it wasn't enough. Nothing could wash away the filth. I was living in a nightmare and didn't know how to wake up.

I stayed in my cabin for three days, avoiding any chance encounters with John and the gang. I would've preferred not to venture out for the rest of the journey, but that wasn't possible since I had to join the family for dinner every night. After a week of successfully sidestepping the outside world, I had no choice but to leave my safe haven for The Crossing of the Equator ceremony. It was supposed to be the best part of the trip. Even Joe took a break from gambling to join in the fun. I was delighted by the chance for a family activity, all of us happy together in earnest, but the idea that I might see John put a damper on things.

I still couldn't believe I'd had sex with someone else, and to make matters worse, I couldn't remember a thing. *Does it count as a betrayal if I have no memory of it?* I yearned to confide in Joe, as crazy as that sounded, but he seemed to have forgotten all about it. It would be best for me to do the same, I thought, to act as though it had never happened, but that was easier said than done. It tormented my every waking moment.

A loud knock on the door made me jump. *Who is it? John? Does he know my cabin number?*

'Who's there?' I called out, my voice wobbling.

'Mummy, we want to go to the party.'

I let out a sigh of relief at hearing my son's voice and opened the door with a big smile. 'Hello, darlings, don't you look nice?'

The children had combed their hair and were wearing their best clothes. Boris looked dapper in his white shirt and dark trousers and Lorraine was an angelic picture in a pink dress, a matching ribbon in her hair. They had been looking forward to this day since the start of the trip.

'Did you put the ribbon on yourself, Lorraine?' I asked my little daughter.

'I did,' she said proudly, 'but Boris helped a bit.'

'Well done. Daddy's in the shower. He won't be long. Come and tell me everything you've been doing with your friends.' Putting my arms around them, I led them to the sofa. Lorraine and I sat down while Boris faced us, jumping up and down, a big smile on his face.

'Mummy, Mummy, I can't wait to go to the ceremony,' Boris said, 'When you cross the equator, they make you dirty and throw you in the pool, and then you have to go to King Neptune, who decides if you are seaworthy. My friend Roger has done it twice.'

'Well then, let's hope Daddy will hurry up and we can go and watch.'

Once Joe emerged, ready to go, we left the cabin. I walked along the corridors, glancing left and right, alert the whole time.

Streamers and balloons adorned the upper deck around the pool, and the ocean sparkled as flying fish skimmed the blue surface. The sun warmed my skin as I looked around. The crowd's excitement was palpable as they craned their necks to get a glimpse of King Neptune sitting on his throne, awaiting his victims. I kept my head low to avoid recognition while

King Neptune's helpers selected innocent bystanders from the crowd. First was a chubby, middle-aged woman. They picked her up, holding her arms and legs, and carried her over to the barber, who smothered her hair and face with spaghetti. She shrieked with laughter as they threw her into the pool, sauce flying everywhere. A beefy man wearing nothing but his swimming trunks suffered the same fate.

The children squealed and clung to my arms whenever the crew came near, not wanting to be taken but secretly hoping they might. Laughing, I spotted a familiar face across from us. The tanned, wealthy-looking woman I'd seen around the bar. She looked over and winked at us. I stole a glance at my husband, my stomach somersaulting when he waved back.

'Do you know her?'

'Yeah, that's … Who?' He stopped himself, a guilty look settling on his face.

'The lady over there. She winked at us, and you waved.'

'Don't be ridiculous. Christ Irene, let's just try to have a good time, okay?'

What's wrong with me? Is my mind playing tricks? They couldn't possibly know each other. She sunbathed on the deck all day, and he gambled day and night. *I need to pull myself together.*

Looking back at her, I studied her face. *Did she just nod her head?*

The woman turned and left. Joe put his hand on my arm. 'I'm going for a piss, luv. You enjoy yourselves. See you later.'

Oh my God, what if she bumps into Joe and tells him what I've been doing at the pool? 'Children, you stay and have a good time. I have something to do, but we'll meet up at dinner.' They were so engrossed in the festivities that they didn't even acknowledge me.

As I raced towards the cabin, I saw two people standing in the corridor. To my horror, I recognised Joe and the suntanned woman.

Hands clenched to hide the shaking; I approached them with a hard smile.

'Hello, darling.' My voice sounded stilted.

They both turned and glared at me.

'Hello, luv,' Joe returned the forced smile, 'This is Marjorie. She was asking if I knew whether it was a formal dinner tonight or just a regular one.' Joe popped a Polo mint in his mouth. 'This is me wife, Irene.'

'Yes, I've often seen her sunbathing at the pool,' Marjorie said with a raised eyebrow.

I smiled and looked into her eyes, pleading with her not to say anything. 'Yes, I've seen you too. And as for tonight, I understand it will be formal. Lovely to meet you, Marjorie, but we must run.' Grabbing Joe's arm, I steered him towards our cabin, praying they would never meet again.

Chapter Seventeen

JOE

After talking to the entertainment officer on the first day, I learned about a private lounge on a lower deck. Only people who knew the password, '*winnings*', could enter. I found my way there no trouble and double speed. I happily uttered the password and a wonderful new world opened up for me. It was exciting. Red curtains— drawn closed— and dim lighting gave the illusion of night-time all day. The seats around the six tables had thick red cushions, perfect for long periods of sitting. Cigar smoke drifted in a haze and the warm, peaty smell of whisky rose from the bar. I felt at home immediately. Besides eating and sleeping, I spent all my time around the tables playing poker or rummy games, and it didn't take long before I knew everyone there. It was like belonging to one of those secret societies, like the Freemasons. No one was allowed to know what we did in there.

One night, I was sitting at the poker table having a shitty time. The money we'd brought with us from England was practically gone. Every hand had been a disaster, and yeah, as usual, the loser of the evening was me. *Can I help it if Lady Luck isn't on my side?* I had no choice but to give it one last shot with what remained in my pocket. Nodding at the dealer, he dealt me another hand. *Damn.* They were crap. The next two were no better. *What the fuck am I going to tell Irene?* Letting out a loud sigh, I was lighting a cigarette when a shadow fell over me.

'I always find it helps to take a break when one is losing. Don't you agree? Have a drink and return as new.'

Looking up, I saw an effortlessly glamourous woman standing beside me. Bloody hell, the way she spoke, you'd think she was the queen or something, at the very least, someone on the BBC radio. Thick red hair framed her face, and she glittered with the gold of her jewellery, oozing wealth. It wasn't just the way she spoke or the diamonds hanging from her; it was her presence. I couldn't explain it exactly. I just knew she was worth a pretty penny.

Compared to her, I felt like I had 'World's Biggest Failure' etched on my forehead. I wondered why she was taking the time to talk to me. It had to be my good looks, or maybe she recognised me and was a fan. She seemed friendly enough, and there was no harm in being polite— better than wallowing in the doom and gloom and working up a temper.

'That sounds brilliant.' I guided her to the bar, where we perched on high stools. 'What's your poison?'

'An Old Fashioned, thank you. My name is Marjorie Sloan.' Her bright smile was a charming contrast to her dark tan.

'Joe Leslie.' I smiled back.

Gesturing to the barman, I ordered her drink and me a lemonade.

Who is this woman? She had the look of someone wise beyond her years, experienced, yet there was something youthful in how she dressed. She was wearing a light pink ruffled shirt that showed more than ample cleavage. Together with her tight, dark trousers, she could have been mistaken for a far younger woman, but I suspected she had mileage on her that most cars didn't.

Flipping her hair and crossing her legs so that our thighs were touching, she bit her lip. I was sure she was flirting with me. It was flattering, but the feeling wasn't mutual.

Leaning closer, she whispered in my ear, 'Why don't we go for a stroll on deck? The sea air can be revitalising.'

Why not? I thought. Escorting her out of the games room, I nodded to a few men we passed, who smiled back at me, one of them winking. What they had in mind was the furthest thing from mine. I just needed some air and to forget my worries for a while.

We went through the large glass doors, onto the deck, and out into the warm night. Leaning over the railing, I gazed at the smooth, glistening ocean, losing myself in its infinite calm. I could stare at it forever.

Marjorie's deep, throaty voice hummed. 'I always sail to Australia at this time of year. That way, summer is constant, and I avoid the endlessly grey British weather. Ever since my husband died, I have kept busy travelling around the world, meeting handsome gentlemen like yourself.

Though I must admit, you look awfully familiar.'

I smirked. 'Well, me dear, I'm a TV star. You've probably seen me on the box.'

'No, I don't watch television. It ruins the mind for other things, but I am prepared to make an exception in your case.' She tittered while patting her hair.

Bloody hell. My stomach turned over, but, with all that blatant wealth, I thought she might come in handy, so I played along. 'What did your husband work in when he was alive?' I asked, showing her my most charming showbusiness smile.

She laughed. 'Honestly, he never told me, and I didn't bother asking. As long as my bank account was full, I was happy.' Her hand fluttered to her chest, displaying the impressive diamond rings on her index and middle fingers. 'Hector was so generous and never minded my spending. He always said, "Thy cup runneth over, for eternity," and it still does.'

The sky was getting lighter, reminding me I should scarper back to Irene, so I stretched my arms and stood. 'Lovely talking to you, Marjorie. Maybe I'll see you on deck or in the games room.'

'It was such a pleasure, Joe. I am certain our paths will cross again soon. I can't wait to hear more about you. No doubt you have had a fascinating life,' she purred, stroking my arm.

I winked. 'You can say that again. Bye for now.'

Marjorie appeared every night after that, insisting on buying me drinks and cigarettes. With the little money I had left, I'd managed to win back the rest of it, which swelled my enthusiasm and drove me on to take bigger and bigger risks.

Feeling optimistic a few nights later, I gambled a larger sum than usual, convinced I could triple my earnings, but in a flash, it vanished into thin air. *What will it take for me to learn my lesson once and for all?*

Marjorie's white-gloved hand squeezed my arm. It felt like a lifeline to my drowning despair. 'Let's sit somewhere and talk. I have something that may interest you. Come on, let me put a smile on that handsome face of yours.'

I suppose there's no harm in listening to the old girl. Walking over to the bar on shaky legs, I chose a table away from all the eavesdroppers as

Marjorie ordered coffee for both of us.

'My dear, it's always rotten when one loses, but do not despair,' she said in a gentle voice. Opening her handbag, she took out a glittering diamond bracelet. Placing it in my palm, she closed my fingers over it. 'This item, I'm told, is rather valuable. My darling Hector gave me more jewellery than I could ever need. I won't miss this one.'

I cocked my head. 'Not sure I follow.'

'This is my suggestion. Use this to win back your losses—you never know, you might even double it— and you can repay me at your convenience. How does that sound?'

Too good to be true. There has to be a catch. She sat there, wearing a soft and understanding expression, while I studied her. I suspected I might go down a rabbit hole if I accepted, but I didn't have much choice. I was dead broke and terrified of facing Irene.

'That's very nice of you, Marjorie. Let me pop over to see a mate of mine. I'm sure he'll give me top dollar for this.'

After pocketing Marjorie's bracelet, I headed over to find my new friend Sam; he was always eager for some wheeling and dealing. I'd met Sam on my first day in the games room when I was on a winning streak. The man was as bald as a newborn baby, with a giant mole sprouting on his forehead. It was always a challenge not to stare at it. He chattered on about his wife and kids at first, which just about put me to sleep, but my ears perked up when he went on to more interesting subjects. 'My job as the food and beverage officer is very important, but the pay isn't great, so let's just say I often need to supplement my income with a bit of trading, if you know what I mean.' I did, indeed.

I knew having a friend like that on my side would be useful. Sam took one look at the bracelet and gave me a thick wad of cash, which brightened my mood no end.

I was sure I'd been careful with the money, but it disappeared like my mother-in-law's smile after she'd heard one of my jokes. Within a week, I'd managed to flush it all away. With the money gone, I spent my days walking around, my mouth dry and legs shaking, jumping if any redhead approached me. Marjorie had been absent for several nights, and I prayed she'd fallen overboard, but no such luck. On the day of the Equator crossing, there she was, standing across the deck, flashing me a warning signal with her eyes. Just from her look, I knew she meant business.

I muttered some excuse to Irene and went below deck to find her. Sure enough, Marjorie approached me, glittering with jewels as she grabbed my arm.

'Joe, there has been ample time for you to reimburse me. I'm here to collect. Otherwise, your wife will have to be informed.' Her voice was unusually loud and I looked over my shoulder in case anyone had heard. *Doesn't she understand how gambling works? I just need some more time, that's all.*

I fidgeted with the coins in my pocket. 'Marjorie, you know I'm good for it. Give me a few more days, and I'll have it all sorted. I've a strong feeling that me luck has turned.' I tried to keep the pleading out of my voice, though I wasn't too successful.

She leaned in close, pressing herself against me. 'Do we really need to argue? We are such wonderful friends, aren't we? I am confident we can come to some kind of arrangement.' She flashed me a predatory smile. 'Why don't we discuss this in my cabin?'

I shuddered in understanding, picturing the old bag with her clothes off. *Ugh!* She might look a million dollars in her glad rags but naked? It would be the stuff of nightmares. *What choice do I have? I have to get rid of her.*

'Okay, but later tonight, when me wife has gone to sleep,' I agreed just as Irene turned up. Seeing her walk toward us, I almost passed out on the spot. Thank goodness for my impeccable acting ability and supremely quick thinking, or who knows what she would've thought was going on.

With one final glance, we parted ways. I was dreading what I had to do later on, but needs must, right?

Chapter Eighteen

IRENE

Hiding away in my cabin, at least I had my romance novels to read. I devoured one after another, escaping into a world that was the polar opposite of my life. Joe and I never gazed into each other's eyes with passion. On the rare occasion he had the fancies, it was very much 'wham bam, thank you, ma'am'. Maybe it had been better with John, but I wouldn't know, unless my memory returned.

I yearned for a fairy-tale romance, where the man, maybe even Joe when he was charming, would be tender with me, desperate to please me. He would bring me roses and expensive chocolates that melted in my mouth. When I said something funny, it would make him roar with laughter, and he would think I was ever so clever. In the evenings, he would lay petals on the bed before lifting me into his powerful arms. Gently laying me down, he would slowly remove my white lacy negligee while kissing my neck and murmuring how much he loved and desired me.

The sound of the toilet flushing brought me back to reality as Joe walked out of the bathroom. 'That was a great shit!' he announced as he went over to the cupboard to get something to wear. *Really romantic.*

It was time for dinner. I hated leaving the room, but I had to eat and behave somewhat as usual so as not to arouse any suspicion from my husband. We left the cabin and knocked on the kids' room next door.

'Grub time,' Joe shouted, and they rushed out, bouncing and chattering.

'Food. Yes, I'm starving,' said Boris.

I took Lorraine's hand, and we headed along the corridor.

'Mummy, I have new friends, Sarah and Caroline and Wendy. They are ever so nice, and we play lots of games together.' Lorraine prattled away next to me, swinging my arm. While it was nice to hear my daughter so happy, I couldn't engage with her in earnest. I felt too exposed. I kept looking over my shoulder, scared of bumping into John or anyone from his group.

My head flicked left and right as we walked into the dining room. There was no sign of him. *Thank goodness.*

We joined a table with two elderly couples, who Joe immediately began to entertain with his stories. They seemed enamoured with him, but I needed to hush the children a few times. Nothing should interrupt my husband when he had an audience.

Amidst the conversation, I scanned the room discreetly. *So far, so good.* When the food arrived, I picked at my salmon and vegetables with little appetite. It was hard to enjoy the cuisine when danger could strike at any moment. Giving the area another sweep, I froze. I had caught sight of a man in the far distance who looked a little, no, a lot like John. I held my breath. He was way across the dining room, so I couldn't be sure, but it was enough for my heart to skip a beat. I knew I couldn't take a chance and stay if it was him.

'Darling,' I said to Joe, 'can we go back to the cabin? I've got a bit of a headache and need to lie down.'

'Oh, you poor thing. It's a bit early for me. I think I'll stay and have dessert, perhaps get in a game or two. You get your sleep. You need it.'

The man was coming closer, so I had no choice but to bolt. 'Alright then. Come on, kids, bedtime. I'll see you later, darling. Bye.' I kissed Joe on the cheek before taking the children's hands and hurrying away as fast as possible.

After saying goodnight to the children and settling them into their beds, I went into my cabin, lay on the bed, and picked up my book. Lost in the pages, I relaxed, losing track of time.

Joe arrived some hours later and went straight into the bathroom. I heard the rushing of water. *How odd.* When he came out, I remarked, 'I don't ever remember you showering before bed.'

He looked away and lit a cigarette.

'Oh,' he mumbled. 'You see, I was so full cos I ate two helpings of apple pie and cream so I decided to walk it off fast around the deck, and then I ran up the stairs. Made me all sweaty.'

I supposed that made sense, but it was the first time I'd ever known

144

him to do any exercise. Still, I had enough of my own problems, so I let it go. Besides, we were due to dock in Australia's first port of call the following morning and I wanted to divert my energy into enjoying our time on dry land. Beauty sleep was calling.

It was another glorious day with a cloudless blue sky. I stood on deck, Joe's arm resting on my shoulders, as the ship approached Fremantle Harbour. It appeared as a small dot on the horizon, growing larger every minute until we arrived at the port. It was exciting seeing the country I was to live in, for the first time. The warm breeze fanned me as I looked over at the crowds standing and cheering. I planned on exploring the town with the family while trying my best to forget my troubles. Looking around, I breathed a sigh of relief. John and the gang were nowhere to be seen.

Joe put his arm around me. 'Sorry, luv, if I left you alone a bit too much, but from now on, I won't go gambling for a while, so we can all be together.'

Why does he suddenly want to be with us? That's very strange after being absent most of the voyage. Joe never had a change of heart without reason. But the sun was shining and I had my family's company. To question him now would only flare his temper and ruin the day.

A massive banner with *Welcome to Western Australia* flapped in the wind above the customs building across the way. A band played while crowds threw streamers or waved balloons in a sea of rainbow colours. It was a contagious, festive atmosphere. Once ashore, I noticed passengers falling into their families' arms, crying tears of joy. The touching sight made me smile until my parents' faces flashed in my head. A sharp pain pierced my chest as I wondered when I would see them again.

With only a few hours ashore, we took a taxi to the nearest shopping area. Exotic birds flashed from tree to tree, flaunting their dazzling feathers and whooping their strange calls as we strolled along, so unlike the hushed chirping of sparrows and the chatter of starlings in England. We gazed up at magnificent blue, yellow, red, and green parrots perched on enormous red trees, screeching and squawking. It was so loud we had to raise our voices over the racket. Joe loved the sound and tried to imitate them with his whistling, making us giggle.

He wrapped his arm around my waist. 'Don't you look pretty? Is that a new dress?'

'No. You got me this a year ago, but thanks.'

'Daddy, look.' Boris pointed at a restaurant in the shape of a giant kangaroo.

'Well, I'm famished. Let's check it out. I just hope kangaroo isn't on the menu.'

Joe grabbed a discarded newspaper as we followed the hostess to a booth, and she handed us some menus. Our mouths watered in anticipation as we scanned the selection. The children chose hamburgers and chips, but I wanted something healthier, like a large salad.

'Will you look at this?' said Joe. 'What a choice. I want the T-Bone steak, and don't you try to stop me.'

The waitress took our order and brought us our drinks in the meantime. When our food arrived, we all tucked in. It tasted as good as it looked. I could really get used to Australian food, though I would have to watch my weight — the portions were huge. The children chatted as they ate, while Joe buried his nose in his paper. Letting my guard down, a sense of calm swept over me, and I started to enjoy our time together.

'Yes!' Joe yelled out.

'Joe! Are you alright? You look very flushed.' His outburst had startled me and I watched him with worry.

'Never been better. Hey, kids, how about ice cream for dessert?' he said with a huge smile.

Folding the newspaper, he placed it on the table and started tickling the children. Giggling, they tickled him back. It was such a pleasure to hear his belly laugh. *Who is this man?* I didn't know what to make of his unusual behaviour, but I liked this husband and father. If only he could stay this way all the time.

Chapter Nineteen

JOE

To avoid bloody Marjorie, I spent as much time as possible with the family. I hated living like that, always looking over my shoulder. I was used to doing whatever I wanted, but I didn't dare go anywhere that old prune face might be. Yet again, I found myself in *schtuck*, beating myself up over my own stupidity. *Why did I trust the old hag? She's got me by the short and curlies, that's for sure.*

We'd been eating in the dining room when Irene suddenly got a headache and wanted to leave. I couldn't go with her since I, unfortunately, had a duty to perform. One I was determined to get over and done with as quickly as possible and settle my debt. Marjorie turned up a short while after Irene left. Catching my eye, she nodded her readiness, then disappeared. Excusing myself from the old couples, I trudged along the corridor, my fate hanging over my head, till I found her cabin. I knocked on the door.

'It's open. Come in,' she called.

It was everything I had feared. And worse. Marjorie lay on the bed, stark naked, looking like a corpse with skin hanging off her bones. *Oh my god.* The dinner I'd eaten earlier, plus breakfast and lunch, were about ready to erupt from my mouth. *What is going on with her tits?* They were like two giant bowling balls sticking out of her rib cage, underlined by vivid red scars underneath. She must've had some kind of operation. No woman her age had breasts like that naturally. *Yikes.*

Looking around the room, I grew increasingly pissed off. I'd thought I had the best cabin, first-class, but hers was even bigger. It was like two cabins in one. I had a good mind to complain.

'Joe, let me see you in all your glory.' She flashed me a coy smile. *What the fuck does she think I have down there? The crown jewels?*

147

In no hurry to start, I took my time getting undressed while she looked at me like a dog waiting for its dinner. She was practically drooling.

Opening her legs, she purred, 'Touch me, Joe.'

I shuddered. I would've preferred to be at the dentist having all my teeth out without anaesthetic than touch that. Marjorie pulled me on top of her, but my plumbing just wasn't working.

'Let me help you. I am quite experienced in these matters.' She took hold of my privates, rubbing up and down so fast I thought it would drop off. Try as she might, she would've had better luck getting Jesus Christ to come back from the dead.

I couldn't take any more. I was red, sore, and my cock felt like it had been circumcised a second time. I pulled her hand away and sat up. 'Sorry, Marjorie, it's not going to work.' Seeing her disappointed face and determined to stay in her good books, I added, 'It's not you. It's me. You are a gorgeous woman, but I've got a lot on my mind.'

She pursed her lips, the wrinkles making her look ancient. 'I must say, I am most disheartened. I expected an earth-shattering performance from you.'

Desperate to leave, I stood up and snatched my trousers off the floor and put them on. I fastened the belt as tight as possible. 'Well, I usually deliver the goods, but all me money worries are affecting me. Of course, if I didn't have such problems, then—'

'Oh, is that your game?' She yanked the sheet up to cover herself. 'Don't think for one moment that you are off the hook. I still expect full payment.'

I was well and truly fucked. Not in the literal sense, of course.

'Could I at least get a discount? I did try, you know,' I said with a cheeky grin.

She'd shot me a threatening glare, so I'd bolted out as quickly as possible, hoping never to see her again.

After days of endless sea, sky, and avoiding Storm Marjorie, we finally arrived on dry land. I stood in line at Fremantle Harbour, aching for a change of scenery. The weather was great. I'd almost forgotten the daily grey drizzle of England. A pang of guilt cut through me as I glanced at the kids. It wasn't right of me to neglect them for most of the voyage. Still, they looked happy enough. I vowed to be a better father and husband after that stomach-churning event, and I meant it.

Irene wore a new flowery pink dress, looking lovely as usual. When I asked her about it, she blushed, silly thing. *At least she still fancies me.*

Walking hand in hand, we checked out the local shops. It was kind of nice. Irene was very interested in the fashions and remarked that Australia wasn't as up to date as London. Apparently, they were still wearing last year's styles. I preferred to scan the street, hoping for a local betting shop, but no such luck. The kids ran ahead. Boris pulled leaves off the trees while Lorraine climbed up and walked along a brick wall. Irene was having none of that, 'Lorraine, come down at once.' Lorraine pouted for a minute, but when Boris pointed to the kangaroo restaurant, she perked up.

Having heard good things about Australian meat, I ordered the biggest steak on the menu, eager to try it. It was top-notch, I tell you. Clearing my plate, I sat back and opened the newspaper. Skimming the headlines, I found little of interest, until I turned to the following page. My eyes nearly fell out of my head. Sitting up straight, my pulse racing, I gripped the newspaper. The article concerned a huge jewellery robbery in London. They estimated the loss in the millions. Photographs of the stolen collection dotted the page, and there, in the middle, larger than life, was a closeup of Marjorie's bracelet, the one she'd given me to sell. I almost jumped out of my seat. It all suddenly fell into place. Marjorie, with all her airs and graces, was a thief. *There is a god, after all. Watch out, Marjorie, the ball's in my court now.*

When we left the restaurant, I tucked the newspaper under my arm for safekeeping. I couldn't wait to get back to the ship.

After dinner that night, I raced over to the games room and sat at a far table by the wall, waiting in anticipation for Marjorie. The old cow turned up a short time later. 'Why don't you join me for a coffee?' I asked with my signature smile.

She seemed surprised at my willingness to talk and her behind had barely touched the chair before she attacked. 'I have been looking for you everywhere. You owe me, and it's time to collect.'

'Really?' I smirked, pulling the folded newspaper article out of my pocket. Opening it up, I showed it to her. 'I've notified the police. You might want to pack your bags or jump overboard. Enjoy the nick.'

Bursting with satisfaction, I got up and strode out, but not before witnessing the colour drain from her face.

Bluffing was yet another of my many talents.

Chapter Twenty

IRENE

1965, Melbourne

Opening the curtains, I gazed out at the tropical oasis. Green leaves the size of dinner plates filled the trees, and birds hopped from branch to branch as a chorus of their high-pitched squeaks and squawks filled the air. My doubts about living here disappeared two months ago when we moved into this charming four-bedroom brick house with a large swimming pool in the backyard. It became a source of pride for me. Our home was in an affluent area, close to St. Kilda beach. I was too afraid to let the kids go into the sea after hearing about the sharks, but staying home and sunning by the pool was no hardship. Beautiful homes lined our street, and there were plenty of upmarket shops and restaurants nearby. There was an enormous selection of food I had never tried before. I even gave Chinese a go and found myself enchanted by the fresh, sweet flavours. My favourite was Dim Sum, little dumplings with meat and vegetables inside. Even the kids loved them, always eager for more. We tried chocolate malted milkshakes for the first time, too. I had felt like a child again, slurping it down through a striped paper straw.

There was a world of difference between the Australians and the English. They were so friendly, with their thick accents, always saying 'G'day'. They had different words, too, like 'arvo' for afternoon and 'fair dinkum' for genuine. It fascinated me. They guzzled beer like water and carried around six packs wherever they went. It was common to see people driving with a beer in their hand, tossing the empty can out of the window. The other day, the newspaper's front-page headline read, *'Australia leads the world in drunken driving'* as though it was an accomplishment.

The whole mess with John on the ship still tormented me. It ate me up, turned my intestines into mush, and made my head throb. I tried to convince myself that if I couldn't remember it, then nothing happened. I didn't entirely believe it, of course, but immersing myself in our new life helped.

Every morning, after the children left for school, I would go to Jazz and Modern dance classes, which I had recently enrolled in. During those three hours, I focused on what I loved most— dancing. At home, I would watch shows on TV with the current styles, copying the moves. On my own, I was free to go wild. I would turn the radio up and whirl around the room, making up my own routines while dreaming of performing in front of an audience. It was my favourite time of the day.

On the weekends, the kids jumped and splashed in the pool, while I stretched out on a deckchair, slathering on oil, focused on tanning my body. The sounds of their laughter echoed through the garden as Joe sat in the shade, reading the newspaper.

Joe would stay in most evenings, watching cartoons with the kids or playing a game he named 'Octopus'. He would crouch on the floor with the children on his back while he stuck out his arm and grabbed their legs. They would shriek and giggle as he tried to catch hold of them. After they had gone to bed, we would watch TV together. On a few occasions, he actually rubbed my feet. The man I fell in love with had returned.

Over time, a sense of peace flowed through me. The pain and loneliness had disappeared, and I became full of optimism for the future.

We'd been settled three months before Joe invited a few people from the studio home for dinner. It was my first time meeting his workmates, so, after cleaning the floors and windows till they shone, I put on an elegant black dress and high heels. With my hair up in a tortoiseshell clasp, I carefully applied my makeup. Looking my best, I went downstairs to make sure the food was ready. I stirred the beef consommé, gave it a last taste, then turned down the flame, allowing it to simmer until it was time to serve.

I heard the front door unlock.

'Irene, you here?' Joe shouted.

'Here I am.'

I ventured out of the kitchen with a big smile.

Oh my god! No! I grabbed the hall table to steady myself as blood rushed to my head.

'Darling, meet John and Stewart. They're from the studio. Be nice to them so they can be nice to me, eh?'

No. No. It can't be John. The John. Words lodged in my throat.

'Hey, cat got your tongue? Say hello, then bring us a drink, woman.' Joe rolled his eyes at the men.

'Err … Of course … What can I get you?' I squeaked.

'Beer, please, if you have any,' Stewart asked politely.

'Anything dark and wet suits me just fine.' John smirked.

Racing to the cabinet to fix their drinks, my hands shook to the rhythm of my heavy, pounding heart. *This is a nightmare.*

'Hey, darling, John here is our cameraman.' Joe slung his arm around him. 'You won't believe what he told me. He just returned from England, and you wanna hear a coincidence? He was on The Majestic too.'

Hundreds of people were on that ship; out of everybody, why did it have to be John? I choked out a laugh, wanting to cry. 'Well, the Majestic was so big. It's no wonder we never met everyone.'

Staring at John, I urged him with my eyes to keep quiet.

He grinned. 'Well, I'm sure I would've remembered you, laying out on the deck like a mermaid.'

Joe chuckled, lighting a cigarette. 'Hey, watch it, mate. She's taken.' He glanced at me. 'When's the grub ready? I'm famished.'

I served the food like the dutiful hostess I was, then sat at the table with a forced smile on my face. The men talked shop, ignoring me, which was just as well as I picked at my food, feeling sick. I looked up at John and for a fleeting moment, our eyes met. I tried to read him, but he had already turned back to the conversation. Starter and mains passed in a blur of chatter I didn't hear.

Collecting the plates, I went into the kitchen to prepare dessert.

The door swung open, and I almost jumped out of my skin as John walked in. His voice boomed, 'Brought these dirties in for you. Can I help make the coffee?'

After putting the dishes in the sink, he turned to face me. 'Well, well, well, hello, pretty lady,' he said in a deep, hushed tone.

My stomach clenched as I whispered, 'Please, John, I'm begging you, forget us. Joe must never know. It was a mistake. It should never have happened.'

John's handsome face broke out into a broad smile. 'Of course, it should've. This is fate. Don't you worry. We'll be discreet.'

'You don't understand. I am devoted to my husband. It's over.' I peered at the door, petrified. Joe might walk in at any moment.

John leaned against the counter. 'No. It's not over. It's just beginning. You wait and see.' With a wink, he turned and walked out of the room.

I stood there, helpless and lost. I had no idea what to do. I knew I needed to behave as normal as possible, so, with clammy hands, I piled chocolate eclairs onto a plate and prepared the coffee, then retrieved my freshly made ice cream from the freezer and scooped it into the bowls.

Looking back, it was clear that I just needed some appreciation and attention, something I'd never received from Joe. I knew it was foolish to flirt with John, but he'd filled a huge void in my life. *Oh, if I could only turn back the clock.*

Knowing I couldn't stay in the kitchen forever, I took a deep, steadying breath before bringing the dessert into the dining room.

Joe looked up as I entered. 'Darling, I've got a wonderful surprise for you.' He winked at his guests. 'Wait till you catch the look on her face when I tell her the news. We've decided to have an addition to the show, a group of dancers. And guess what? You're gonna be one of them.'

Speechless, I forced a weak smile. 'Oh … uh … That's lovely, Joe, but are you sure that's what you want?'

'Of course it's bloody well what I want. Now I can keep an eye on you. Make sure you stay out of trouble.' Lighting another cigarette, he winked and turned to the men. 'Keep the old ball and chain close, so it doesn't get rusty.'

They all burst into laughter, everyone except me.

That night, as I lay in bed next to Joe, a thousand thoughts raced through my head.

'Darling,' I said, tentatively, 'can we speak for a moment?'

'Yeah, sure. What's going on?'

'It's lovely that you want me to be one of the dancers, but I'm not good enough.' I clenched my fist, resisting the urge to bite my nails.

'Course you are. I've seen what you can do.' At any other time,

Joe's confidence in my dancing might have made me glow with pride, but tonight I felt nothing but fear.

'But, isn't there an audition to get the job?'

'Yes, but not for my wife. You're gonna be great. Relax. Now, let's go to sleep. We have a big day tomorrow.' He switched off the lamp on his side and closed his eyes. The conversation was over.

I lay in the dark for hours, knowing I would be a wreck in the morning. My head spun round and round as I swirled my curls around my index finger and bit my lip so hard it almost bled. If John told Joe about us, Joe would explode. Burns would be mild compared to what Joe could do to me if he knew. *What am I going to do?*

Chapter Twenty-one

JOE

I loved Australia. No more umbrellas or having to wear a suit for work.

The ugly Marjorie debacle was over, thank goodness, but I needed to swallow a pill anytime I thought of that shitty business in her cabin. Eventually, the memory faded till I convinced myself that maybe it never happened and was just a figment of my imagination.

The only painful part of my life was not having my dogs, who I missed daily, but there'd been no way to bring them with us. I'd left them with some friends and hoped they were okay. After dropping them off, I felt like I needed windscreen wipers for my eyes as I drove home. A sharp pain pulled at my stomach every time I thought about that day.

Despite the pups, life was grand.

What I liked most about working in Melbourne was the respect my co-workers gave me. My being British made them think I was royalty or something. They even gave me a personal assistant on my first day. Jenny was a gorgeous young thing who catered to my every need. Well, not every need. That's what the wife was for. When I could be bothered. The boss, Marvin, was a good guy. He wasn't much older than me but was already in a high position with the network. I respected that, and we got on well. He was a savvy businessman but not one of those stiff, over-serious types. He told me that as long as I stayed within budget, I could do what I wanted with the show. That was easy enough as the budget was huge.

My show, *Feel the Beat*, promised to be a big hit. The studios were excited. They loved the idea of pop singers performing their latest hits while the resident girls, who I nicknamed 'The Movers', danced around the stage. The audience could also get up and join in if they wanted.

While working on the show, I studied the director's every move. It was something I wanted to learn, to add yet another notch to my belt. I felt like I would be a natural, and it looked easy enough. All you had to do was bark orders at the cameramen. I could do that. I was sure it wouldn't be long before I could have a chance to direct.

While I sipped my coffee in bed one morning, I was deep in thought. *Something's missing. The show needs to stand out. I know, what if the girls wear sexy costumes with their names written on their chests? Yes, that should turn a few heads.* After making a mental note to talk to production, I got myself ready for work. As per my contract, the network had to provide a car, and I insisted on a Jaguar. I was used to its high standard and comfort and wasn't prepared to accept anything less.

It was only a short fifteen-minute drive to the studios, and I arrived even before Jenny, so I popped into the cafeteria for another coffee. Two blokes sitting at the table beside me were talking so loudly that I couldn't help but listen.

'I just got back from England on the Majestic,' said the blonde, muscular one.

My ears pricked up.

'Sorry to interrupt,' I said with a smile. 'Were you on The Majestic? So was I.'

'Great, wasn't it? What's your name? I'm John, and this is Stewart.' He pointed to the man sitting with him.

It wasn't long before we were trading stories and laughing at my jokes, of course, but John had one story that made the air freeze in my lungs.

'There was this sexy English woman who was a fucking cock tease most of the voyage. All over me, she was. Then, when I finally landed her in my cabin, the bloody sheila passed out on me. Now, I'm no pervert, so nothing happened, and she goes rushing back to her husband, the stupid bird. If I were him, I'd keep an eye on her.'

The memory of Irene coming back late at night, her hair in a mess, smelling of booze, flashed in my head. As I laughed along with the lads, an uneasy feeling swept over me. I had to find out if I was crazy, or if the woman he was talking about was actually my wife. I mean, there were plenty of women on the ship. *Why do I think it was Irene?* Something kept nagging at me, remembering her that night, spewing everywhere and lying to me. It was so unlike her. I fished in my pocket for a Valium as sweat dripped down my neck. The fake smile on my face was hurting my jaw.

By the end of our coffee break, I had an idea.

'So, guys, this has been great. What do you think about carrying on the conversation at my house tomorrow night for dinner?'

Stewart looked eager. 'Yeah, I'd like that. What about you, John?'

'I'm available. That would be nice. Thanks a lot.'

'Good. Let's meet here after work at seven, and you can follow me in your cars to my place.'

When we walked into the house, it all became crystal clear. Irene looked like she was going to faint as I introduced her to John.

As I sat at the dinner table, I almost choked on my food as I watched him looking over at her, but I tried my best to carry on the conversation as normally as possible.

'So, I figure we should use four cameras if we want to cover every angle. What do you think, John?'

He prattled on while I resisted the urge to smash him to smithereens. I blinked away the vision of *my* wife naked on his bed and his filthy hands all over her.

When Irene got up to take the dirty dishes away, he practically undressed her with his eyes, the fucking bastard. What did he think? That I didn't notice? A minute later, he picked up some plates and went into the kitchen. I almost lost it right then and there, but I needed to keep my cool. I had to be clever and take my time to figure out what to do. I sat talking to Stewart, who was about as interesting as a librarian and was droning on about some documentary he filmed. Something to do with ancient trees or something.

John came back and sat down.

'Hey, I've been thinking,' I said, 'I've decided to put Irene in the show as one of the dancers. She's trained for years, and with her looks and moves, she'd be a great addition. Now don't say a word because I want to surprise her with the news. Okay?'

John nodded. 'That's a great idea. And nice to have your wife at work every day too.'

'Yeah,' I said, lighting a cigarette and imagining me stubbing it out in his eye.

It would be good to have Irene nearby so I could keep an eye on her and him. I'd be watching. One wrong move from either of them and they would regret the day that they were born. And if I had to sit in jail for the rest of my life, it would be well worth it.

Chapter Twenty-two

IRENE

After tossing and turning most of the night, I was twitchy and drained when I accompanied Joe to the studio. A pretty, young girl with straight blonde hair and a cute pixie nose bounced up to us, hugged Joe, then turned to me.

'Hi, you must be Irene. I'm Jenny, Joe's personal assistant. So nice to meet you.' She had a radiant, welcoming smile. 'If you need anything, just let me know, alright?'

'Thanks,' I replied, smiling back.

Jenny took hold of Joe's arm. 'We have a lot on today. There is a production meeting in fifteen minutes, the choreographer is coming in to work with the girls, and the costume designer's in after that.'

'Okay, me lovely, let's go to the office. Irene, see that bloke over there?' He pointed to a man with a huge mop of messy brown-grey hair, a clipboard in his hand, and a cigarette dangling between his lips. 'That's Harry, the floor manager. Tell him who you are, and he'll fix you up. Got to run.' After giving me a quick peck on the cheek, he strode away.

All alone, I realised I'd better find Harry. Before I could move in his direction, a tap on my shoulder startled me. It was John.

'Hello, mermaid, how are you today? Want some coffee?'

'No. I am fine, thank you,' I bristled.

I rushed across the studio floor, glancing behind me as I walked. John was still there, smiling, his eyes fixed on me. *Ugh!* I wanted to scream but took a deep breath instead, then approached the floor manager. I didn't have time to dwell on things after that. There was work to be done. Harry took me to the rehearsal studio, where I met the other dancers. They were all mortifyingly beautiful and very fit. Watching them limbering up, I felt my confidence shrinking by the minute. After changing into my leotard, I joined in, hoping they wouldn't notice the amateur amongst them.

One girl with short blonde hair gave me a big smile. 'Welcome to our flock. It's going to be such fun. I'm Anne.' She pointed to each girl. 'That's Gina with the straight black hair. Over there is Nancy, the redhead, and the blonde is Lizzy.'

'Nice to meet you all. I look forward to working with you. I'm Irene.'

'Tell me, Irene,' said Nancy with her leg stretching on the bar, 'what's it like being married to the producer? Does he boss you around at home?'

Everyone laughed, so I joined in. If only they knew how true that was.

A gorgeous, sculpted man wearing a shiny purple leotard pranced into the room.

Lizzy called out, 'Gavin, the boss's wife is here. Her name's Irene.'

'Oh, how lovely to meet you. I'm the choreographer. I just want to say it's an honour to have you with us.' He reached out his hand, which I shook.

'Well, girls, make sure you limber up properly before we begin.'

I hurried to begin my stretching routine, glancing over at the others to make sure I was doing it correctly. We did the splits, which was easy as I did it every day. Then we went into first position with our feet turned out. Bending our knees, we went into a plié, then on to second position, our feet apart.

Gavin went over to the table and turned on the tape recorder. Loud pop music blared from the speakers. 'Alright,' he said over the music as he walked back to us, 'the start is easy, but then we will be doing some elaborate moves, so pay attention. And a one, and a two...'

My muscles were sore and aching after several hours of dancing. I did my best to keep up with the other girls, but it wasn't easy. They were so polished, taking instruction with ease, while I felt like a bumbling idiot. As the hours went by, I slowly started to trust my ability and found myself enjoying every minute. I'd dreamed of becoming a ballerina when I was a little girl. What I was doing here wasn't quite the same, but it was close enough for me.

At one point I noticed John standing in the doorway watching me, but I ignored him. I wouldn't let him spoil my concentration. The next time I looked up, he was gone.

Our costume fittings followed rehearsal, and I adored the outfits. We would be wearing a bare midriff top with our names embroidered on the front, and each of us had our own colour of hot pants. Mine was red. The outfit was so revealing that I was curious as to why Joe didn't mind me wearing it. Perhaps he thought differently when it came to show business.

Once we were finished, Harry gave me directions to Joe's office.

As I neared the door, I could hear Joe screaming at the top of his lungs. 'Listen, you bastard. Try anything again with my wife, and you'll regret it. I can fix it so no one will ever dare hire you again. Is that clear?'

I froze.

'You don't scare me, pom. She was begging for it. Everyone said so.' *Oh my god, that's John's voice.* 'I told you; she'd had too much to drink and passed out. I didn't touch her.'

'According to you! How do I know you didn't cop a feel while she was unconscious? How do I know you didn't stick your filthy cock in her?'

'I didn't, but obviously, you're not enough for her. She's a sex kitten, and you can't handle it. You're nothing but a sissy boy.'

I gasped, rubbing the scars on my arm.

'I'm going to fucking kill you!'

Sounds of a scuffle, then a loud crash echoed out into the passageway.

I stood there shivering, biting my nails.

'You're fired!'

The door opened with such force, and John dashed out, holding his nose as blood dripped over his hand. Crashing into me, he shouted, 'You fucking cock teasing cunt!' Then ran down the corridor.

Incredible. I'm innocent. I've been beating myself up for nothing. Tears streamed down my face. I wanted to run in, take Joe in my arms, and kiss his face, grateful he had uncovered the truth, but I hesitated. I couldn't be sure how he would react.

Knowing I had no choice but to talk with him and see how things stood, I bravely entered his office and walked over to him. I let out a breath and gently stroked his arm. 'I'm so sorry. I didn't mean anything by it.

Please forgive me.'

He glared at me; his eyes cold.

'Sit down. Now.' His lip curled.

I did what I was told, and he pulled up another chair, sitting opposite me, cracking his knuckles. It was the only sound in the silent room.

'Why the fuck did you go to that ponce's cabin?'

I was finding it hard to breathe.

'Answer me, you cow. What were you doing lying on his bed stark naked?'

'It wasn't like that. I'd had a lot to drink,' I pleaded, my hands in front of me as if in prayer.

'Oh, drunk, were you? Great excuse.' His voice got louder with each word. 'Did you let him touch your tits, your fanny? Did you touch his cock?' he shouted, spittle flying from his mouth.

Sobbing, I cried, 'I'm so sorry. It was a big mistake.'

He lunged out of his chair, grabbed my throat, and pulled me close to his face.

'You ever so much as look at another man, and you'll be *brown bread*!'

I tried desperately to pull away, but it made breathing harder.

Seeing the look in his eyes, I realised he was capable of anything. 'Yes. Yes.'

He held me a moment longer, glaring at me, then, with a loud sigh, he dropped his hand. I whimpered and massaged my neck, gulping in mouthfuls of air.

Walking over as calm as you like to the mirror behind the door, he fixed his tie as though it was just a regular day. Soon he was back to looking like Joe Leslie, the popular entertainer and TV host.

'I deserve a treat after all this carrying on, so I'm going to the pet shop. I want to buy a couple of dogs,' he said with a smirk, then left.

After a storm came the calm, and it was the same with Joe reverting to his charming ways, but it didn't fool me this time. I knew only too well that he could become vicious in the blink of an eye, so I vowed, once and for all, to take the children and leave. I couldn't say when or even how, but it would happen. First, I needed to work out how to find enough money.

I entered the studio's production office the very next day.

'Hello, I'm Irene Leslie. I was just wondering about my wages. How do I get paid?'

The middle-aged secretary looked up from her desk.

'Oh, you're Joe's wife. Good to meet you. What a lovely scarf. You find few women wear them anymore.'

I smiled at her, adjusting the flowery silk, hoping it still hid the bruises.

'For your salary, I suggest you speak to your husband. He told us to pay him instead.'

'Of course, silly me, I forgot. Sorry to bother you. Bye.'

I walked back down the hallway, fuming. *What am I going to do now?*

After dinner, I entered the living room with a tray of coffee and chocolate biscuits. Joe was sitting in his favourite chair. Pouring his coffee, I smiled sweetly.

'Darling, I never asked you how much I'll be earning.'

'You don't have to worry about that. I take care of the money around here,' he said, reaching for his coffee.

I took my cup and sat down on the sofa. 'I just thought it might be nice to have my own bank account.'

He laughed. 'No need for that. Women shouldn't have money, anyway. Makes you too independent. Besides, you have more than enough with the housekeeping allowance I give you each week.'

My blood was boiling, but I had to restrain myself to achieve my goal.

'Yes, but could you increase it a little more? I'm having trouble keeping up with the food prices around here.'

'Of course, me lovely. Now, let's watch the box. Gotta make sure the competition doesn't get too good, right?'

Sitting back in my chair, I came up with a plan. I would siphon off whatever I could and put it somewhere secret. One day, I'd have enough to leave with the kids. It might take a while, but it would be worth the wait. In the meantime, I needed to continue my act as the dutiful wife, so I offered Joe a biscuit with a charming smile. He took two, stuffing them both in his mouth before turning back to the TV.

~ * ~

We had become popular with the other local celebrities. They were only too happy to turn up at our house with a case of beer and laze around the pool most evenings. Jack and Karen were our favourite new friends. They were both in their fifties but behaved like teenagers.

Karen had a habit of losing her bikini top whenever she jumped in the pool, and Jack would often turn up with some young blonde on his arm. They would sometimes bring a young man along. It was common to see Karen dancing seductively with her young thing and Jack with his. Often Karen, Jack, and their dates would drink to the point where standing up was a challenge and going home was even more so. I got used to eating my breakfast in the garden to the sounds of snoring coming from the lounge chairs. Their behaviour shocked me at first, but as time went on, my innocent ways became corrupted, and I started to consider myself a modern, sophisticated woman.

Joe's show had become a smashing success, and the network had approved another season. I loved working on TV, especially with a live audience. The girls and I would keep the atmosphere upbeat by dancing our routines to live music, encouraging the public to join in. With our names embroidered on the front of our costumes, often someone from the crowd would shout out, 'Gina', 'Lizzie', 'Irene.' Yes, that's right, me. Joe would make sure I had plenty of closeups, and soon I became so used to the cameras that I didn't even notice them. It was exhilarating but exhausting, and dinner wouldn't cook itself— something my family expected even after taping a show, which often took over eight hours of hard work.

Joe was his happy old self again, which made life much easier. I was sure he wasn't gambling. He was home every night. I also couldn't remember the last time he'd taken a pill. He started spending time with Boris, even buying a BB gun for them to play with. I was concerned at first as it looked so real, but Joe assured me it wasn't dangerous since it only fired pellets, not bullets. I stopped worrying but made him promise to keep it tucked away somewhere neither Lorraine nor I would see it, like in the glove compartment of his car.

On the days Boris went with Joe to shoot at trees in the woods, I would take Lorraine out for a mother-daughter day. Sometimes, we would go shopping, and I would buy her a new dress or books she wanted. Other times, we went to the hairdressers and had our hair styled for a treat. But if I really wanted to have a chat, the best place was a restaurant. Then we could take our time and talk about everything. It wasn't always easy, as it depended on her mood. She would often ramble on about a book she read or a show on TV, but at other times she could be silent and sullen, which was difficult for me. It was important to see how she was settling down in Australia. It was a big upheaval for her, moving halfway across the world, and I wanted her to know that she always had her mum.

I looked at my daughter as we sat in a coffee bar one afternoon. At seven years old, she was turning into quite a beauty with her blonde curls and blue eyes but, like me, she was painfully shy. I wished I could help her, but I knew from experience it would get easier as she grew up. She was quiet. I was worried something was bothering her. After ordering her favourite banana milkshake, I asked, 'How is school going?'

'It's okay,' she mumbled and went back to her drink.

Determined to get her to talk, I smiled warmly. 'You know, darling, you can tell me anything. Good or bad. Sometimes it helps to talk about things that are bothering you.'

She looked at me for a few moments, her lip quivering.

'I hate it,' she snapped, bursting into tears. 'They call me a pom and make fun of my English accent.'

A fiercely protective feeling overwhelmed me. I wanted to march right into that school, straight over to the schoolgirls and slap them silly.

'Oh, sweetheart. That's awful. What does that word mean? Do you know?'

'No, but it's not nice, I know that.' She sniffed while wiping away tears from her blotchy face.

I took her hand and gently squeezed it. 'There must be some nice girls. Have you made any friends at all?'

'Well, Sandy is nice to me. We play skipping rope. And sometimes Anne talks to me when we have lunch.'

'That's fun.'

'I hate the boys. They pull my hair even when I tell them to stop.'

'It's because they think you're pretty. They're trying to get your attention.'

'Well, I don't like boys. I think they are horrible.' She crossed her arms in a huff.

I laughed. 'You'll change your mind one day.'

'No. I'm never getting married.'

'Why?' I asked with an indulgent smile, but her reply soon wiped it off.

'Because you have to do everything, and if your husband doesn't like it, you get punished. I want to be alone so no one can tell me what to do or burn my arm.'

My heart stopped. *Oh my god, what have we done?*

I had tried my best to shield the kids from Joe's rages, but it was clear I hadn't been as careful as I should have. *What effect will this have on them? How can I fix this?* I could only hope we'd heal when we were away from all the turmoil.

I changed the subject to one I knew Lorraine enjoyed talking about: animals. We discussed Australian marsupials, and as she chattered on about koalas and how cute they were, I tried to ignore the feeling of deep sadness pressing on my heart.

Chapter Twenty-three

JOE

My talents always amazed me, but I had one that shone above all others— the gift of the gab. I'd been watching the director wank his way through the show, and I couldn't take it anymore. He was bringing the standards down. I marched straight into the production office where all the big nobs were sitting around the table having a meeting.

'Hey, Joe. Do you need something?' one of them said as he looked up.

'Yeah. Sorry to interrupt, but this is important.' I sat down in an empty chair and poured a cup of coffee from the pot on the table.

'Look, it's like this. I'm going to take over from the director because, to be perfectly frank, I can do a better job than Simon. It's my show. I know it inside out and what it needs.'

They all looked at each other, and then Marvin turned to me.

'I don't mean to be rude, Joe, but you are not a director. You don't have the training. We took you on as creator, producer, and of course, the host.'

'True. But some people like myself have a natural ability.' I ran my fingers through my hair. 'Let's make a deal. Give me one show to direct. Just the one. And if you don't like it, I won't ask again. But if you do like my work, I'll take over from Simon from then on.'

'I don't know, Joe.' Marvin said, 'You don't have the experience, and we are not willing to take the chance. You know how much each episode costs us.'

I gulped down the rest of my coffee and stood up. 'Yeah, I do, and I know it'll cost you a hell of a lot more if I pull the show.'

They all looked shocked. Marvin came over and put his hand on my arm. 'You don't mean that. I'm sure we can come to some agreement.'

I brushed his hand away and glared at him.

'Joe. Think of the consequences. There is a contract, and you wouldn't want to risk everything, would you?'

'Try me,' I said and headed to the door.

Marvin came running over as I grabbed the doorknob.

'Joe. Wait.' He sighed. 'Fine. One show, but if it doesn't work out, then I want your word that you will never speak of this again.'

'Sure, but don't worry. There will be no need.'

~ * ~

'Okay, that's it, everyone. We're done for the day. Thank you, you were all great.'

I stood in the middle of the studio, clapping loudly, a broad grin on my face as crew members passed by, giving me a thumbs up. I approached the band as they were packing up their gear and shook each of their hands. 'Thanks, boys, you were fucking amazing.'

'The Frenzies' had been number one in the charts for the last two months, guaranteeing high ratings for our show. When they performed their hit song, *Don't You Love Me, Baby*, the audience went wild, joining in with the gorgeous 'Movers' on the dance floor. Shooting angles from way down on people's feet up to their nostrils, I zoomed in on the band's eyes and the girls' arses. It was wild.

The network's executives filed in and shook my hand with big smiles. 'Wow, Joe, your direction was great, and the camera work; amazing. Ahead of its time.'

Marvin came up and slapped me on the back with a wide, sparkling smile. 'What can I say? You were right. You *are* a natural. Okay, we have a deal. You're taking over from here on out, and if you keep up such high standards, I can assure you of another season.'

Even Simon came over. 'I've got to hand it to you, Joe. I might have the training, but you've got talent. I could learn a lot from tonight. Good luck with everything.'

All the praise felt incredible and I lapped it up, revelling in the warm glow.

As Irene turned up, I gave her a kiss, 'Join me once you've changed, yeah?' She nodded before heading back to the dressing rooms.

I strolled along to my office and, like always, swelled with pride at the plaque on the door: *Joe Leslie. Producer. Host.* I couldn't wait for *Director* to be added. I went in, plonked down on the leather sofa, and put my feet up. I glanced at the huge, framed photo of my new bulldogs, Mabel and George, on my desk. They were so beautiful. There was another small photo of Irene and the kids, but they weren't as photogenic as the dogs.

Who'd have thought that little old me would be living the life of Riley, eh? I had my dogs, sunshine year-round, and crowds of people worshipping me. I would walk around the studio with people asking, 'Joe, can we get you anything?', 'Joe, is everything alright for you?', Joe this, Joe that. *What can I say? I've never been better.*

I worked non-stop, but that's how I liked it. Sometimes I felt knackered and a bit out of breath, but one of the crew had snuck in a few little pills, which instantly boosted me back up. Add in a lot of coffee, and I was raring to go. The pill supply that I'd brought with me from England had almost run out. I was okay without them for a while, but once stress kicked in, that was another matter. I didn't bother telling Irene; I was never in the mood for one of her lectures. Our marriage worked best when I left her in the dark about things, like the demands of my job. She didn't understand that I had to live up to my name and reputation, and if I needed a bit of help, like pills, then so be it.

My kids were growing up, and their one redeeming feature was that they were rather good-looking. I wished they would shut up though, rabbiting on about nonsense most of the time. They had started speaking with a hint of an Australian accent, which was weird. I wasn't sure if I liked it or not. But all in all, I wasn't complaining. Life had finally delivered me a great hand. It was no less than I deserved, after all.

Irene came in, and I pulled her onto my lap. Feeling great, I gave her a cuddle and tickled her stomach.

'Stop.' She laughed. 'I can't take it. I'm going to wet myself.'

Cracking up, too, I gave her a big smooch. *I do love this woman, my beautiful wife.*

Chapter Twenty-four

IRENE

1968

Three years had passed: three years of dancing, partying, and sunshine.

The show was still on top, boasting the highest ratings on prime-time TV. As Joe was the host and I was one of the dancers, we would often get recognised while we were out at the shops or having dinner at a restaurant. My husband was used to the attention and thrived on it. I, on the other hand, cringed with embarrassment every time someone approached to fawn all over us. Often, I would have liked nothing more than for the ground to open up and swallow me.

We had a new friend, Gareth, who loved to turn up at our place unannounced with a six-pack of beer and several girls on his arm. He was great fun and, at six foot five of pure muscle with long blonde hair, bright green eyes, and a soothing voice that he used while working as a DJ on the radio, he was quite a hunk. I liked to listen to his morning show when I got the chance. He would talk about current activities and events around the town and play the latest hits. Occasionally, he would say, 'Joe, Irene, get the barbie on. I'm coming round.' Then later, the garden gate would creak open, and there he was. He'd strip down to his bathing suit and dive into the pool.

I often saw little Lorraine sitting in the garden, gazing at him with starry eyes. When he crouched down and asked if she had a boyfriend, the poor thing blushed even more than I did. Whenever he came over, she'd be outside, lying on one of the deck chairs in her green two-piece bathing costume, studying him. Other times, she would jump into the pool, splashing him like crazy and giggling loudly.

The months and days sped by, and my children were getting older. Soon they'd be teenagers. *How can that be? I'm only thirty-one.* The kids had settled well in school, and new friends always came over to swim on weekends and school holidays. It seemed Lorraine's issues with bullying had ceased. Once their schoolmates realised who Joe and I were, Boris and Lorraine became extremely popular. Everyone wanted an invitation to our house. I imagined the kids enjoyed their new status, but to my surprise, Lorraine was unhappy about it. 'How can I know if my friends really like me, or just because Dad's famous?' she grumbled to me one evening while we painted our toenails. I assured her that her friends loved her because she was wonderful, not for any other reason, but she wasn't buying that and refused to have anyone visiting from school. It was a shame she felt that way, but what could I do? Boris didn't mind at all. In fact, he loved that we were famous. I was certain it had plenty to do with the attention he received from the prettiest girls in his class.

I'd been careful about putting away money each week, accumulating a decent amount, enough to make our move if things turned sour, but I wasn't in any rush to leave. Even when it wasn't ideal, the familiar felt safer than the unknown. I knew what to expect with Joe, and when I played the dutiful wife, he was charming. The fact was, I was terrified of change. *What if we leave and we're miserable? What if I can't manage to support the kids and myself? What if I never find another man and become destined to be alone for the rest of my life?* Despite all the what-ifs, I kept on saving. I liked the security of knowing I had it ready if I really needed it. Just in case.

It was Wednesday, my day off, and I was sitting at the breakfast table drinking my second cup of tea, looking forward to my morning. After cleaning up the kitchen, I planned on taking a relaxing bath before dragging the dogs to the park around the corner. Bulldogs are never ones to lead the charge, preferring to waddle and huff their way along, stopping dead every few yards to plant their feet and snort. I often ended the walk more worn out than Mable and George.

The phone rang. I thought it might be Karen. We'd planned to meet for coffee later, so she was probably calling to confirm.

'Irene, it's Jenny.' She sounded panicked. 'I'm so sorry, but Joe's been taken to the hospital, the one by the studio. You had better get there as soon as you can.'

I froze. My inertia lasted seconds. Then I was moving, fast. Bolting upstairs to throw on some clothes, I ran out of the house and hopped on the tram for an agonising twenty-minute ride.

Arriving at the hospital, I dashed through the corridors, following the signs for the emergency room, where I found Jenny pacing the hallway.

'Irene, so good that you're here.' She hugged me tightly. 'It was awful. One minute he was fine, and the next, he was clutching his chest, white as a sheet. I rang for an ambulance immediately. He gave me quite a scare. He's in that room, right there,' she said it all in a rush, then pointed to the bright white door across the hall.

I burst in to find Joe lying in bed, looking very pale and shaken. He was hooked up to a monitor that beeped, echoing throughout the room. The smell of disinfectant filled the air, and I understood why Joe always hated it. It was horrible.

'What happened? Are you okay?' I asked, looking down at my husband with concern.

'Doc thinks I had a heart attack, but he's wrong. They don't know everything. It was probably just indigestion.' He reached over to the side table, opened the drawer, and took out a cigarette.

The door swung open as the doctor walked in.

'Mr Leslie, put that down,' he commanded. 'I told you; you will need to adjust your ways.'

'Is my husband going to be alright?' I asked, biting my lip.

'He's had a coronary, but a mild one, thankfully. He was lucky to get here in time.'

Joe huffed.

'I am prescribing bed rest for at least a month, and your diet and habits need to change drastically.'

'I can't take a month off,' Joe shouted, struggling to get out of bed. 'I've got a show to tape.'

I reached out and took his hand, trying to calm him down.

The doctor gave him a stern look. 'Mr Leslie, please try to relax.

These outbursts are not good for your heart. You are not well, and if you continue behaving this way, your wife will become a very young widow. It is non-negotiable. You cannot return to work.'

Sighing, Joe pulled his hand away from mine and lay back on the bed. 'That's it then. I'm a fucking invalid. The show is screwed, and so am I.'

Chapter Twenty-five

JOE

It didn't matter what anyone said, nothing made me feel better. I wanted to smash everything in sight, lash out at whoever was nearby, but the doctor warned me about my temper. Ultimately, it could kill me.

After spending two days in that depressing hospital with the smell of death in the air, they allowed me out on the condition I rest. When we drove back home and parked outside, Irene tried to help me out of the car, but I wasn't having that. The kids were at the door, shouting, 'Dad' and 'Daddy', so I needed to stand straight, I'd be damned if they were going to see me as a weakling. It was a bit of an effort, but I didn't tell them that. At the entrance, I gave the kids the dutiful peck on the cheek, then Irene told them not to tire me out, so they went to their rooms.

I was happy to get home and see the dogs. They went crazy when they saw me, yelping and jumping. Poor things wouldn't have understood why I wasn't there for a few days.

Refusing to stay in bed all day, where I was certain I'd die of boredom before my heart killed me, I settled on the sofa in front of the TV instead. It was much better. I had the dogs to cuddle up to and I could fart as much as I wanted because no one could tell who had let off, the dogs or me. Irene wasn't pleased, but she couldn't fight with me; it might up my blood pressure. She had no choice but to agree to all my demands.

After two weeks of being nursed around the clock by Irene, the novelty had worn off, and I was left feeling suffocated. The bloody kids always made a racket, so Valium became my friend again. Luckily, the doc had prescribed me some, so I didn't need to sniff around to find them elsewhere.

Jenny came to visit one afternoon with an enormous bunch of roses. Kind of weird a girl giving that to a fella, but hey, times were changing.

I gave her a peck on the cheek.

'Thanks, luv, for taking such good care of me and calling the ambulance.'

I didn't remember much of that day, but I did remember her worried face. It was sweet of her to be so concerned. I figured she probably had a crush on me. It was only natural.

Irene went to make the tea, and I cornered Jenny as soon as she left the room.

'What the fuck is happening with the show? I haven't heard anything.'

Jenny looked sad. 'I hate to be the bearer of bad news, but they are not renewing for another season. I am so sorry. The producers tried to convince the network to hold off for a month, but they refused.'

She looked like she was going to cry. I didn't want that to happen. I hated pity. Some blokes thrived on it, exaggerating whatever was wrong with them to get sympathy. Not me. No way. It made me feel like a puny, weak nobody. I needed to be strong to feel good.

I pretended like it was no big deal. 'Don't worry. I'll be back soon, better than ever, with a new show I have in the works.' It was a downright lie, but it sounded good.

Eventually, after sitting, making small talk, Jenny got up, 'I must be going now. Feel better, Joe.'

Irene stood up too. 'I'll show you out.'

With them gone, I sank back on the sofa to lick my wounds.

What the fuck am I meant to do now? Sit at home twiddling me thumbs like a bloody old man? Where are my cigarettes? I don't care what the fucking doctor said. I need them. Doesn't he understand that the stress of not smoking could give me another heart attack? I went upstairs to search through my jacket pockets for a pack but couldn't find any. Bloody Irene had obviously thrown them all away.

'Boris!' I yelled. 'Come here now!'

'Yes Dad? What do you want?'

'I need a favour,' I whispered, pulling him into the bedroom. 'Listen, you gotta do something for me, but you mustn't tell anyone, okay?'

'Alright.' He nodded.

I found my wallet on the bedside table and took out a few notes.

'Go to the corner shop and buy me a few packs of Benson and Hedges.'

'But Dad—' He looked alarmed.

'It's fine. Your ma is just overprotective. You know how women are.' I gave him a weak smile, hoping I sounded convincing.

After hesitating for a minute, he took the money, stuffing it in his pocket.

'Mum's the word,' I said, tapping the side of my nose with my index finger.

He opened the door, shouting out, 'Just going for a ride on my bike. I'll be back soon.'

I was back in the living room when he returned twenty minutes later. After seeing I was alone, he handed me the goods and a few leftover coins.

'Thanks, mate. You did good.' I patted him on the back. 'Keep the change. Get yourself some sweets or something.'

I stashed the cigarettes in the cabinet behind the record player since Irene never opened it.

After dinner that night, I told her I needed a stroll in the fresh air. She looked surprised, as it wasn't like me. She insisted on coming, but I stood my ground, explaining I needed time alone. Once outside, I walked around the corner and out of sight. Leaning on my neighbour's wall, I lit up. It was fantastic. It made me a bit dizzy at first, but by the second cigarette I could feel my brain unwinding, the stress falling away. From then on, I took advantage every time Irene left the house or was busy doing something to sneak out and have my fix. It was the only way to keep from going insane.

Two days later, after spending the morning staring at the TV, I realised I couldn't take much more. I was useless lying here day in and day out doing fuck all. *We need money, or how will we survive?* I had to get out, go somewhere, do something, but my mind came up empty. I knew what would fix things— a few hands of poker or blackjack. Just a little game, nothing big. It had been ages since I'd treated myself, not since I left the ship, but with all the shit that had been sent my way, I decided I deserved it.

Casinos weren't legal in Melbourne, and as for illegal activities, I hadn't bothered making the right connections with work being so frantic.

They did have greyhound racing, though. Jack was there most weekends, and he'd told me how exciting it was. I'd never tried it, but why not? The same game, isn't it? Odds, adrenaline, the thrill of chance, the rush of winning. For the first time in ages, I had a rare smile on my face, the kind that lifted my heart and made me feel like life might not be complete shit.

After catching a whiff of myself and almost passing out from the stink, I decided I better get ready if I wanted to go out, so I went upstairs to complete the three S's (shit, shower, and shave). Once dressed, I headed back down and pulled out the yellow pages from the hall table, flipping through till I found the full-page ad for the races.

'Hey, Irene,' I shouted from the front door. 'Where're the car keys?'

She came out of the kitchen, looking worried. 'Joe, the doctor said you had to rest for at least a month.'

I couldn't stand that fucking nursemaid's voice of hers. It wasn't attractive.

'I'm not a fucking cripple, so stop treating me like one. Now, bring me the bloody keys.'

'Where are you going?'

'Over to Jack's. It wouldn't interest you. We have to talk shop.'

She pursed her lips. 'Well, if you must,' she pointed at the hall table. 'The keys are right there in the drawer beside you.' *Damn. If I'd known that, I wouldn't've needed to deal with her at all.*

'Thanks, luv,' I shouted, slamming the door behind me.

Fuck the heart attack.

Heading to the dog track, I realised I'd passed it many times on my way to the studio but never really noticed it. Parking, I made my way over to the entrance of the huge stadium, which was packed full of loud, red-faced Aussies enjoying the sun and half-cooked on beer. My pulse raced with excitement at hearing bookies shouting out the odds as the smell of alcohol and cigarette smoke filled the air.

I stood, cigarette in my mouth, scanning the afternoon schedule when one of the dogs' names caught my eye. Brit-bull. *It has to be fate— British and bulldogs, a perfect combination.* With a massive grin on my face, I marched over to the counter and placed most of my cash on her. *She's sure to be a winner. I just know it.*

I took my seat in the arena. The geezers next to me were halfway to oblivion and still had three six-packs on the floor. It was ridiculous. Even if they won, they wouldn't know it, nor care if they lost their shirts. I, on the other hand, was as sober as a nun and would stay that way. I never needed to drink to blot things out. Pills and gambling did the job just as well, if not better.

An announcement came over the loudspeaker. 'The three o'clock race is about to begin.'

I turned my attention to the track as the greyhounds took their positions at the starting gate. I recognised Brit-bull by the Union Jack flag she wore. The stadium buzzed in hushed anticipation as the crowd narrowed their focus on the dogs.

With a loud bang, they were off. The stands erupted with cheering and shouting. I joined in as much as the next man. 'Come on, Brit-bull. Come on, girl!'

Yes, she's in front. I moved closer to the edge of my seat, puffing away on my cigarette. *No. Shit. The other dog is passing her. Fucking hound.* I stood up when Brit-bull started lagging behind the others into third to last place.

'Hurry up, Brit-bull. Come on, old girl, you can do it.'

Bloody hell. My stomach clenched as the first few dogs reached the finish line. Brit-bull was nowhere near it. As everyone else collected their winnings, I ripped up the betting slip and let it float to the floor. *What a fucking idiot. I never learn, do I?* I felt a throbbing pain starting in my temples. Rubbing my head, I figured I might as well head home. *Why does this shit always happen to me?*

Chapter Twenty-six

IRENE

I was worried when Joe stormed out of the house. *What if his temper triggers another heart attack?* It took a near-death experience to make me realise that despite everything, I still loved him. It was crazy. I should hate him after everything he'd done to me, but he was in my veins, my soul, my heart. Leaving needed to be a last resort, and I hoped it would be an unnecessary one.

I needed to take my mind off my troubles, and Jenny was the perfect diversion. We had become friends since the show ended. She'd taken me out for coffee on several occasions, and sometimes we perused the local boutiques. I never ended up buying anything as they were usually too expensive, but it was fun having a friend to spend time with and a blessed relief to be away from Joe's foul moods. That day, we were going to a lecture on women's independence. I couldn't imagine what they would talk about, but Jenny's enthusiasm was contagious. She said that women had a right to be their own person. I wasn't sure what that meant, but it was intriguing and would beat the monotony of housework and childcare.

I'd told Joe a few days before that I was going to a lecture while he was engrossed in a TV show. He didn't react, so I presumed he hadn't heard me, but I didn't bother repeating myself. It was easier if he didn't know. I was sure he wouldn't approve. I didn't enjoy doing things behind his back, but I needed to have something just for myself. It wasn't quite lying, since I had told him where I was going. It wasn't my fault if he hadn't paid attention.

I met Jenny at the coffee shop near the studio before we took a short bus ride to the hall where the speech was taking place. 'Lily McGillis is great,' Jenny told me as we sat on the bus. 'This is my third time attending her lectures. She really explains it so we can understand our rights. She has changed my life. I'm now an independent woman with a job, and I am respected.' She straightened her shoulders with a look of pride.

'What do your parents say about you working?' I asked, shivering at the thought of Mum's reaction if I went and got a job on my own. Dancing on the show didn't count because my husband was still in charge of me.

Jenny looked puzzled. 'What does it matter what they think? I'm twenty years old with my own flat. I do whatever I choose.'

'You live on your own?' I gasped. 'Isn't that scary, being all alone? What's it like?'

Jenny smiled, her eyes lighting up with excitement. 'It's great. I love it. Away from my parents always telling me what to do, I answer to no one.'

My eyebrows knitted together. 'But don't you want to find a husband? Someone to look after?'

Jenny laughed. 'Why would I choose to become an unpaid servant?' Reaching for the bus handle, she stood up. 'Come on. This is our stop.'

My mind raced as we walked down the street. I had never even imagined that there were options other than marriage. No one I knew had done that. Straight from family home to husband, that's how it was, and we never questioned it.

We arrived at a plain grey building belonging to the Young Women's Christian Association; the letters YWCA hung above the door. Inside, women of all ages filled up the hall, chattering with excitement. We made our way through the crowd, apologising as we accidentally knocked over a few handbags, until we found empty seats in the back row. After sitting down, I removed my coat and pulled up my sleeves. It was stuffy and warm in the large room. Beautiful murals of inspirational women from the past were displayed on the walls. I recognised Cleopatra in Egypt and Amelia Earhart beside an aeroplane. I wasn't sure about the other portraits, but they looked important. I made a mental note to ask Jenny about them later. I was sure she would know.

The crowd burst into an enormous round of applause as a woman in her mid-forties with bright red hair and a vast bosom approached the stage.

Jenny nudged me, whispering, 'Here she is!'

I craned my head to get a better look.

'Today's subject is obedience,' Lily McGillis began, plunging the room into silence. *Obedience, huh? I certainly know all about that.* 'They taught us to obey,' Lily continued. 'Obey our parents, obey our teachers, and ultimately obey our husbands.'

The crowd murmured in agreement.

'What we will learn today is that obedience is for oneself. Obey yourselves and no one else.' She pointed her finger at the audience. 'Until we can look at ourselves, respect ourselves, we will never be free.' Lily paced up and down the stage, scanning the audience. 'Being downtrodden by our partners is humiliating and cruel. If we do not take a stand, we will always be prisoners to other people. Be it a parent or husband, tell them, shout out, I will not obey! You are not my keeper! I am my own person!' She raised her fist in the air as hoots and cheers echoed around the room.

I was mesmerised. *Not obey? How? Hasn't that been my whole life?*

With the lecture over, we made our way outside. I overheard countless voices praising Lily, preaching about the change she had brought to their lives. Enthusiasm and positive energy filled the air. It was electric.

'That was incredible,' I said as Jenny and I walked to the bus stop. 'I have never heard anything like that before. It was inspiring.'

Jenny laughed, taking my arm. 'Oh, this is just the beginning. You wait and see. I'll soon have you realising there's more to life than boiling eggs for breakfast.'

Her bus arrived first, so we hugged and promised to see each other soon. Waiting a few more minutes for my ride, I was deep in thought during the journey home. Never had I heard anyone like Lily McGillis. So often, I'd wanted to shout out, 'No, don't speak to me like that. Don't treat me that way.' But I'd learned to keep it all bottled up. I knew the consequences only too well.

Stepping off the bus, I walked to my house, wondering if Joe was home yet. A part of me hoped I still had some time for myself. I would've liked nothing more than to sit with a nice hot cup of tea and think about all the new things I had learned, but the children would be back from school soon, so I needed to get dinner started. *Why do I have to prepare the food? What would happen if I said I didn't want to cook, clean, or do anything?*

I laughed just imagining Joe's face. I was sure the kids would have lots to say too.

The dogs lunged at me as I opened the front door, slobbering all over my white trousers.

'Get down, Mabel. George. Oh, damn!' The entire floor was covered with rubbish. They'd got into the bins once more. 'Not again.' I knelt down to pick it up. 'This is not my job, Lily McGillis said so.'

The dogs watched me with dumb expressions, tongues hanging out.

'And I suppose I'm your slave, too.'

Cleaning up, I noticed the Yellow Pages lying open on the table, and an advertisement caught my eye. Outlined in blue was the Melbourne dog track. I sighed, shaking my head. Joe lied. He didn't go to Jack's. He went gambling. *Damn! Damn! Damn! I thought he'd given that up.* Sitting back amid the rubbish, I scowled.

The front door clicked open, and Joe came in, tense and sullen etched on his face. He looked down at me, oblivious to his surroundings.

'Come here, woman. I got a splitting headache and need a neck rub.'

I hesitated for a second. 'No.'

'What did you say?' Confusion etched his face.

I sat up, pulled my shoulders back, and crossed my arms. 'I said no. I am not your slave. I am busy cleaning up the bloody mess *your* dogs have made.'

He frowned. 'You on the rag again?'

I glared at him. 'No, I am not.'

'Well, get up and do as you're told then.'

Standing up, I faced him, and after taking a deep breath, I shouted at the top of my lungs, 'I will not obey! You are not my keeper! I am my own person!'

He looked stunned for a moment, then went bright red. His jaw jutted out as he raised his fist in the air.

Bracing myself for the attack, I scrunched my eyes shut.

Nothing happened.

I peeked out of one eye as he slowly lowered his hand, glowering at me.

'Fucking cow,' he muttered as he turned and stalked into the kitchen.

I stood a moment, my whole body shaking. I couldn't believe it. For the first time ever, I'd had the courage to stand up to him. It was amazing. What freedom. Feeling powerful, I smiled so hard I thought my mouth would crack.

Thank you, Lily McGillis.

Chapter Twenty-seven

JOE

I wasn't sure I could stand many more endless days of fucking boredom, stuck in the house with Irene's sour face. She'd been acting strange the last few weeks. It took every ounce of strength to resist throttling her, but I had no choice. I didn't fancy another heart attack.

'What's the matter, for Christ's sake? It's like I don't exist. I won't stand for it. Talk to me already.'

She looked up from one of those books she always had her nose in. This one was called 'Women's Rights'. *What the fuck?*

'You want me to talk? Okay, let's talk about the bill collectors knocking on the door demanding money we don't have.'

I gritted my teeth. 'Thanks very much. I thought wives were meant to be loyal and supportive of husbands, especially if they'd fallen on hard times. For better or worse and all that crap, or did you forget that?'

She looked at me with disgust before turning back to her book.

Digging my fingers into my palm, almost cutting myself, I clenched my jaw shut, then opened it to swallow a Valium. Choosing to ignore her, I leafed through the newspaper, but nothing held my interest. *What am I meant to do? Sit and stare at the walls like an idiot? Maybe I could make a few calls. See if anyone can help.* I got up and went to the hallway. Picking up the telephone, I dialled Jack.

'Hello Joe, old boy, how are you?' he answered in a friendly voice.

'Not too good, I'm afraid, Jack. Funds are low. I got to find some work. Got any ideas?'

'It may just be your lucky day. I heard about something, though I'm not sure if you will like it. My friend manages a strip club. I saw him yesterday, and he told me he's looking for a host. The last one had a drinking problem and collapsed on stage. All you have to do is warm up the audience before the girls come in and strut their stuff. Fancy it?'

'Does it pay?'

'Of course it pays. Don't know how much, though. If you're interested, give him a call. His name's Frank Malone. Here's his number.'

'Thanks, Jack. You're a good mate.' I jotted the number down on the writing pad.

'Sure. Just a little advice. Watch your back. Some of those club people can be a bit dodgy.'

I dismissed Jack's warning. 'No worries. I can take care of meself.'

A glimmer of hope had emerged. I could host at a strip club. In fact, I would be bloody brilliant at it, and most importantly, I needed the work.

As soon as I finished talking to Jack, I called Frank Malone.

'My name's Joe Leslie, and Jack Parker suggested I call you about the hosting job for your club.'

'Am I actually talking to *The* Joe Leslie? TV star?' he asked in a deep voice.

'Yep. I'm the one. Anyway, is the job available?'

'For you? Of course. You would be a hell of an attraction for my place. I would love that.'

'Great.' I said,

'But I'm sorry, I will have to audition you, I've got to see if you can fit in with the girls and audience. I hope you don't mind.'

'Not at all. I understand, but no worries, I can manage any crowd, no matter who they are.'

'Good. The club's called The Passion Pit, and we pride ourselves in having the biggest tits in Melbourne.'

I laughed, 'Really? Well, that's something to boast about, I suppose.'

'Come over around seven, and we'll take it from there, okay?'

'Sure. Look forward to it.'

I was excited about the audition for the evening show, but I still needed to come up with an excuse to get out of the house without Irene knowing why. I had no intention of telling her about the club. She'd hit the roof, going on about naked girls, morals, and bad influences on the kids, blah, blah, blah. There was no point in getting her knickers in a twist when the job wasn't even mine yet. I missed the old days when I told her I was going out without explanation, and she just had to lump it, but things had changed recently. If I did something she thought was wrong, she'd sulk or ignore me, which I didn't like one bit. It took all my patience not to give her a good hiding to remind her who was boss.

After convincing Irene that I needed a little drive to relieve my boredom, I almost got lost trying to find the bloody place. I drove around in circles until I spotted a small arrow pointing down a gravel driveway with a bright red building at the end. *Classy.* Once parked, I stepped out of the car and grabbed my suit jacket from the backseat, shaking out the wrinkles before slipping it on.

Walking to the front, I noticed enormous pictures of naked women covering the walls and a massive gold door with a pair of cement tits in the middle. Chuckling, I straightened my tie before pressing the nipple. The doorbell rang loud and low, then a wide panel slid open, and a dark, rugged face looked out.

'We're closed. We open in two hours. Come back then,' the man growled.

'No, I'm not a customer. Joe Leslie. I have an audition for the host job.' I gave him my award-winning smile.

He looked me up and down, eyes narrowed, before snapping the panel closed. The heavy door opened into a dark, musty hallway.

'I'm Larry. Security.'

He was over six feet tall with a huge muscular frame. Not one to get on the wrong side of.

'Go down the stairs over there, and you'll find Frank in his office.' He pointed to some worn-out, red-carpeted stairs to the right before locking the door and walking in the opposite direction.

I made my way down the steps and into a dimly lit corridor lined with doors. One had '*F. Malone*' etched onto it. I knocked.

'Come in.'

I entered as a short, balding man with heavy glasses smiled up at me from his desk. The voice on the phone made me picture a tall, heavyset man, but this guy looked like a leprechaun.

'Ah, Joe Leslie in the flesh. I'm Frank.'

Shaking his hand, I took in the room. Papers and an overflowing ashtray cluttered Frank's desk, while on the threadbare sofa in the corner lounged an overweight, ageing blonde. She had the most enormous tits I'd ever seen.

Frank looked over at her. 'Meet Betty, my wife. Betty, this is Joe. He'll be hosting tonight's late show.' She gave me a coy smile, revealing a gap in her front teeth.

'Want something to drink, Joe?' He didn't wait for a reply. 'Honey, go get us a coffee. There's a good girl.'

She sauntered off, leaving a whiff of cheap perfume behind her. It amazed me how easily she walked away without toppling over.

I turned back to Frank as he started to speak.

'First of all, it's an honour to meet you. I loved *Feel the Beat* and was sorry when it went off the air. What happened?'

'Oh, bureaucracy and other stuff with the network,' I said, brushing it off. 'It was a shame, but life goes on.' I wanted to change the subject as quick as possible. 'So, can you tell me about the show and what you need from me?'

'Sure.' Frank smiled. 'We get the girls to drink with the men before the show; that's where we earn our best money, so what you're dealing with is a crowd of randy drunken idiots. You keep 'em laughing and having a good time.' I nodded. 'We'll talk about money later, but don't worry, it's not bad, and you can always enjoy the girls' company.' Frank winked.

I laughed. 'Not me. I'm a happily married man. I look but don't touch.' A sudden flashback of naked Marjorie lying on the bed, her legs apart, appeared in my head. *Never again.*

'Suit yourself.' He shrugged. 'But if you ever change your mind, you let me know. Now, let's take you through to the stage, and I'll introduce you to our girls.'

Chapter Twenty-eight

IRENE

I felt like I had been reborn after Lily McGillis's lecture. It was as though I needed to learn how to think and talk all over again. Only this time, it would be different.

Jenny and I had long discussions about my life, and I came to some startling realisations. My mother had been controlling me since the day I was born. I remembered having to speak and think as she did; any other way was unacceptable. It was so ingrained that, after a while, I believed her thoughts and feelings were my own. I had learned to fear men, starting with my father and the pain of his belt on my backside, then Joe, who used violence as a means of control.

Jenny looked puzzled. 'You don't approve of these people, so why would you seek approval from them?'

That was a good question. *Why do I?*

Jenny took me to other lectures on women's liberation. I couldn't get enough of them. The winds of change blew in through the door, and I welcomed them.

I spent my time reading books, picking up every relevant title that Jenny recommended, that had changed so many women's lives. They all maintained that men had been repressing women throughout history. I agreed. I'd been repressed my whole life, letting everyone walk all over me. *Why, as women, do we have to accept what men say? They are no better than us. Who made them the boss? Enough.* The time had come for me to take a stand.

At his last check-up, the doctor said that as long as Joe stayed calm, he could resume all activities, so I tried making love with him, but he was unsure and wanted to wait. I was still a young woman, and it was the only affection I received from my husband. I craved physical contact. I noticed how men looked at me when I went shopping or for a walk. I wanted Joe to appreciate what he had and know that other men desired me. Maybe then he wouldn't take me for granted.

If Joe continued to gamble, we could end up on the streets. I panicked every time I opened the post, fearing the dreaded eviction notice. Since the show had ended, the network no longer paid the rent, but we could stay in the house as long as we covered the payments.

One day, as I sat reading in the living room, Lorraine came in and stood in front of me. 'Mum,' she said with a worried look on her face, 'Are we going to move again? Only I heard you and Dad fighting over money.'

'Oh no darling, that was nonsense. We are not going anywhere. I promise.' I gave her an encouraging smile and she went back upstairs, looking relieved. I hoped I could keep my word.

The dogs suddenly jumped up and raced out of the room. With their internal antennas, they could sense when Joe was arriving home long before I did. I never knew where he went lately. I figured to the poker clubs or maybe the dog track. Our debts were growing larger, and I had no idea how we were going to pay them. It wasn't Joe's fault he had lost the show, but with his health returned, he needed to find another way to make money.

Joe appeared in the doorway with a huge smile on his face.

'Hi, doll. I have something to tell you.' He sat on the sofa opposite me, laughing as the dogs crawled all over him, licking his face and neck. 'You gorgeous things. You wonderful doggies,' he crooned, rubbing their fur and kissing their heads.

Snapping my book shut, I looked on with disgust.

'Do they have to jump up on the settee? I can never get rid of the fur.'

'Don't worry, luv, I like it hairy.' At least he was in a good mood. That was something. 'Anyway, listen. Got me a job!'

My shoulders dropped in relief. *At last.* 'Really? What wonderful news. Where? What?'

'I'm hosting a show in a … club every night.'

His pause made me suspicious. 'A club? What type of club? What's it called?'

'The Passion Pit,' he mumbled. 'It's great. Lots of people go there.' Looking away, Joe placed his feet on the coffee table as Mabel chewed on his ear.

'That's a strange name for a club. What sort of shows do they put on?'

'Can't hear you, darling,' he shouted. 'Ow. Mabel, stop.'

I narrowed my eyes. 'Joe, I asked you something.'

He pulled Mabel off to tickle her belly as George jumped up to chew her leg.

'Please, Joe. Talk to me.' I huffed.

Joe looked at me. 'Just a club with girls performing. Aren't you pleased? Now we can pay off our debts.' He gave me a cheeky wink. 'Come on. Give us a smile, luv. Let's see your pretty teeth.'

His charm did not sway me. 'I'm glad you have a job, but I'm not sure I like the sound of this club. What do you mean girls perform there? What do they do?'

He got up and brushed the hair off his trousers, still not quite meeting my eye. 'I don't need to explain anything. I got a job, so just be happy and shut up.'

I wasn't going to allow that.

'No. You talk to me with respect. I am your wife. If I ask you a question, you should have the courtesy to answer me.'

Joe studied my face, then groaned. 'Bloody hell, not that time of the month again.'

My jaw tensed. 'No, it's not and even if it was, so what? Things need to change around here. If you do not treat me with dignity, then maybe... I don't need to be here anymore.'

Joe paled. 'What the hell do you mean by that?'

'I think you know.'

Standing up, I left the room, but not before seeing his stunned face. *This new power is addictive.*

That night in the bedroom, I sat at the dressing table while Joe lay in bed smoking. He kept looking at me and sighing. I knew he hated silence.

Joe sat up. 'Okay, Irene. Listen, I've got to take the job in the club, if only for a while. That way, I can bring in some money. We've almost run out.'

'Really, Joe? Well, maybe we would have more if you didn't

gamble,' I snapped, while carefully applying my face cream.

He looked puzzled for a moment, trying to work out how I knew about the races.

'Okay, point taken. I won't do it again. I'm still taking the job, okay? Darling?' He gave me one of his endearing smiles, but I didn't react.

He sighed heavily. 'Just tell me what you want then.'

'I want you to answer the questions I asked you earlier. What type of club is it? What do the girls do?' I turned around, legs crossed, my gaze fixed on him.

'Alright. If you must know, it's a strip club, but just a few tits here and there; they don't even show their down-belows. I have nothing to do with the girls. All I do is introduce 'em.'

Fuming, I didn't say anything.

'Christ, Irene, I've got to do it for a bit. I promise you, in the meantime, I'll look for something else. Now, enough of this. Give us a kiss. It'll all be okay.' He patted the bed next to him, but I didn't budge.

'Come on, me lovely woman. Pretty please, sweet lady of mine.' He crossed his eyes and stretched his lips while pushing his teeth out, making that stupid face which always made me laugh.

I wasn't going to allow him to soften me up, but damn, it was happening.

I walked over to the bed and sat on the edge. 'All right, Joe, if it's only for a bit, but you need to find something else soon. Something to be proud of.'

Reaching over, he put his arms around me and pulled me close. 'Don't you worry, gorgeous.' He opened my robe. 'Now, take your clothes off, and let's see if we can manage a bit of the old one-two.'

What could I say? I weakened, but at least I was happy for a while.

Chapter Twenty-nine

JOE

1971

Busty Betty was The Passion Pit's leading act. Her proportions were not in the least bit proportional. At five foot one, she should've been a petite woman, but her forty-eight triple-G bust put an end to that idea. The audience went crazy for her. I couldn't understand it myself; I thought she looked like a freak.

'Bloody hell,' I told Jack on the phone when I called to thank him. 'You got to come and see Busty Betty. I tell you, she's not normal. Her tits walk in the door before she does.'

Jack chuckled. 'You've got to be kidding. I better come and see for myself. Save me a seat.'

Busty Betty believed every man desired her. It was clear she'd taken quite a fancy to me, as she wouldn't leave me alone, but discretion and subtlety were beyond her. She would throw her arms around me whenever I entered the club, her gigantic tits crushing against my chest, almost knocking me over. She thought this turned me on, but the more she pushed, the more disgusted I became. I tried to avoid her, but when Betty wanted something, she made it her life's mission to get it.

I began to really appreciate my lovely Irene. She was a class act and nothing like those slags, riddled with diseases, strutting about with their sagging boobs.

Irene had asked if the girls had tried anything with me. I told her they were all lesbians and hated men. *I wish*. If Busty Betty wasn't after me, it was Naughty Nelly who had the worst case of B.O. ever encountered on the planet. They should've called her Smelly Nelly. Her hanging tits, covered in large silver stars, just about swept the floor. She also liked to give me a hug when I arrived. It was a hell of a challenge trying to fend them off.

I dreaded going to work each night. Besides the fact that I had to deal with revolting smells, I also had to make up answers when Irene questioned me over what I did exactly. I couldn't tell her that I basically had to hang out with a bunch of drunks and tarts.

I missed the glamour, class, and prestige of the studios, and the satisfying sense of creating quality work. The only thing The Passion Pit created was alcoholics and scumbags.

The one bonus was being on stage. It gave me such a rush when the crowd laughed as they hung on my every word. I felt like a king again, but it was short-lived. I returned to feeling like a sleazeball as soon as the show was over.

Frank came into the dressing room as I was relaxing on my chair.

'We've got a full house tonight, Joe, and I want you to be at your best. The owner is going to be in the audience. Okay?'

'I'm always at my best. You know that,' I said, admiring myself in the mirror.

'Yeah. You are. Also, I need you to stay after the show and meet the big boss.'

I hoped it wouldn't take too long; I liked to arrive home before Irene fell asleep.

'Fine. Now let me prepare for my act.'

I'd been performing for almost a year, yet the mysterious owner had never appeared, not even once. I didn't really care, as long as I had a job to come to and a cheque to put in the bank.

The music started as I entered the stage to a round of applause.

'Ladies and gentlemen, welcome to The Passion Pit, where your evening will be filled with excitement and wonder.' Flashing my famous smile, I waited for the buzz to die down. *They obviously can't believe their luck at seeing me in the flesh.* 'We've got girls galore and fun games, too, so sit back, relax, and allow us to entertain you. First, let me introduce meself. You've all heard of Elvis the pelvis. Well, I'm Enis... the penis.' The drummer performed the ba-dum-bum-ching drum roll while I made wanking motions with my hand.

The audience cracked up.

The band started to play as a procession of half-dressed girls strolled onto the stage.

I winked at the crowd. 'Not bad, eh, boys?'

They hooted and clapped wildly as the girls made their way back offstage.

'Drum roll, maestro.' I raised my arm in the air. 'And now, ladies and gentlemen, the one, the only, Busty Betty!'

Betty sauntered onstage, batting her eyelashes at me. That was my cue to exit. I stood at the side to watch the show, bored after seeing it so many times. The crowd went wild as Busty Betty danced, removing her bra to the sound of wolf whistles. She stepped down to the audience and made her way through the tables, blowing kisses and smiling. She stopped in front of one middle-aged, balding geezer and picked up his beer. 'This seems a bit flat, doesn't it?' she asked as he laughed, nodding in agreement. Lifting one of her colossal tits, she tried to squeeze it into the glass as if mixing a drink. 'Here you go. It should be better now.' She handed it back to its drunken owner, who lifted it in the air before drinking it down in one.

The other men roared, shouting, 'My beer's flat too.'

Betty 'mixed drinks' at two more tables before returning to the stage for her last dance.

Once she'd finished, I reappeared to introduce Naughty Nelly, who was dressed as a nun. 'Do we have any volunteers in the audience?'

Several men raised their hands. I picked a very boozed-up, sweaty creature who mounted the stage. *Let's see how Nelly likes his pong.*

'Naughty Nelly is very hot. Do you think she should take off some of her clothes?' The man nodded his head up and down, his eyes wide open. 'But Naughty Nelly doesn't know how. Perhaps you could show her.'

The band played strip music as he attempted to dance seductively and remove his trousers at the same time. It wasn't a pretty sight. Nelly, wearing a pious expression, clasped her hands in front of her as if in prayer. When the man got down to his underpants, the audience shouted, 'Nelly, Nelly, take it off, take it off!'

In a flash, her expression turned to lust. Biting her lip, she slowly removed her habit, and her long bleached blonde hair tumbled out. Lifting her tunic inch by inch while swaying her hips, she pulled it over her head to reveal her milky white body, naked except for a black sequinned G-string and glittering stars on her nipples.

The cheering grew louder.

With her dance over, she bowed to the audience as I came back on stage.

Man, I love a full house. The audience cheered and laughed as though I was the best performer in the world, but I suppose it wasn't an accurate gauge of my talents as they were all drunk out of their minds.

'We'll have a fifteen-minute intermission and be back with more gorgeous girls soon.'

Entering the dressing room, I loosened my tie and undid the top button of my shirt. When I found out they only had one dressing room for all of us, I had a flashback to when I was a young lad in the theatre. It felt so long ago. I was a different person then, so naïve and innocent. Not like the man I'd become, who was no longer impressed with a room full of naked bodies. I hardly even noticed them most of the time.

I was soon back on stage to kick off the second half. After a few jokes to keep the audience alert and amused, I brought on all the girls dressed as innocent, shy schoolgirls. I didn't stay to watch the act. I had a brief break to relax in the empty dressing room before racing back to the stage at the familiar sound of the band's closing number.

'Let's have an enormous round of applause for our sexy ladies.' I swept my arms out to the girls. 'That's it from me. Have a great night, and don't forget to recommend The Passion Pit to all your mates.'

At that point, I would usually leave the club as fast as possible, desperate to wash away the grime and leave the sordid dump behind. But tonight, I had to wait around and meet the big boss, especially if I wanted to keep my job and salary, which was two months past due. Frank kept telling me the money would come any day, but so far, it hadn't. Maybe buttering up the owner might help.

Frank was sitting in the VIP booth, wearing a new suit. I guessed he was trying to make a good impression.

Frank waved me over. 'Joe, come say hello to the boss.'

Fixing my famous smile firmly on my face, I sauntered over and stopped dead in my tracks as all the blood drained from my face. I couldn't believe my eyes. Marjorie Fucking Sloan.

'Why, hello, Joe. Good show. How very entertaining,' Marjorie said in a sultry voice.

Shaking, I ran one finger around the inside of my collar and straightened my tie. 'Hi, Marjorie. How are you?'

'You two are acquainted?' asked Frank, looking between us.

'Yes. We go back a way,' Marjorie said, puffing on her cigarette.

'Sit, Joe. Want a drink?' Frank offered.

'No, thanks. I can't stay long. I must get home.' Pulling out a chair, I perched on the edge.

Marjorie smiled. 'How are your dear wife and children?'

'Fine, thanks. So, how long have you owned this club?' I glanced at the exit. *I need to get out of here.*

'I just bought it. I thought it would be fun.' She waved her cigarette around as she spoke. 'I enjoy acquiring new businesses. I intend to own an entire chain of clubs all over Australia.'

She leaned forward, smoke curling around her. 'We should meet and talk about this some more. Perhaps next week?'

'Erm … Sorry, Marjorie, I'll be busy.'

Frank gave me a stern look. 'I'm sure you can make time for our boss. You do like your job, don't you?'

I sighed, understanding Frank all too well. 'Yeah, I suppose I can move things around.' Rising from my seat, I looked at Marjorie. 'Frank can let me know when, and I'll be there. Night.'

I ran out of the club, burning more than ever with the urge to take a shower and wash the slime off me.

My job was not the kind of work where you could call in sick. I had to show up no matter what. *Damn Marjorie. I know she's a crook, but how do I prove it?* I hated to admit it, but she scared me. Who knew what she was capable of? The worst part was, I couldn't talk about it with Irene without spilling the beans, so I had to keep it all to myself and try to numb the worry with pills.

The following afternoon, the dogs and I were cuddling on the couch while my children sat on the floor watching cartoons on the TV, something I usually enjoyed doing with them. It was the one activity I could share with my kids, but I couldn't concentrate because of stupid Marjorie. Her smug face swirled round and round in my head.

Irene shouted from the hallway, 'Joe, telephone call from overseas.'

I jumped up and rushed over to her, taking the receiver from her outstretched hand. *Who is it? Is Ma unwell?*

'This is Joe.'

'Mr Leslie, my name is Jerry Barnes. I am calling from Toronto.'

'Toronto, Canada?'

'Correct. I'm a producer at Channel 9. We have been watching *Feel the Beat*, and we love it. We were sorry to see it go. We are interested in producing the show here. Would you be open to directing and hosting it?'

'Really?' My eyebrows hit the roof. 'Nice to learn I've got fans around the world.' I relaxed against the wall. 'So, you're interested in the show? Well, I don't blame you. It's fab, if I may say so meself, but if I'm to consider it, and of course, I'm not committing to anything yet, I'll need to see your facilities. The show needs a large studio with a top-notch crew.'

'Of course, Mr Leslie. I'm sure you'll find our studios here up to your standards.'

I cleared my throat. 'You should know, I don't come cheap. Best to be upfront about it.'

'I'm certain we'll be able to deal with everything. We are eager to meet with you. If you are willing, we can send you a plane ticket. You can tour our facilities, and we can discuss the details. Is that all right, Mr Leslie?'

'Please call me Joe. When would you like to meet?'

'As early as possible. We want to get this rolling.'

'Well, like I said, I'm not committing to anything, but your timing is lucky— I'm between jobs. Send me a ticket, I'll take a look and let's take it from there. Good talking to you, Jerry. See you soon.'

Replacing the receiver, I breathed an enormous sigh of relief.

'Irene. Doll. Come quick. Our problems are over.'

Irene raced over to me, the children behind her.

'Great news. We're moving to Canada,' I said with a huge smile, expecting them to jump up and down with joy.

'Canada?' All three repeated.

'Yeah. They want me to direct *Feel the Beat* in Toronto.' *I can finally stop working in that shitbag club.* I waited for them to tell me how brilliant and amazing I was.

Lorraine pouted. 'Mum promised we wouldn't move again. You

know I have the lead in the school play. Everyone will be watching.'

Boris smirked. 'Yeah, right. Who'd waste their time watching you?'

'At least I'm not spotty. No one likes looking at your oily, pimply face.'

'Watch it,' I warned them both. 'I'll give you a good hiding if you don't shut up.' *What an ungrateful family. Where's the admiration and awe? I've just saved the day, after all.*

Irene pointed upstairs. 'Go to your rooms. Daddy and I have things to discuss.'

Sulking, they turned and walked away.

We returned to the living room and sat down on the sofa.

'Look,' I said, putting my hand on Irene's thigh, 'nothing's final. They're just sending me a ticket. I'll go check it out. Make sure the moneys decent. Don't worry. It's good news, eh?' I nodded my head happily.

She kissed me on the cheek but didn't seem pleased. *Oh well, she'll come around eventually. She always does.*

'I'll make us some tea,' she said and left the room.

I sat back with a huge grin. I would carry on at the club until I knew whether I had the job in Canada. I still needed to get my overdue salary. Then I could bid Marjorie, Busty Betty, and even Smelly Nelly farewell. *Won't that be grand?*

Chapter Thirty

IRENE

Balancing the tray full of tea and biscuits in one hand, I let myself into the living room. Moving aside Joe's legs resting on the table, I poured him a cup and silently offered him a biscuit, which he grabbed and stuffed into his mouth.

'Great news, doll, isn't it?' he said as crumbs flew out of his mouth and landed on his lap.

I shook my head. 'No, darling. It's not. We can't just up and move again to another country. We're settled now, and things will get better soon.'

'How?' he asked. 'The fuckers haven't paid me in months. At least those Canadians sound serious and are prepared to put out big bucks. And for a decent gig, not clown work.'

I sat in silence, not knowing what to say. Joe always got swept away by new opportunities, excited as a schoolboy. He never stopped to think.

'Look, maybe my wages will come in soon,' he said after taking another biscuit.

'I hope so. In the meantime, I still think you should start looking for another job.'

'Fine. But at least if push comes to shove, there's always Canada.' He picked up the newspaper and turned away from the conversation.

I sipped on my tea while fighting the urge to bite my nails. Not knowing what more to say and wanting to put the worry aside, I got back to the letter I had been writing.

Mum had phoned long distance last week, but we spent three minutes talking about the weather. Seeing as it was so expensive, I'd put the phone down, frustrated, and decided to write to her instead. I didn't tell her too much about our life in Australia. She would've had a fit if she knew where Joe worked, so I avoided the subject and wrote about the children. I wrote about Lorraine having the lead in the school play and how she took it so seriously, rehearsing her lines every evening in her room. I explained how much it had boosted her confidence, transforming her from a shy, introverted child to an outgoing pre-teen with her own opinions and desires.

I didn't have too much to add about Boris, as he was moody most of the time. I tried talking with him, worried issues were lurking behind his gruff exterior, but I was lucky to get a grunt in reply, so I gave up after a while. I did write about how he was doing in school and his adequate report card. Finishing the letter by sending Mum and Dad my love, I put it in an envelope and sealed it.

With that task completed, all my worries about Joe, Canada, and the club came flooding back. I wished I could feel calm and carefree, but so many things were niggling away in my head: Joe being around all those naked girls every night, knowing how his ego always needed stroking, I worried they would try something with him; he would certainly enjoy the attention. Joe just laughed when I brought it up. 'Don't worry, luv. They're all lesbians. They hate men.'

I barely even knew what a lesbian was or if I'd ever met one before. I spoke to Jenny about it, and what she said made me almost faint. 'I've slept with several women. It was great, but I prefer the ruggedness of a man.' She rolled her eyes at my shocked expression. 'Irene, you need to be more open-minded.'

She was right. I was tired of being so naïve, so I decided to work on myself, to improve and learn about current events. I started reading the newspapers daily and watched the news each night. I realised I had been living in a bubble of pleasing Joe and the kids. Looking back at my behaviour, I thought it was pathetic, but I had learnt that way from Mum, who had drummed it into me. No one had ever told me to broaden my horizons before Jenny.

I could see that the change in me had affected the family. Joe often looked uncomfortable when I reacted in a way he didn't like, but it was too bad. He would just have to get used to the new me.

Neither did the kids know what to make of it. They had become accustomed to me always picking up after them, catering to their every whim. I shouldn't blame them for being spoilt; they didn't know any different. When I informed them I wasn't their servant, they stared at me like I was an alien from outer space. They stomped their feet or threw a tantrum, but I didn't react. I calmly let them know they were capable of making breakfast and lunch at their age as I opened the fridge and pointed to the ingredients inside. I made it clear that if they would not make their own food, they could just starve. Of course, I had to listen to their rants and protests, saying how I was such a terrible mother, but I stood my ground. They had no choice but to learn how to fend for themselves.

It made me proud to watch them becoming independent. I had finally broken the chauvinistic and corrupt education of women passed down from generation to generation. It stopped with my daughter. I took pleasure in knowing that her daughters would not have to endure the abuse and degradation women had suffered before her.

My next task was to work on getting Joe to look for a better job. One that we could be proud of, where he could hold his head up high. It wouldn't be easy, but I welcomed the challenge.

What is Joe thinking, moving yet again? Canada? He has to be crazy. Under no circumstances would I allow it, especially after I had promised Lorraine. With that decided, I picked up the letter and headed to the post box down the road.

That night, we were watching the news when a segment about mobsters being arrested at their strip club appeared.

'Oh my god, that's not your club, is it?' I gasped.

'Nah. Don't worry, that's in a totally different part of town. Nothing to do with The Passion Pit.'

'But what if gangsters also run your club?'

Joe laughed. 'You've got a hell of an imagination, darling. If you saw Frank, the boss, you'd feel stupid even suggesting it. He's the size of a dwarf and a real family man. Now, let's watch something else before you start imagining werewolves or something.'

He switched the channel to *The Beverly Hillbillies*. I tried to concentrate on the show, but I still couldn't relax. My head rang with the imagined headline , 'Famous Host, Joe Leslie, Arrested at Strip Club'.

Chapter Thirty-one

JOE

Someone knocked on my study door.

'Come in if you must.'

Irene walked in, holding her handbag and waving away the smoke. It made me want to light up another while I was already smoking one.

'Are you sure you don't want to come with us to the cinema? You kept saying how you were dying to see the film.'

'I changed me mind. Please, just go and leave me in peace.'

'Very well. We'll see you later,' she said in a clipped voice and left the room.

'Kids, time to go,' she shouted, and the ceiling above me rattled as they clomped down the stairs. Only when I heard the front door closing did I lean back and continue staring at the walls, as I'd done for the past few hours.

George and Mabel were snoring away at my feet, oblivious to my turmoil. If I were a cartoon, smoke would be coming out of my ears from the rage I felt towards fucking Marjorie and Frank, who still owed me several months' wages. *The bastards.*

I thought about my talk with Frank in his office the other day.

~ * ~

Stomping down the corridor to Frank's office, the door swung open just as I knocked. Two gigantic men in dark suits walked out. One of them nodded to me as he passed.

When I went in, I asked Frank. 'Who are those blokes I just passed by now?'

'Oh, they're just my cousins, asking for tickets for the show,' he said dismissively. *His cousins? Yeah right. They were at least six feet and built like a ton of bricks, knuckles dragging on the floor and all. They make Larry the bouncer look like a toddler.*

'Anyway, what brings you in today?' he asked.

'It's about me pay. Three months overdue, Frank.' I tried to keep the frustration out of my voice.

'I told you, I'm having a bit of a cashflow problem. I'm sure you understand. Any day now. Trust me.' He put his hand on his heart.

'I have bills to pay. You owe me.' There was no hiding my tone.

He leaned back in his seat. 'Give me a couple of days. I'll sort it out. I got a few things in the works.'

I sighed. 'Okay, but only two days. I'm serious, Frank. Otherwise …' I shook my finger at him.

'Otherwise what, Joe?' A snarl replaced his usual smile. 'You don't have any idea who you're dealing with, do you? I'd tread carefully if I were you.'

A shiver ran down my spine, and I started to wonder just who Frank was and who he and Marjorie were really working for.

'I … I just mean I need to be paid as soon as possible.'

'Of course. I will do my best.' His smile returned.

Swallowing my growing fear, I turned and left his office. *What have I got myself into?*

~ * ~

That had been three days ago, and still nothing. I was fucking fuming. *Is it because of Marjorie? Is she holding back my wages to spite me? Well, fuck that.*

I grabbed the car keys from the hall table and dashed out, driving like a lunatic as I headed towards the Passion Pit. I parked the car and stormed out, pounding on the front door.

Larry let me in. 'What are you doing here, Joe? Isn't it your day off?'

'Yeah, but I need to speak to Frank. Is he in his office?' My whole body was vibrating as I looked down the hall.

'No one's here. Just me and the cleaning lady.'

I stood a moment, my mind racing. *That money is mine. Fucking bastard owes me. Marjorie owes me.*

I had an idea. 'I need something from the stage. Won't be long.' Trying to look casual, I patted him on the shoulder as I walked past.

The smell of stale cigarettes and beer filled my nose as I switched on the main lights and looked around. Spotting what I was looking for in the far corner of the stage, I unplugged the fancy high-tech sound system and picked it up.

Moving fast, I carried the equipment to the entrance, going straight to the car. I ignored Larry sitting on a chair in the hall, but he was hot on my heels.

I jumped in the car, threw the device in the back seat just as Larry grasped the door handle.

'What've you got there, Joe? Hey, you can't take that. The boss will kill me.'

I quickly pressed the lock, but his arm squeezed through the crack in the window, and he tried to grab my neck. I reached over to the glove compartment and whipped out the BB gun, aiming it at him.

'I'll fucking kill you. I'm only taking what's owed, so fuck off.'

Larry backed away with his arms up, eyes focused on the gun. 'You're going to regret this, Joe. Mark my words.'

Starting the ignition, I put my foot down and sped away. *Fuck. What've I done?*

The house was silent when I let myself in. I carefully placed the BB gun on the top shelf of the downstairs cupboard. Confident it was safely hidden, I went into my study, took out the wad of cash I'd gotten for the stereo, and shoved it in the desk behind a whole lot of papers.

After leaving the club, I'd driven straight to the pawnshop. They'd given me over three thousand dollars for the stereo, more than I imagined it was worth. It would cover a few expenses and leave some over to line my pocket as well.

The dogs charged at me as I entered the kitchen.

'Down. Down. I'm not in the mood for you two.'

Ignoring them, I walked to the side cabinet, opening every drawer, desperate for Valium, but there was none. Bloody Irene forgot to refill my prescription. *I bet she's done it on purpose, the cow.* I slammed the last draw shut.

Sitting at the table with shaking hands, I lit up a cigarette. I couldn't relax. I kept imagining police sirens every time a bird chirped. *Fuck. How do I get out of this mess? Wait a minute. What time is it in Canada?* I had no idea, but hell, I had to make the call.

Dialling the international operator, I gave her Jerry Barnes' number. There was no answer from the studios, so I tried his home.

A groggy voice answered, 'Hello?'

'Hi, Jerry, this is Joe Leslie from Melbourne. How are you?' I did my best to sound calm.

'Joe, it's three o'clock in the morning. Is everything all right?'

'Yeah, fine. Sorry to ring so late or so early.' I laughed. 'Anyway, wanted to let you know I've decided to come over and check out the facilities.'

'That's great news. When were you thinking of coming?'

I paused, pretending to think for a moment. 'How about two days from now? Is that okay?'

'Yes, that can work. I'll get my secretary to arrange your ticket.'

'One more thing. I want the wife and kids to come too. They don't like me travelling alone, you see. Can you arrange that?'

'I suppose that will be fine. I'll take care of it in the morning. For now, though, I'm going to say goodnight.'

'Goodnight, Jerry, and thanks.'

Grinning, I put the receiver down. *Problem solved.*

Chapter Thirty-two

IRENE

The kids and I came home in a great mood. We'd been to see the movie *Fiddler on the Roof* and had a wonderful time.

Lorraine was delighted. 'Oh, I just loved it all, especially the music. *Matchmaker, matchmaker, make me a match* ...' Lorraine sang, and we all joined in.

It was such a lovely time, just the three of us without a care in the world.

'Mum,' Lorraine said as I put the key in the front door, 'I want to act in a film like that one day. My music teacher told me I have a sweet quality to my singing, and I'm really good at getting into character.'

'Yes, you are, darling. You never know. It might just happen.' I gave her an encouraging smile. It was good to see her so confident and full of life.

The house was dark and quiet. I switched on the lamp on the hall side table and called out.

'Joe, are you here?'

'I'm here,' came a voice.

The kids ran upstairs as I went into the kitchen. Joe was sitting at the table with a half cup of coffee and an overflowing ashtray in front of him. The smoke filling the air stung my eyes. I opened the window.

'Everything all right, darling?' I asked, sitting down opposite him, brushing away the film of ash covering the table.

'Yeah, all's fine,' he said.

I wasn't so sure.

'Hey, doll, you know how we talked about me going to Canada to check it out?'

'No. I thought we decided against that.'

'We didn't. We just put it on hold, right? And I've been thinking. There's no work here, so why don't we just go and live there? I think it could be good. Canadians love the British.'

I lost it.

'You can't do this to us again. We followed you here to Melbourne. Settled in. Adjusted. I'm sorry you had a heart attack, but it's not our fault. I will not move the kids every time you need a change. You should consider the family, not just yourself.'

Joe sprung from the table, grabbed his chair, and flung it across the room. One leg broke off and lay in pieces on the floor, while the seat hung off the empty frame.

I flinched. He looked like a madman. *Will he throw me across the room as well?*

'We're going, and that's that. Start packing. We leave the day after tomorrow.' He snatched up his pack of cigarettes and lighter and stormed out.

I sat there, stunned, feeling as though he had hit me, but without bruises. The ache was internal but just as sore as if he had belted the living daylights out of me.

I watched him go but didn't care. I wouldn't run after him this time. Never again. If he wanted to fly off to Canada, then he could, but alone. I wouldn't budge.

That night, I couldn't sleep. I slipped out of bed and went downstairs to make myself a cup of tea. It was clear what I needed to do. I had enough money saved for the children and me to take off and start afresh. It tore at my heartstrings, but I had no choice. I refused to continue on Joe's crooked, unpredictable path.

I would do everything in my power to look after the kids and give them a sense of home and security. I would need to find a job, though I had no idea what I could do. But I would take whatever was available to provide for us. I only hoped I could find a place nearby, the least disruption, the better. I had noticed there were flats for rent near the school. I didn't know if they were suitable, but I would enquire.

The doorbell rang, interrupting my thoughts. *My God, who on earth could that be in the middle of the night?*

The dogs woke with a snort and tumbled off the sofa, barking.

'Quiet, Mabel. George.' I tiptoed to the front door. 'Who's there?'

'Melbourne police. Open up, please.' *The police! Whatever for?*

Joe appeared on the landing wearing only his pyjama bottoms. 'Who the hell is that?'

'The police,' I hissed.

With a strangled expletive, he leapt down the stairs two at a time and ran to the cupboard. Pulling out the BB gun, he shoved it into my hands.

'Hide this somewhere, anywhere, just so it's not found.'

I stood, paralysed.

He pushed me frantically up the stairs. 'Hurry!'

The doorbell rang again, jolting me into action, and I raced upstairs into Boris's room. He was fast asleep but sat up with a start as I entered.

'Mum? What's going on?'

'Shush,' I whispered. 'I need you to do me a favour.' I handed him the gun. 'Hide this for me. Don't ask me why. I'll explain later.'

Boris smiled. He actually looked like he was enjoying himself for once.

'Sure, I'll put it in my boots in the wardrobe. No one will find it.'

'Thanks, darling. Just pretend to be asleep and don't come out of your room until I tell you.' I planted a kiss on his forehead and went back downstairs.

Joe and two burly policemen stood by the front door.

'Hey, darling, these men seem to think we've got a gun here. You've not seen one around, right?'

I kept my shaking hands behind my back. 'A gun? Whatever for? We would never keep a weapon in the house with children around.'

The policeman narrowed his eyes as he looked at me with suspicion. I felt my face grow hot.

'Mind if we look around?' the other one asked.

'Of course not.' Joe smiled. 'Be my guest, but please, try not to wake the kids.'

Joe led the policemen through the house, starting in the living room, where they opened up draws and felt behind the pillows on the sofa. I wanted to scream, 'Take your filthy hands off my things,' but I stayed silent, trying to look innocent as I followed behind them. They searched the kitchen next, again opening and closing doors and cabinets, then moved on to Joe's study to do the same.

They finished their inspection. 'We'd like to go upstairs.' Following them, I whispered, 'Please, if you don't mind being quiet, as my husband said, the children are sleeping.'

'What's in here?' One pointed to Boris' door. It stood ajar. I hadn't shut it completely when I left.

'Oh, that is my son's room. He'll be fast asleep.'

As the policeman opened it, I flashed Joe a terrified look. He grabbed my hand behind my back and gripped it tightly.

Satisfied, the policeman closed the door.

I breathed a silent sigh of relief, but it was short-lived as Lorraine's door opened, and she came out, rubbing her eyes.

'What's going on, Mum?'

'Nothing, sweetie pie, just a few friends. You go back to bed.' I put my arms around her and led her back to her room.

The policemen searched the other rooms but came up empty. Disappointed, they made their way to the front door.

'This is not over yet. You'll be hearing from us.' the broad-shouldered policeman threatened.

Joe let the officers out. Closing the door behind them, he leaned against it and let out an enormous breath. His face was white as he slid down to the ground, shaking.

'Bloody hell, that was close.'

I looked down at him. 'Joe Leslie, you'd better tell me what's going on,' I demanded.

Joe grunted as he got up off the ground. 'Let's go in the kitchen. I need a cup of tea.'

I put the kettle back on and made two steaming mugs of dark, strong tea. Putting them down in front of us, we waited for them to cool down enough to swallow.

In the silent room, the clock on the wall ticked loudly. *What on earth is going on? What has he done now?*

Joe took a long, deep breath before taking a sip of his tea, wincing as the liquid burned his mouth. 'The fucking club owner must be in bed with the Mafia. How was I not aware of that? I must be dense. I've heard before that the Mafia and police work hand in hand here, but I never connected it to the club. Jack warned me, but I didn't take it seriously.' He shook his head before turning to me. He tried to act nonchalant, but I could see fear in his eyes. 'I might as well tell you. I had a bit of a to-do with the club today. They hadn't paid me for ages, so I said fuck it and took something on account.'

'You stole something?'

'I didn't steal. I just took what they owed me in the form of a sound system. I was sure I could get it out quick, but the fucking security guy came after me, so I whipped out the BB gun and aimed it at him. I would've been *brown bread* otherwise.' He brushed his hand over his mouth and rubbed his chin. 'How was I to know they were bloody gangsters?'

For a moment, I felt a pang of sympathy for him as he sat there, afraid and, for once, honest about his mistakes. I reached out and held his arm.

He took my hand. 'So now you understand why we have to leave and fast. Luckily, I spoke to the guy in Canada, and our tickets should arrive tomorrow. We'll be out of here the day after. We just need to avoid the police till then.'

Well, that was it then. I didn't have a choice. Who knew what gangsters might come after us if the children and I stayed here? We had to follow him to another unknown country for the second time. It just wasn't fair.

I shook my head as the mounting fear crept cold fingers over my scalp. 'I can't believe this mess. What should I tell the kids?'

'Nothing. Just that we have to leave.'

'Boris hid the gun. He knows something's up. I have to say something.'

'Fine, fine, he's a sensible kid, but make sure he doesn't say a word to anyone, especially that we're leaving. Keep them home from school till we go. And don't tell Lorraine anything. I don't need a hysterical teenager on top of it all.'

I placed my hand on the table, realising I'd been biting my nails. 'The kids are on holiday, but they have summer school tomorrow.' I sighed. 'I'll cancel it. Oh, Joe, what about the dogs? We can't take them. We don't have time to find out about quarantine and all that.'

'Shit! Shit!' He put his head in his hands, his eyes glazing with sadness. I was glad that something, at least, was bringing home the gravity of the situation, even if, yet again, it wasn't his family. He shook his head. 'I'll never find a home for them at this short notice. Don't worry, luv. I'll deal with it, somehow. Now, let's try to get some sleep.'

We turned out the light and headed upstairs.

I popped into Boris' room to thank him. He was sitting up in bed with his headphones on, plugged into the record player beside his bed. He took them off and looked at me, winding the curling wire around his hands.

'Mum, what was that all about?' he asked, a quizzical look on his face.

'Dad had a bit of trouble with the club. I'll tell you more in the morning. I'm too tired right now.' Giving him a weary smile, I tried to sound casual. 'Oh, by the way, no summer school tomorrow. And go to sleep soon, okay?'

Boris beamed. 'Okay. Thanks, Mum. You're the best. Night.' He put his headphones back on and lay down.

The next day, while Joe was out making arrangements for our imminent departure, I sat down with the kids for a heart-to-heart.

'Dad got into a bit of trouble with his work, which means we need to leave the country.'

Lorraine jumped up. 'No. You promised we wouldn't move again. I'm not going anywhere. I don't care what you say.' She crossed her arms, her eyes blazing.

'Darling, there isn't any choice,' I said as gently as I could.

She put her hands over her ears. 'No! No! I'm not listening to you. You're a liar.'

Boris growled, 'Where to this time, Mum?'

'Dad took a job in Canada. Toronto. I'm so sorry, but we have to go. Maybe it won't be too bad.'

Lorraine burst into tears, sobbing in the most dramatic manner she could muster.

'It's not fair. I hate you.' She ran upstairs to her room, the house rattling as she slammed the door shut.

I shook my head. *This isn't easy for me, either.*

I looked at my son. 'I want you to know that if it were possible to stay, we would, but it's too dangerous.'

'Is it to do with the gun?'

'Yes, I'm afraid so.' I bit my lip, reluctant to say any more.

He laughed. 'It's fake, you know. It only shoots pellets.'

'Yes, I know. But the people in question don't. The bottom line is that we have to leave as soon as possible.'

To my surprise, he came over and put his arm around me. A rare occurrence, if there ever was one.

'It's okay, Mum. We'll be okay. Just tell me how I can help.'

At least I had him on my side. It was hard enough just getting through the ordeal.

I wondered what the next days would bring, praying I could handle it.

Chapter Thirty-three

JOE

Well, there we were, tucking into our dinner on the flight to Toronto. Everyone except Lorraine, who'd been sniffling for almost half of the journey. We still had over ten hours to go. She was getting on my nerves.

'This is why I prefer ships. You take your time, no jet lag, and you're not stuck with ungrateful children. Millions of kids would want your life, Lorraine. To travel around the world instead of the same boring routine, but not you. All you think is *poor old me*. If we weren't flying right now, I'd really give you something to cry about.' I resisted the urge to whack her one.

'But Daddy, Mabel and George are family. How could you just throw them away?' Tears rolled down her cheeks.

I swallowed a Valium and lit a cigarette. 'I told you. They wouldn't allow dogs to come with us to Canada. I found them a great place on a farm with lots of animals. Now, shut up and eat your food.'

I couldn't tell her the truth. She would've had a fit. I hadn't really found them a home. I didn't have the time to. There was only one solution. I had them put down. It was what any humane person would do. The vet refused at first, but everyone had a price, and once I upped the amount, he agreed. Irene was horrified when I told her, though I couldn't understand why. I did the kindest thing.

I was so relieved the police hadn't returned. The night they'd turned up at the house, I'd felt like all my blood had drained from my body, leaving my arms and legs like jelly. Thank goodness I was a great actor. I should've got an award for my performance as a calm, decent man above suspicion.

It seemed like I had aged thirty years by the time they left and I was even more determined to get the fuck out before we all ended up in the river with cement boots. I even considered dyeing my hair and growing a beard, but I was reluctant to spoil my good looks. For the next couple of days, I only went out to deal with the vet and over to the chemist to refill my Valium prescription. Other than that, we all stayed home and packed. I was really only able to calm down once the plane had taken off. I kept my fingers crossed that Toronto would be a decent place to live. *I wonder if gambling is legal there.*

After sleeping for almost nine hours, I woke up to an announcement over the speakers telling us to put our seats upright as we readied for our descent. As an air hostess passed by, I tapped her arm. 'Could I get a cup of coffee, please?'

'Sorry, sir, we've closed the kitchen. Please fasten your seatbelt.'

If that wasn't enough, the no smoking sign came on, and it made me damn irritable.

'Look at that,' Boris said as he looked out of the window. 'Everything is white. I've never seen so much snow before. Lorraine, take a look.'

She shrugged, 'No thanks. I'd rather stare at the ceiling.'

I felt a bump and then another, which meant we had landed. 'Great,' I mumbled as the plane slowed and came to a stop. The ping of the seatbelt sign turned off, and it was time to get our hand luggage from the overheads and get out.

Retrieving our hold luggage, we trudged out of the terminal, only to be greeted by over two feet of snow covering the ground.

'Bloody hell, it's colder than a witch's tit.' I shivered, pulling my collar up to try and keep warm, but it was useless. 'Where the hell is the driver the studio sent over?'

We had to wait a whole hour for him to arrive, our hands and feet going numb.

'So sorry. The roads were closed because of last night's heavy snowfall. Here, let me take your bags.'

'Is this unusual?' I asked the driver as we all buckled up.

'Nah, every year it's the same.'

Even in the car, with the heat on full blast, I was still miserable. 'Christ, I can't stand the bloody cold. We left England because of the weather, and that wasn't half as bad as this.'

We drove along in silence. The children looked out the window at the Christmas lights sparkling, lighting up the city, but I didn't give a shit. I just wanted to get into the warm.

Irene tried to cheer us up. 'I'm sure we'll all feel a lot better once we've had a hot bath and a good sleep. Things will look much nicer tomorrow. You have your meeting in the morning, Joe, and I will register the kids for school.'

'But, Mum,' Boris whined, 'we're on summer holidays.'

'It's winter in Canada, and they only break up for Christmas.'

'Shit,' Boris mumbled under his breath.

'I heard that,' Irene scolded.

The car pulled up outside a high-end building. A doorman welcomed us and picked up our suitcases. Jerry Barnes had arranged for us to stay here and said that once I signed the show's contract, the rent was free of charge.

'This is nice, isn't it, Joe?' Irene said.

I didn't reply, just hurried to the entrance.

Once inside, we retrieved our keys from the front desk and rode the lift to the twelfth floor, letting ourselves into our new home. It was a roomy flat with three bedrooms and a large sitting room. The sweeping, floor to ceiling windows looked out onto the snow-covered skyscrapers of the city.

I flopped down on the sofa and stared out the window.

'I'll just go and check for supplies,' Irene said and headed to the kitchen.

I could hear Boris shouting, 'This one's my room. You get the smaller one.' Then Lorraine crying, 'I hate you. I hate everyone,' and a door slammed.

Irene came out with a note in her hand. 'This was on the table. Listen, *Welcome to Toronto. We look forward to seeing you tomorrow. We've stocked the kitchen with some food for you and your family. Jerry Barnes and all the crew at Channel 9.* That's nice of them.'

'Yeah, nice,' I said, lacking enthusiasm.

She went back to prepare the food. After a short while, she called out, 'Come and eat.'

We sat down and had cheese sandwiches with some hot tea. I ate without an appetite, avoiding Irene's eye. I knew what she was thinking. How I'd shlepped them halfway across the world to this arctic country and was still complaining. *It's not my fault I'm not a genius in geography.*

I hardly slept a wink, tossing and turning all night. It took two coffees and a shower to make me halfway decent in the morning, but I was on time for my meeting at the studios.

I met Jerry Barnes in the lobby. He looked to be about forty years of age, with a full head of light brown hair and a face which was kind of nondescript: broad, symmetrical, and toothy.

He shook my hand with a big grin. 'Nice to meet you, Joe. Hope you found everything to your satisfaction.'

I nodded, 'Yeah, thanks. It's very comfortable.'

'Great. Let's go upstairs to the boardroom, and I'll introduce you to the producers.'

We entered a room filled with men in suits. When I walked in, they all stood up and smiled. One of them came over and pumped my hand. 'Mr Leslie, so pleased to see you. I'm Barry Smythe, head of light entertainment.'

I shook some more hands, and they were all full of praise for me. '*Feel The Beat* is a hell of a show. We can't wait to get started on it.' 'Just brilliant.' they said.

It was like being back on set in Melbourne, people fawning over me, complimenting my work. Of course, it was flattering, filling that part of me that had been missing after working in that dump of a club, but I still didn't feel like I usually did after lapping up so much attention.

We discussed the show in detail throughout the day. They were ready to start production and just needed my signature on the agreement. It looked like they were more than willing to provide anything I needed, from crew to props. I kept adding more demands, like a cocky asshole, but they weren't fazed. They wanted my show and would do anything to get it.

Yet, I had an undeniable sinking feeling in the pit of my stomach. It all seemed too good to be true. Apart from the freezing cold, I couldn't understand why I didn't feel happy, optimistic, or even remotely smug. On any other occasion, I would've been thrilled with all the VIP treatment, but something was missing.

By three that afternoon, the jet lag had reared its head, and I was exhausted.

'Sorry, guys, but I'm fading fast.'

'No worries,' Barry said, 'We'll continue tomorrow morning.'

Jerry walked me out of the building. 'We are hopeful you'll give us a positive answer.' He smiled and shook my hand.

'Let me sleep on it, okay, mate?'

I decided to brave the climate and walk home. It was only a few short blocks away. *Maybe the frigid air will wake me up a bit.* With my arms crossed around my chest, I strode along the street, hugging my thin coat.

We'd have to buy warm clothes for this weather, but I had no desire to do that. *What's the matter with me? The job is mine. The pay is great, but I still can't say yes. I must be going bonkers.*

Passing several buildings, I kept my head down, shielding my face from the driving snow when an enormous gust of wind almost blew me over. As I staggered and looked up, a sign on a building caught my eye.

The Jewish Agency for Israel.

Well, that's something new. Israel. The homeland for us Jews.

Almost without thinking, I opened the door and went up the narrow staircase. A huge blue and white Israeli flag covered the office door, and posters of the land of milk and honey hung proudly on the walls. A warm feeling washed over me, and I knew I was in the right place.

'Hello, luv.' I smiled at the dark-haired girl sitting at a desk. 'Who do I talk to about Israel?'

She laughed. 'We only talk about Israel here.' She had a strong accent, and I realised I'd never met an Israeli before. She opened a door behind her and spoke to someone in Hebrew.

'You can go in, please.'

A balding man in an open-neck white shirt rose from his chair as I entered. 'Shalom, how can I help you?'

I sat down and took a deep breath. 'I'll get straight to the point. My name's Joe Leslie, and the family and I only arrived here yesterday from Australia. Even though I got me a good job, something's missing. I just know in my gut that this country is not the right one. I never thought about Israel before, but something tells me it's the place to be.'

'Mr Leslie, if you only arrived yesterday, how do you know this is not the place for you?'

'I just know it.'

'If I may ask, what do you do?'

'I'm a TV director and host with lots of experience. I'm sure I could find work in Israel. I'm in big demand. The TV station brought me here to direct a show,' I said smugly.

A small, concerned frown settled on the gentleman's face. 'Mr Leslie, Israel is a new country, and television is only a few years old. It would not be near your usual standards. They also speak Hebrew, which I presume you do not. We try to encourage all Jews to immigrate to Israel. That is your right, but we want to make sure that you integrate successfully.'

The obstacles just made me more determined. 'Look, I'll be frank. I've run out of countries. I'm not staying in this igloo. My next home is either Israel or the moon.'

The man smiled and inclined his head. 'I can see you are intent on moving, and of course, I would never stand in the way of a Jew returning to his homeland, but I must clarify that Israel is not as luxurious as Toronto, not by a long shot.'

'As long as there's no snow, I'll be happy. Now, where do I go from here?'

I left the office whistling *Hava Nagila* while clutching the pamphlets and forms.

Israel, here we come.

Chapter Thirty-four

IRENE

Toronto

I stood outside the local high school, the children at my side, waiting for the taxi we'd ordered. Boris kicked up a pile of snow, which drifted straight into Lorraine's face.

'Careful!' I gave Boris a disapproving look.

He scowled back at me. 'I'm sick of new schools. Why can't I work instead? I don't need an education. I want to do what dad does, and he never finished school.'

'We've gone over this. You are going to school. It is not open for discussion.'

'I don't want to go to this school either, I want my school in Melbourne with all my friends, not here where they speak weird....' Lorraine piped up. I narrowed my eyes at her, which made her snap her mouth shut.

When the taxi finally arrived, our hands were numb from the cold, and we were all shivering. We'd require plenty of warm clothing if we were to survive a Canadian winter.

Back home— if I could call it that— I unlocked the door and the kids ran to their rooms without a word.

'Hang up your wet clothes and take off your shoes,' I called after them, but they ignored me.

'Hi, darling.'

I jumped.

Joe was sitting on the couch with a broad grin on his face.

Something was strange. He looked happy. Too happy. Before he'd left in the morning, he was in a foul mood and cursing the moment we landed in Toronto.

'Oh, Joe, I didn't notice you. How was your day?'

'Fucking fabulous, me love. How was yours?'

I walked over and sank down wearily next to him. 'I'm exhausted. Registering the children for school took hours. The place was massive. Anyway, tell me, how was it at the studios? What's it like?'

Joe put his arms around me, squeezing tight. 'Do you believe in destiny?' he whispered in my ear.

I pulled away, a warning bolt of suspicion flashing through my chest. 'Destiny? What do you mean?'

'That sometimes things happen for a reason. If I hadn't walked home today, our lives wouldn't be about to change.' He looked me straight in the eyes.

The word 'change' caused alarm bells to go off inside my head. 'You are not making sense. This is change. Here. In Canada. It all feels strange right now, but we haven't given it a chance. I'm sure it will get better after a while.'

He laughed. 'This place is shit. We're not polar bears. We need the sun. To be where we belong. Like Israel.'

'What are you talking about?'

For once, Joe spoke in a quiet voice. 'I met with someone from the Jewish Agency today. Did you know that because we're Jews, we can immigrate to Israel, and they give us all sorts of stuff, like apartments, help finding a job, and free education?' He patted my leg and chuckled. 'You know how we always feel like outsiders? Having to make sure we say and do the right thing? Well, we *are* the outsiders. We don't belong anywhere except our home, Israel, the land of the Jews.' He emphasised the last words as though he were giving a speech in front of an audience.

'As new immigrants, we'll have three months in an absorption centre, where we can learn the language and explore the country. I can't wait. So, what do you think? Great, eh?' he said, beaming.

'What?' I threw my hands up in the air as my voice raised to a high-pitched scream. 'You cannot do this again. No, this place is not ideal, but we are not ping-pong balls you can bounce around. We know nothing about Israel. You have a job here, a flat, and good pay. Stop with all this nonsense at once.'

Joe stood and yelled, 'Don't you tell me what to do. We're leaving for Israel, and that's final. I make the rules, and you obey!'

I jumped up and faced him, drew a deep breath and shouted the words I had held back for far too long: 'Screw. Your. Rules!'

Joe stared at me, his eyes wide, mouth open. I could almost smell his fear.

I held his gaze, feeling the power of my rage radiating from me in waves.

He slumped back on the sofa, his previously red face drained of all colour.

I put my hands on my hips and looked down at him. 'You want to go to Israel? Then go, but we will not follow you all over the world every time you have a whim. I've had enough. Do what you want, but don't expect me to come crawling along behind you, the obedient wife.'

As I walked toward the bedroom, still furious, Lily McGillis appeared in my head, her fist in the air as she cheered me on. I turned and strode back to him.

'And one more thing. You are a bloody hypocrite. You stopped Shabbos dinners, saying it was a bunch of crap made up by rabbis wanting to control us. Now suddenly, you're sprouting the importance of being Jewish and returning to our homeland. Now *that's* a bunch of crap!'

The children must have heard our raised voices and crept into the living room.

Boris shouted, 'Israel? The place from the bible? Screw that. I'm not going, and you can't make me.' He crossed his arms and stuck out his chin.

'Me neither. I want to go home to Melbourne,' Loraine sobbed loudly before running down the hallway.

I fixed Boris with a steely look and pointed after her. 'Go to your room now. This is a discussion between your father and me. Go!'

Glowering, he left the room.

Joe put his head in his hands. 'I'm sorry, okay?' His voice was small. 'I find it hard to imagine us staying here. I know I'm not religious. I don't even believe in God, but something about Israel feels right. Dad always told me to be a big fish in a small pond. Well, TV's only a few years old there. I can be a big star.'

I looked at my husband, hunched over like a lost little boy. *How can I be so angry with him one minute, and the next, he manages to tug on my heartstrings?*

My voice softened. 'Look, I understand this is important to you, but we have to think of the children. We can't just land in a strange country knowing nothing about it except that everyone is Jewish. Isn't it dangerous there? Isn't there a war going on?'

I reflected for a moment. 'Why don't you go to Israel and check things out? I can take the kids to England in the meantime and stay with my parents. It'll be the Christmas holidays soon, so they won't miss too much school.'

It was an attractive solution. I needed time. Time without him, to sort out the mess in my head and try to decide about our future.

Joe didn't answer at first, then let out a huge breath. 'I suppose you can call that a compromise, right?' He gave a short nod. 'Okay, I'll go find out if I can start work immediately as we don't have a lot of cash. I can give you a bit, but I'm going to need most of it to get us a place to live. You and the kids can come once I'm settled, but I won't wait long.'

'It's for the best.'

'Kids, come back. We've got something to tell you.'

Boris and Lorraine shuffled in, looking dejected.

'Listen up. You're going to England with your mum, while I go to Israel to get things ready for us. Then you'll join me there.'

'England? Groovy! We can see Grandma and Grandpa.' Lorraine jumped up and down, a smile on her face for the first time in ages.

Boris turned and trudged back to his room in silence.

Joe took my hand in his. 'I'm gonna miss you, darling, but it won't be long, just a few weeks, and then it will be paradise. I just know it.' He looked brighter. 'Now, what's for dinner? I'm starving,' he said, summoning again, without fail, his cheeky grin.

Joe was on the phone arranging our flights to England while I prepared the meal. As I stirred the soup, I felt a growing optimism I hadn't felt before. Joe was right when he said that things happened for a reason. He didn't realise it, but he had just given me a ticket to freedom.

Chapter Thirty-five

JOE

I'd managed to get Irene and the kids a flight to London for early the next morning. At the crack of dawn, I helped them into a taxi to the airport. Waving them off, I braved the cold and walked to the Jewish Agency to wait for them to open up. It only took a few minutes before the Israeli bloke I'd spoken to arrived. I followed him up the stairs and sat myself down on the chair.

'I've decided to immigrate to Israel,' I announced.

'Mazal tov, but are you sure?' he said, moving papers around his desk.

'I am one hundred per cent certain,' I said, crossing my arms.

'Very well. Have you filled out all the forms?'

Nodding, I handed him the paperwork.

He glanced at it and set it aside in an in-tray. 'Good. Leave them with me. I will get it all sorted and ready for you in about two weeks.'

I leapt to my feet. 'Two weeks? No, that won't do. I have to fly tomorrow,' I shouted. 'You don't understand. I won't have anywhere to live because I'm giving up the job they offered me. The family has already gone to England to visit family. I'm alone now. You gotta make it happen.'

He looked confused and raised his hands to calm me. 'Mr Leslie, these things take time.'

'Look, from one Jew to another, I might do something drastic if I stay here a moment longer.' I clutched my hair in dramatic appeal.

'I am sorry, but I cannot do what you ask,' he said, shaking his head.

'God created the world in seven days, and you can't send one Jew back to his homeland in one? Come on.'

He looked like he wouldn't budge, but I wasn't having that. 'I'm begging you. Please, I'm desperate.' I went down on my knees, my hands clasped together, and looked up at him with my most pleading expression.

He looked down at me and burst into laughter.

'Alright, Mr Leslie, you can get up now. This has never happened to me before. Come back at four pm, and with God's help, I will have it arranged.'

I skipped out of there, mentally ticking off the tasks for the day. *Two down, one to go.*

All that was left was a visit to the studios to give them my answer. I was nervous about speaking to Jerry, afraid he might hit the roof or try to change my mind, but he surprised me once I mentioned Israel.

'Of course, I'm not happy about your decision, but being Jewish myself, I understand. I'm almost jealous.'

'No hard feelings?' I asked with a smile.

He shook my hand. 'No. I wish you all the luck in the world, and we'll be here if you change your mind.'

I couldn't believe my luck. It was all meant to be.

I couldn't relax until I sat in my aisle seat on board the crowded El Al flight to Tel Aviv the next day. Once the plane took off, I could feel my neck muscles loosening. I became fascinated by the orthodox Jews in their long black coats and hats, tassels peeking out under their sweat-stained shirts. I'd seen the religious before in the East End, but I never really gave them much thought. As I looked at them, it was like seeing aliens from another planet. *Hard to believe these geezers and I are from the same tribe.*

They stood at the rear of the aeroplane, absorbed in their morning prayers, paying no attention to the other passengers. Swaying back and forth, they chanted ancient Hebrew prayers. Strangely enough, it gave me a sense of security. *Glad someone's praying, making sure we all get to the promised land safe and sound.*

Looking around, I smiled at the man next to me. 'This is great, isn't it? No goys judging our every move. Just us Jews here together. I tell you, if I never have to speak to one again, life will be perfect.'

He closed his book. 'Actually, I'm studying to be a Catholic priest, and I'm going to Jerusalem for my final year, before I take holy orders.'

'Oh.' I laughed. 'Well, I didn't mean holy men like you, of course.'

He nodded and returned to his reading.

Fuck that for luck. One goy on the plane, and he has to sit next to me. Shrugging to myself, I settled down for a nap. When I awoke, there was still another hour to go, so I ordered a coffee and watched my devout neighbour mumble to himself, rolling some beads between his fingers. I was about to ask him why he did that, when it occurred to me that the answer would probably bore me. I opened the newspaper instead, but it was hard to concentrate. My mind was racing as I imagined my new life. *Do palm trees line the streets? Will I be walking on the same stones that Moses and all the other blokes from the Bible did?*

My ears popped as the fasten seat belt sign came on. Some Israeli folk song started playing through the sound system. Most of the passengers joined in singing while I fidgeted impatiently in my seat.

The soon-to-be priest closed his book and crossed himself as the aeroplane touched down and sped along the runway.

Everyone clapped as a heavy Israeli accent announced, "*Shalom*, and welcome to Israel. Please stay seated until the plane comes to a complete stop."

No one paid attention. Everyone was too busy grabbing their bags from the overhead compartments.

Once the doors opened, I walked down the stairs at Lod airport and into the bus waiting to take us to the terminal. I hung on to the strap as they crammed us in, trying not to topple over. I felt like I was coming home as we approached the terminal building, the towering, bold sign *Welcome to Israel* beckoning to me. *This is it, my final resting place.*

An hour later, my back was dripping with sweat as the taxi wound its way to the absorption centre in Carmiel, a development town nestled in the Galilee hills of northern Israel. The radio blared as the muggy, humid air blew through the cab's windows.

'Hey, mate,' I shouted above the noise. 'Is it always this hot during the winter?'

Without turning down the radio, the driver yelled, 'No, this weather is called a *hamsin*. It is a hot wind that blows from the Arab countries in the east. They send it to us many times a year. Tomorrow it will be cool.'

'Your English is good,' I said, surprised. I only knew two or three words in French, yet he was rabbiting away like there was no tomorrow.

'Thank you.'

Tilting his head, he turned the radio up even louder to concentrate on the broadcast. 'This is not good, not good at all,' he muttered.

'What's wrong?' I sat upright, the muscles in my neck tense. *Irene might have a point about the war.*

'It's Egypt, not good for us, but it will be okay. Don't worry. You see that over there? That's Carmiel.'

I followed the driver's pointing finger to a desolate street. A scattering of dirty concrete apartment buildings, two storeys high stood alongside the road. The road itself was nothing but sand, with a few dried-out eucalyptus trees lining it. I wasn't impressed. The guy in Canada had said not to expect luxury, but this was ridiculous. I'd seen slums that were more elegant.

The driver slowed to a stop.

Uneasy, I got out, paid, and then carried my suitcases to a shabby-looking building. The sign above the entrance read *Absorption Centre Office*, in Hebrew and English. A young man in a short-sleeved white shirt and khaki shorts stood outside wearing a crocheted kippa on his head and holding a clipboard.

'*Shalom*. My name is Yacov. Your name, please?'

'I'm Joe Leslie.' I shook his hand. 'The rest of the family will arrive soon.'

'Welcome. Your name in Hebrew is Yosef, so I shall call you that. Please come with me, and I will show you to your apartment.'

'Great, but I must make a call to England first.' I looked in the office's direction while making the hand gesture for the telephone.

'I am sorry, you can only call from the office tomorrow. Now, we go to your new home.'

Yacov picked up one of my cases and led the way. *Damn!* I wanted to speak with Irene. Let her know I'd arrived. I needed to hear her voice, to know she was as desperate to be with me as I was with her. I told everyone that the wife and kids hated me to travel alone, but, in truth, it was me that couldn't stand it.

There were groups of people hanging around on the pavement, talking as we passed. A few turned to me and smiled.

'*Shalom.*'

I smiled and returned the greeting. 'Shalom.'

It was nice to see friendly faces.

'Is it always like this here?' I asked Yacov.

'Yes. People like to meet up with friends in the early evening. There is not much else to do here. Our town is quite small, with two coffee shops and one cinema. If you walk straight, you'll find them all in five minutes. If you want to enjoy more, you need to go to Akko, twenty kilometres away. There is a bus once a day.'

We arrived at a building identical to the others. Up a short staircase and to the right, Yacov opened a door and then handed me the keys.

'You should lock the door because sometimes the Arabs come with a knife. It is best to be safe.'

The smell of fresh paint overpowered me as we entered the apartment. The walls had obviously just been whitewashed. There were two tiny bedrooms with wooden beds and thin mattresses. The bathroom had a shower, sink, and toilet crammed into one tiny area, and the living room was only slightly bigger, with an uncomfortable-looking sofa. You couldn't even swing a cat in the kitchen. It was deeply depressing. *Irene's not going to like this at all.*

'You get the big apartment because you have children. It is nice, no?' Yacov smiled.

I didn't know what to say.

As we sat around the small Formica table on plastic chairs, he handed me a printed sheet of paper. 'This is your schedule. You will study Hebrew at the *Ulpan* Sunday to Friday, from eight until twelve. You are free after that. The dining room next to the office is for breakfast at six-thirty, lunch at twelve-thirty, and dinner at six. On Shabbat, we also have prayers and songs. Do you have any questions?'

'Yes. Are you sure I can't make a call now?'

Yacov got up. 'I am sorry, but we only allow it during office hours.'

'I wouldn't ask if it wasn't really important, but it could be life or death.' I gave him a look of dread and covered my mouth with my hand, doing my best to make my eyes water convincingly.

'Okay,' he said and patted me on the back. 'Come now. I take you to the office, but you must make a collect call.'

Yes.

228

~ * ~

After sitting for three bloody hours on a wonky wooden chair as the teacher droned on and on in Hebrew, I thought I would drop dead of boredom. I went cross-eyed staring at the lines of scrawling, indecipherable letters and couldn't get my tongue or teeth around a single word. When the class was finally over for the day, I walked out with the others, stretching my aching legs. I wondered how Irene would handle the studies. *She would take it seriously and end up teaching me as well.* The thought of her caused pain in my gut, making me desperate for a cigarette.

One man from my class, a tall American, leaned on the wall, smoking. I joined him.

'Ulpan. How long does it take to learn Hebrew? Two weeks in, and all I can say is please and thank you. Ironic, considering the Israelis don't use them.' I laughed. 'I was standing outside the other day, minding me own business, when this young fella comes up to me and points at my cigarette and says, "Give me one." No, please. Nothing. Being a decent guy, I hand one over. The fucker just takes it and leaves.'

The American chuckled. 'So true. I can barely string a sentence together. The good news is that most Israelis speak English. Especially if you find the right place to live.'

'Where are you going after the absorption centre?'

'We're moving to Netanya. Really nice, by the sea, filled with lots of Anglos, and it's only a half-hour drive from Tel Aviv.'

'That sounds wonderful. What's the name again? Netanya?'

With nothing else to do, I figured it would be worth checking out. *Anything's better than this shit hole.*

'I'm off. See you tomorrow.'

I headed over to my new blue Peugeot. It wasn't a Jag, but it worked. I needed to be careful with funds if I wanted to bring the family over.

I drove up to the office and shouted out the window to Yacov, 'Shalom. How do I get to Netanya? Is it far?'

'No, only about an hour and a half, an easy drive. I will draw you a map.'

Driving in Israel was a challenge. They were on the wrong side of the road, and as manners were non-existent, things like indicating and slowing down didn't happen. It didn't stop them from honking every two seconds, though. It was like going out to war. You had to be alert at all times, ready for an attack.

Parking the car in Netanya's city centre, I strolled down the bright boulevard, smiling. *Now, this is more like it.* Coffee shops packed with people laughing and chatting lined the main street, and there were all kinds of stores on either side, including several bakeries. I inhaled the delicious scent of cakes and freshly baked bread as I passed by. *Irene will love this.*

I kept walking as the sun warmed my face and soon arrived at the waterfront. Leaning over the railings, I looked down at the deep blue Mediterranean Sea as it glistened and twinkled in the sunshine. Even though I wasn't quite dressed for it, I went down the steep stairs to the beach, the sand trickling into my shoes. I didn't care. When I reached the bottom, I sat myself down and watched the locals as I enjoyed the warmth of the soft sand underneath me. *This is way better than Brighton.*

I felt wonderful. The only thing missing was Irene, but I would persuade her to fly over at once. She was probably suffering, what with her parents' nagging, plus rain, sleet, and whatever the fuck else. She would jump at the chance to come here. It really was the best place on earth.

Determined to get her here as soon as possible, I leapt up and took the stairs two at a time, but I was so out of breath when I reached the top that I had to lean against the railings.

An old geezer said something to me, but I didn't understand.

'I'm sorry,' I gasped, 'but I don't speak Hebrew, only English.'

'I say, you have no air. You walked up too fast.'

I chuckled. 'I'll be okay in a minute, *todah*. That's Hebrew for thank you, right?'

The man nodded and shuffled away.

Breathing normally again, I hurried down the street until I found a real estate agency.

'Shalom.' The sales lady smiled at me.

'Do you speak English?'

'Yes. How can I help you?'

'I'm looking for an apartment for rent, three bedrooms, as soon as possible. Do you have anything available?'

Chapter Thirty-six

IRENE

London

After countless hours, the plane touched down in the wintry darkness of England. The three of us yawned, stretched and wearily collected our luggage. Once outside, I scanned the crowds of people.

'Grandma. Grandpa,' Lorraine squealed.

My heart filled as I spotted my parents waving frantically with warm, loving smiles. I parked my luggage trolley to one side and rushed over to them. Mum embraced me so tight I almost couldn't breathe. I felt a rush of warmth and safety. I'd finally come home. I hadn't realised how much I'd missed them until then.

Dad grinned, looking at the kids. 'You're all grown up. Look how tall you've got.'

Mum couldn't stop smothering them with kisses. Boris wrinkled his nose, trying to pull away, but she wasn't having it.

'Come here you. You're going to have to put up with your grandma's smooches. I'm making up for all the years you've been gone.'

Lorraine and I chuckled.

It was so good to see them. I noticed they looked smaller and a little older, but they weren't a single jot different.

We got into the car and drove to their new home. They told me that Brighton wasn't the same after we'd left for Australia, so they'd moved back to the East End, where Mum had always been happiest. The house was cosy but cramped, with only two bedrooms, so Lorraine and I shared one, and Boris slept on the sofa in the study. None of us minded too much and Mum spoiled us with all my favourite meals. I couldn't stop stuffing my mouth. It was heaven.

I realised after a few weeks that I no longer had neck and jaw pain from tension. I'd been walking around sore for so long that I'd become used to it, but once it was gone, I had a lightness in my step. I'd even stopped jumping at any little noise. For so many years, I worried constantly whether what I said or did would make Joe lose his temper. It was such a relief to be able to speak freely, about whatever I fancied and worry only about what I planned for the day.

The children seemed more relaxed too. Boris had already met up with his former pals, and Lorraine was content to stay in and read. I couldn't help but notice the change. We were so much lighter and more optimistic without Joe around. No more worrying about him and his problems. It was strange for a while, like something was missing, but settling into life without him came as a relief.

Joe had called me the day after we arrived in England, saying Israel was paradise on earth and I should fly over at once. But I was not ready to go anywhere, if at all. We needed some time to reunite with family and friends, and I needed to decide, one way or another, about our future. Joe would just have to wait. I stalled him by saying we weren't budging until he'd settled in with a job and a home, hoping it would take him time to get it all arranged. He sounded agitated, but I didn't care. I was far away. He couldn't hurt me.

I helped Mum with the household chores and spent hours simply talking with my parents. I told them about Joe's erratic moods and impulsive decisions and that I couldn't keep moving the children around the world. Dad suggested we stay with them for as long as we liked. They had certainly changed their tune. Having them on my side bolstered me, gave me strength and confirmed that I was doing the right thing.

It was a bitterly cold Saturday night, with ice and sleet covering the ground. The temperature didn't bother me as my family warmed me with love and affection, welcoming me into their arms at my aunt and uncle's golden anniversary party, held at Cohen's restaurant. The place was full to capacity with over one hundred guests at several large tables. The clinking of silverware and the hum of my raucous relatives occupied every corner of the private room.

Seeing Lorraine and Boris full of life and laughter, at ease as they reconnected with their cousins, I sat down next to my parents. Uncle Percy was, yet again, telling us how he discovered a way to hypnotise chickens by drawing a chalk line on the ground. We had all heard it many times before. Our performances of false amazement were well polished.

'Silly old goat,' my aunt whispered next to me, 'He didn't discover a thing. It's been done for generations. Psht.' She dismissed him with a wave of her hand as I hid my laugh behind my handkerchief.

Looking around at the many people, most of whom I hadn't seen since childhood, I spotted a familiar face on the far table across the room. Something about her made me shiver, but I wasn't sure who she was. Then it dawned on me as I recognised the cruel, sadistic woman with the thin, hooked nose. The wicked witch who still made me shudder after all these years. *No, I am an adult now, and it is time I tell her exactly what I think of her.*

I got up and headed over in her direction. She couldn't put me in a cupboard anymore, but I could put her in her place. I stopped in front of her as my stomach clenched. *Could this be the same woman that terrorised me?* The nose was the same, but the rest of her was barely human. Her hands were twisted into claws, and her previously thin frame looked like it could break in two as she sat in a wheelchair, staring into space.

I took a deep breath. 'Hello, Aunt Sarah. How are you?'

She didn't react. Her eyes were like sea glass, milky and opaque.

'No point trying to talk to her,' said Aunt Gladys. 'She's been away with the fairies for years since her illness. She doesn't know who anyone is. I took her out of the nursing home for today, but I suppose there was no point, really.'

'Oh, that's sad.' I meant it in a warped kind of way. As horrible as she was, I wouldn't wish such a thing on anyone. Still, I was angry as I returned to my table. I would never get the chance to stand up for the little girl that had suffered at her hands.

As I sat down, Uncle Morris, my dad's brother, stood up and cleared his throat. 'Thank you all for coming to celebrate this very special day with my dear Rachel and me. She has given me fifty years of joy. Without her, I would be only half a man. Thank you, Rachel, my love.'

Fifty years of wedded bliss. I couldn't imagine Joe and me lasting that long. My eyes filled with tears. Holding them back, I sipped my orange juice while listening to the animated conversations around me.

The man opposite offered me a plate of blintzes. 'Would you like one?' His voice was deep, his accent refined. He looked to be in his mid-forties, with greying sideburns. He was attractive in a British sort of way. I had no idea who he was. No one had bothered to introduce me, though he had been glancing over throughout the evening.

'No, thank you.' I smiled at him. 'Not really hungry, I'm afraid.'

'Well, that is a shame. I always enjoy good food.' He gestured to the empty seat next to me, wanting to move closer. 'I'm Samuel.'

After nodding my agreement, he pulled out the chair.

'Nice to meet you, Samuel. I'm Irene. Who are you related to? I've not seen you before.'

He chuckled warmly. 'I'm not part of the family. I am Morris and Rachel's doctor. They insisted I come and join their celebration.'

'How lovely. I hope you are enjoying yourself.'

He looked to the corner of the room where several men were standing with drinks in their hands. 'Which one is your husband?'

I felt my face get hot, although I wasn't sure why. 'Oh, he's not here. He's abroad at the moment.' My body tensed.

The waiters placed more pastries on the table, and arms desperately reached over to grab them.

Laughing, I leaned into Samuel and whispered, 'You would think the poor things hadn't eaten for ages.'

'Nothing wrong with a good appetite,' he said with a smile.

We spoke for some time: about his love of museums and how he spent his weekends strolling around, contemplating all the wonderful works of art.

'Do you like the arts, by any chance? Personally, I cannot get enough and have season tickets to the Royal Ballet.'

My face lit up. 'How wonderful. I adore ballet. I studied it when I was a child. Actually, I became a dancer while we were in Australia. Not ballet, but modern jazz. Dancing is my favourite thing in the world,' I said shyly.

'Then you must accompany me to the next performance.'

My heart skipped a beat.

He moved closer. 'I do enjoy talking to you. I hope I don't sound too forward, but there is a charming tea house that I like to visit on the weekends. Perhaps you might do me the honour of joining me tomorrow afternoon?'

I smiled. 'Thank you for the invitation, but I'm not sure I should.'

He cleared his throat. 'Just as friends, of course, nothing more. Two people enjoying a pleasant conversation.'

Samuel was everything that Joe wasn't: sophisticated, cultured, educated, and, based on the expensive-looking suit he was wearing, quite well-to-do. As enticing as he was, I knew I shouldn't go out with him. I was a married woman. It was wrong, but I wanted a chance to spend time with someone who treated me with respect. I deserved it. Besides, it was purely innocent. What harm could it do?

Chapter Thirty-seven

JOE

Israel

I sat in Yacov's office, trying to get him to understand.

'You're not hearing me mate. I can't learn the bloody language. I just don't have a head for it.'

'But Yosef,' he placed his palms on the desk and leaned towards me, 'you need to give it more time. You have only studied for two weeks. You need a minimum of three months. Otherwise, you cannot get a job if you don't speak Hebrew.'

'Don't worry. I'll be fine.' I stood up and reached in my pocket. 'Now here are the keys to the flat, and thanks for everything.'

'Please, Yosef. You need to think about this.' he said as I picked up my suitcase and went to the door.

'Shalom Yacov. Thank you.' I headed out to the car. *Netanya, here I come.*

Compared to how I'd lived in the last few weeks, the new flat I'd rented was a colossal improvement. That whole absorption centre business was crap. I don't know, maybe I was spoilt, but any more of that and I would've done meself in.

Netanya was something else. I could smell the sea air from the balcony, and the entire place was full of light. I had to wait at home for a delivery of some temporary furniture that the lady in the real estate office had helped me arrange, but once it arrived, I felt right at home. It wasn't cheap, and I worried I wouldn't have enough money to get by if I didn't get a job soon, but I would get that sorted. I had to.

After finding out where the main offices were, I drove to Tel Aviv and met with Yossi Cohen, the head of the Israeli broadcasting association.

It had been absurdly easy to get an appointment.

I sat down in his office, crossed one leg neatly over the other, and grinned.

'I've just moved to Israel, and I'm ready to start work.'

He stared back at me. 'Do you have any experience?'

'Experience?' I laughed. 'Where do I start?' I was a bit insulted. He should've realised a star was sitting in front of him, but he soon came to his senses when I rattled off all my previous productions, his face going from blank to flushed and eager in a second.

'You trained in London?'

'Of course.'

'You can go track forward, track back?'

'Yeah. Obviously.' I snorted, rolling my eyes.

He smiled, showing pearly white teeth. 'How soon can you start?'

I walked out of there whistling. It was all going my way. I had a flat and a job. It was time to call my wife and let her know she could come on over.

Back home, I sat on the new sofa, held the telephone to my ear and lit a cigarette, waiting for the international operator to connect us. My foot tapped the floor until, at last, Irene came on the line.

'Hello?'

'Irene, darling, how are you? Everything is great. Listen, doll. It's all working out. I went down to the TV station, and they hired me. You wouldn't believe how thrilled they were to have a talent like yours truly.' I flicked my cigarette towards the ashtray. 'I'm on salary, and they're giving me an assistant to translate everything. I start tomorrow on a show, some folky music thing. Oh, and guess what? Got us a lovely flat in a wonderful seaside town called Netanya. You can walk to the beach in a few minutes. You're going to love it. Go to the travel agent today and book your tickets, and I'll see you in a few days.'

Silence.

I frowned. *Why isn't she saying anything?*

'Irene? Are you there?'

'Yes … Joe … I am.'

I huffed. 'You don't bloody well sound too excited over all this great news.'

'I need to think about it.'

'What do you mean? What's to think about? Get your arse and the kids on the plane. I'll be waiting.' I clenched my jaw.

'No. We are not ready. You have to give us more time.'

'Time? I went and got it all arranged, and you're giving me conditions. Fuck that. Come here. Now!'

'I've got to go. I'm sorry. We can talk in a few days.'

She hung up.

My heart raced as I threw the telephone at the wall. Sliding to the floor, I cradled my head in my arms. *This doesn't sound good. Not good at all.*

~ * ~

A couple of weeks later, I sat in the control booth at the television studios in Herzliya, studying the monitor in front of me.

'Zoom in, camera one. Fuck. Zoom in.' I shouted into the headset.

'What's the matter with these guys?' I said to my crew sitting next to me.

Jumping out of my seat, I stepped out of the booth and charged into the studio, heading straight over to Shlomo, the cameraman. Slinging my arm over his shoulder, I pulled him close. 'Listen, mate, when I say zoom in, I mean zoom in, not stay on mid-shot.'

Shlomo shook his head. 'I do not think it is a good idea. Better to stay mid-shot on the singer.'

'What!' I shouted. 'Are you telling the director, me, how to direct? That's not your job. You know what? You're fired. Fuck off.'

The producer came running over. 'Joe, what are you doing?'

'What am I doing? This guy is not following directions and dares to tell me what to do, so I fired him.'

He pulled me aside and whispered urgently, 'You cannot fire him.'

'What do you mean?' I hissed.

'We don't have another cameraman.'

I shook my head in amazement. This obviously wasn't the BBC. 'No other cameramen? What type of television studio is this?'

The producer and floor staff stared at me blankly.

'What the hell. Okay, I'm going back.'

Ettie, my young and pretty assistant, was waiting for me when I returned to the booth. 'Can we finish the show? I'm hungry.' Her red lips parted in a wide smile.

Laughing, I lit another cigarette and sat down in my chair. Ettie was button cute and deadly sexy with her tight, short skirt and long eyelashes. She took away my anger in an instant. *What does it matter if we lack cameramen? I have a job in TV, paying me good money. To hell with anything else.*

The show I was directing wasn't exactly my cup of tea. Some musical trio singing about the hills of Jerusalem and stuff like that. Gone were the exciting days of pop groups and loud music, but it was a job, and I would do my best because I was a pro.

'Okay, camera one, do what you want. Let's just get this over with.'

With the day's production done, I had nothing else to do but return to the empty apartment. I wasn't sure when Irene and the kids would come. She'd ignored all of my calls. Another few days and I would send a telegram telling her to call me urgently.

Ettie sashayed past.

'Want to come out for falafel?'

'Well, I'm not sure what that is, but it sounds tempting. Where are we going?'

She smiled. 'It is food. I come in your car and show you the way. Not too far.'

Ettie waved to a few crew members as we walked to the parking lot. She was a friendly girl. I noticed some blokes checking her out, then smiling at me as though I'd won a prize.

Directing me through the town, Ettie chatted on as we drove along the main highway.

'I was born in Tel Aviv, but my parents immigrated from Yemen.'

'Wow. I never even knew there were Jews in that part of the world.'

'Yes, many, but they came here for a better life. To be safe.'

'Yeah. Away from the fucking goys, right? I know all about that. That's why I came here.'

Ettie laughed. 'I think the life my parents lived in Yemen was a little different from yours in England or Australia.'

After about ten minutes, she gestured to a group of cars lined up on a sandy road by the waterfront.

'Park anywhere.'

Ettie found us a seat at the Mifgash Hafalafel restaurant, a shabby hut with wooden folding chairs and tables outside. Most of them were occupied.

I looked around. 'This isn't exactly the Ritz.'

'This is the best in Israel. Sit down. I will bring you the food.'

I did as I was told and gazed out at the ocean. The sun was setting, the sky a glorious orange with red streaks. There was a lot of noise from the other tables. The sounds of families eating and laughing surrounded me, making me painfully aware that my own family was absent. *I wonder what the kids are doing. They must hate being suffocated by Manny and Pearl.* I knew I was a fun, hip dad, letting them do whatever they wanted. Unless they made a racket, then I gave them one. I bet they missed me like crazy.

I couldn't understand what was going on with Irene. *Why won't she do what I ask?* It was really pissing me off, and I hated the evenings at home all alone, with nothing to do but chain smoke.

Ettie returned holding what looked like a kind of bread pocket filled with strange-looking brown balls and a sauce poured on top. It didn't look tempting to me, more like a specimen you might need to take to the doctor.

'Here, eat. You will love this.'

'What is it?'

'I don't know what it is in English, but it is healthy and tastes so good.'

'I don't usually put anything in me mouth that I can't identify, but in this case, I'll make an exception.' I winked at her, and she giggled.

With some hesitation, I took a bite. It was bloody good. Turned out I liked pita bread stuffed with falafel, salad, and tahini. I tucked into my food with relish, realising I hadn't eaten much in the last few days.

Ettie joined in.

'You know, you are a handsome man. Where is your wife? Why is she not with you?'

'She's coming over soon, just visiting her parents in London.' I tried to keep the agitation out of my voice.

'If I were her, I would not leave you alone for one second. Some other woman could take you away.' She batted her eyelashes as she picked up her napkin and wiped the sauce away from the corner of my mouth.

Why can't bloody Irene appreciate me the way Ettie does? She better watch out, or I might have to replace her with someone who values me.

'How do you say, I think I love you, in Hebrew?' I asked with a sly smile.

Chapter Thirty-eight

IRENE

London

The tea parlour was hung with soft yellow curtains at the painted sash windows. Silver bowls filled with cream and jam were arranged on the lace tablecloth, ready to be spread on our scones. Samuel sat opposite me and, on that first outing, we talked endlessly about art and museums. I thoroughly enjoyed myself.

On our second excursion, we went for a stroll in Regent's Park. Even though it was a cloudy day, walking with Samuel, with all his gentlemanly charm, made me feel like the sun had come out. As we walked along, I told him about life in Melbourne, the pool parties, dancing on the TV show, and how everything was so laid back. He seemed to listen to my every word. I couldn't remember being able to talk so much without being interrupted.

On our third meeting, we went out for dinner at a very expensive-looking restaurant, and over our boeuf bourguignon, he asked me about my marriage. I was reluctant at first, but with his gradual coaxing, I began the story of a young girl in awe of a famous actor. Once I got talking, it was as though the gates had opened, and I poured my heart out, even telling him about Joe's temper and the violence.

Part of me felt disloyal to Joe, but the other part enjoyed seeing Samuel's shocked face.

'That man should be in jail. What he has done to you is atrocious.' He took my arm and lightly stroked the burn scars. 'You deserve to be treated with the utmost kindness. His behaviour is unforgivable. You are terribly brave.'

Moved by his compassion, I almost burst into tears.

243

'I know we've only just met, but sometimes one knows when it's right. I know you are unsure whether to remain in England.' He leaned closer, looking into my eyes. 'Please don't go. I would love to get to know you and your children better.'

'I … oh.' I didn't know what to say.

'If it is too crowded at your parent's residence, you are welcome to stay with me. After my wife died, I was left alone in an enormous house with a lot of empty rooms. It would give me immense pleasure to have it full of laughter and joy again. All proper and above board, of course. I will behave like a perfect gentleman.'

I smiled, speechless, but flattered, nonetheless.

'Thank you. That's ever so generous. We are fine at my parents' house, but I shall certainly keep it in mind.'

Straightening the napkin on my lap, I changed the subject. 'Does anyone ever call you Sam? I cannot imagine they would.'

'Absolutely not. I am Samuel and always will be.'

The time passed, and I was sorry to see that I needed to get home.

We stood outside my parents' house.

'This has been the most enjoyable evening. I do hope I can see you again very soon,' he said, looking into my eyes. I looked back, taking in the calm warmth that shone from them. It was mesmerising.

'Yes,' I said eventually, 'that would be nice. I look forward to it.'

I spent a lot of time in bed that night thinking about Samuel. I wanted to keep seeing him. He made me feel special, not asking for anything except my company, but an uneasy feeling of guilt cut through my stomach. *I'm not doing anything wrong, am I? No, it's all innocent. It is.*

We went to the cinema the following evening to see the new film *Cabaret*. As I sat in the darkened movie theatre, enchanted by the actors and singers on the screen, I felt Samuel's hand touching mine. I wasn't sure if I liked it or not. I moved my hand away. If there wasn't any touching, then I wasn't doing anything wrong.

As the weeks passed, we fell into a pattern of meeting almost every day.

Mum was ecstatic, encouraging me to keep seeing him. 'What a catch Samuel is, and he wants you, my beautiful daughter. I have never been happier.'

'I'm still married to Joe, don't forget.'

'Married.' She waved dismissively. 'To what? A brute of a man that cannot give you a stable home. You need to be concerned about having a comfortable life, and Samuel is just the one to fit the bill.'

The next time Samuel arrived to take me out, I introduced the kids to him. Although he was very polite and shook their hands, they didn't seem to be too pleased. Lorraine hurried upstairs, while Boris refused his handshake and walked away. I was sure they were just being loyal to Joe. I knew I should be too, but I was having too much fun.

Every time I saw Samuel, he always brought up the subject of moving into his house. I turned him down each time. I just wanted to enjoy being courted.

'Irene, your friend is here,' Mum shouted.

I proceeded downstairs. Samuel stood waiting for me in his three-piece suit, his hair neatly combed. I smiled as he kissed my cheek.

'Hello, Samuel.'

I turned to Mum. 'Please make sure the children are in bed by eleven. I'm certain I won't be much later than that myself.'

We walked outside and over to Samuel's Bentley. He was such a gentleman, holding the car door open for me. I could never remember Joe doing anything like that, even when I was nine months pregnant.

We drove maybe fifteen minutes from my parent's home before Samuel pulled into a long, elegant driveway lined with well-maintained trees. He jumped out, went around to my side, and opened the door.

'Madam, your new home,' he said with a flourish.

I laughed. 'I haven't decided yet. You need to be patient.'

'Oh, I am, but once you see this place, I am sure you will agree.'

Stepping out of the car, I gasped. I'd visited many lavish homes but none like this. The house was massive. The brick was a rich red and covered in ivy. Huge pillars framed the wide walkway in front of the solid wood doors, which had a large brass lion door knocker.

Samuel held out his arm for me to take. 'My lady, I hope it is to your liking.'

I looked up and marvelled at the ceiling as we entered the grand foyer. It reminded me of Sheila's home, but this place made hers look like a cheap imitation.

'There are eight bedrooms, plenty of space for your children, and the master suite has its own floor. Allow me to show you around.'

It was enchanting. Every bed had big fluffy duvets, fine lacy curtains adorned the windows, and there was a different colour scheme for each room. It was like something out of a Country Houses magazine. Living in such a palace would be a dream come true.

'My family has lived here for over a hundred years, since the 1860s, after they immigrated from Germany. I come from a long line in the medical profession. My great grandfather was famous and made his fortune by attending to Europe's aristocrats.'

I was impressed. That was quite different from my ancestry. As far as I knew, my parents were born in the East End. Their parents had been poor farmers from Poland who came to England for a better life. I remembered my old grandmother, who we called Bubba, sitting in the kitchen, wearing dark clothes and a scarf on her head. She always seemed depressed. Before taking a single bite of food, she would softly recite the ancient prayers to herself. She hardly spoke English but conversed in Yiddish, which I didn't understand. Bubba died when I was a small girl, just before the war. I think she was the reason Mum always had a fierce determination that we would never be penniless.

Samuel put his hand on my shoulder. 'We can get a cook, a maid, anything you might need. So, what do you think, my dear?'

'I think I'm in love,' I said in awe.

'I hope it's not only the house. Perhaps a little with me as well?'

'Perhaps a little.' I murmured with a smile, as my bond with Joe slipped further away.

We sat down to wine and cheese in the pale green drawing room. After some time, I decided I didn't want to wear out my welcome.

'Samuel, thank you so much for a lovely evening, but it's time for me to go home.'

It was a quiet journey. I had a lot to think about. Samuel, with his class, breeding, and grand home, made me look at my life with Joe. I still hadn't decided if I would go over to Israel, but I knew for the foreseeable future that I wanted to stay put and not make any rash decisions. Returning to England had been the right choice.

I arrived back to find the children still up.

'Hi, darlings. Where's Grandma and Grandpa?'

Lorraine didn't look up from the TV. 'They went to bed.'

I sank down onto the big comfy sofa and removed my shoes. 'I would like to speak with you both. Can you please turn off the television?'

Boris groaned. 'We're in the middle of a show. Can't it wait?'

'No, it can't. Switch it off,' I demanded.

They did as they were told, but not without frowning.

I looked at my children, paused a minute, and then took the plunge.

'What do you think about staying here for the time being? I know you both weren't too happy about moving to Israel, so why don't we give England a chance?'

'For how long?' Lorraine asked, biting her lip.

'A while.' I gave her my most encouraging smile.

'So, when's dad coming back?' Boris asked.

'Not right now. He's busy with work.' I hated lying to the children. 'Anyway, we can stay with Grandma and Grandpa a while longer and see what happens after that.'

Boris turned the TV back on. Apparently, the conversation was over.

I stood up, grabbed my shoes, and went upstairs to my bedroom. I had so many things to think about and decide. *Is Samuel the one? Yes, he's classy, refined, a doctor, but Joe has been my life for so many years. He's the father of my children and has been my everything, and also my nothing. If I divorce him, the kids and I can have stability with Samuel, but is it right? Oh, I just don't know.*

I tossed and turned most of the night, trying to make sense of my life as images of Aunt Sarah, Dad, Joe, and even John appeared in my head. My anger bubbled over. *I have had enough of being dictated to, burned, strapped, and put in cupboards, all by people who have taken advantage of my insecurities.*

In the early hours of the morning, as I watched the grey light of dawn filter through the window, I made my decision. From then on, it was easy. I spoke to Samuel, who put me in touch with a solicitor so I could start divorce proceedings that week. Then, I called Joe. The conversation was short.

The following day, he rang me. His voice was icy and had the nasty tone I knew so well.

'You want a divorce? Fine, give me the kids,' he stated.

'What?' I said, shocked. 'You don't mean that!'

'Oh yes, I do.'

'You wouldn't be able to handle them. You never have. What makes you think now will be any different?'

'That's not your business. I'll wait for your answer.'

I lost it. *How dare he try to manipulate me like this?*

'My solicitor will let you know. Goodbye.' I hung up the phone and bit my nails. *Damn!*

Mum wasn't deterred when I told her about the phone call that evening. 'Let's look at the worst-case scenario. The children are practically grown. If they go to Israel, you will have more time to be a wonderful wife to Samuel. It would give you a chance to entertain, throw extravagant parties, really *enjoy* life for the first time.'

'How can you say that? I love my children. I couldn't bear not being with them,' I said, horrified at the idea.

Mum exhaled. 'Stop being so dramatic. The time has come for you to really start living. If anyone deserves it, it's you.'

Boris appeared in the doorway, fully dressed and pulling on his jacket.

'Where are you going? It's bedtime.'

'Jeez, mum, I'm not a kid. I'm going out for a bit.' He waved me off.

'Oh no, you are not, young man. Go to your room right now.'

'Get stuffed,' he yelled, his contorted face a mirror image of his father. He darted out the front door, slamming it behind him.

I burst into tears.

Mum put her arms around me. 'You see, darling. It will be easier without them.'

~ * ~

The weeks turned into months since we had been back in England, and Mum still couldn't stop going on about Samuel.

'He is all the things that Joe is not,' Mum exclaimed once again, after taking an enormous vase of perfect white roses from the delivery boy and placing them on the hall table.

Snatching the card attached, she read aloud, '*Dearest Irene, these are to match your beauty. Samuel.*'

She stood back to admire the beautiful flowers. 'What a gentleman he is. You have finally come to your senses and got yourself a proper man. Now, why is this divorce taking so long? You need to hurry up so we can start planning your wedding.' Her eyes lit up.

I lifted my hands in the air. Sometimes she was just too much. 'What's the matter with you? Samuel hasn't even proposed. Don't you think you're jumping the gun?'

'Nonsense. It's just a matter of time. Play your cards right, and he'll be popping the question before you can blink.'

She put her face in the flowers and breathed in deeply.

Samuel invited me to his house a few days later. When I arrived, he ushered me into the dining room, where elegant red and gold plates were laid out beautifully on the large oak table. A matching vase filled with roses— deep red this time — stood in the centre, and on either side, a pair of crystal candlesticks with long red candles cast a soft glow as classical music resonated throughout the room.

Samuel pulled out my chair, and I sat down. *What is going on?*

Sitting opposite me, he picked up a silver bell and shook it. A young woman wearing a white, lace-bordered apron walked in.

Samuel nodded to her. 'You can tell the chef we are ready for our soup.'

I watched her leave, then turned to Samuel. 'Well, this is quite a surprise. A chef? A waitress? How did you arrange it?'

He smiled. 'Not a waitress, a maid, and it's just for tonight, but it can be permanent. I would move mountains for you.'

Taking the silver holder, I pulled out the napkin and placed it on my lap, listening with appreciation to the beautiful violin strings reverberating from the record player.

'You are amazing,' I said.

He blew me a kiss, and I smiled, feeling like a princess.

The maid returned with a silver tureen and a large ladle, filling my bowl with a mouth-watering French onion soup.

'Bon appetite,' Samuel said.

I picked up my spoon and tried a mouthful. It had to be one of the best soups I'd ever tasted. 'This is incredible. I want the recipe.'

Samuel laughed. 'Don't eat too much. There are plenty more dishes on the way.'

After gorging myself silly on roast lamb, crispy potatoes, and vegetables, I sat back, too full to move. Samuel refilled my wineglass, and as I sipped, I listened to his soothing voice.

'A new art gallery recently opened in the West End. I would love us to go and see what paintings they have for sale. Maybe I could add to my collection.'

When the crème brulée was brought in, Samuel moved next to me.

'I can't eat any more. I'm going to explode.' I chuckled.

'Take your time, but before that, there is something I wish to ask you.'

My eyes widened as he got out of his chair, dropped to one knee, and took my hand.

'My dearest Irene, I have loved you from the moment we met. Will you do me the honour of becoming my wife?' He removed a small box from his jacket pocket and opened it. Inside was an enormous sparkling diamond ring. I had never seen anything so beautiful.

'Please say yes,' he begged.

I beamed. My smile couldn't have been bigger, but it soon faded as Joe's face appeared in my head. My mind swam.

'Oh, Samuel, I don't know what to say. I'm still married.'

'I know, but if you say yes, I will put the ring away until the time comes for you to wear it.' He cupped my chin and looked straight at me. 'Now, please tell me what I want to hear.'

Why am I hesitating? If I say yes, I can have the ring, the house, the stability, and everything Mum wants for me. But what about me? What do I want? I bit my lip. 'Can I think about it?'

'If you must,' he said. Standing up, he pocketed the ring and, with a sigh, went back to his original seat opposite me.

We ate the rest of our meal in silence.

I panicked as we drove to my house. I could see he wasn't pleased by the thin line of his mouth. I desperately hoped I hadn't humiliated him. I didn't want to lose him and all his finery, leaving me with nothing but a dream of what could have been.

'Samuel,' I whispered, 'please understand. I'm not saying no. I just need a bit of time. It's all so sudden. Please say you will be patient, just for a while.'

He cleared his throat. 'I would be lying if I said I am not disappointed, but I will respect your decision for now.'

The initial relief at his acknowledgement faded as I sat back and stared out of the dark window. His last words rolled around my head. *I will respect your decision. For now.*

Chapter Thirty-nine

JOE

Israel

The furniture had finally arrived from England. We'd left it in storage when we moved to Melbourne, and I'd called a friend to get it sent over. I was proud of myself for unpacking everything all on my own. *No one can accuse me of being lazy.*

The flat looked perfect. There was comfort in having familiar things close by, like my desk, books, and ashtrays. I placed Irene's make-up table and chair in the bedroom, and our lovely, comfortable bed filled the rest of the room. Looking at it prompted a flood of memories from the old days. I smiled as I remembered how Irene, the dogs, and I would cuddle in that bed, lazing on a Sunday morning. I couldn't wait for her to arrive, then I could set about getting another dog or two. *Do they have bulldogs in Israel? Jewish bulldogs. Ha!*

The first day I moved into the new flat, the front door swung open, and a complete stranger walked in. As he shook my hand, I made a mental note to keep the door locked in the future.

'I am Menachem. I live upstairs.' He pointed to the ceiling. 'Nice place. How much you pay?'

Later, another family on the third floor, directly above me, invited me in for a delicious dinner of roast chicken and potatoes.

'Where is your family?' the man asked.

'Oh, they'll be coming over soon.'

The lady of the house said, 'Maybe your wife does not come so fast because she finds a better man in England.'

They all laughed. I didn't find it funny.

'Don't be silly. She knows I'm the best,' I bragged, trying to keep the doubt out of my tone.

The woman started fussing over me. 'Maybe if you brush your hair and take a shower, she will come over quicker.'

I worried she was saying I smelled, but that couldn't have been the case as they all hugged me when I was at the door saying goodnight. Besides, they invited me back many times after that. Still, I wasn't going to take any chances, so I'd gone out and bought the strongest deodorant I could find. With the intense humidity, one needed to be prepared.

My wife still hadn't arrived. We'd had a deal. Once I had a flat and job, the plan was for her and the kids to come over, but it had been months already. She never seemed to be available when I called, and I needed her to know what I thought. On top of that, she ignored the telegram I'd sent, demanding that she ring me. In all honesty, I was a touch shaken up. *What if she doesn't come back? Nah, that can't happen. Can it?*

I'd recently had a phone line put in. From what I understood, phones were rare, but I had learnt a new word in Hebrew, *protecksia*, which came in handy. It meant if you knew someone who knew someone, it could open doors. As it turned out, Ettie had a cousin married to someone in the phone company, who pulled some strings, and voila— I was the proud owner of a new telephone. Unfortunately, it came at a price. Having the only phone in the entire block of flats, my doorbell chimed several times a day with neighbours asking to make a call, always for emergencies. *How many bloody emergencies can there be in one building, for Christ's sake?* I chuckled as I remembered my pleas to Yacov on the day I arrived at the absorption centre. Life or death, I'd said. I let them use the phone.

That morning, I'd raced to answer the ringing, hoping it was Irene. No such luck. It was some old geezer demanding to speak to the lady in apartment three— another "emergency"— I didn't bother to rush when the phone rang again. I was sure it wasn't for me.

'Shalom. What is your emergency? Which apartment do you need?' I asked politely.

'Joe? Is that you?'

A wave of relief washed over me.

'Irene, me luv, how are you? I've been waiting to hear from you for so long. Are you ready? Did you buy the tickets? When do I pick you up from the airport?'

'Joe, I need to tell you something.' Her voice sounded frosty. 'I want a divorce,'

My pulse was racing so fast that I thought I was having another heart attack. 'What? Irene, you don't know what you are saying. What divorce? Don't be an idiot. Stop this nonsense right now and get yourselves on the fucking plane already,'

Irene sighed heavily. 'You are not hearing me. I am serious. My solicitor will contact you regarding the divorce. Goodbye.'

The phone went dead.

What the fuck? I shook my head, trying to make sense of what had just happened. *She can't mean it. She's just gone bonkers for a moment. She'll call back, saying it was a mistake.*

I stood next to the phone, hands on hips, waiting for it to ring. A voice sounded in my head. *She's not going to call. She's serious this time, and you know it. You've gone too far, pushed her over the edge. There's no going back.*

I paced the room, taking deep breaths while trying to steady my trembling hands. My eyes stung something horrid. Dad's voice continued in my head. *Don't be a sissy.*

'Fuck off,' I shouted to the empty room. *I won't cry. No fucking way.* But it was too late. The tears poured out of me like Niagara Falls.

'No. Irene. No,' I sobbed, my chest heaving as I fell to my knees. 'Please come here. I need you. I'm sorry. Please.'

Unable to stand the pain, I swallowed three Valium, praying they'd kick in before I did something I'd regret. Drained and weak, I lay on the floor, rubbing my stinging eyes.

And then, in an instant, something changed in me. Yes! I knew what the problem was. Her fucking parents. *It's all their fault, brainwashing her against me.* The heat rose from my chest to my face. Furious, I jumped up and hurled a coffee cup across the room. It shattered against the wall.

As I looked at the broken pieces scattered on the floor, coffee seeping into the rug, I felt the anger melting away. Sighing, I bent down to pick it up, but my legs gave way, and I collapsed to the ground. That's where we slept that night, the cup and I, broken into a thousand pieces.

Sitting on the balcony a few weeks later, I smoked a cigarette as sweat trickled down my back. It didn't matter how many showers I took, the minute I came out and dried myself, boom, wet again. I mostly wore nothing but a towel wrapped around my waist when I was at home. I looked down at the street below, watching people walk by, greeting their friends as they strolled along. Israelis were so loud, such a difference from the reserved English. I could be myself here and not worry about what anyone thought of me.

After that awful crying episode— which scared the living daylights out of me— I decided to get a grip. I would never be a sissy like that again. Once was enough.

I missed Irene so much it hurt, but at the same time, I wanted to bloody strangle her. *How dare she turn away from me? No one rejects Joe Leslie. No one.* I told her if she wanted a divorce, she would have to give me the children. I knew she would never let them go, so she'd have no choice but to join them. *Problem solved.*

Until then, I had Ettie catering to my needs. She was devoted to me and knew how to look after a man. After that first meal we'd had together on the beach, she was always ready to join me for a bite. That suited me fine; I hated being alone. She was all over me by the second meal. Being a man, I couldn't refuse her advances. She knew I was married, but it didn't seem to put her off. I told her point blank that my wife would be coming over in a short while, but as time went on, she saw that wasn't happening.

I liked Ettie, with her thick black hair and dark eyes. Sure, she wasn't as good looking as Irene, but if a man couldn't eat steak, he would have to make do with some chicken. Ettie was always full of energy and would do anything I asked. I just had to say 'neck', and she'd stand behind me and massage away all the tension. She would even come over to cook a meal and clean the place up, but as amazing as she was, she wasn't Irene. There were times when I felt guilty at her attentions. I knew I couldn't give her what she really wanted, a husband. Still, we had good times, enjoyed each other's company and she reassured me that she was happy.

Later that day, we went to the Be'tehavon Inn. Everything social in Israel revolved around food. If I wasn't at somebody's house for dinner, I was at one of the outside coffee bars or at a restaurant. I loved it.

'How do you pronounce this again?' I pointed to the dish in front of me.

Ettie laughed. 'Hummus.'

'Hoommouss?'

'No, Joe. You must make the "Ch" sound in your throat.'

'Bloody hell, it seems you have to smoke three packs a day to speak the language. Choooo mooos.'

'You are so funny. Maybe that is why I love you.' Ettie grinned.

My face froze. *Love me? She loves me? No, no, that's not good. Love is for Irene only.*

'Joe, you okay?' Ettie looked concerned.

'Listen, luv. I think you are a smashing girl, lots of fun, and I really like you, especially your tits.' I chanced a brief glance at her chest before I saw the hurt in her eyes. 'Now, don't look sad. I didn't mean that, though they are great.' I winked. 'Look, we work together, and it would complicate things if we got all lovey-dovey. Know what I mean?'

She didn't look too happy. Her dark brows furrowed and she folded her hands in her lap.

I panicked. I didn't want her getting in a huff and leaving me all alone. I couldn't stand that. I did my best to rescue the situation.' I mean, we're friends, right? Let's just stay how we are for now. We can talk about it another time.'

Ettie seemed to accept this and returned to her food with a shrug. 'Okay, Joe. For now. And then we shall see.'

I breathed a silent sigh of relief.

I needed time to change Irene's mind. Make her come to her senses and fly over with the kids. Until then, I would let Ettie and her youthful body fill the void.

Chapter Forty

IRENE

London

Samuel's house had such elegance, such class. It was everything I could have ever wanted and more. Butterflies filled my stomach. *This could all be mine.*

I was finding it hard to separate my own feelings from Mum's, who didn't let up about his wealth and breeding. It was confusing, but I decided to give Samuel a chance and take it one step at a time.

A few weeks after Samuel proposed, I laid across the red velvet chaise lounge in the living room, a box of exquisite chocolatier's truffles balanced on my lap. Samuel sat opposite, pouring the tea. He placed a cup on the side table next to me.

'Enjoying the chocolates, dearest?'

'Oh yes, delicious. Thank you.' I bit into another one, enjoying the feeling of it melting on my tongue. *Strawberry, my favourite.*

'I thought they may not be to your liking. You have left a lot half-eaten in the box.'

I laughed. 'You'll think I'm silly, but I saw this movie once. Can't remember the name, but the woman in it was ever so rich. She always took a small bite out of each chocolate and left the rest. To me, that was the height of luxury, and I always wanted the opportunity to do the same.'

Samuel chuckled.

Putting his cup down, he moved over to me, sliding my legs onto his lap. I shivered as he caressed my feet but let him continue, despite feeling like spiders were crawling over me. Inch by inch, his hands crept up my legs, onto my thighs and under my dress.

Panicking, I stood up, smoothing my clothes. 'It's late.'

'You're always running off,' he said. His tone was suddenly harsher. His frown was one of genuine displeasure.

'I need to get home. My children are waiting.' Refusing to look at him, I stepped into my shoes.

'Calm down. The children are with your parents. You must stop fussing over them. They are not babies anymore.' His voice was softer. 'Now, allow me to give you a lovely foot rub. I promise to behave myself.' With mournful eyes, he held his hands up in surrender.

I didn't know why his touch repulsed me. Even though I craved affection, something about him made my skin crawl. I couldn't understand it. I was fond of Samuel, and him being so sophisticated and well-to-do should've turned me on, but it had the opposite effect. *Maybe I can overcome it?*

With a slight nod to indicate the end of my internal debate, I removed my shoes, sat back down, and placed my stocking-covered feet back on his lap. He kneaded my prominent arches before moving on to my toes and the soles of my feet. I tried to enjoy it. *Joe would have never done this*. He always demanded that I rub his neck. It never crossed his mind to ask if I would like a massage as well.

'Isn't this nice, my lovely lady? Enjoy the sensation.' His deep and soothing voice calmed me, and I relaxed into the soft cushions at my back. His hands stroked my ankles as they worked their way up my legs. Soon they were past my knees, creeping up towards my thighs again.

I stiffened. 'Please stop. It's wrong.'

'I just want you to feel pleasure.' His voice was gentle. 'Of course, if it's not what you want, then might you allow me a little enjoyment?'

'What do you mean?' I asked.

'I want you to stand up in front of me. I promise not to touch you. Go on, be a good girl and do what I say.' His commanding tone didn't allow any refusal.

I sat up. 'I don't understand.'

'I just want to look at you, that's all,' he coaxed.

I hesitated a moment. It was a strange request but seemed harmless enough and I needed to please him. A man like Samuel didn't come along every day. If I refused him, he might leave, and I would never hear the end of it from Mum.

Taking a deep breath, I stood in front of him.

'Good girl,' he muttered while looking me up and down. 'Now, take off your dress.'

'Excuse me? I'm not doing that.' I crossed my arms over my chest.

'For me, you will.' Sternness coloured his tone. 'Come on, dearest, show me. I must look at your beauty.' His eyes were dark and threatening.

Fear shot through me as I stared at him, trying to comprehend what was happening. *I could leave now, but that would be the end of this house, this life, this dream. The end to a future where the kids and I live in stability and comfort, never having to worry about money anymore. If I try and leave, will he hurt me?*

I chewed on my lip, uncertain. Mum's voice popped into my head. *Just do what he says and get it over with.*

With resolve set in my shoulders, I lifted my dress over my head. Placing it on the chair, I stood before him in my black lacy bra and matching underwear.

Samuel's voice was husky and low. 'You are so beautiful.' He looked at me with such reverence.

I smiled, rather liking his adoration.

'Now, remove your bra. Show me your breasts. I know they will be delicious.' Samuel licked his lips.

Why not? I undid the clasp, freeing my breasts.

'Perfection, as I suspected. Now, my dearest, take off your knickers. I want to see it all.'

I had never stood completely exposed in front of a man before. When Joe and I had been intimate, we'd always had the lights off. I wasn't even sure if Joe had ever seen all of my naked body, let alone expressed a desire to see it. Samuel was so different. It would be stupid of me to deprive him.

I shimmied out of my knickers.

'Oh, yes.' His breathing accelerated.

I felt wicked, sexual, wild.

'Sit in the chair opposite me, then open your legs and touch yourself,' he commanded.

I stopped dead in my tracks. *This is too much.*

'No. I'm sorry. I refuse.' I pulled my knickers back up.

259

'You can. You will. For me,' he said breathlessly while unzipping his trousers and exposing himself.

Alarm bells rang frantically in my head. *What on earth am I doing? I'm a married woman with two children.*

I grabbed my clothes from the chair and started getting dressed. 'Samuel, stop that. Take me home right now, and we'll forget this ever happened.'

'Oh no, no, just a little more, my sweet Irene.' His breathing grew heavy as he stroked himself, the pace quickening.

'Stop that. I want to go home. Now.' I tried to look anywhere but at the man sprawled out on the chair.

'Just … one … more … second. Yes, yes, yes!' he shouted, ejaculating into the air, spraying the carpet and his trousers.

Looking at him in disgust, I felt filthy, tarnished and so ashamed. Memories of John and the Majestic came flooding back. *How have I let this happen again? No, that's not right. I did not let it happen. I'm not to blame.*

Once fully dressed, I grabbed my handbag and raced out of the room. I stood waiting for him at the front door, unable to meet his eyes when he appeared a few minutes later.

We went out to his car and sat in silence all the way home. Thank goodness it was a quick trip.

When we approached my parent's house, I didn't even wait for the car to come to a complete stop, but jumped out, mumbling a hasty goodbye.

Letting myself into the house, I hoped everyone had gone to bed so I could spend a little time collecting my thoughts. No such luck.

Mum rushed towards me, looking worried. 'Darling, I'm so glad you're home. Boris hasn't returned. I sent your father out to find him.'

'What? It's almost midnight. Where's Lorraine?' My shame was instantly replaced with a surge of fear.

'She's in the living room. She's fine.'

I hurried into the next room to find Lorraine lying on the carpet, reading a book.

'Where's Boris?' I hissed.

'How should I know?' She sat up. 'Why are you having a go at me? It's not my fault. I'm not his keeper.'

'Sorry, darling. I'm just worried.'

I sat on the sofa as beads of sweat dotted my forehead. *Where on earth is he? I'm going to give him such a talking-to when he returns.* I felt a moment of panic. *My God. What if I'm being punished? What if something has happened to him because of what I did? What if it is my fault after all?*

I dissolved into tears.

Mum brought in some tea, setting it on the table before handing me a cup. 'Drink this. You'll feel better soon.'

The clock on the mantlepiece ticked loudly as each painful minute passed. No Boris. It was almost too much to bear. If I hadn't been so selfish, running off to Samuel's house to do such disgusting things, then Boris would've been home. *I've been blind to what I've put the children through, moving them about, wanting to divorce their father. Please, God, don't let anything happen to my son.*

The clock read one thirty, and still no sign of Boris or Dad.

Mum dozed in the armchair while I stared into space.

'How much trouble is Boris in?' Lorraine whispered, standing in the doorway in her pyjamas.

I rubbed my forehead. 'Shouldn't you be in bed?'

She moved further into the room.

'Please, Mum, let me stay up until Boris comes back,' she pleaded.

All the fight had left me.

'Oh, all right,' I conceded.

'Thanks. You're the best mum in the world,'

No, I'm not, but all that will change.

We both leapt to our feet when we heard the front door unlock. Mum woke with a start.

Boris and Dad walked into the hallway, and I raced over to my son, hugging him as though I never wanted to let go. 'You're home. Thank goodness.'

'I'm sorry. I didn't mean to scare you. I just…needed to be alone for a bit,' he said, his voice breaking.

'I found him in the park, just sitting on a bench,' Dad said.

'Why?' I asked.

Boris was silent, but I could hear his heavy breathing, and then his face went red.

'Why? You ask why?' he exploded, kicking the wall. 'You never spend any time with us. You're always with that creep.' Boris's eyes filled with tears. He angrily wiped them away, like they had no place being there. 'I miss my dad.'

'Me too. We don't like Samuel. He's weird,' Lorraine added with such conviction.

Mum interrupted, 'How can you say that? Samuel is a perfect gentleman. He's a—'

'Mum, please leave us alone. Why don't you go up to bed? I'll deal with this.'

Her eyes narrowed.

'Yes, it is late. Come along, Manny. I can tell when we're not wanted.' Huffing, she grabbed my dad's arm and led him upstairs.

'Let's go into the living room.'

Boris and I sat down on the sofa while Lorraine took the armchair.

I looked at my sad, worried children.

'What do you mean Samuel is weird?'

'I don't know. There's just something about him.' Boris shrugged.

Wasn't I having the same thoughts earlier?

Moving closer to Boris, I put my arms around him. He tensed but didn't move away. 'I'm so sorry. I didn't realise the damage it's caused you. I promise it's going to be different from now on. Tell me what I can do to make you happy?'

'You getting back with Dad,' he said, his chin jutting out.

'But I thought you didn't want to go to Israel?'

'I don't, but if Dad won't come here, then I guess we'll have to go to him.'

'I agree.' Lorraine nodded. 'I want us all to be together again.'

I felt a sharp pang of sadness. I had done this. Taken my children away from their father, selfishly chased my own dreams under the pretence of making them happy, ignoring what they truly wanted. What they needed.

'I'm so sorry I put you through this, but things are going to change. I'll make sure of it. Now, let's get some sleep. We all need it,' I said wearily.

I had a lot to think about. I knew what had to be done.

Chapter Forty-one

JOE

Israel

I was walking on air at hearing Irene's voice over the phone.

'Joe,' she said, 'I've been thinking about cancelling the divorce.'

My face almost split from smiling. 'That's fucking great, darling. I knew you'd see sense.'

There was silence for a moment.

'If we come over to be with you, I need your word that things will be different.'

'Of course,' I said. 'I'll be a model citizen. I'll even wash the dishes and sweep the floor. Whatever you want.' And I meant it. I'd do anything for that woman, even grovel.

'Seriously, Joe. I need your word that you will *never, ever* lay a finger on me again.'

I hung my head in shame. I wished I could erase that part of our history.

'I promise, darling, never again. I will treat you like a delicate flower.'

She actually laughed a little. It was music to my ears.

'There's no need for that. I'm stronger than you think. One other thing…'

I held my breath. 'Yes, Irene, whatever you want.'

'I need to know that you will not gamble anymore. I think I should be in charge of our money. Is that acceptable to you?'

'Of course, me darling. I give you me word, hand on me heart. Oh, I can't wait to see you.'

'The children are excited to see you too.'

'Look, I'll take care of the tickets, don't you worry. How about you fly here in a couple of days?'

'That will be fine. See you soon then.'

'I love you, Irene. I really do,' I said, but she'd already hung up.

I had so much to do to prepare for our new life together, starting with Ettie. I wasn't looking forward to it, but it had to be done. The following night, after she had cooked us dinner and cleaned up, I drove her home and parked in front of her apartment building.

I lit a cigarette and, with an apologetic look, told her straight. 'Sorry, luv, but the wife and kids are coming back, so we need to be workmates only from now on.'

'What? No, no, no.' She shook her head. 'You cannot do this to me. I love you. I am good to you. You told me you are happy with me.'

'You're a wonderful woman, but me family comes first,' I said in a soothing voice.

She glared at me. 'You know what, Joe? You are a cold British bastard. I hate you.' She got out of the car, spat on the ground, and then slammed the door shut.

I groaned. I would have to ask for another assistant. Best if she were ugly. It would make things easier with Irene. But those problems could wait. My only priority was my family. I'd already been to the travel agency and booked their tickets, getting a great bargain on some new charter flight no one had ever heard of. It was almost half the price of the Israeli airline, and I figured why pay double when it was probably the same thing?

Looking back, though I hated admitting it, I hadn't been the best of husbands. Maybe I took Irene for granted, just a little. Well, all that was in the past. I promised myself I would give her my full attention. I never wanted to go through the pain of her leaving again, so I'd make it up to her every day if I had to. Maybe it sounded soppy, but it was the truth.

Chapter Forty-two

IRENE

London

We pushed through the crowd at Gatwick airport. Hundreds of people, laden with suitcases rushed in every direction. The loudspeaker announced boarding for flights, and the echoes of people laughing and talking filled the terminal.

Dad and Boris, with their trolleys full of luggage, followed Lorraine, Mum, and I, as we headed over to the Coach Airlines ticket booth and stood patiently behind a long line of people.

'I've never heard of this airline before. Is it new?' Mum asked.

'I don't know. Joe bought the tickets. I'm hoping it will be comfortable.'

'Comfortable, eh?' Mum spat. 'You could've been comfortable married to that wonderful Samuel, living in a mansion and having dinner parties. Instead, you're throwing it away for that waster, that gambler.'

'I'm doing it for my kids. Be happy for me, Mum.'

'How can I be happy when my daughter is a *meshuganah*?'

We moved up as the people in front approached the counter.

Dad looked sad. 'You're off again, just when we got you back.' He wagged his finger, smiling. 'You tell your husband I said to behave himself.'

I felt a rush of warmth towards him.

'But don't come crying back to me when it all goes wrong.'

The feeling quickly evaporated.

Dad put his arm around Lorraine. 'This is for you, *bubalah*. To keep you safe.' He handed her a little box.

She opened it with great excitement and pulled out a silver chain with a Star of David pendant. Smiling, she hugged him. 'Thanks so much, Grandpa.'

'It's called a Magen David. You should wear it at all times. It will bring you good luck.' He fastened the necklace around Lorraine's neck.

'You will come and visit, won't you?' I asked Dad.

Mum butted in, 'Of course, we will. If we were considering travelling all the way to Australia, then this short flight is nothing. Besides, we have always wanted to see Israel.'

She pulled me over to one side. 'What about Samuel? What should I say when he calls?'

'Tell him the truth, that I am with my husband and children, and to leave me alone,' I snapped.

He'd called the day after that disgusting night, wanting to see me. I told him I was busy all week, making up a story about having to go away to visit some ailing relative.

Mum pursed her lips. 'If you insist, but just know that I think you are making a big mistake.'

'I know you do, but I have to do what I feel is right.' My eyes pleaded with her to understand, but I knew it was pointless.

I looked up as an announcement crackled over the loudspeakers. *'Coach Airlines is ready for boarding.'*

We all hugged and said our goodbyes. Mum's embrace was so tight that it felt like all the air was being squeezed out of my lungs.

'I'll send you a letter as soon as we arrive. I promise,' I said and gave her a kiss.

My parents looked so old and sad standing there as we walked away. *I hope I'm doing the right thing.*

Once onboard, we made our way to our seats, stowing our bags in the overhead compartment. Keeping my handbag on my lap, I buckled up in between my son and daughter, then slumped back in my seat as all the energy left my body.

The last few days had been exhausting. I chose to go back to Joe because I knew it was what the children needed. My feelings were not as important as theirs. With that settled, I went full steam ahead, not allowing any other thoughts to distract me from my mission.

I'd called Joe first thing. He was overjoyed. He told me he would take care of the tickets and arranged for us to fly two days later. I just needed to get on with the packing without any interruptions. That was easier said than done because when I told Mum, she hit the roof. She practically became hysterical, all but accusing me of outright insanity. It took hours to calm her down, and then she walked around the house with a wrinkled mouth, only talking to me when absolutely necessary.

At least the kids were in a good mood. They were full of happy anticipation at the thought of seeing Joe. I didn't quite understand it. He'd hardly ever given them any attention except to tell them off, yet it didn't stop them from wanting their dad.

As more and more passengers came aboard, chatter filled the air. All I wanted to do was doze until we arrived. It was a short flight— only five hours— and before we knew it, we would be beginning a new phase in our lives. I had no idea how it would go. I prayed Joe would behave himself for once. He gave me his word, but he had done that before. I would only believe it when I saw it with my own eyes.

Boris looked out the window, cupping his hands on the glass, while Lorraine relaxed, reading her book. Allowing myself a little quiet time, I closed my eyes, trying to ignore the surrounding noises as I felt the plane race down the runway and lift off the ground. The gentle vibrations lulled me to sleep.

A loud voice jolted me awake.

'Everyone, sit down and stay in your seats. Do as I say, or you will be sorry!'

I opened my bleary eyes. My heart leapt into my mouth. A man with a dark black moustache stood in the aisle, waving a gun. Passengers screamed, cowering in fear as three more men with guns stood up.

Lorraine grabbed my hand. 'What's happening?'

'I don't know, darling, but let's just keep quiet and do as they say.'

I looked over at Boris and whispered, 'You alright?'

'Yeah, I'm okay,' he said with a wobble.

As the armed men moved into the aisles, I noticed that one of them was wearing a *keffiyeh* on his head. I'd once read about the Arab's headdress in a magazine; a black and white cloth fastened around the head with a black band.

The first man continued to shout in a heavy middle eastern accent,

'We are from the Anti-Zionist Organisation. We demand our brothers' freedom from the Zionist jails. Until this happens, you are our prisoners. You will remain in your seats and do as you are told.' He pointed his gun at a young man in front of him.

An elderly man behind me muttered, 'It's happening again. I knew it would, but no one would listen.'

I turned to him as his wrinkled wife nodded in agreement. The old man, his face drawn and sorrowful, pulled up his shirt sleeve to display the numbers tattooed on his inner arm. Not knowing what to say, I gave him what I hoped was a strong, compassionate look, before turning back to my family, who were silently staring at the men with guns.

Another man shouted, 'Everyone, give us your passports. Hold them above your heads.'

I opened my handbag with shaking hands and took out our three British passports, which he yanked out of my grip as he passed by. When the basket was full, he handed it to another man, who began searching through them. *Will it help to be British? They won't do something to an English citizen. Right?*

I turned back to the old couple behind me to whisper, 'Why do they need our passports?'

'It is not good,' he replied, shaking his head. 'I thought I was finally safe after the camps. They didn't get us then, but maybe they do now.'

'We are British. They won't hurt us,' I said, trying to reassure myself.

'Maybe you will be lucky. We shall see.' He shrugged as though resigned to his fate.

I sat back in my seat and slowly exhaled, fighting to slow my racing heart.

Lorraine whispered in my ear, 'Mum. I'm scared.'

'I know, darling. Let's just do what they say. I'm sure it won't be long before it's over.'

As I patted her hand, she grabbed mine and held it tight. I could feel her shaking.

'Yeah, right,' Boris hissed. 'These guys are never happy until they've killed everyone. I watch the news. I know what's going on.'

'Boris, stop scaring your sister,' I scolded. 'Everything will be fine.

It has to be.'

Frowning, he turned to look out the window.

Time passed slowly, and what felt like hours had only been minutes.

I was painfully aware of every movement in the aeroplane. Outside, the skies were quiet, but inside, the terrorist's footsteps vibrated through my head as they paced back and forth along the aisle.

I figured the man with the moustache was the leader as the others were asking him questions, then cocking their heads while waiting for his reply. He looked up and gripped his gun, his eyes scanning the terrified passengers.

'I will be calling names. If you hear yours, you will go and sit in the back.'

The old man groaned. 'They will be calling Jewish names, you will see.'

Boris whispered in my ear, 'Leslie's not a Jewish name. It'll be okay.'

I nodded in silent agreement.

One of the other terrorists started shouting out names in alphabetical order, 'Cohen, Cornblum, Dolinsky, Dreyfus.'

I clasped Lorraine's and Boris's hands in mine, watching people getting up and moving to the back.

'Frank, Finkel,' the man barked.

The old couple behind us rose slowly, and my eyes filled as I watched them gather their belongings.

'Katz, Kazan.'

Oh God, almost at the L's. It's going to be fine. Our name will not be called.

'Klien, Lazar, Leibowitz.'

I held my breath.

'Lerner, Levine, Levy.'

Thank God.

Breathing a deep sigh of relief, I glanced behind me and saw the old couple huddled with the others. I was overwhelmed with guilt, but I had to protect my family. *My children come first. Always.*

'Persky, Pachulsky, Rabinovitz, Rubin, Rosen.'

There were almost no passengers in the surrounding seats. Over three-quarters of them sat at the back, and the names were still being called out.

'Shapiro, Sachs, Shulman.'

What will happen to them? What will happen to us?

Chapter Forty-three

JOE

Israel

I bounced out of bed at the crack of dawn. I'd never been an early riser. Normally I needed at least two strong coffees and three cigarettes to get me going, but today was different. Irene was coming home.

I'd scrubbed the flat, checking every nook and cranny, making sure there wasn't a speck of dust, then did the same with my body under a hot, steaming shower. I'd even splashed on some cologne. I wanted Irene to find everything, including myself, spotless.

To make sure I had the right directions to the airport, I stopped by the neighbour's house. I couldn't risk getting lost.

'You look very happy,' Menachem said with a smile.

'The family will be here soon. Oh, you're going to love them. Irene's gorgeous and kind. What can I say? She's amazing, and she's coming home.' I beamed.

'And your children?' he asked.

'They're, you know, kids. Anyway, I'm off now, and thanks.'

Heading outside, I opened the door and got into the car, smiling at myself in the rear-view mirror. *She won't be able to resist me.* I pulled away from the kerb, whistling a merry tune. Menachem's directions to the airport were easy to follow. I would have plenty of time until the plane landed to have a coffee and read *The Jerusalem Post*, the English language newspaper.

Driving along the coastal road onto the main highway, I wound the windows down, and the hot *hamsin* air blew in. It was sweltering. Even the birds seemed to be flying in slow motion, struggling against the thick air. Looking out at the dunes of Israel as the palm trees swayed in the wind, I realised that I was finally at peace, that I had come home, as corny as that sounded. I prayed Irene would feel the same way. Sure, Israelis weren't the easiest and had no tact, saying exactly what they thought at any given time, but at least you knew where you stood with them.

I parked the car and headed towards the terminal. Ignoring the busy coffee bars and shops, I searched for the incoming flight board. *That's strange. There's nothing listed for Coach Airlines.* I made my way to the information desk and waited until someone could help me. When it was my turn, the woman behind the counter smiled.

'How may I assist you?'

'I can't find any information about the Coach Airlines flight.'

She paled. 'You haven't heard the announcements? You must go to the VIP room.'

I chuckled. 'I know *I'm* a very important person, but how did you know I was coming?'

She spoke to the girl beside her in Hebrew. I couldn't understand what she was saying, but I knew something was wrong. Her brow was wrinkled. She wasn't smiling anymore.

'Please follow me,' she said, leaving the information booth.

I had a hard time keeping up with her. 'Hey, is everything okay?' I asked as she rushed through the airport.

She didn't turn around. 'You just come with me. They will tell you everything.' Her voice was tight, almost breezy.

Turning down a corridor, she buzzed a door open.

Inside was a large room, a few chairs and tables pushed against the white walls. Groups of people of all ages were standing, speaking loudly to each other, clutching onto each other, pacing. Several were crying. The few that were sitting down held their heads in their hands. My stomach plummeted. Something had happened. I didn't know what, but I knew it couldn't be good.

A man in a white uniform stood behind a table.

'The passenger's names, please.'

'Irene, Boris, and Lorraine Leslie. My wife and children. What's going on? Will someone please explain?' My heart started beating wildly.

'Mr Leslie, there is a ... problem. The plane has been hijacked.'

'Hijacked?' I shouted, almost pissing my pants. 'How?'

'We do not know all the details yet. We have learned that the plane will land shortly, and as far as we know, no one is hurt.' He pointed to a row of seats. 'Please sit down and wait until we have more information.'

Moving aside, I found a seat and frantically fished in my pocket for a Valium. *Fuck.* I had bought a brand-new pair of trousers, and they were empty. *Am I being punished for something? Sure, I may not be husband of the year, but I'm a decent bloke.*

With shaking hands, I wiped the sweat off my forehead and rubbed my neck, which had started to ache like crazy, but nothing helped. My jaw was also sore, and there was something familiar about the way the pain travelled down my left arm. *Oh no, not again. Not now.* Sweat drenched my forehead. I tried wiping it away again, but I was having a hard time catching my breath. *Maybe I'll stand by the window and get some air.*

As soon as I stood up, my legs gave way. The last thing I saw before the dark circle closed in front of my vision, was a bunch of strangers staring down at me. *Irene. I need Irene.*

Chapter Forty-four

IRENE

Looking down the aisle, I studied the terrorists' angry faces. I couldn't understand how they were prepared to kill because of their faith. I'd always believed that human beings, no matter where they were from, or what religion or colour they were, were all the same.

'Be silent, and no one will get hurt,' the man with the keffiyeh reiterated. 'We will land soon, and when the Zionist pigs let our brothers go free, you will be released. Until then, stay in your seats.'

'I need to use the restroom,' one woman called out.

'Shut up. No one gets up, or I will shoot.'

Sinking down in her chair, she whispered, 'I'm pregnant. I must go to the toilet. I cannot hold it anymore.'

A kind lady beside her wrapped her arms around the unfortunate girl.

As I watched all this in horror, a sudden voice in my ear startled me. 'What's this?'

I whipped around, my heart pounding in my chest.

Lorraine screamed as the terrorist held her by the throat and pointed to her necklace.

I jumped out of my seat. 'No, no, it's a mistake! We are British. It was just a gift.'

'You are lying, you Jew,' he roared.

Lorraine squealed as he gripped her tighter, her neck turning bright red.

'Shut up!' He pushed her away, hard. 'Go to the back, and do not lie again.'

I grabbed the children and our bags, and we bolted to the back of the plane. *Why did I not think about her necklace? I'm such an idiot. We all but wrote 'Jew' on our foreheads.*

The other passengers tried to make room for us, but it was cramped. There were more Jews than non-Jews on the plane, but the terrorists expected us only to occupy six rows. We squeezed ourselves into two seats with the old couple sitting beside us. The man looked at us with such kindness. It hurt me to know that he carried the weight of history on his shoulders.

'Don't cry, my dear. Your tears are wasted on them. We must be strong. What are your names?'

'I am Irene, and this is Boris and Lorraine.'

'Boris?' the old man asked. 'Are you Russian?'

'No, my husband wanted to name our son after Boris Karloff, the actor.'

'Could've been worse,' Boris muttered. 'They could've named me after W. C. Fields.'

I gave him a warning glare, then turned back to the old man. 'What are your names?'

He smiled. 'We are Shimon and Ester Finkel. So nice to meet such handsome young people, even under these circumstances. Where is your husband?'

'We are on our way to meet him in Israel. He went over first to get everything ready.'

My ears popped, letting me know the plane was descending. I held Lorraine tight and stroked her hair. I knew I had to be strong for my children, but I so wanted to curl up and cry like a baby.

As the plane shuddered, landing on the tarmac, the leader waved his gun again. 'Stay in your seats and be quiet. No one move. You will do what we say.'

Several babies were crying as their mothers rocked them, and a young girl of maybe five or six clung to her father's arm, whimpering as the plane sped along the runway. Shimon quietly prayed in Hebrew beside me as I peered out the window. In front of me was a large concrete building with a sign.

Welcome to Israel

After a few hours, they finally gave us some water and apples, which we devoured as though we hadn't eaten in days. No one seemed to know what was happening until a man called Moshe, who supposedly held a senior position in the military, addressed us in Hebrew.

'What is he saying?' I asked Shimon.

The old man sighed. 'He thinks we are in trouble because Israel does not negotiate with terrorists, so maybe they will kill us, maybe not.'

'What? He must be wrong. Surely, they will come to an agreement.'

Shimon looked straight into my eyes. 'I am a fatalist. I was sure I would die in the camps, but that did not happen. Maybe it will now.'

Desperate to ignore reality, I changed the subject. 'Your English is excellent. Where are you from?'

'I grew up in Poland. After the Liberation, they sent me to Rhodesia, where I learned your language. I came to Israel in 1948, just after Independence. What a land it was then.' His eyes glazed over as he lost himself in his memories. 'All swamps, mosquitoes, and Arabs trying to kill us.' Frustration filled his voice. 'We finally have our homeland, but they still want the Jews dead. What Hitler did not finish, the Arabs will. You are young, but you will learn.'

'Shut up and listen!' the terrorist shouted, standing with his comrades. 'We are in contact with your Prime Minister. We have given her four hours to release our brothers. If she does not, we will blow up this plane. Now we wait.'

Lorraine looked terrified. 'I don't want to die.'

The little old lady, Ester, put her hand on my daughter's shoulder. 'Shhh, *maydaleh*, it will be fine, do not worry. Our Golda will know what to do.'

Chapter Forty-five

JOE

Israel

I opened my eyes, then quickly closed them again. The light was too bright. *Where am I? What's going on?* My chest was on fire. *Fuck. I think I passed out or something.*

I lay in pain, listening to rhythmic beeping from nearby. *Shit, the hijacking. Bloody hell. I have to talk to someone.*

'Hello?' I called out weakly.

A nurse came over. '*Shalom Yosef. Ma shlomcha?*'

'Do you speak English? I have to get to my wife. I need to go to the airport.'

'No English. Minute.' She walked away and returned a moment later with a young man.

'Shalom, I am Dr Geffen. How are you feeling?'

'I've been better, Doc. Listen, my wife is on the hijacked plane. I've gotta find out what's going on.'

'You need to rest. You were brought here, to Tel Hashomer hospital, after a major heart attack. You are lucky to be alive.'

'I have to know what's going on. Have you heard anything?'

'It will be okay, you will see. You must not think about it right now. Your job is to get well.'

'Is there a radio or something? Please, Doc, I promise to rest, but I must know what's happening.'

'Okay. I will see what I can do.'

A nurse came over and plugged a radio in on the bedside table next to me. I reached over and turned the dials. I needed the BBC world service if I was going to understand anything. Finally, I found the familiar station and waited for the news. *Please, God, I know I never believed in you before, but I'm starting now. I'm begging you, keep my family safe. I will change, I promise. No more gambling, whatever you want, but please let me see Irene again.*

The radio beeped five times, followed by a newsreader. 'This is the BBC World Service. Now for the news. Israelis are awaiting Prime Minister Meir's decision regarding the Coach Airline hijacking earlier today. The plane landed at Lod airport a few hours ago. Several terrorists from the Anti-Zionist Organisation are holding the passengers hostage onboard. The AZO are demanding the release of two hundred Arab prisoners from Israeli jails. So far, there has been no official statement by the Israeli government. The deadline for a decision is an hour and a half from now.'

I'd never felt as scared as I did at that moment. *Why the hell did I have to scrimp on cheap tickets? Fuck, shit, and bollocks. Have I killed my family?*

Chapter Forty-six

IRENE

'One and a half hours left,' the terrorist yelled. 'You stupid people with your stupid leaders. Do you think we want to kill you? No, but we will if we have to. We must make the world understand that we are serious.'

The heat in the cabin was unbearable. We had already stripped down to the minimum garments modesty allowed. There was nothing to eat, either. I'd handed the children a few sweets I'd found at the bottom of my bag an hour ago, but that was it. The only thing we could do was wait. It was agonizing. Each minute seemed like an eternity; the minutes ticking closer to our possible execution.

The children were quiet. Even Lorraine, who usually chattered nineteen to the dozen, was silent. I think we were too afraid to voice the obvious— that no one had a solution for our bleak predicament.

Moshe, the military man, stood up and stormed over to the terrorist.

The terrorist gripped his gun, moving it closer to Moshe. 'What do you want? Go back to your seat.'

'You say you do not want to kill us. You are just making a statement. If you are so humane, why are you letting the children go thirsty?' Moshe demanded. 'There is nothing to give them, and the heat is making it worse.'

'We gave you water and apples. There is nothing more. Now go.' With his spare hand, the terrorist pointed towards the hostages.

'We need water now. A pregnant lady is back there.'

'We have finished all the drinks. That is how it is.' He moved even closer to Moshe, pushing the gun into his stomach. Moshe took the hint and returned to his seat, but not before giving the gunman a look of disgust.

The hijackers conversed in Arabic, then, the leader strode over to the captain and aimed his gun at him. 'Come with me to the cockpit.'

I looked at my watch. One hour and ten minutes left. The sweeping of the second hand hypnotised me. One hour and nine minutes. One hour and eight minutes…

The terrorist returned.

'I have arranged for water to be brought onto the plane soon. Now you can see that we are fair people,' he said before returning to the front of the plane.

Moshe whispered to the others in Hebrew.

'What is he saying?' I asked Shimon.

'He says if they come aboard with water, maybe we can make a run for it. He's crazy. People always got shot when they tried to escape from the camps.'

'Shimon, can I ask you something?' He nodded. 'The Prime Minister cannot let us be blown up, right? She wouldn't let that happen, would she?'

'I cannot believe she would allow that, but if we meet their demands, that is two hundred more terrorists out for our blood. Let us preserve our energy and just wait.' He gave my arm a little squeeze.

Forty-five minutes left. Forty-five minutes to determine if we would live or die.

I hugged my children close. Boris suddenly reached out and grabbed my hand. He looked at me with a quivering lip, and for a moment I saw the little boy he used to be. 'Mum, I'm scared,' he said in a wobbly voice, and I saw tears glistening in his eyes. 'I know darling.' I stroked his face gently. 'So am I, but we must be strong and believe that all will work out in the end. Okay?' He nodded back at me and laid his head on my shoulder.

There was a noise outside the main door. One of the terrorists shouted in Arabic to his comrades, and they all raised their guns. A low murmur went around the plane as everyone held a collective breath as they stared at the door.

'*Mayim*,' Moshe whispered to us.

Shimon translated, 'Water.'

After a loud hiss, the cabin door slowly opened.

The terrorists aimed their guns at us.

A group of soldiers raced in, and I stood up to get a better look.

One yelled, '*Koolam laredet miyad!*'

People suddenly threw themselves to the floor as gunfire echoed around the plane.

Frozen in place, I watched as several terrorists fell to the ground, before a searing pain pierced my chest, knocking the wind out of me. As I slumped down onto the seat, I could hear Lorraine crying, 'Mummy, no!'

Then, darkness.

Chapter Forty-seven

JOE

Israel

Even though my voice was not much more than a raspy whisper, I managed to muster up enough strength to call out, 'Nurse, nurse.'

It took a while, but eventually, one turned up.

'Yes?' she asked.

'I gotta call someone who knows what's going on. I need to find out what the bloody Prime Minister plans to do.'

'You must rest. This is not the time.'

'Not the time? There's less than an hour. Don't you understand? I gotta find out about my wife.' My heart rate rose, which I knew wasn't good for me, but I didn't care. I struggled to get up, but I was so weak. She patted my shoulder and I slumped back without a shred of energy.

'All will be okay,' she said and left, leaving me to my helpless fear.

I stared at the white walls as the radio droned on. Tuning it out, I listened instead to the machine that was attached to me with wires. *Beep, beep, beep.* My heart beeping in time with the clock's tick, tick, ticking. *Why don't they bloody well release the hostages? Those bastard Arabs. Let Irene come home to me. She's the only woman I've ever truly loved, but like a fool, I almost let her get away. I swear, if she makes it back, I'll be a new man. Hell, I even miss the kids. I'll be a better dad to them, and then all will be perfect. It has to be.*

The radio interrupted the regular program. 'This is the BBC World Service. With forty-five minutes left to the AZO deadline, the Israelis led a daring operation today at Lod airport. Commandos, posing as the catering crew, stormed the aircraft and shot all four terrorists dead, releasing the passengers and flight crew. We have reports of one passenger being wounded and in critical condition. The identity of this person has not yet been released. We will bring you more coverage as soon as we have more details. Now, back to our scheduled broadcast.'

It's over. Thank you, God! For the first time in I don't know how long, I actually managed a smile. I wanted to celebrate. Those bastard terrorists were dead; good riddance to them, and thanks to those amazing Israeli commandos who were heroes, everyone on the plane was released. I felt a bit sorry for the poor bugger who got hurt, but it was probably some old geezer in the way. *Oh well.* All I needed to do was wait, and soon I was sure someone would bring Irene and the kids over to see me. I knew that once I had my family back, I would be good as new, and we could start our new life together.

After dozing for a while, I woke up to someone standing by my bedside.

'Oh, Dr Geffen. Did you hear the good news? All's fine now. Everyone's safe.'

The doctor pulled a chair over and sat down. He didn't look happy. His mouth was set in a grim line and his eyes were grave.

'Joe, I have a bit of bad news, but I want you to listen till I finish.'

'Okay,' I said, wondering what the hell was going on.

'I'm sorry to tell you that your wife was shot. Please don't worry. She is going to be fine. She had an operation here, in the hospital. You will be able to see her in a few days.'

I felt like someone had sucked all the air out of me.

'What? She's okay? You sure about that? Where did she get shot? Will there be a scar?'

'We are sure that she will recover completely. You will see for yourself in a short time, and you can ask her all those questions. Now, you must rest. It is the most important thing you can do to get better. I will be back later. *Shalom.*'

I lay in bed, trying to digest the news. *I can't believe it. Shot. Irene was shot. Hell, at least she's alive.* I couldn't wait to see her, and hopefully, she would be on her feet again in no time. As to her looks, even if she were maimed, I would still love her and think she was beautiful. Unless it was on her face, of course, but then I guess I would have to get used to it. I closed my eyes and tried picturing her without an eye or nose, knowing in my heart that it didn't matter. I would be happy as long as I had her back.

Just before I fell asleep, I realised I hadn't asked about the kids. *No worries. I'm sure they're fine.*

Chapter Forty-eight

IRENE

Israel

I let out a groan of pain as I touched my chest, only to realise it was swathed in bandages. That was when it all came back to me, the plane, the terrorists, the shooting. *Thank goodness I'm alive.*

A moment of panic engulfed me. *The children. Are they okay? I have to find out.* I tried lifting my head but it seemed to weigh me down like concrete. I was too weak. I squinted, the room swimming in and out of focus as I tried to get my bearings. To my left lay a woman, countless tubes and wires connected to her body. To my right was another woman, but she was sitting up, reading a magazine.

'*Boker tov*,' she said with a smile.

'Sorry. English only.' My voice was hoarse.

'I said good morning. How do you feel?'

'Not too good.'

'It's okay.' She nodded. 'I will get someone for you.'

Laying back in bed, I struggled to recall what had happened. I remembered being on the plane and the doors opening, then nothing.

A young, pretty nurse walked over to me and lifted my arm to take my pulse. 'Shalom Irene. My name is Shula, and I will help you. Do you have pain?' she asked in a soothing voice.

'Where are my children?'

'You don't worry. All is good. Dr Levy will be here soon to talk to you about your condition, and someone will come and speak to you about your children. Now, you must rest.'

I dozed on and off until I heard someone nearby. Next to my bed stood a short, bald man wearing a white coat, focusing on the machine attached to me.

'Oh, you are awake. Good. I am Dr Levy. I operated on you when you arrived at the hospital.' He smiled. 'You were very lucky. You were shot in the chest, but the bullet missed your heart by a fraction of a millimetre.' He held his fingers up to demonstrate. 'Any closer, and you would not be with us. That is what we call *mazel*. Luck.' He looked pleased with himself. 'I am confident you will make a complete recovery. Now, do you have any questions?'

'Yes, I need to know about my children,' I said, straining to speak.

'Of course, but they are fine. Do not worry. Also, your husband is here.'

'Joe's outside? Can he come in?'

'No, no. You see, your husband is a patient at the hospital. Unfortunately, he suffered a major heart attack, but he is recovering in the ICU. He will need to be here for some time. You may visit him when you are able to get out of bed. I will come back later and see how you are. *Shalom.*' He patted my hand and left.

I couldn't make sense of it. I had been shot, and Joe had another heart attack? Both of us had nearly died. *But we didn't. Surely that has to mean something?*

Hours later, a woman wearing a red patterned scarf around her head came over and sat by my bed.

'My name is Aviva, and I am a social worker. I want to tell you about your children.'

'Oh, yes, please. Tell me they are okay.'

'Yes, yes, they are fine. Do not worry.' She smiled. 'Both of them have gone to a kibbutz. Do you know what that is?'

'No, I don't.'

'It is a wonderful place where they grow fruits, and everyone lives together helping each other. Your children are very happy and have made friends. They pick oranges during the day, and in the evenings, they sing, dance, and eat.'

It sounded like an idyllic place, but I couldn't imagine Boris being too pleased about it.

'You sure they are fine?'

'Oh yes, of course. Everyone loves beautiful Lorraine and funny

286

Boris.'

Boris, funny? That's a first.

'They can stay on the kibbutz until you and your husband can take care of them again.'

I wasn't exactly in any condition to do anything about the situation, so I just had to accept it and hope for the best. It was such a relief to learn that they hadn't come to any harm.

Three days later, feeling stronger and after getting approval from the doctor, I visited Joe in the ICU. When the nurse wheeled me into his room, I was shocked to see Joe looking so small and vulnerable. Tears sprung from his eyes as soon as he saw me, and he started sobbing uncontrollably. I had never seen Joe cry before, and it tore at my heart.

The nurse parked me next to his bed, and I took his hand.

'Irene, me darling, I want you to know how sorry I am for all the pain I've caused you.'

I found it hard to catch my breath and didn't know what to say. *Who is this man? Where is the bastard that is my husband?*

I squeezed his hand. 'All that matters is that you are alive and getting better by the day. Everything else is in the past. We can look forward to good times from now on.'

'I'm so relieved to have you here. I thought I'd lost you. I can't go on without you. I love you. You know that, don't you?'

A nurse approached, interrupting our conversation.

'He must rest now. I will take you back to the ward.'

My recovery took time, but I improved bit by bit. Although I was in a lot of pain, I got up every day and walked a few steps. Before long, I was walking on my own to the bathroom.

Dr Levy was pleased with me. 'If you continue like this, you will not have to be here so long.'

When the stitches were taken out, I was pleased to see I wouldn't have a large scar, and what there was could be easily covered up with the right make up.

I stopped all pain medication, disconcerted by the wooziness it caused, and I found I was able to function much better without.

Joe's recovery was not so easy. He was in a lot of pain, and from years of smoking, he'd developed a nasty cough which exhausted him. The doctor said it was imperative he get up and walk around, but he was too weak.

I encouraged him to take the smallest steps, just to get out of bed and sit in the chair. A few days later, he managed to stand up and walk slowly to the other side of the room.

'You're doing really well, Joe.'

His face lit up at the praise.

It was good to be needed. It gave me a purpose and made me feel important. I made sure to visit him daily. In an effort to please me, he tried his best, and I was happy to see his pallor gradually brighten to pink in his cheeks.

I had become somewhat of a local celebrity as the only passenger to be shot in the hijacking. I was even photographed for the newspapers, and people who saw me would shake my hand when they visited other patients.

The doctors released me after two weeks, and I took a taxi to the flat, which was bright and spacious with a view of the sea from the balcony. All our familiar furnishings were there and as I stepped through the door, it almost felt like home.

I was still somewhat weak and sore, but several times a day, the neighbours knocked on the door bringing food and cleaning up the place. I was barely alone for a moment. I could see why Joe loved Israel. People were so welcoming. I was suddenly very popular, especially with Menachem, who, despite having the worst comb-over I'd ever seen, and trousers buckled so high it made him resemble either Tweedledee or Tweedledum, flirted with me non-stop. He turned up at all hours, and I had to make sure the door was locked, or he would just barge in.

I grew stronger by the day and, within a few weeks, I was almost back to my old self. I visited Joe every couple of days, and he, too, was making progress, though he still had a long way to go until he could come home.

While I missed the children and worried for Joe, I enjoyed the time alone. I was free to do whatever I wanted, and I took advantage by going to the beach, lying on my towel as I relaxed in the warm sun.

One afternoon, a muscular, tanned lifeguard crouched down next to me. 'You are so pretty. I cannot stop looking at you. Marry me and make me a happy man.'

I laughed. 'Sorry, but I don't think my husband will be a happy man if I do.'

Another day, a different lifeguard handed me a Turkish coffee as he sat down.

'Thank you.'

'If you come to my house tonight, I will make you more than coffee.' He said, his bright blue eyes matching his swimming trunks. 'I will give you also a massage. You will be pleased.'

'I don't think so. I'm married. Didn't you see my ring?' I held my hand up to show him.

'So what?' he said. 'So am I, but no one needs to know. You come to my place, yes?'

'No,' I said, then picked up my book and pretended to read. Eventually, he left, and I giggled to myself. It was such great fun and a tremendous boost to my ego. *Is this how it would be if I were single? Would I have my choice of so many men? I think I might like it.*

Six weeks after I had been in Israel, I went to visit Joe and found him full of beans. 'Doc says I can come home tomorrow. I can't wait to be alone with you all the time,' he said with a wide smile, looking almost like himself again.

'That's great news. I'll go and find out what time I can pick you up.'

I squared my shoulders and held back the sigh. *Back to being a wife again. Oh well.*

The following day, I helped Joe up the stairs to the flat. He was still a little weak and it took a while. When we entered our home, he went straight to the sofa and settled himself down.

'Can you turn on the TV for me, darling?' He said in a weak voice.

'Of course. Would you like a cup of tea?' I asked.

'Yes, please, and I won't say no to any biccies you have. The hospital food was awful.'

I brought him what he asked for, placing it on the table in front of him.

'I'm going to pop out now and buy some food for dinner. I won't be too long.'

In an instant, his eyes filled up with tears. 'Oh, please, darling, don't leave me alone. I might fall over and break me neck. Anything could happen.'

'We have to eat. You'll be wanting dinner.'

'Just stay, and we can have an egg or something light. Please, me love. I couldn't bear it if you went out.'

The same thing happened the next day. He wouldn't let me out of his sight.

'Joe, this is ridiculous. I have to get some food. There's nothing in the house.'

'Oh, alright then, but don't be long, and make sure you get some hummus and the newspapers.'

'Fine. See you later.'

Heading outside, I strolled down the road in the sunshine, feeling like I'd been let out of a cage. It was short-lived. When I returned home with the shopping, Joe was waiting at the front door.

'What took you so long? I've been so worried.'

'What do you mean? I was gone less than an hour.'

His eyes narrowed. 'Did you talk to any men?'

'Just the shopkeeper, but he was about eighty-five and deaf in one ear.'

Seeming satisfied, Joe took the newspaper from the basket and settled at the kitchen table while I unpacked the food.

~ * ~

A letter arrived a few weeks later. 'Joe, look, it's from the kids.'

I opened it in a hurry, excited to hear from them. '"Dear Mum and Dad, just to let you know all's fine and we should be back next week, on the seventeenth. We will tell you all about our adventures when we return. Love Boris and Lorraine." Isn't that wonderful? They'll be back next week.'

Joe grunted and continued flicking through the pages of the newspaper.

To prepare for their arrival, I cleaned the flat and put fresh sheets on the kids' beds, trembling with excitement.

Finally, the doorbell rang, and there they were.

'Darlings,' I cried, racing to hold them in my arms. 'It's been so long. Three months. I can't believe you are here.'

Lorraine wiggled out of my embrace and tossed her backpack on the sofa. 'Where's my room?' she asked with a sneer.

What's going on?

'It's down the corridor, but don't you want to say hello to Dad?'

'Yeah, okay, where is he?'

'He's having a nap but should be up in a few minutes.'

'Call me when he's awake,' she said, then traipsed toward her room without a backwards glance.

I turned to Boris and almost fell over when I noticed a kippa on his head.

'Boris! Why are you wearing that?'

'It has great importance and meaning for me.'

'What do you mean? I don't understand.'

'I have *Hashem* with me now and forever.' His eyes sparkled as he looked up at the ceiling.

'Oh,' I said, not making any sense of what he was saying. 'Well, come in and let's get you settled.'

Joe shuffled out of our bedroom and gave us a feeble wave.

'Darling, come and greet your kids.'

He plodded over and gave Boris a pat on the back, then sat down on the sofa. 'What time's dinner?' he asked.

I ignored him. 'Lorraine, come and say hello to your father,' I shouted.

When she still hadn't come out after five minutes, I knocked on her door, but she didn't answer. I turned the doorknob, but there was resistance. I knocked again.

'Lorraine, please open the door.'

'Yeah?' she said, poking her head out.

'Come out. Your dad is awake.'

'Okay, in a minute.'

As she went to close the door, I smelled something familiar. I pushed past her and entered the room, which was thick with cigarette smoke.

'Oh, Lorraine. What are you doing?'

'Nothing,' she said, rolling her eyes.

'We'll talk about this later. Now, come out, your father is waiting.'

I had spent the afternoon preparing a special meal of roast chicken for the kids, their favourite, and was really looking forward to having a family dinner together after such a long time without them.

'The food is ready. Come and sit down.'

Joe was first at the table. Boris went over to the sink and washed his hands while mumbling a prayer.

I hissed at Joe. 'Do you see that?'

Joe just shrugged. 'I think he's gone a bit doolally if you ask me. Anyway, I'm famished. Let's start.'

Boris finished his ritual, then came over and sat down.

'Mum, do you have any paper plates? I can't eat off these. They aren't kosher.'

'You've got to be kidding.' After seeing the determined look on his face, I went over to the cupboard and grabbed a few disposable plates. *This is turning into a fun evening. I wonder what other demands he will have.*

Boris inspected his food. 'Did you use any dairy products? Because there's chicken, and you mustn't mix meat with milk.'

'I don't know, Boris. Let me think. Yes, I may have added butter to the peas and potatoes.'

'Well, I can only eat the chicken then.'

I noticed Lorraine was wearing eyeliner as she parked herself at the table. I was starting to accumulate a list of things to talk with her about later.

'Here, darling,' I said, handing her a plate.

'I can't eat *that*.'

'What? Don't tell me you're religious as well?' I looked over at Joe, but he was busy scarfing down his food.

Lorraine rolled her eyes yet again. 'Religious? No way. I won't eat it because that poor chicken was once a living creature who was brutally murdered by greedy bastards. I am a strict vegetarian.'

I shook my head. *This is all too much.*

'Since when?' I asked.

'Since I became aware of the cruelty of human beings.'

'Fine,' I said with a sigh. 'Lorraine, you eat the vegetables, and Boris, you can have the chicken. At least your father is enjoying his food.'

As Joe let out a loud burp, Lorraine sniggered. I tried not to burst into tears.

And so, our new life in Israel began.

Boris would spend every Friday night at the synagogue and all day long on Saturdays until dusk. To be honest, it was a relief to have him out of the house for a while. There was only so much weirdness I could take.

Lorraine wasn't home much either, which worried me. She barely ate and looked horribly thin but refused to talk about it. I tried, but I had no control over her. One word from me, and she would shout, 'Shut the fuck up! echoing her father. She returned at all hours of the night but wouldn't tell me where she'd been, and no amount of threats deterred her.

I tried discussing the problem with Joe, but he just lay on the sofa, showing no interest.

'Joe, you have to help me with Lorraine. I can't handle her.'

'It's not me fault she's turned into a slag. Anyway, all that matters is that you and I are together again.'

'Oh, for god's sake. If you won't help me with our daughter, then at least get up and go for a walk or something. Isn't it time you went back to work?'

'I'm still too weak. I don't want to risk another heart attack. Can I have a cup of tea, darling?'

Boris came out of his room with a serious look on his face.

'Mum, I was speaking to the rabbi, and he says you must instruct Lorraine to cover herself up. It's immodest how she dresses.'

I could feel the heat rising to my face.

'I'm not a bloody magician! I can't do everything! I've had enough of all of you!' I exploded.

Grabbing my handbag, I stormed out and headed down the road until I reached the beach. As I sat alone in a secluded area, watching the magnificent orange and red colours streak across the sky, I realised nothing had changed. I was back to being a servant again. *Why did I come here? To be taken for granted by everyone once again? No more. I am done being a doormat. I do not need a man. Not Joe. Not Samuel. Not anyone. I can be by myself and flourish.*

With renewed energy, I started planning my new life.

First thing the next morning, under the pretence I was going food shopping, I headed to the bank and checked the balance. Relieved that there was enough money for what I needed, I withdrew some cash and stashed it in my purse.

In the days that followed, I carried on as usual, before finally gathering the courage to have a heart-to-heart with my husband. I sat in an armchair facing him while he lay in his well-worn spot on the sofa.

'Joe,' I began, 'I need you to listen to me. I'm overwhelmed and exhausted, and I need time for myself. I came here, got shot, and yet you all still place demands on me that I can't handle. I looked after the kids for months alone. Now, it's your turn. I've made a decision. I'm going back to England for a while.'

Joe sat up, looking horrified. 'You don't mean that. You can't.'

'I do, and I will.'

Tears poured from his eyes as he reached out to me. I moved backwards. I was determined to maintain my strength in the face of his emotions. Joe and all his violence, temper and domineering ways had been terrible, but this weakened, helpless Joe was somehow worse.

'Please,' he begged. 'Don't do this. I can't live without you.'

'Yes, you can,' I said. 'You have to.'

'No! I'll kill meself. I swear.' He jumped up and clutched his chest as though he was having another heart attack, but I wasn't fooled.

'Stop that. You're pathetic. I will be leaving at the end of the week. It's time for you to take responsibility and look after the kids and yourself. There is nothing more to say.'

I got up and headed to the door.

'Promise me it's only for a short while,' Joe shouted as I closed the door behind me and walked down the road to the travel agency.

~ * ~

I had a spring in my step as I walked through the airport terminal. It was a new day, a new beginning, and I knew in my bones that this was absolutely the right move.

I held the ticket to my freedom in my hand as I approached the El

Al counter. No charter flight this time. I was determined to get to London bullet free.

The desk clerk looked up. 'Mrs Leslie, no return ticket?'

'No.' I smiled. 'Just one way only.'

With the plane in the sky, I let out an enormous sigh of relief. From that point onwards, I only had myself to look after. The smile on my face lasted the entire five hours of the flight.

Life is going to be wonderful. I just know it.

Acknowledgments

Writing a book is never easy and I couldn't have done it without the amazing support of family and friends. I'd like to begin by thanking my incredible husband, Gil Beckenstein, for patiently listening and providing invaluable feedback as I read each chapter aloud night after night. I'm so grateful to my amazing aunt, Sandra Hale, for always having my back, going through every draft, and giving me priceless advice. Heartfelt thanks to my sister-in-law, Tamara Langford, and to my dear friends, Jane Windsor, Eileen Mamanov and Johanna Petree, for their brilliant advice. A huge thank you to my editors, Rachael Hedges and Miles Hawksley, who deserve applause for their insightful criticism. I want to give a shout-out to Gubby Beckenstein, my incredibly talented stepdaughter, for designing such a fabulous cover. Lastly, I want to acknowledge Rogue Phoenix Press for giving me this wonderful chance to bring Irene and Joe into the imaginations of readers.

About the Author

Caroline Langford was born in England, grew up in Australia and Israel, and now resides in Los Angeles where she performs as a stand-up comedian and actress. After a lifetime in show business, she discovered storytelling as her new passion. *Walking on Eggshells* is her debut novel.

VISIT OUR WEBSITE
FOR THE FULL INVENTORY
OF QUALITY BOOKS:
http://www.roguephoenixpress.com

Rogue Phoenix Press

Representing Excellence in Publishing

Quality trade paperbacks and downloads

in multiple formats,

in genres ranging from historical to contemporary romance, mystery and science fiction.

Visit the website then bookmark it.

We add new titles each month!

www.ingramcontent.com/pod-product-compliance
Lightning Source LLC
Chambersburg PA
CBHW061941170626
46813CB00006B/2492